THE THRONE OF THE EMPEROR

PART FOUR OF EMPIRE OF THE SUN AND MOON

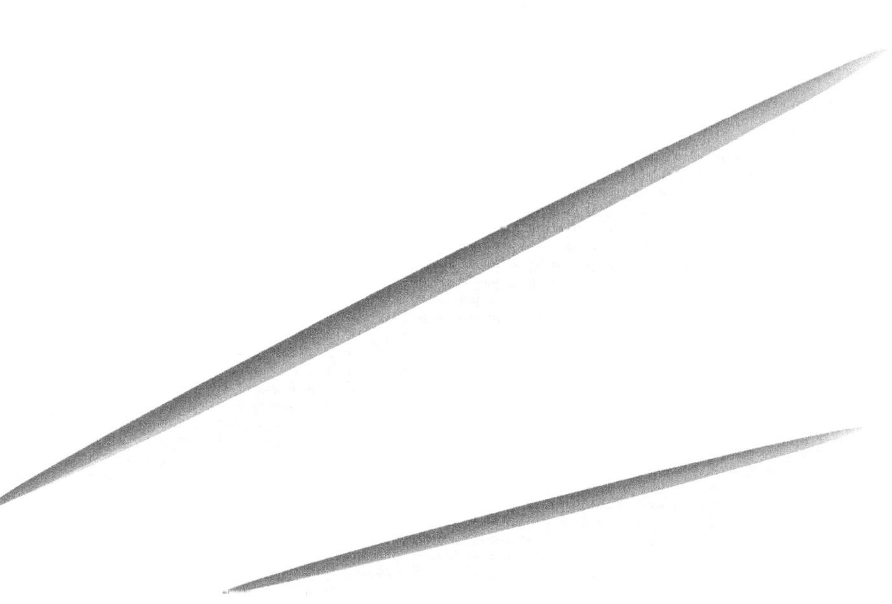

THE THRONE OF THE
EMPEROR
PART FOUR OF EMPIRE OF THE SUN AND MOON

ROB HOBART

ISBN: 978-1-7322899-7-0 (Paperback)

ISBN: 978-1-7322899-6-3 (eBook)

Front cover image by Nino Vecia.

Book design by Logotecture.

To Kathryn. Some•ay you'll be ol• enough to rea• this!

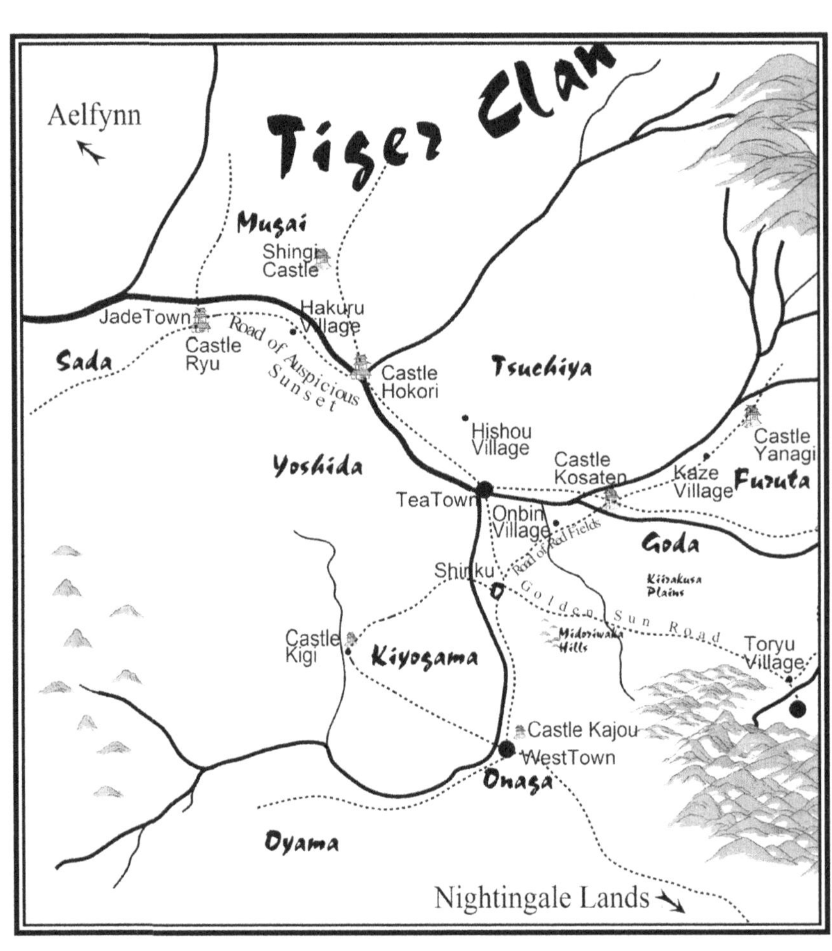
Tiger Clan
Aelfynn
Mugai
Shingi Castle
JadeTown
Hakuru Village
Castle Ryu
Sada
Road of Auspicious Sunset
Castle Hokori
Tsuchiya
Hishou Village
Yoshida
Castle Yanagi
Castle Kosaten
Kaze Village
Furuta
TeaTown
Onbin Village
Road of Red Fields
Goda
Shinku
Kiirakusa Plains
Golden Sun Road
Castle Kigi
Kiyogama
Midoriwaka Hills
Toryu Village
Castle Kajou
WestTown
Onaga
Oyama
Nightingale Lands

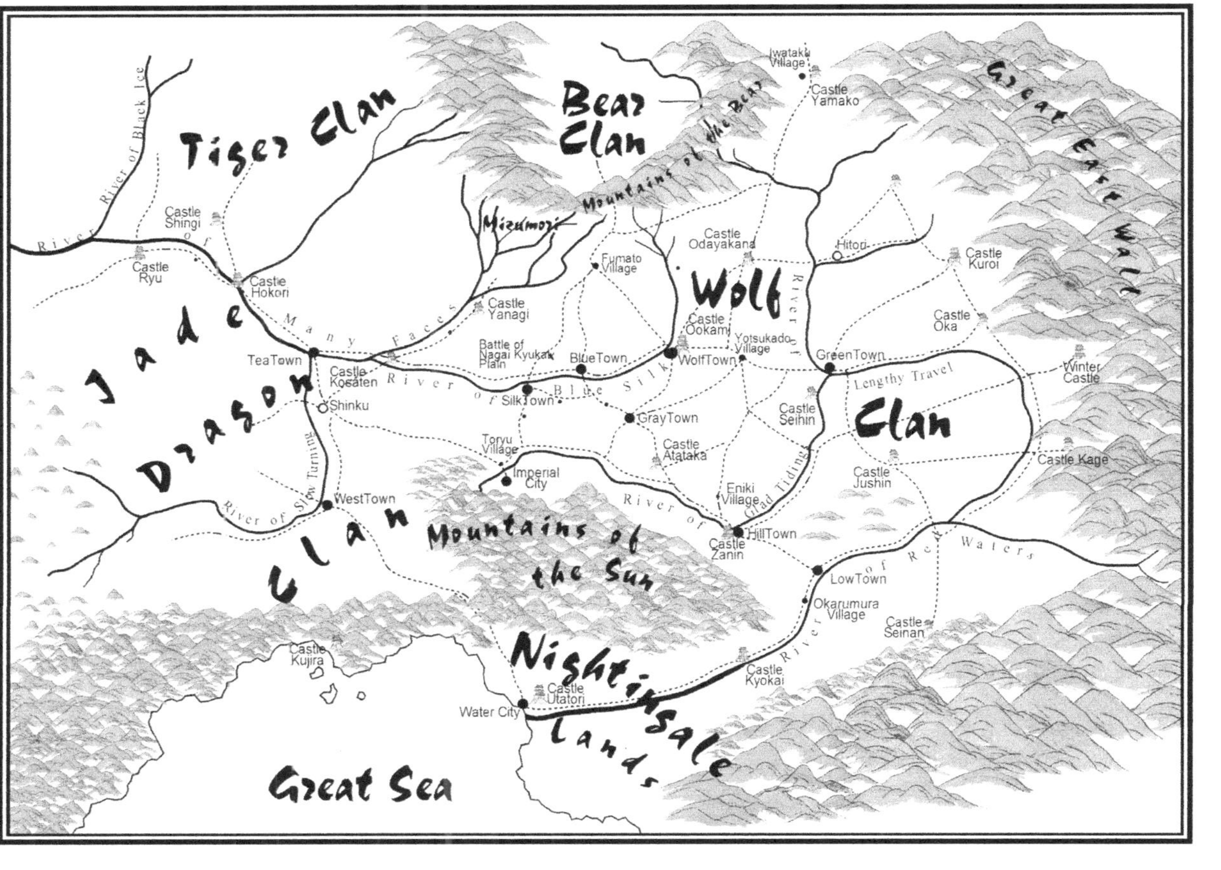
Tiger Clan
Bear Clan
Wolf Clan
Jade Dragon Clan
Nightingale Lands
Great East Wall
Great Sea
Mountains of the Bear
Mountains of the Sun
Mizumori
River of Black Ice
River of Many Faces
River of Blue Silk
River of Lengthy Travel
River of Glad Tidings
River of Red Waters
River of Slow Turning
Castle Shingi
Castle Ryu
Castle Hokori
TeaTown
Castle Kosaten
Shinku
WestTown
Castle Yanagi
Battle of Nagai Kyukak Plain
Fumato Village
BlueTown
SilkTown
Toryu Village
Imperial City
GrayTown
Castle Atataka
Castle Ookami
WolfTown
Castle Odayakana
Yotsukado Village
Eniki Village
HillTown
Castle Zanin
Iwataku Village
Castle Yamako
Hitori
Castle Kuroi
Castle Oka
GreenTown
Castle Seihin
Winter Castle
Castle Kage
Castle Jushin
LowTown
Okarumura Village
Castle Seinan
Castle Kyokai
Castle Utatori
Water City
Castle Kujira

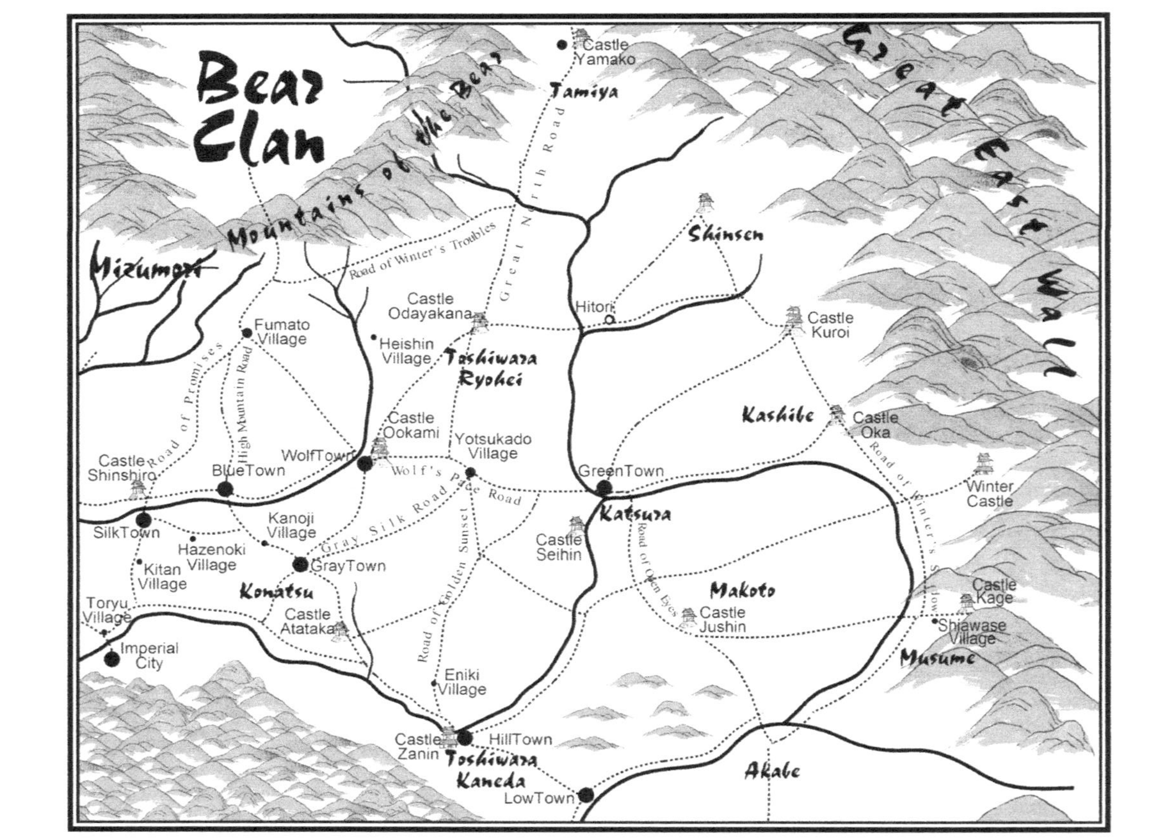
Bear Clan
Great East Wall
Mountains of the Bear
Mizumori
Castle Yamako
Tamiya
Great North Road
Shinsen
Road of Winter's Troubles
Castle Odayakana
Hitori
Castle Kuroi
Fumato Village
Heishin Village
Toshiwara Ryohei
Road of Promises
High Mountain Road
Castle Ookami
Yotsukado Village
Kashibe
Castle Oka
Castle Shinshiro
BlueTown
WolfTown
Wolf's Pace Road
GreenTown
Road of Winter's Shadow
Winter Castle
SilkTown
Kanoji Village
Gray Silk Road
Katsura
Castle Seihin
Hazenoki Village
GrayTown
Kitan Village
Road of Golden Sunset
Road of Open Eyes
Makoto
Castle Kage
Konatsu
Castle Jushin
Toryu Village
Castle Atataka
Shiawase Village
Imperial City
Musume
Eniki Village
Castle Zanin
HillTown
Toshiwara Kaneda
Akabe
LowTown

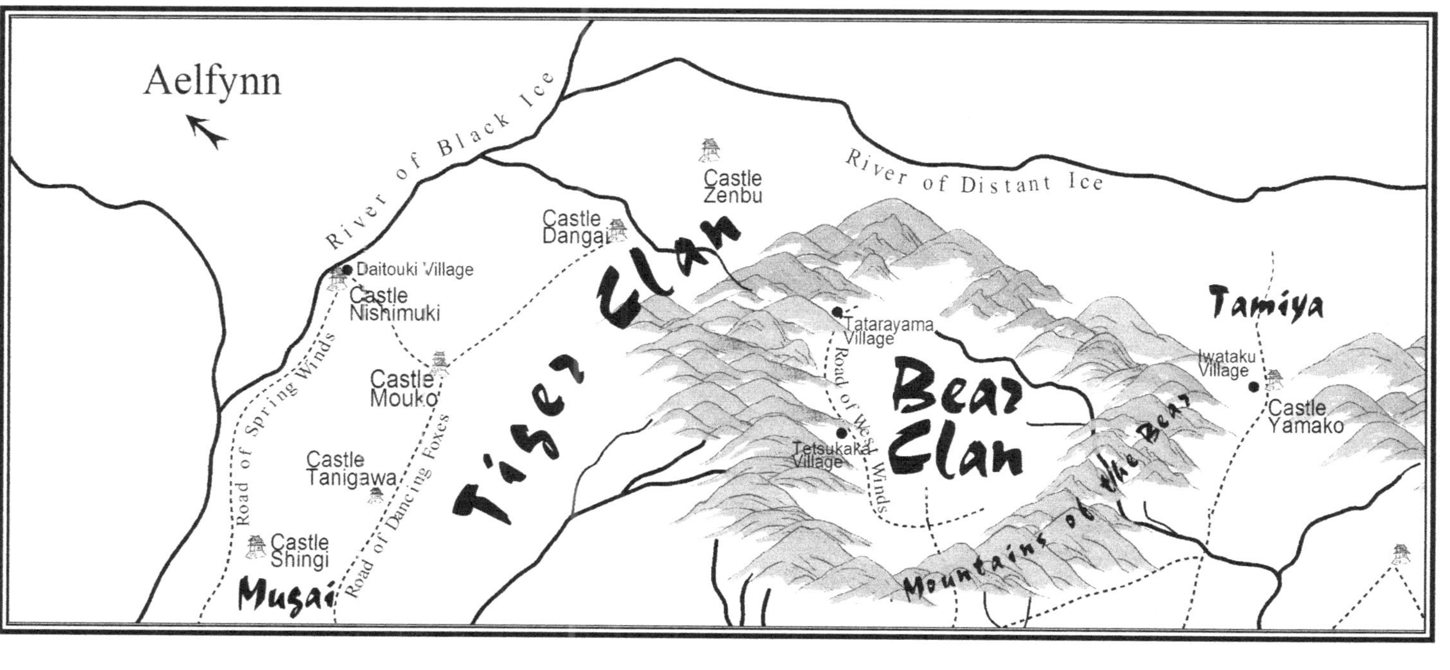
Aelfynn
River of Black Ice
River of Distant Ice
Castle Zenbu
Castle Dangai
Daitouki Village
Castle Nishimuki
Castle Mouko
Castle Tanigawa
Castle Shingi
Mugai
Road of Spring Winds
Road of Dancing Foxes
Tiger Clan
Tatarayama Village
Tetsukaka Village
Road of West Winds
Bear Clan
Mountains of the Bear
Tamiya
Iwataku Village
Castle Yamako

CHAPTER 1

THE FIRST ONE TO see the strangers was Tsugo, the dung-collector. He was always up early, rolling his hand-cart through the streets of Aotouki Village while the sky was barely turning gray, early because most folk didn't want to see him – or smell him. By the time the Sun was over the horizon and everyone else was starting on their day, he was already pushing his cart back home, which was not quite as far as the local mortician clan but closer to their dingy settlement than to the rest of Aotouki. No one wanted to live near a dung-collector's hut, fearing both the stench and the spiritual contamination that could accompany it; the farmers who bought his dung to fertilize their fields and rice-paddies would only visit when they had to, and paid as little as they could manage.

Tsugo had resented all that when he was a young man. He had resented having to marry the plain-faced younger daughter of a servant at the village inn, because no other woman would marry a dung-collector. These days, a widower well past his thirtieth year with three children to feed, he no longer had time or energy to resent anything beyond the ruts and sloughs in the road that kept threatening to bog or knock over his cart. The rain two days ago had turned the road halfway to mud, and the samurai who marched through that same day had finished the job. Then yesterday a merchant caravan had come down from the north, pushing their ox-drawn wagons hard even when they churned the soft road to porridge, dragging the wagons through nearly axle-deep in the slough.

Inconsiderate oafs, Tsugo thought, grunting and gasping with effort as he wrestled his cart out of the mud and onto the sparse winter-yellow grass alongside. *They didn't even set up any stalls.* When merchants came through town they always seemed to think their dung didn't stink, but they did buy loads of the pottery that was Aotouki's main product, sometimes picked up other things as well, and usually brought interesting things to sell. Tsugo had bought his wife a comb one time when a merchant came through, years ago when she was still alive – an indulgence she had scolded him for afterward. These fellows, though, had just taken all the rooms at the village inn and put their wagons in the stables without so much as a word to the curious townsfolk and eager potters who had gathered outside. Some of the villagers had even talked to Tsugo about it when he came by this morning to empty their chamber-pots. *You know it's strange when folk'll lower themselves t'gossiping with t'dung-collector,* he thought with a faint echo of his youthful bitterness.

Tsugo shrugged to himself and leaned on the handle of his wagon, blowing out long breaths and waiting for the pounding of his heart to ease. The rising Sun, peeking in between the clouds that cluttered the sky, was warming the contents of the cart and intensifying the odor, enough that even Tsugo's long-numbed senses could pick it up. It was the growing clouds of buzzing flies that really annoyed him, though; flies always got worse during the warmer hours. He mopped his face with the sleeve of his baggy gray overcoat and then adjusted the headband on his forehead, wishing he'd brought a canteen. He could just see the distant shape of his house across the fields, a half-mile away. Not a daunting distance on a normal day, but the road today might as well have been created by the Demons themselves…

He blinked and squinted. A pair of human shapes had appeared on the road, emerging from the background of distant trees. Momentarily he thought it was the morticians – their dwelling was somewhere beyond that treeline, though he'd been careful never to visit it himself. No chance he would risk being dragged down to their lowest spiritual level.

No, it isn't them, he realized. *Travelers, I think. Strange for folk t'be on t'road this early.* The next village was miles to the north, so anyone leaving there in the morning would take hours to reach Aotouki… *Well, no matter. I've rested long enough, and no telling what trouble t'boys might be getting into by now.* His eldest child and only daughter, Chio, kept the two younger ones in hand while Tsugo was working, but it was a struggle, especially with the youngest who had a wild streak so broad that Chio sometimes accused him of being a fox spirit born into a boy's body.

Tsugo took a deep breath and gripped the wagon's handle tightly, pushing it back onto the road and then grunting with effort as it tried to slew back and forth in the mud. For a few minutes he was conscious only of the strain in his arms, the mud churning under his feet, and the buzzing of the flies. A distant clanging noise teased the edge of his senses, but he was too focused on the wagon to pay attention to it. Finally he reached the side-path to his own house, which was still mostly dry, and stopped there to rest again.

That was when he realized the travelers had nearly reached him, and that one of them was the source of the metallic sound. He didn't look directly at them – that would rude in the best of circumstances, and a dung-collector wasn't supposed to be too forward even with other commoners. Instead he observed them sidelong, keeping his head pointed toward his cart and slightly lowered.

A Priestess, he thought, as the Sunlight glinting on her prayer-staff caught his eye. *That's what was making t'noise.* Aotouki Village did not have a Priestess of their own, but one visited from Daitouki Village every season to lead the festivals. Those were usually older women – once it had been an outright tottering crone who could barely speak the mantras – but he thought this one was young. The shaved head and thick saffron-and-yellow robes made it difficult to be sure. Those robes were rather ragged and muddy, he realized, and she looked tired and unkempt; even her shaved scalp showed some stubble. She walked close by the taller stranger, a young man.

Sellsword, Tsugo thought, feeling a prickle of alarm. The fellow wore samurai blades, one on each hip, and was dressed in baggy pleated pants that hung down to his shins and a loose shirt with open-ended sleeves that extended to his wrists; a broad sash around his waist held the swords in place. A samurai's casual clothing, rather than the short-sleeved overcoats and knee-length pants that peasants wore. The garments were mostly ragged and dirty, even more so than the Priestess' robes, though the shirt was fairly clean. The man's hair was a loose greasy tangle that hung down his back.

Scars on his face, Tsugo thought, feeling his nerves clench. *And his eyes… something wrong with 'em.* They caught the Sunlight oddly, seeming to almost glow.

The man's gaze snapped toward Tsugo. The dung-collector gulped and lowered his head, leaning over the cart's handles, focusing on showing nothing but deference. Sellswords were trouble, always, even at the best of times – which these were not. He'd heard stories about remote villages and farmers that killed any sellsword they found, pawning their armor and weapons, and at times like this he couldn't blame them for committing such crimes.

The strangers stopped walking, mud squishing up around their filthy sandals. This close, Tsugo could see their clothing was completely soaked below the waist. *Did they cross t'river?* The River of Black Ice that lay on the west side of Aotouki Village was too deep to cross here, but he'd heard there was supposed to be a ford somewhere upstream.

The swordsman took a step closer, and Tsugo could see his hands were on his hips, close to the hilts of his swords. "A dung-collector, no wonder I thought something was stinking. You just come from the village up ahead?"

"Yes, honorable swordsman," Tsugo mumbled, tightening his grip on the cart-handle. He kept his voice low, expressionless, speaking in the most submissive manner possible. "This one's called Tsugo. This one just finished his duties there, honorable swordsman."

"Huh. Yeah, I can small that," the swordsman sneered. The Priestess murmured something, her staff chiming once, and the swordsman let out a snort and then continued in a more normal voice: "What's wrong with your damned river? It was full of dead bodies."

Tsugo blinked. "Honorable samurai? I... I'm just a dung collector. Ain't heard nothing about dead bodies." Though now that he thought about it, he remembered hearing the village's potters complaining that the river was full of filth, making the water unfit to use in their pottery clay.

The swordsman squinted past him, his pale eyes flashing again. Tsugo felt an odd chill run up his back at the sight. "Yeah, that's the place. Somethin' ain't right there."

The Priestess shifted, making her staff chime again. "Kenji? Are you sure?"

"In the village. There's... shadows." The swordsman – *Kenji?* – rolled his shoulders like a woodsman getting ready to cut down a tree. He headed down the road, walking on the thin grass at the edge of the slough. "Let's go."

"Wait, Kenji! What do you mean—" The young Priestess started to follow him, then paused briefly to bow at Tsugo. "Lady watch over you, honorable Tsugo." She hurried after the swordsman, her staff chiming discordantly.

Tsugo watched them go, his immediate fear fading into confusion. *What a strange pair. That fellow was... scary, and those eyes!* He glanced toward the distant village, noting the faint haze of charcoal smoke as women cooked the morning meals. *What'd he mean, shadows? Was he seeing t'smoke?*

Then he shook himself and took a fresh grip on the handle of his cart. *Well, they've moved on, and no harm done, thank t'Goddess' Compassion. Time t'get back t'work.*

⛩ ⛩ ⛩

THE SECOND ONE TO SEE the strangers was Ryoga the Potter.

He was not the only pottery worker in his family by any means, let alone in all of Aotouki Village. There were six families of potters in Aotouki, and while Ryoga could boast that he was the elder of his own family he could not even claim to be the oldest potter in town. That was Manji, who was so old that his eyesight was gone and he shaped his pots entirely by feel.

Aotouki was not as well known for its pottery as the larger town of Daitouki, ten miles downriver next to the big samurai castle. Ryoga had been bitter about that when he was younger, believing Aotouki's pottery was just as good and deserved more success. Old Manji had told him once that Daitouki's pottery was actually better, because their clay was dug from hills full of cleansing hot springs, and Ryoga had been so angry he hadn't talked to the man for a month. Besides, water was more important to a clay than the stone that was pounded into powder to form its base. The waters of the River of Black Ice came from somewhere in the far north, unlike any other river in the Empire, and that was the real reason why local pottery was better.

These days, well into middle age and with a back that ached more often than not, Ryoga was more resigned to things. Daitouki was next to a castle, which meant more roads went there, which meant more merchants went there, which meant its pottery was more successful. Nothing to be done about it; no man could defeat Fate, however much he might have tried when he was younger. Ryoga still thought water was more important than rock to the quality of clay, but at the moment there was no way to appreciate the debate properly. For the last two weeks the river had been foul, not just muddy as it often was in early spring but full of dead animals... and the occasional human corpse.

Ryoga frowned at the rows of wooden molds in his shed. Each of them contained dried blocks of clay base; to make that base into proper pottery clay, it would need to be crumbled into powder, mixed with water, and then strained to remove grit and impurities. The process was laborious and would require the assistance of Ryoga's brother-in-law Daizo and his boy Kanta for a day or more. And it used water – a lot of water.

In these last two weeks the town's potters had used up their reserves of prepared clay. Now the majority of them were idle, working on odd jobs, mining extra stone to stockpile for the future, or simply relaxing in the town's teahouses, drinking wine and gossiping fatalistically about the river and what it implied.

"Bad times are coming," old Manji had muttered last night, holding out his cup for his son Hideji – himself no young man but a crease-faced grandfather – to fill it. "All those samurai passing through town. Strangers on t'roads. I had a dream, a warning from t'Lady. Bad times."

Ryoga had snorted and said nothing. Bad times were always coming, to hear old Manji tell it. Bad times had always been coming. When the town had a record harvest five years ago he had spent the festival predicting famine for the next year.

To be sure, yesterday a big troop of samurai had indeed passed through, marching northward all grim-faced and silent. More samurai in one group than Ryoga had ever seen. Presumably that meant a war somewhere, though it was odd for them to be marching north – Ryoga had always had a vague impression that wars happened in the south, where there were – supposedly – other samurai who wore different colors and swore allegiance to different Lords. It was all very abstract to him, hardly worth thinking about. Samurai did what they did, and it was no concern of his. It was only fretful old men and women like Manji who tried to see meaning in it.

The same war was doubtless why there were more travelers on the road than usual, all of them heading south. Like that merchant caravan that had come in last night, though the cheap scum hadn't done any buying… not that Ryoga had much he could sell them right now. It was like that drought year, when the river had shrunk to a muddy trickle and no one could do anything but pray there would be enough rice to keep them alive…

Enough thinking, the potter told himself. *I have work t'do.* He looked at the boxes of dried clay-base a moment longer, then shrugged. *I'll go check on t'river. Maybe t'water's cleared overnight – there was rain a couple days ago, after all.* He picked up a bamboo yoke that leaned on the wall, slung it across his shoulders, and hooked a wooden bucket onto each end. Thus burdened he set out from the shed, trotting along the path toward the distant waterway, his thin sandals scuffing on the bare damp earth of the footpath. The route snaked between tussocks of thick grass, brown and dead now at the tail end of winter, and headed toward the dense bamboo grove that crouched above the riverbank.

A faint sound impinged on Ryoga's ears, something unfamiliar, and a subtle prickle of unease went through him. He looked to his right, where the main road could just be glimpsed through gaps in the brush and tall grass. Two people were just visible there, walking briskly up the road, passing in and out of sight as the undergrowth intervened. At this distance they were little more than silhouettes, but Ryoga could see the distinctive shape of a Priestess' staff and realized it was the noise he was half-hearing above the cold morning breeze and the rustle of grass and trees.

Ryoga relaxed. Unsettled times meant more people on the road, but a Priestess would be no danger. *No reason t'be afraid of everything… I've spent too many evenings listening t'old Manji telling stories. And t'past is dead, not coming back.* He turned back to the path, resettling the yoke on his shoulders, and trudged forward into the bamboo grove. *Perhaps the Priestess'll give us a blessing t'help clear t'river.*

The cloudy morning light turned dim, almost shadowy, as the ridged tubes of the bamboo trunks enfolded him on all sides. He could hear a faint steady creaking from the trees as they swayed in the wind, and beneath it a subtle rushing noise that was the river. He couldn't see the water from here save for a faint impression of brighter light and motion in between the trees.

He did see, as he always did, a slight depression amid the trees, a place where the ground had settled. Enough years had gone by that he no longer let his gaze linger on it, even when no one else was with him.

Ryoga paused, frowning to himself. Had he heard something else? He stood still, head cocked, listening. Then he resumed his walk, swinging the yoke forward to dodge a grove of trees that crowded close onto the path. A minute later he emerged from the bamboo onto the riverbank.

It was an overhang here, a shallow cliff with grass and brush atop and a scoured-out arc of bare earth and naked roots descending to the water. The path turned left and followed the top of the embankment; Ryoga knew it would descend to the water a hundred paces downstream. But he had no need to follow it further. He had known the moment the smell hit him.

The brown churning surface of the river was covered with pale bobbing oblongs. *Fish,* Ryoga realized, feeling a surge of unease. *Dead fish.* Dead for days, judging from the rancid odor that rose from the water.

As he watched, a dark bloated shape floated past him. A facedown man with a black samurai topknot on the back of his head. Several thin sticks – arrows-shafts, the potter belatedly realized – stuck up from his back. The body went past him, slowly turning in the brown current, and after a minute a second corpse appeared upstream, this one face up and with the river half-filling the gaped-open mouth.

Water's no good today, Ryoga thought through a faint buzzing that seemed to echo within his head. *Might not be good for a long time. What could kill all t'fish upstream?*

Somewhere in the distance, a voice rose in a scream.

卄 卄 卄

THE THIRD ONE TO SEE the strangers was Sakura, the innkeeper.

She frowned to herself beneath the pleasant smile she was showing as she carried the breakfast trays out to the common room. *There is something wrong with these people,* she thought.

The merchants had come in yesterday evening, driving a trio of ox-drawn wagons, everything covered in mud from the road. Four men, all of the sort she recognized from a lifetime of experience as belonging to the merchant class – soft-looking fellows in middle age, well-dressed in an understated way designed not to offend samurai, carefully avoiding the mud that spattered and smeared the rest of their caravan. Accompanying them were over a dozen younger folk, men and a few women, dressed in simple commoner garb made desperately filthy from the road.

She had been too busy last night to pay close attention to individuals – it had taken all her energy to deal with the sudden influx of guests. Getting the wagons and oxen stabled and scrounging up help to clean them; readying enough space for all the guests, which had meant emptying out the rooms where she and her family usually stayed; preparing food and drink for all of them, and enough water and charcoal to the bath-house for them all to wash up, and making sure all their dirty clothes were soaked and scrubbed so they would be dry enough by morning. It was the first time in a year that she had found herself missing her late husband; he had been callous and indifferent to the point of cruelty, but he had always worked hard and knew how to do everything in the inn, and the extra pair of reliable hands would have been very useful. As it was, her son Buso had called in his cousins to help in the stables, her younger son Kaji had spent all evening in the kitchen with her, and she had sent runners to summon her daughters Harue and Naoko from their own houses and bring along anyone they could to help with the cleaning. She would have to pay all the extra help, but these merchants were spending money like water. One of them, a man who called himself Raizo, had simply tossed a loaded money-string at her last night and said "bring food."

The one thing that had struck Sakura as odd from the beginning was their complete disinterest in meeting the local potters and shopkeeps. Usually any merchant who went through town made at least a gesture at doing both, even if they were in a hurry. Still, it was very early in the season and there was clearly trouble up north with all the samurai passing through in that direction, so perhaps it wasn't that strange for them to show no interest in local opportunities.

This morning, though…

She knelt by one of the tables and handed out the bowls and plates – grilled pieces of chicken and bean curd, rice with raw eggs, sliced pickled vegetables and spring onions. Her daughters and her eldest granddaughter – that would be Kaya, just turned eleven this year – did the same at the other tables. The merchants nodded and grunted, but their entourage of guards and laborers accepted the meals in complete silence, not even looking at the young women handing over their food. Which was… *Strange, thoroughly strange.* Not that Sakura appreciated the leers and intermittent gropings male customers often bestowed, but such behavior, distasteful though it was, was *normal* – it was what men did, especially traveling strangers with no connection to the local community. And the ones who didn't behave badly still showed appreciation for being served by an attractive female.

These fellows, though… her daughters might as well have been old men for all the attention they got. Even the merchants themselves, who at least acknowledged the arrival of their meals, showed none of the focused attention that was normal for men. *I suppose they could all be the sort who prefer other men, but... what would the odds of that be?* She vaguely knew such people existed, especially among the samurai, but it seemed highly unlikely that a whole group of them could have shown up at once. Besides, the lower-ranking fellows didn't seem to show much interest in anything – they were eating with dull mechanical motions, like flesh-and-blood waterwheels.

And the smell... There was an odd tone to their body odor, even after bathing last night. A rancid note that somehow put her in mind of the feral dog that had troubled the town last year.

Definitely something wrong, though I don't know what. Sakura rose and tucked the tray under her arm, shooing the others ahead of her back into the kitchen. Harue reached for the teapots there, but Sakura waved her off. "Stay back here with Kaya and clean up," she murmured, and while Harue looked confused and almost rebellious, Naoko nodded firmly. *Ah, she's picked up on it,* Sakura thought, obscurely pleased. Naoko had always been the more sensible of her daughters, marrying the son of the town's best potter and keeping a solid household there.

Sakura collected a teapot herself and headed back out to the common room alone. The men were still eating stolidly, not even looking at her as she refilled their cups. The merchants, crowded around a single table – one of them had pulled over a bench from another table to sit end-on – spoke together in low voices. They fell silent as she approached, watching her with expressions that felt... measuring, almost predatory. She avoided their gazes, pouring the tea quickly and proud that she did so without wavering or spilling.

One of the merchants – the one called Raizo – cleared his throat. He did not touch his teacup. "Honorable innkeeper."

Sakura didn't like the way he said it. The honorific seemed mocking rather than polite. But she bobbed her head politely. "Yes, honored guest? Is there anything else you need?"

"Is there a landholder here?"

"No, honored guest," Sakura answered automatically – merchants often asked about that, since samurai landholders were potential customers and were also the local authorities to report any problems. And it was true, there was not a samurai residing in Aotouki Village... But even as she answered her prickle of unease intensified. She set the pot back on its tray and rose to her feet, holding the tray in front of herself instead of at her side. "Is there anything else you require before your departure, honored guests?"

The merchant smirked. There was no other word for the unpleasant smile on his face. "You will stay here, innkeeper." He nodded at the other three, two of whom stood up. None of them had touched their teacups.

Sakura's unease blossomed into fear. She started to back away, and Raizo lifted one hand and made an odd grasping motion.

Her legs locked, the muscles refusing to answer. The merchant's smirk broadened. Sakura's chest tightened and she let out a whimpering noise as she struggled to move; the tray in her arms tilted slightly, the teapot sliding toward one edge.

"We'll start with this place," Raizo said, speaking not to her but to the others, as though she wasn't even there. "Keep the children for the Lords, and dispose of the rest."

Sakura heard a noise around her, a wood-on-wood rumble of benches moving, and realized all the laborers had stood up at once. The merchant rose as well, and as he did for a brief moment she could move, her whole body jerking violently. The teapot dropped off the tray and smashed on the floor, hot liquid splashing and a shard slicing painfully across the top of her foot, and she stumbled backward until her back struck a table. She gasped for breath and shouted: "Kaya-*chan*, run—"

The merchant stepped toward her and lifted his hand again, and Sakura whimpered as her shout died in her throat, all her muscles locking and spasming in agonizing immobility. As though from a great distance she heard Harue come out of the kitchen, calling her name and then screaming aloud as two of the laborers seized her, three others shouldering past her through the kitchen door. The other merchants and their followers were moving toward the inn's front entrance, and knives had appeared in their hands... where had those come from?

Sakura knew with sudden certainty that they were going to kill her, and Harue and Naoko and Kaya and *everyone* in the village. *Amatsu, blessed Lady, help me,* she prayed, lips barely moving, the rest of her straining against whatever force it was that clutched her body.

"No, no," Raizo smiled, and he lifted his other hand – the one not making the strange claw-like gesture – and stroked his fingertips across her face. She shuddered and her stomach lurched and try to empty itself. There was something *wrong* with his touch, as though his fingertips were slugs crawling over her face. "No, the False Light can't hear you, won't help you. It never does."

"—it's in here, I'm tellin' you," a rasping male voice declared.

Sakura's eyes darted sideways, as far as the unnatural force would allow, and she saw a silhouette in the front door, resolving into a long-haired man who brushed past the hanging half-curtain and then stopped dead. *A samurai,* Sakura knew, seeing the outlines of the sword-hilts projecting past his hips.

The merchants and their workers went silent and still. For a long moment nothing happened, and then a voice called from outside, a young woman's voice: "Kenji?"

The samurai – not a proper samurai, she realized, he was filthy and unshaven – suddenly grinned, teeth white against his dirty face. "I must be doin' what She wants, to find all this scum in one place."

And then *light* flashed from him, as though a lantern had briefly opened behind his eyes.

Sakura felt a prickling run all over her skin, a sensation like she had felt once when a lightning strike had landed on the tree behind her outhouse. Merchant Raizo turned sharply toward the newcomer, and Sakura felt the… force… holding her falter; instinctively she jerked back and then she was free, scurrying back toward her daughter. No one reacted; their eyes were all fixed on the tangle-haired swordsman.

"Kill him!" Raizo shouted, and his men surged forward, knives glinting as they lifted them overhead to stab and slash. The samurai's long sword came out of its sheath in a ringing blur.

The strangers holding Harue released her and rushed past Sakura; she caught her daughter around the waist and dragged her toward the kitchen door, looking back over the younger woman's shoulder. She glimpsed a spray of dark red hazing across the roof of the dining room, followed an instant later by the tumbling shapes of severed hands and arms and heads. The rush of motion suddenly reversed itself, men stumbling back and leaving others on the floor, screaming in bewildered agony or silent and still.

"I said *kill* him," Raizo shouted, though his voice had gone oddly shrill. He stepped forward, lifting both hands with fingers crooked, as if to claw at the swordsman from halfway across the room.

The samurai's eyes flashed again, the light stabbing-bright. Sakura let go of her daughter and clapped her hands over her mouth, weeping. For a moment she could not see the inn or the blood or the merchant waving his hands as though they were claws; she was a young woman again, alone in the forest beyond the town's edge, burying the child she had smothered to death because there was not enough food to last until the harvest.

⛩ ⛩ ⛩

RYOGA THE POTTER EMERGED FROM the bamboo grove, moving at a shuffling trot, straining to hear more as he wove in between the view-obscuring tussocks. *Screams, yes, those're definitely screams,* he thought, panting as he tried to move faster despite the weight of the yoke and buckets. He couldn't recognize the voices or even tell if they were the cries of men or women. Ryoga knew true agony sounded the same regardless of the person; a decade ago his cousin Tojiro's leg had been crushed by a panicked ox, and the man had shrieked as wildly as any woman.

A small corner of his mind wondered: *Why run* toward *the screams?* He grimaced and shunted the thought aside. Common folk might not be samurai, but that didn't mean they had to be weaklings; he had always despised those of his neighbors who cowered and hid the moment there was trouble.

He reached the shed and dropped the yoke off his shoulders, grimacing as the buckets clattered and one of them made an ominous cracking sound. *Worry about that later.* Beyond the shed a shorter path snaked between two small clumps of trees to the back of his house. Most houses had a vegetable garden behind them, but his had not since his wife had... left, a decade before – he got vegetables from his sister's garden across town. The back yard of his house was just bare earth, weeds, and a two-wheeled hand-cart that he used to take his pots to market. He scurried past the cart and swung right, turning down the narrow, muddy alleyway between his house and his neighbor's dwelling – he didn't want to run through the interior in his dirty sandals. Clots of half-dried mud flew up behind him as he pushed past a tangled shrub at the front of the alley and into the street. People were there, neighbors, farmers' wives. Some looking to the right, while others were running from that direction. The inn was there, fifty paces away, perched on the southern edge of the town proper with a clump of trees beyond it. Someone was standing outside the front door, a robed figure holding a tall stick whose circular top glinted in the Sunlight. *A Priestess*, Ryoga realized. *Must be t'same one I saw on t'road.* As he started forward, another scream echoed, and he saw two women come out from behind the inn and run toward him – well, no, they weren't running, they were tottering and staggering as though drunk.

Closer, and he recognized Sakura the innkeeper and one of her married daughters. They were both weeping, clutching each other like drowning people holding a rope. He started to ask them what was happening, then realized it was useless – they were hysterical, barely able to stay upright. He joined the others moving up the street toward the inn. His brother-in-law Shoma was there, his hands all covered in gray clay – had he been holding out, keeping enough clay to make more pots? The blacksmith Teiji held a blank piece of iron whose tip still glowed hot-orange from the forge. A couple of farmers arrived from the fields, mattocks clutched in both hands.

Another scream echoed, clearly from inside the inn, and Ryoga was sure it was a man's voice driven to shrill pitch by sudden agony, sounding almost exactly like poor Tojiro had done. The Priestess had stepped away from the front of the inn to follow Sakura, but now she turned back.

The wooden slats covering the inn's front window exploded outward, driven by a human shape that sailed awkwardly through the shower of wooden fragments. The man hit the ground and rolled a couple of times, limbs flopping loosely. The Priestess flinched away, raising her staff in a defensive gesture.

Ryoga and his companions drew up, still a dozen paces from the inn, those with improvised weapons clutching them tightly. Ryoga squinted at the fallen figure, noting the rapidly spreading dark red stain around it, mixing with the damp earth of the road. *One of t'strangers from last night,* he realized. *What—?*

Someone came out of the inn's front door, a slightly plump man in a merchant's garb, staggering away but looking back wide-eyed, not even noticing the villagers in front of him. His lips were peeled back from his teeth, like a wild dog baring its fangs, and his eyes were so wide they seemed to be bulging out of his head. He did see the Priestess and made a brief gesture toward her, a swing of the arm as though trying to shove her away, and she stumbled and clutched her staff as though a wind had struck her.

Two others came through the door, men in simple laborers' clothing, plain jackets and white leggings and bare feet. One of them was clutching an arm that ended at the wrist, leaving pulses of red on the ground as he wobbled backward and then sank to his knees, his face going slack. The other held a knife in an awkward overhead pose, stabbing erratically into the doorway, yelling wordlessly with each blow.

A third man came through the door, loose hair and baggy pants and loose-sleeved shirt, and he had a samurai's swords in his hands, long and short blades held to either side, the steel red in the sunlight and the dark sleeves of his shirt sodden and red-dripping too, and his teeth flashed as he laughed aloud.

The laugh was storm-thunder and joy and Sunrise and madness, all wrapped together, and Ryoga took a step back, feeling an almost uncontrollable urge to cover his ears and shut it out. He heard Shoma let out a grunt, heard a clatter and sizzle as Teiji dropped his iron blank.

The knife-wielding man screamed, shrill and insane, and staggered forward with his blade rising and falling spasmodically. Then he was in pieces, flying apart in sprays of crimson, and the laughing swordsman walked through the ruin toward the merchant. "Just you left now, scum," he called, and spread his swords apart to either side, holding them down and away. Red droplets ran off their ends and left a trail behind him. His sandals left red prints behind as well, though he walked lightly, like a hunting cat.

The merchant held out both hands toward the swordsman as though he were trying to push the man away. His voice was shrill and wild, almost gibbering. "What are you? How can you resist the Lords?" He shoved his hands again, and Ryoga thought the fingers looked like claws.

The swordsman's eyes flashed, like a mirror catching the Sunlight, and then they *flared* and the world filled with *Light—*

—Ryoga knelt over the body of his wife, shaking, his knuckles stinging where the blows to her face had split the skin. He whispered her name hoarsely, his dwindling rage curdling into nauseating fear. He hadn't hit her that hard, she had just made him so angry, all her cutting words always slicing away at his dreams, and she'd been so much worse since the miscarriage—

—his daughter Minami knelt sobbing in the back room of the hut as he told Teiji and Manji and Headman Asao the story he had rehearsed. "I knew she'd been bad in t'head since she lost t'baby, didn't matter that it had no soul yet, but I never expected her t'run off and leave me." They nodded sympathetically, everyone knew women could be faithless, Asao had lost his first wife to a traveling musician—

Something hot and sticky spattered across Ryoga's face and neck, and the merchant's head bounced off the ground in front of him and rolled away. The Light, the terrible clarity, had faded. Ryoga realized he was sobbing, clutching his hands together as though he could squeeze the remembered crime out of them. The swordsman loomed over him, wiping his blades on the clothes of the fallen merchant, and now his eyes did not shine, though they were still... unnatural, ghostly pale.

"Kill me," Ryoga whispered.

The swordsman looked down at him, his blood-spattered face scowling. "What? You've got a shadow... you one of them too?"

"Kenji," the Priestess called. She hurried toward the swordsman, her staff clanging. "He's just a villager." She knelt in front of Ryoga, her left hand holding her soft-chiming staff upright as a brace. "Are you hurt? Do you need help?"

Ryoga realized she was actually young, maybe as young as his daughter.

He slammed his fists against his own numb face. "Kill me," he said again, louder this time. His voice was hoarse, a rasping croak.

The swordsman broke into a crooked grin, white through the pattern of red. "Nah. Your shadow's weak. So you ain't one of those Mask scum." He finished cleaning his swords and slid them into their opposite-hip sheaths, not even looking to guide them, the motions oil-smooth. "You want to die, do it yourself."

The Priestess caught Ryoga's wrist with her free hand, the slim fingers halting his blows as though they were made of steel. "You are no samurai, to seek penance through death. And no Sin is unforgiveable."

Ryoga shut his eyes, and felt a hot prickling gather in their corners. "I can't ask forgiveness of... of someone who's dead."

"No, you cannot," she agreed softly. "Not in this life. But the Lady's Compassion is infinite. There is always a path to redemption."

Ryoga thought of the place in the bamboo grove, and of what it would cost him to take his son-in-law and daughter and newborn grandson there, to tell them the truth. "I can't," he mumbled.

"You can," she told him, and recited a mantra as she set her fingertips on his forehead. They felt oddly warm, and his eyes opened in surprise.

She rose, her staff chiming again as she pulled herself upright with it. The swordsman was standing next to her, his posture casual but a little closer than was proper. Ryoga noticed he was holding a blood-stained money-string in one hand, and realized it must have come from the now-dead merchant. "You done? Let's go find the Wolf Lord's men. I'm not stickin' around for these peasants to try to kill me." He half-turned and took a step, signaling the desire to move.

The Priestess glared at him. "Why in Amatsu's name would they do that after you just—?" But she followed him, and the pair walked down the road, past the inn and on south, their voices receding.

"You know how many times peasants have tried to kill me? They act all cowardly until your back is turned—"

"That's a horrible thing to say. Why do you—"

Ryoga stared after them, breathing deeply, trying to get his thoughts under control. Slowly he realized a substantial portion of the village population had gathered around him, staring in awe and not a little fear at the bloody slaughter in the street. Sakura and her daughter had returned, now joined by the rest of her family and in-laws, and they were haltingly describing what had happened inside.

"The honorable Priestess was talkin' t'you, Ryoga. What'd she say?"

It was Headman Asao who asked, but when Ryoga turned to answer he saw his daughter, standing alongside her husband Shoma and holding their infant son in the crook of one arm. Her eyes were wide in her heart-shaped face, and in that moment she looked very much like her mother had, long ago.

"Yes, what'd she say, Ryoga?" It was Teiji the blacksmith asking now. "That was… that was all so strange, felt like I was dreamin' for a moment. Did she tell you something?"

Ryoga looked at all of them, ending at last on his daughter. Her eyes widened slightly as she took in his expression. "Honored father..?"

The Lady's Compassion is infinite.

Ryoga knelt forward, pressing his face into the earth, his hands to the ground before her feet. "Minami-*chan,*" he whispered. "Please, forgive me. I killed your mother."

CHAPTER 2

OOKAMI KAEDE, HIGH LADY of the Wolf Clan, paused just inside the main doors of Castle Ookami's inner keep. The guards escorting her on either side and the small legion of servants following her also paused, silently awaiting her command. She still occasionally found that unsettling, though far less often than in the past. *One can get used to anything. I'm even getting used to being married to Akira. Is that a good thing, or a tragedy?*

Kaede moved her hands subtly, checking one last time on the arrangement of her robes and sash. She wanted to check her hair again too, despite having watched in the mirror while the maids meticulously combed out the four-foot-long glossy black strands and placed the golden pins and headdress that was her inheritance from the Black Wolf Clan into which she'd been born. *It's perfectly fine*, she told herself, *and if I fuss with it here where everyone can see, it will be a loss of face.* Still, the urge to check once more was powerful. It was so important for the High Lady to appear flawless in public...

She brought her hands together, clasping them inside her sleeves, and nodded to the two servants who knelt waiting on either side of the doors. They rose and pushed the heavy oak valves open, and bright early-morning Sunlight made her blink even as the chill air made her skin prickle and tighten. For once Kaede was grateful for the numbing effect of the thick cosmetic powder that covered her face. Grateful, too, that her husband had accepted her insistence that their son Basho remain inside for the departure ceremony. Even if Spring had officially arrived, the weather was cold and she was not going to risk her only living child falling ill for the sake of appearances.

Though there might be another child soon. Her moon's blood was late, and that had been a reliable predictor both times before.

Both times... She advanced down the steps from the keep's doors to the parade ground outside, keeping her pace slow and hieratic as the occasion demanded. It was an effort not to stumble when the memories surfaced. She had lost her second pregnancy, and nearly her life, to a virulent fever. Ritsuko, the bitter old Priestess who had nursed her through that misery, had told her it was a miracle that her fertility cycle had resumed afterward. And had blamed the lost pregnancy on Kaede's covert affairs with the now-dead Katsura brothers.

Stay focused, Kaede told herself firmly, still advancing at a steady pace. *Ritsuko is with the other Priestesses in the Temple, praying for the army – and Akira already knows about the affairs and doesn't seem to care.* She had confessed the truth in a moment of fearful weakness last spring, half-expecting him to divorce her or order her to slit her own throat, but he had done nothing.

The long shallow steps clacked softly beneath her sandals. *This is important, we are going to war and if there is a bad omen at the departure – like me stumbling right now! – it will hurt our chances.* It was strange to her that such things could matter when it might be weeks until the actual fighting happened, but the historical books she had read in her youth agreed with her allies in the court that it was true. Her former handmaiden Tokage Miyako – Kuroi Miyako now, after her marriage – had told her stories about such incidents during the reign of the previous High Lord, Akira's father Lord Okaro. Omens could haunt armies for weeks afterward. She had seen it herself, for that matter, when Dowager Lady Toride had cursed Lord Okaro and committed suicide in open court, and the subsequent military campaign had been plagued with ill luck and high casualties.

Kaede stepped out of the shadows of the entrance and into the view of the waiting army. A surf-roar of noise struck her like a blow, a thunder that resolved into bellowing words: "Ookami! Ookami! Ookami!" She paused, almost stumbled, feeling an odd warmth run through her. *Are they cheering for... me?* She actually shook her head very slightly before she schooled her features. *No, of course not, don't be a fool. They know nothing about me. They're cheering for... what I represent. I'm just a symbol.*

She focused herself, letting the cheers fade into the background, and walked toward her waiting husband.

Ookami Akira, High Lord of the Wolf, was in his early twenties but with broad white streaks in his hair that created an impression of age, clashing oddly with his smooth expressionless face. It was a face that in the abstract could be considered handsome; Kaede had become resigned enough to their arranged marriage that she could admit that, if only to herself, but the stony lack of expression somewhat undercut the appeal. For this occasion he was dressed in the Wolf Clan's ancestral full armor, a gaudy bulk of gray-and-red lacquered shoulder plates and waist guards layered over the simpler greaves and back-and-breast he wore by preference. The helmet, a gigantic metal dome topped with gaudy feathers and a double-half-moon clasping a steel-rendered snarling wolf's head, was tucked under his arm to let the army see his face. The ensemble did look imposing, especially from a distance, which she supposed was the point.

His face remained unmoving as she approached and made a deep bow. Not a full prostration – her status as his wife meant she was not required to do that – but deeper than his return bow. His expression did not change, his face as rigid as if it had been carved from wood or Nightingale ivory. By now she was almost accustomed to that inhuman blankness; the very rare and brief spasms of real emotion she had occasionally glimpsed were actually far more unsettling.

There was no such crack in his inhuman self-control today. He stood aside and let her take her place at his left, facing the army that stood in blocks and rows within the castle's massive parade-ground. They were alone, since the other two high-ranking officials who might have been expected to stand alongside them – Ookami Tokage, the captain of the castle guard, and Ookami Amano, the Seneschal, both of whom Akira had inherited from the court of his late father Okaro – were both absent on a mission to negotiate with the foreign spirits called Aelfynn. A few letters from Amano had trickled in since their mid-winter departure, but the last one had been almost a month ago.

Just as well Amano's gone, really, Kaede thought. Amano was also the Wolf Clan spymaster, and in his absence she had been reading the spy reports before passing them to Akira. She would have questions to ask honorable Amano, when he returned...

Akira faced the army and shouted, his voice projecting across the parade ground with the force of a temple bell. "We march for the Imperial City!"

That met with an instant of stunned absolute silence, the soldiers trying to comprehend something that had been unthinkable for generations. Kaede could see some of Akira's favored officers in the front ranks, and she could tell they were not surprised; instead, their faces were exultant. *He must have already told them.*

The High Lord drew his sword and raised it overhead. "The Lady with us!"

That was the traditional cheer of the samurai since the days of the First Emperor, and the ranked soldiers broke from their amazement and bellowed it back.

"THE LADY WITH US!"

Despite herself Kaede swayed on her feet as the vast shout repeated three times, buffeting her like a strong wind. The soldiers' faces were rapt now, all sense of self lost in the moment. *They all worship him like the Emperor come to life,* she thought, the knowledge still tinged with an embittered bafflement. Akira was as cold and inhuman toward them as he was toward her… *But he wins battles,* she reminded herself. *He wins when everyone thinks he will lose. To a soldier that must seem wondrous.*

And now we're going to war again, but this time Akira is starting it, instead of reacting to others… and he's doing something no one has dared to do for centuries. The Imperial City had remained unclaimed since the death of the last Emperor four hundred years before; during that time the Empire's twelve samurai Clans had dwindled to five.

The cheers finally ended and Akira sheathed his sword. Kaede waited for him to turn toward her, afraid he would forget and shame her in front of the whole army – his attention seemed to be on the soldier bringing his horse. But finally he did look at her, and Kaede bowed again, and recited: "Amatsu watch over you, honored husband." She said it as loudly as she could without sounding shrill or manly – that would defeat the purpose.

For a moment he just stood there, but then – thank Amatsu – he bowed as well. "Thank you, honored wife." His voice was stone-flat, devoid of sincerity – but he had said the words, maintained etiquette, which was what mattered in the end.

The soldier halted at Akira's side with the horse, and the High Lord swung into the saddle with almost casual ease despite his confining heavy armor. A brief jab with his heels put the beast into motion, trotting toward the passage that led through Castle Ookami's layered defenses to its outer gate. The officers mounted as well, shouting orders, and the whole army began stirring into motion, a ripple from the front to the back of each column of men. One by one the columns flowed through the gate after Akira, descending the switchback ramps to the castle's outer gate. Kaede waited, silent, shivering a little as the cold almost-spring air began to seep through the layers of her robes. It would not do for her to go inside before the last of the men had departed.

This isn't even most of the army, she reminded herself. *Just a chosen few brought here to witness the High Lord's departure. There are many more camped outside the city, and others from the Lords' provinces that will join the army as it marches. Thousands and thousands of men.* That would have been a meaningless phrase to her in former years, but last spring she had accompanied Akira to the battle against the rebel Lords led by his mother-in-law and had seen first-hand what "thousands of men" actually meant. It had been an alarming experience, especially the bloodthirsty enthusiasm of soldiers before and after they slaughtered each other.

Akira's army had been outnumbered at that battle, and she had more than half expected they would lose and she, her son, and everyone she knew would die. Instead, somehow, Akira had won.

The army was nearly all gone now, and Kaede drew a breath, fighting not to shiver openly, eager to return inside. *How will this war turn out?* Fear colder than any winter air wormed through her heart whenever she thought about it. *Akira has never lost a war… but this is different. This means we could wind up fighting* everyone. *Can he really do this? Priestess Ritsuko keeps saying he is mad, and half the time I am sure she is right, he is so strange… but could a madman really win wars as he does?*

She shook her head very slightly. *Well, Priestess Ritsuko says horrible things about everyone, actually. That shouldn't count.*

Kaede turned and re-entered the keep, moving with the same grave pace even though her shivering was now almost uncontrollable. *I will go upstairs and see Basho, she told herself. The court can wait, this once.*

⛩ ⛩ ⛩

THE BEAR SAMURAI TURNED THE paper over in his hand, frowning deeply. "Am I supposed to care about this?"

Kobayashi Mitsui had gone through many experiences in the last four years. He had seen dying men walk like puppets on strings, seen a man hurl fire from his hand. He had seen a Demon walk the earth. Even so, he felt an inner shock at a samurai speaking in public with such blunt rudeness.

I suppose I am less hardened than I imagined myself to be, he thought ruefully. Aloud he spoke carefully: "It is my authorization from the High Lord of the Wolf Clan. Is that not sufficient to permit my companion and I to pass through your waystation?"

The samurai grunted and scratched the fingers of his left hand in the scruffy beard on his cheek. He was a burly man, no taller than Mitsui but broader and more heavily muscular, his skin swarthy and roughened by weather. His brown-lacquered armor – back-and-breast, greaves on arms and shins, waist-guard and shoulder-guard plates – was more extensive than the basic protection typically worn by waystation guards, and lacked any decoration beyond its color. His helmet, a plain open-fronted dome of brown-lacquered steel, did at least have a small crest on the front, a dark yellow disk with a snarling bear's head rendered in black.

"An authorization from the Wolf Lord. Hm. That would mean something in the Wolf lands, samurai. But in case you haven't noticed, samurai—" the guard jerked his head backward, toward the walls of the border station behind him, "—this isn't the Wolf lands."

He didn't even call me 'honorable.' Mitsui felt a surge of anger, mingled with a sharp twinge from the shortened finger on his right hand. He had lost the end of it in a fight with Mask cultists three weeks ago. He opened his mouth, then shut it again, controlling his breathing and thinking carefully. *It took me months to find this trail to follow. I can't let myself be deflected so easily.* "Honorable samurai, I understand you have a duty to fulfill. So do I, my duty as a Magistrate."

The guard went silent, staring hard. By invoking his status as a Magistrate, Mitsui was asserting a claim to higher authority, suggesting the Bear samurai did not have the rank to obstruct him. It was a political ploy, and using it made Mitsui clench his teeth. *But what is the alternative? I have only this one lead left, and to follow it I must enter the Bear lands...*

Mitsui could hear shuffling and soft murmuring from the line of people waiting on the road behind him. From the border waystation, the road – wide enough for a merchant's wagon to traverse comfortably – swung down a long curve on the inner side of a hill that extended down into the Wolf Clan lands below. The slope was very shallow; Mitsui judged the patchwork of woods and farmlands below was no more than a hundred yards down. In the opposite direction, beyond the border station, the road grew steeper as it climbed the shoulders of the Bear Mountains toward a pass so distant that he perceived it only as a hazy gap in the line of jagged peaks.

The road's outer edge was lined with small piles of stones, some of them clearly the remnants of old posts and roadside shrines from centuries past, others merely shapeless stacks of rocks. Crowded between that tattered gesture of an outer barrier and the wooded inner slope that climbed up the hill, a long line of wagons and mounts and people snaked away downslope for a half-mile or more. Mitsui and Satoshi had waited in that line for almost two hours before reaching the gate of the border station.

The Bear post was considerably more formidable than the provincial waystations Mitsui had passed through so many times in the Wolf lands. It was almost a fortress, tan-stuccoed walls zig-zagging up and down the side of the hill, archers peering over the tile-lined tops. A three-story tower, nearly big enough to be called a keep, loomed above one corner of the enclosure, and a gatehouse nearly as large crouched over the main entrance. The gate, a twelve-foot-high valve of thick oak beams fitted together into a single whole, was propped half-open, granting a limited view of the interior.

"Not very welcoming," Satoshi had observed as they had inched their way up the road. "Are all the roads into the Bear lands defended like this?"

Mitsui had felt vaguely embarrassed that he did not know. "The Bear are known to be suspicious of outsiders," he had said neutrally.

"Well, I shall endeavor to be thoroughly unsuspicious," Satoshi had declared. "Of all the sordid and pointless deaths we could suffer, getting cut down by a border guard would surely rank near the bottom."

True to his word, the horse-faced samurai was holding a dour silence, refraining from his more typical preference for odd remarks. Mitsui was grateful for that, since the Bear samurai did not seem like the sort to find humor in Satoshi's quirks.

The guard's fingers had tightened on Mitsui's paper, making it crinkle slightly. "Do you think you can give me orders… Magistrate?"

Stay calm. Mitsui breathed in slowly, fighting to keep his face smooth. "Not at all, honorable samurai," he said, and felt brief pride in how even his voice was. "Perhaps… perhaps my companion and I could discuss this matter with the officer in command, so as not to further delay those waiting behind us?"

The guard visibly considered saying no. Mitsui wondered what he would do if he did. Try to escalate? The Bear looked like the sort who would not take that well. Go back to the end of the waiting line, and hope for a different man at the gate when they reached it again? Retreat to the lowlands and find another road?

The Bear grimaced and shoved the paper back at Mitsui. "Fine," he grunted. He half-turned and made a sharp gesture to the soldiers atop the walls. "Go through and wait in the yard to the right side. Don't go anywhere else or you'll catch an arrow, understand?"

"Thank you," Mitsui murmured. He and Satoshi bowed, low enough to show respect without being servile. The guard grunted again, made a bare-minimum head-bob, and called the next person in line forward.

The two Wolf samurai walked through the gate, blinking as they passed into the rectangular tunnel that pierced the wall and the bright late-morning Sunlight momentarily cut off. "That was interesting," Satoshi murmured. "I was always under the impression that my behavior was unusual for a samurai. Perhaps I was just born into the wrong Clan."

Mitsui chuckled despite himself. It was true that Satoshi often said things that were strange, inappropriate, or even shocking… but he was always polite about it.

They emerged from the tunnel and squinted again as the Sunlight returned. Beyond the gate, the road passed through the center of the border station to another gate on the far side. On their left the path was defined by a four-foot wall of close-fitted stone, pierced by stairs in a couple of places; the flat space above the wall was crowded with buildings, including the tower and various other structures Mitsui recognized as barracks, storehouses, a training hall, and a shrine – dedicated to the Lady, as was typical for castles, with a statue of Her visible through the open front doors.

On the right, the ground extended flat to the outer wall, and in that space Mitsui could see a small stable, an obvious bath-house with steam rising from its roof, and a bland undecorated two-story structure that he decided had to be an inn for travelers staying the night. In front of the inn was an open space, all flat tight-packed stone, half-full of wagons and lowing oxen. Mitsui hesitated, then led Satoshi to the far corner of the open space, well away from the noisy, stinking beasts of burden.

They waited while the Sun crept higher and other travelers passed through the border station or visited the inn. Outside, the cold winds blowing down from the mountains had been unpleasant, but here the walls cut off the chill and allowed the early-spring Sunlight to warm them. Mitsui tried to release his impatience by focusing on the mountains that loomed above those walls. The thickly-forested peaks of the Mountains of the Bear filled the western horizon from end to end, looming like a second wall above the modest border station. Mitsui was not sure if they were taller than the Mountains of the Sun in the south of the Empire, but from this angle they certainly felt taller, an imposing barrier to any army. *No wonder the Bear Clan has held on to its lands through all the wars, though…* Mitsui frowned to himself. *I seem to recall they did not do so well when fighting outside of their mountains.* He had only a vague understanding of the wars that had wracked the Empire in the four centuries since the Dread Eclipse.

"Who is this man who demands to see me?"

Mitsui blinked back to himself, straightening and bowing at the man approaching from across the road. The newcomer was short and thick-bodied, with a face that was clean-shaven and heavy-browed but shared the weathered outdoor look of the gate guard. He was not armored, but the simple leggings, shirt, and overcoat he wore looked more like a sellsword's garb than the clothing of a samurai officer; the only real indicator of his rank was the embroidery on the breasts of the jacket – a Bear Clan crest done in dark thread that made it difficult to see against the brown linen, and a smaller crest above it comprising five black circles on a field of tan. That, and the obvious high quality of the swords tucked under his sash.

Mitsui and Satoshi bowed, low enough to show respect for a man of station. "I am honorable Kobayashi Mitsui, Magistrate of the Wolf Clan, and this is my deputy Tamashiro Satoshi."

"I am honorable Captain Chiba Yasuji," the other man said shortly, offering a bow that was just low enough to not be openly insulting. His dark eyes were narrow, full of suspicion. His body language was aggressive, chest out, left hand resting on the hilt of his sword.

Mitsui cleared his throat. "Honorable Captain. We are conducting an investigation into the Cult of the Mask, on the orders of the High Lord of the Wolf Clan." He held out the now-wrinkled letter, presenting it with both hands in the manner of someone offering a gift.

"Yes, yes, they told me about your letter." Captain Yasuji made no motion to take the paper. "I've heard that the… most honorable High Lord of the Wolf is a strange man, but even so I wouldn't have expected him to give out writs of authority to wandering ragamuffins."

Wandering ragamuffins..? Mitsui clenched his teeth and forced himself to think about how he would appear to the Bear samurai. It was hard, because his mental self-image was still lodged in what he had been four years ago, before all of this happened: a plump clean-shaven man in his early thirties, well-dressed and civilized. A man with a wife and son and a respected posting in HillTown.

He had gone into a merchant's shop last week to buy a new pair of sandals, and while he was there he had come across a display of women's hand-mirrors, small ovals of polished silver in hand-carved wooden frames. The image of his face in them had been like a blow to the stomach: raw-boned, haggard, creased with lines of pain and grief that aged it a decade. Sunken grizzled cheeks and baggy, haunted eyes. A tattered, frayed overcoat that no longer displayed any crests, though a close look would spot where the embroidery had been pulled out. There were even a few hints of gray in his hair, now fully grown-out and tied back in a practical topknot; at some point in the last few years he had given up on shaving his temples.

What respectable samurai would ever trust me?

He bowed again, lower than before. "Honorable Captain. I have… I have pursued this investigation for over three years, at great cost to myself, my family, and my companions."

The faces flickered through his mind as he spoke. His wife Akemi, bleeding out from the Mask's knife that had slashed her throat. Deputy Taizaburo, sprawled dead in his office. Bozu the Monk, cut down by a Mask swordswoman in a distant cave. Deputy Mako, burned to death by unnatural power.

"The Masks…They took my son." The shame of the words burned his mouth, but he made himself speak on. "This is the last lead I have. I beg you, in the name of the Lady's Compassion, permit me to follow it." He held the bow, waiting, and realized Satoshi was doing the same.

The Bear officer grunted, sounding irritated. Mitsui could see his sandaled feet shift slightly, conveying discomfort. Finally he growled, "Fine. Fine! Enough."

Mitsui straightened, letting out a breath. "Thank you, honorable Captain."

Yasuji was scowling openly. "You want to search for your son, fine, but you're just a traveler here, not a Magistrate, you understand? I don't care what your precious letter says."

"I understand, honorable Captain."

"Fine. Get on your way, then." The officer gave the briefest departing nod, turned on his heel, and stamped up the stone steps to the station's upper level, marching briskly toward the tower.

Satoshi shifted his shoulders, visibly letting out stored tension. "Well," he murmured, "I suppose that could have gone worse. But I suspect that officer does not really believe your story."

"Probably not," Mitsui agreed, fighting down a grimace. It would not do to let the Bear officer look back and see him frowning. After a moment he lifted the bamboo canteen that dangled from his sash and removed the stopper, taking a sip of water.

"Washing out the taste of humiliation?" Mitsui choked and coughed. Satoshi lifted his own canteen. "A good idea, actually. I suppose this is a minor indignity compared to what else we have experienced, but it does leave a bitter residue." He took a long swallow of the lukewarm water. "I confess I am surprised he gave in."

Mitsui nodded, slowly re-capping his canteen. "He would have felt as though he had dishonored himself if he had continued to deny such a humble entreaty." His mouth twisted. "I suppose I have finally learned to use my own humiliation in my favor."

He had never been good at that, at the simpering self-denial and ostentatious humility that courtiers employed as weapons against each other. He had, in fact, often resisted it disastrously, taken offense when he should have just gritted his teeth and endured. At HillTown he had nearly wound up slitting his own belly in consequence.

"Well, humiliation is something I am accustomed to," the older samurai observed. "Fortunate that he did not ask to search our travel packs," he added thoughtfully.

The gear they carried these days, the result of almost four years hunting the Cult of the Mask, would make a normal samurai accuse them of being burglars or assassins.

"Let us not give him the opportunity to think of that," Mitsui said, and stepped back onto the road, following it toward the exit gate on the far side of the border station.

Satoshi fell in beside him, looking around casually. "Hmmm, the honorable Captain is still watching us. I suspect he regrets giving in."

"No doubt," Mitsui nodded. "He can't stop us now without losing face, though."

"True, but he can cause trouble for us in other ways. Perhaps tell his comrades at other waystations to obstruct us."

Mitsui sighed. "We'll deal with that if it comes."

They passed through the exit, walking in the wake of a merchant's wagon and followed by a pair of traveling musicians with flutes and string instruments strapped over their backs. The Bear samurai on the far side of the gate, checking papers for a line of people waiting to leave the Bear lands, did not even glance at them as they passed.

All right, Mitsui thought, feeling his chest loosen slightly. *One small obstacle surmounted.* He had been worried about the border for days, wondering if the High Lord's writ would be enough, if after all this time his investigation would fizzle out in mere bureaucratic obstruction.

Despite himself he slid one hand inside the opposite sleeve, touching the small bundle of papers that hid in the dangling linen pocket. The last of his surviving notes from GreenTown, identifying a Bear Clan merchant called Goro as a possible Mask cultist, connected to GreenTown's Fuse Iemon by commercial shipments that had carried the cult's notorious white masks and strange foreign-made candles.

If this doesn't go anywhere, what then?

Go back to HillTown and be a Magistrate again, as though nothing happened? The idea was almost physically painful.

Or just kill myself?

Once he would have dismissed that thought out of hand. For most of his life Mitsui had never understood the craving for death that seemed to obsess so many of his fellow samurai. But after the last few years of misery and loss, the idea had a seductive appeal. *Die, and go to the Lady's judgment, and be reborn to a new life without all this pain...*

The face of his dying wife hovered in memory, blood on her lips as she whispered: *I do not forgive you.*

Mitsui grunted softly and shook his head. *If I kill myself, will she be waiting in judgment alongside the Lady?*

⛩ ⛩ ⛩

Captain Ookami Tokage rubbed the fingers of his one good hand through his beard, trying not to let his scratching be too obvious. The inability to bathe regularly and properly was catching up with him, and he felt grubby and itchy everywhere, acutely conscious of the stink of old sweat from his armor and clothes, of the thick smell from the horse and saddle beneath him. On top of that, the inability to properly wash and shave meant that hair kept trying to grow back in on the bare portions of his scalp, and that itched even worse than the rest of him. It was a constant struggle not to scratch at it.

Well, at least I am honorably sharing the suffering of my men, he thought, glancing to his left. The samurai marching past him had the same patchy, bedraggled look to their scalps as he did. Most of them were also growing in facial hair they would have kept shaved under normal circumstances.

No help for it. He carefully pulled his hand away from his beard and picked up the reins he had laid across his lap. *At least we're almost out of this.*

It had been twenty days since the bizarre catastrophe – or perhaps Divine intervention, Tokage still wasn't sure – that destroyed the domain of the nonhuman spirits who called themselves Aelfynn. Seven of Tokage's fifty samurai had perished outright in the supernatural earthquake that had swept the creatures' kingdom away, and eleven more had been seriously injured; two of those had subsequently died as well. It had taken several days for everyone to rest, reorganize, and get the surviving wounded fit for travel before they could begin the journey through the wilderness back to the Empire.

Tokage glanced toward the back of the column, where several ox-drawn wagons labored in the muddy wake of the marching soldiers. *At least the servants and baggage train were outside the… the place, when it happened.* The Aelfynn had allowed only their samurai guests to cross the border of the unnatural domain they had claimed as their home.

Still, even with their supplies the return trip had been challenging. The landscape that had seemed so welcoming and easily traversed on their journey out to the Aelfynn's home had somehow been far more wild and mystifying on the way back. The road-like trails that Speaker to Strangers Oeisen had shown them had seemingly vanished, leaving them to labor slowly through the forested hills with only the position of the Sun in the sky to guide them. The journey that had taken less than a week on the way out had stretched to more than two on the return, stretching their supplies dangerously thin. Tokage had assigned men to hunt for game and birds each day to supplement their dwindling rations. That, at least, had gone reasonably well – they had seen far more animal life in their return journey, as though the wild beasts were reclaiming the land from the vanished Aelfynn.

Well, not vanished, Tokage corrected himself, feeling a slight chill despite the warm spring Sunlight. *Dead, crushed, torn to pieces.* The disaster that had overwhelmed the Aelfynn had left them revealed – or perhaps transformed, or cursed, the whole bewildering event was difficult to comprehend – as small, weak, helpless, and ugly creatures. Many had perished outright with the destruction of their city, and the rest had died at the hands of the men and women who had been their servants. Beaten down, torn to pieces, stamped into the mud in a frenzy of vengeful rage that had been almost as unsettling to witness as the spirits' own transformation.

The day after it all happened, there had been a tense, uncertain confrontation between the samurai and the Aelfynn's former servitors. They were foreign people, their faces squarer and flatter than those of the Empire's folk, their eyes more widely spaced. They spoke to each other in a language Tokage did not recognize, resembling neither the smooth speech of the Empire nor the musical trilling of their dead masters. They had no weapons beyond sticks and rocks and simple tools, but there were many of them, hundreds and hundreds. Their flat alien faces were unreadable, but their postures and voices radiated anger and looming violence; Tokage and his men had waited, hands on weapons, through a long afternoon hour. Finally the foreigners had begun to drift away, by ones and twos and then dozens, until all were gone.

Later, Tokage had sent out spies and confirmed that the foreigners were heading northwest, away from the Empire. *And good riddance to them,* he thought. *Let them return to whatever land the Aelfynn got them from. One less thing for us to worry about. We have too many such as it is.*

He kneed his horse back into motion, noting the slight reluctance from the beast before it obeyed. The horses were as tired as the people. He guided it alongside his marching men, forging through clumps of grass that was starting to green with the warming weather, insects springing up in buzzing arcs. He passed through the shade of a belt of trees, blinking in the sudden change of light, then emerged into another open field and squinted against a distant glitter, two miles away down a long shallow slope of brush and thick grass and scattered trees.

Sunlight on water, he saw, feeling a loosening in his chest that was so powerful it almost brought tears to his eyes. He reined in once more, shutting his eyes until the wave of emotion could pass – it would not do to let the men see him losing control. *The River of Black Ice. We've made it back to the Empire at last.*

Hoof-beats scuffed in the grass, coming up behind and drawing alongside. Tokage took a deep silent breath, clearing his mind, and reopened his eyes. Next to him, an old man in formal robes and a black courtier's cap perched on a sullen-looking pony.

"Honorable Seneschal. You are looking well."

It wasn't entirely a hollow polite remark. The white-bearded courtier had somehow managed to keep himself reasonably clean and well-groomed even during this long wilderness march, though Tokage suspected that was more to the credit of Amano's servants than the old man's own skills. Still, the Wolf

Clan's seneschal and spymaster looked weary, his squinting eyes perched above thick bags, the lines in his face visibly deeper than they had been a month ago.

Well, no wonder. We're going back to report... failure. Complete failure, and we don't even know why, or what really happened. It is entirely possible we will be slitting our bellies at the end of all this.

They had come here at High Lord Akira's orders, to negotiate an alliance with the Aelfynn against the combined threats of the northern barbarians and the Jade Dragon Clan. They were returning with nothing – no, with less than nothing, since the Aelfynn no longer existed at all.

"I thank you for your Courtesy, honorable Captain," Amano murmured. "But I must apologize for requiring it of you."

Tokage grunted. He had never been well-suited to the world of courtly discourse, and was thankful the late High Lord Okaro had known that; after Tokage had lost his arm at the Battle of Green Leaves, Lord Okaro had assigned him the straightforward martial duty of commanding the house guard of Castle Ookami, rather than burdening him with something that would have required diplomacy. Okaro's son Akira seemed to recognize the same reality, or at least had made no changes to Tokage's duties; privately, Tokage and his wife credited that more to Akira's wife, Lady Kaede, who they had aligned themselves with as soon as Akira's older brother died and it became clear that he was the sole hope for the Clan's future.

Seneschal Amano shifted slightly in the saddle, an involuntary gesture of discomfort that meant far more from him than from an ordinary samurai. After a moment he murmured, "It is... unfortunate... that honorable Tora Saneda was not able to accompany us back to the Empire."

Tokage grunted again. Only a lifelong courtier could use 'unfortunate' for a High Lord's brother going mad and killing himself. Tora Saneda had accompanied them to the Aelfynn lands as the representative of his brother, Tora Iesada, High Lord of the Tiger Clan. The Tiger had been allied with the Aelfynn for almost two decades, and the combined pressure from the northern barbarians and the Bear Clan had made them desperate to enlist the Wolf Clan into the same alliance.

Confronted with the destruction of the Aelfynn, Saneda had killed himself, and most of the Tiger samurai who had accompanied him had done the same – including Tora Gentaro, who was a personal advisor to the High Lord. Only twenty-three had chosen to stay alive, mainly to carry the swords and belongings of their companions back to their homes. Tokage could see them now, marching in a tight-crowded group with downcast eyes, holding themselves apart from the larger body of Wolf samurai around them. He suspected their High Lord would order them to slit their bellies as soon as they delivered their news – and if he didn't, they would probably request it anyway.

And what will the Tiger do to us, when we arrive with this news? Tokage was sure that was what Amano was really talking about with his oblique language. He glanced again at the older man, reading the same thoughts hidden beneath Amano's bland expression.

They wouldn't dare kill emissaries from another Clan, would they?

In fact Tokage knew it was perfectly possible. High Lords had done such things many times in the four centuries since the death of the last Emperor. There had even been a few instances before then, though such Lords had been punished by the Emperor for violating the virtues of Courtesy and Honor. *We are bringing back word that his brother is dead and his allies are gone. Death might be the least of what he does to us...*

Tokage snorted at himself. *What am I doing, dwelling on my fears? I am a samurai, and the highest honor I could have is to die for my lord. I would miss Aya, and miss seeing Miyako-*chan *have her children, but the Lady would surely show enough Compassion for us to meet again in our next lives.*

Amano shifted in the saddle, straightened up slightly. "Well, I am glad to see the approach of civilization at last. I am grateful to you for fulfilling you duty and guiding us back here safely, honorable Tokage."

Tokage was no courtier, but even he recognized the unspoken aspect of Amano's words: that with the return to civilization, Amano's authority would now supersede Tokage's and he would become responsible for their future survival. Which was a relief, to be sure. Tokage did not envy Amano the task ahead.

At least it will be a bit easier without... those two, the swordsman and the Priestess.

The strange pair had shown up midway through their journey last winter, insisting on joining the expedition and displaying a letter from the High Lord himself. There had been no choice but to let them tag along on the mission, and now Tokage felt sure there was some connection between their presence and what had happened, though he could not say what it might have been. The Priestess had made some very bizarre statements, both before and afterward...

The two of them had left four days ago, offering no explanation other than a brief incomprehensible remark from the swordsman about "following a shadow." The Priestess had apologized and promised to rejoin them later – not that Tokage would mind if they chose to stay away. "Kenji must follow the commands of the Lady's Light," she had said, which made it sound like the foul-mouthed swordsman was some kind of Heavenly avatar.

The Lady's light...

Briefly Tokage's memory returned to the *light* that had erupted from the heart of the Aelfynn lands, and the shattering sensations and memories that had run through his mind and soul in that instant. As though he was being shown every failure, every sin, every defeat of his life…

The Lady's Compassion is infinite… but She judges each soul before that Compassion can be granted.

He shook his head slightly, nudging his horse into motion once more. *No purpose to thinking about it,* he told himself again, as he had done every day and night since it happened. *Focus on the task at hand. Later, when I'm back in Castle Ookami, I'll talk to Aya.*

CHAPTER 3

THE VOICE OF SELFISHNESS, which sometimes still remembered it was also a man called Ryu Noboru, lifted a piece of raw fish in plump fingers, dipped it in a bowl of soy sauce, and stuffed it past drooping saliva-coated lips. Luxuriant flavors and sensations filled his mouth, making his whole body tremble with pleasure as he chewed and swallowed. Soy sauce and drool spilled from the corners of his mouth and dribbled down his chin, spattering the front of his embroidered silk robe.

A very faint sound came from the two servants kneeling by the door. Suppressing the impulse to retch, Noboru knew, and felt a further wave of pleasure at the thought of their fearful misery. He deliberately turned his head as though idly looking about, letting his gaze track across them, and they trembled and blanched though not daring to move.

The High Lord's chambers in Castle Hokori were divided into several different rooms, and he was eating in the outer one, closest to the hallway and stairs where samurai stood guard. It was physically little different from the others – each a rectangle of slightly differing shape, the only real distinction being whether they had exterior windows or not. When he had taken possession of them, the rooms had all be elaborately, almost gaudily decorated: silk paintings and fine pottery, lanterns of elaborately carved wood frames decorated with gems, gold-plated statues of the Lady and Lord. Such was typical of any wealthy noble's castle, with the most splendid decorations always reserved for the most private rooms where only a few privileged guests might see them. To put such splendor on public display was to lack dignity, after all, thus bringing shame on oneself.

A few weeks ago Noboru had destroyed the artworks in his quarters, reveling in the sensation of beauty and harmony crumbling under the impact of hands and feet, sword and teeth. The pleasure of the destruction had been enhanced by the pleasure of forcing his guest, young Lord Sada Daijiro, to join in the acts; he had reveled in the sense of Daijiro's youthful, fragile soul crumbling even further as he violated the nobility's deep traditions of aesthetic elegance. Later, after he had completed the conquest of the nobleman – barely more than a boy, in fact, which had made it all the better – he had enjoyed watching the servants clean up the wreckage, their eyes downcast, their hands trembling whenever they noticed his gaze. A lesser pleasure than those before, but a pleasure nonetheless.

He couldn't do that in the rest of the castle, of course. That would upset too many samurai who were not yet broken to the yoke of Dakkurru as Daijiro was broken. It would shake their already-weak loyalty, and he needed that loyalty, at least for now. Until he had enough Brothers and Sisters here, until the Tiger were crushed, until enough Lords' souls could be subverted and devoured, he still needed the Jade Dragon Clan's samurai.

That knowledge filled him with rage whenever he let himself dwell on it, a rage that could no longer be distinguished between Noboru and Selfishness. It was infuriating, intolerable that he still had to play the role of the High Lord, still had to speak the empty words, cater to the meaningless, puerile customs and traditions of ephemeral, useless humanity.

Not for much longer, Selfishness knew. The Tiger Clan was crumbling under the assault of the Brothers from the north, the barbarian tribesmen gathered in numbers too vast to be withstood, and led by the two women who channeled Dakkurru's combined power. And here in the Jade Dragon lands the Masks were gathering, hundreds of them, a hidden army now emerging to fight. Soon the moment would come for him to cast aside all pretensions.

In the meantime, playing the role of the High Lord had benefits.

The table before him was covered with plates and bowls, most of them now empty, the remnants of the feast he had enjoyed for the last hour. Droplets of soy sauce and bits of stray rice were scattered across the smooth-polished wood, and a puddle of spilled broth had gathered around the empty soup-bowls. The pleasure of eating was not the greatest one a human body could experience, but it had been a personal favorite of Noboru long before he had accepted the mantle of Selfishness. He picked up a soup bowl that was not yet empty and slurped the remaining contents – chicken broth, with small-diced vegetables and pieces of meat all softened by long cooking. He reveled in the sensations, the rich taste on his tongue, the warmth going down into his swollen belly, the excess spilling out of the corners of his mouth.

A distant corner of his mind briefly thought: *When we are triumphant, this pleasure will no longer exist.* But that thought immediately drowned beneath another, the thought of the greater pleasures which would accompany the ultimate victory of Dakkurru: the endless revel of destruction. To devour and rape and tear and burn and crush, forever, without need of any human host with human limitations.

There was a time when Noboru's own thoughts might have been disrupted by the recollection that *he* was human. That time had passed; now it was rare for him to perceive a difference between his own thoughts and those of Selfishness.

He set down the bowl next to the other empty tableware, wiped his face with the sleeve of his silk robe, the broth staining the delicate embroidery. *Soon all will be as we wish it… but not just yet,* he reminded himself. *Not everything is going well.*

That recollection bit into Noboru's pleasure like a stone lodged in his sandal. He felt his teeth clench, his thick wet lips pulling back to bare them. A distant corner of his awareness noticed the servants openly trembling, trying not to watch.

General Akiyama, his father's most reliable soldier, had fled early last winter – almost certainly to the Wolf Clan, though no one knew for certain. And somehow the two-faced Lord Kiyogama Heisuke had gotten out of Castle Hokori near the end of winter. Noboru had managed to arrest the nobleman's younger son Goichi, who had remained behind as cover for his father's escape, but Goichi's sister Nomi had taken her own life before the guards could seize her. Noboru had killed Goichi as slowly and cruelly as possible, but that could not change the reality – confirmed by the latest reports from spymaster Mugai Soto – that Lord Kiyogama had reached his stronghold at Castle Kigi, where his elder son Daihachi also resided. The nobleman's escape was especially infuriating because Noboru had finally gotten proof of his treasonous plots, tortured out of his fellow traitor Lord Wakita Genki, and had been planning a public spectacle of arrest, confession, and execution to force the rest of the Clan's cowardly, unreliable Lords into compliance.

He would need compliance, because Soto's latest reports from the Wolf lands affirmed the winter rumors that High Lord Ookami Akira was mobilizing for war. The Wolf Clan held an advantage in numbers, though not so great as it had been two years ago. That was when they had defeated the Jade Dragon Clan at the Battle of Nagai Kyukai, and the Jade Dragon – then still led by Noboru's father Akurai – had subsequently collapsed into a months-long civil war. The Wolf had gone through their own civil war last year, greatly weakening their armies; Noboru had read the reports gleefully, the Voice within him taking pleasure at each tale of death and destruction.

Still, the net result remained in the Wolf Clan's favor. If they were preparing to march against the Jade Dragon, Noboru would be hard-pressed to stop them, especially with so much disloyalty within his Clan.

Which was the reason for the visitor waiting outside his chamber.

Noboru pushed himself back from the table, keeping his legs folded as he hunched around to face the door and the two pale-faced servants. He blotted his mouth once more and then picked up the large fan that lay alongside the table. It was over a foot long, made of stiff-folded paper on wooden staves, painted with the Jade Dragon Clan's crest in green shades against a yellow-gold background. Normally he would have carried it tucked under his sash, but the pressure of his food-swollen belly made that uncomfortable.

He swallowed once more to clear the saliva from his mouth. "Young Kuma may enter now," he declared, and the servants quickly bowed and slid open the two thin wooden panels of the door.

Kuma Joji was a young man, plain-faced and short, but nonetheless fit and strong despite having spent the last half-decade and more as a 'guest' – a hostage in all but name – of the Jade Dragon Clan. His shirt, pleated leggings, and overcoat were in the plain brown and dark green colors of the Bear Clan, with the clan's crest, a snarling bear's head viewed straight-on, embroidered in black thread on the jacket's left and right breasts. He bowed low but did not prostrate himself; as the son and heir of the Bear Clan's High Lord he was not obligated to do so. Then he sat back on his heels, regarding Noboru with the blank wariness of a samurai in a hostile court: showing nothing, observing everything.

Noboru felt a subtle irritation at the younger man's exhibit self-control, something he had not always shown in the last year. He lifted his fan and slowly closed it, one vane at a time. "Honorable… Kuma. I trust your father is well?"

The Bear samurai cleared his throat. "Quite well, according to the letter I received last autumn."

Noboru had known about that letter and its contents, of course. Mugai Soto monitored Kuma Joji's communications very carefully. And Joji surely knew that, and was signaling he knew that by referring to the letter.

"A letter, yes. Splendid." Noboru smiled, tapping his folded fan into the opposite palm. "Letters are a fine topic." Kuma Joji's expression did not change, but Noboru could see his pulse in his neck, the mark of growing fear. It was delicious. He gulped and sucked in his drooping lower lip against the urge to drool. "You must send a letter to your father, young Joji."

Joji's face shifted for a moment before he got it back under control. "Apologies, most honorable High Lord. A letter? To my honorable father?"

"Yes, a letter," Noboru repeated, smiling broadly, making an encouraging gesture with his fan. "Requesting the Bear Clan's support in the valiant fight our Clan will soon wage against the Wolves."

"I… apologies again, most honorable High Lord, I do not understand. My honorable father has been fighting the Tiger Clan, as you requested. Now you wish him to fight the Wolf Clan..?"

Noboru felt a surge of rage at the man's stupidity. He leaned forward, feeling his expression start to slip out of his control, and the Bear heir actually shrank back slightly, samurai courage or no. With an effort Noboru schooled his features and changed his motion to one that tapped his fan on Joji's shoulder. Borderline inappropriate, though not a direct touch.

This close, Noboru was aware of Joji's skin, still smooth with youth, and the scent of his fear-sweat. He was really too old and too plain for Noboru's tastes; this close the faint marks of his shaved whiskers were visible. Still, it would be pleasant to hurl Joji to the floor and slake his lusts upon his body, before devouring his flesh and drinking his blood and—

Noboru's mouth flooded with saliva and he had to swallow again. *I cannot do that yet,* he reminded himself. *Not… quite yet. I still have need of armies that will follow my orders. I still need the Bear Clan's armies too.* He felt the pulsing strength of Selfishness, the ravening desire to devour and destroy, recede slightly. His vision cleared and he smiled into the face of the young Bear samurai. Kuma Joji swallowed hard, sweat beading thickly on his forehead.

"The Wolf Clan is marching to war against us, young Joji," he crooned. "I have even heard… rumors… that their young High Lord thinks to seize the Imperial City, to make himself Emperor."

Which was only a rumor, to be sure, but Mugai's spies had heard it several times in the last few weeks. There might be something to it.

The Bear heir's expression changed, fear giving way to shock and anger. For the first time he seemed to be paying real attention to what Noboru said. "They are… that is madness. Does he imagine that can succeed?"

Noboru pulled back his fan, allowing the Bear samurai to relax slightly, and tapped it against his own plump cheek. "Yes, he is surely a madman. But his armies are strong. If he is to be stopped, I must have the support of your… valiant and honorable father, and his warriors."

That wording brought Joji back to the present, his momentary animation fading. He swallowed again, then bowed carefully. "I shall… I shall write it immediately. With your permission, honorable High Lord?"

Begging me to let him leave, Noboru thought contemptuously. The temptation was very strong to refuse, to force the young man to stay, even to…

No, he told himself, or perhaps Selfishness told him. "By all means, honorable Joji."

It was difficult not to laugh aloud as the young man bowed low again – lower than before, in fact – and left the room just slowly enough to maintain face.

⛩ ⛩ ⛩

OOKAMI AKIRA, HIGH LORD OF the Wolf Clan, heel-prodded his horse to the top of a tree-clustered knoll and stopped there, waiting for his escorts and the man carrying the Clan banner to catch up. The hill was only about as tall as a farmer's hut, but it gave Akira a good view of the long lines of soldiers marching past him on the Gray Silk Road. The road here was not particularly wide, allowing only about six men to march abreast, and the column of marching men stretched ahead and behind to the limit of sight. That was not particularly far, since this part of the Empire was a mixture of small open valleys – most of them with farming villages – and forested hills. From here Akira could see one of those villages about two miles southward, buildings clustering on either side of the road, the army flowing through the middle of the settlement in a glittering line of Sunlight on lacquered armor, banners mostly limp in the calm spring warmth. The town was larger than some in this region, and Akira had seen it once before when he toured the border territories last fall. *There's a landholder here,* he recalled. A samurai who lived in a pleasant estate on the west side of the village, keeping to himself except when duty dragged him out of his house. The man had emerged from his residence and prostrated himself when Akira had ridden through.

Northward, the road passed through a narrow divide between two thickly-wooded hills, turning this way and that to avoid the worst of the slopes, eventually emerging into another farming region. Continuing that way for miles, until reaching the city of SilkTown where the army had gathered before the current march. A haze of brown in the air in that direction marked the dust of thousands of marching men; the army was large enough that the back of the column probably had not yet left the camps around SilkTown, even now with the Noon hour approaching.

Not all of his forces were taking this route; there were simply too many men to funnel down a single road. Some of his smaller formations were moving westward on secondary roads and trails; they would travel more slowly, but cut the angle of his own route. And more than a third of the Clan's strength, commanded by his most trusted noble Lord Toshiwara Ryohei, was moving west along the southern bank of the River of Blue Silk. The land there was more rugged than north of the river, where the Wolf and Jade Dragon had clashed three years ago at the Nagai Kyukai Plain, but putting the river between himself and Toshiwara would be a fatal error.

Even with the whole army south of the river, this is dangerous. The knowledge ate at him, a coil of inner tension that was almost physically painful. Extremely dangerous by the standards of warfare he had learned at the Monastery of War. The generals and scholars of battle he had studied back at the Monastery had warned endlessly against the hazards of overcomplicated plans, of dividing one's forces beyond the range of easy communication, inviting defeat of the separated pieces. *The allure of the elaborate plan is the appearance of cleverness, but complexity creates weakness, while simplicity imbues strength.* That was the Second Emperor, who had fought a long series of wars to bring the Empire into unity after his father's defeat of the Demons. Akira had broken that principle, more than once, and he was doing so again… but he needed to move quickly, and he had advantages the Second Emperor had never possessed. Starting with the knowledge he had gained from Akiyama Gakuto, the former Jade Dragon general who had switched allegiance last winter.

He looked west, across the dark brown fields where farmers were busily chopping the soil with wooden mattocks, churning it up before planting buckwheat and soybeans. A quartet of horsemen was riding through those fields, back-banners fluttering where they rose from the backplates of their armor, dirt clods flying up from the horses' hooves. Their armor was in the gray-and-red lacquer of men sworn directly to the Ookami family, and the Clan crest – a snarling wolf's head inside a circle of dark red – decorated the banners.

Akira was using his cavalry both to maintain communication between his scattered forces and to scout for the enemy – the latter an unconventional application of horsemen, who were more traditionally used to make flank attacks, strike at archery formations, or ride down and slaughter an enemy already broken by infantry combat. So far, his enemies had not figured out how to counter his new methods, but that could not last forever.

The four horsemen kicked their mounts into gallops, surging past the alarmed farmers, and crossed the narrow irrigation ditch on the near side of the farmland in impressive leaps. They slowed then, trotting up the hillside to where Akira waited. As they reined up, a brief round of in-saddle bows – more like deep nods – passed between them and the escorts waiting behind Akira, while their leader guided his horse closer to the High Lord before bowing as deeply as the saddle would allow. "Honorable High Lord!"

Kado Kitaro was nearly Akira's age of twenty-four, but looked much younger, his clean-shaven face alight with energy and tightly-leashed excitement. He was the younger son of one of Akira's most loyal provincial Lords and had sworn personal fealty to Akira four years ago, after their first military campaign together. Now he commanded all of Akira's cavalry, over five thousand horsemen.

Akira waited. Samurai were often left nonplussed when he did not answer their ritual salutations, but Kitaro knew him well enough by now that he simply went ahead with his report: "No sign of the enemy within a day's march, my Lord. I have sent squadrons farther west, they should report back tomorrow."

Inwardly Akira felt a little of his constant tension relax, if only for a moment. *So far the Jade Dragon Clan did not seem to be reacting… probably.* He hadn't gotten Lord Toshiwara's latest reports. He shut his eyes, seeking the emotionless void of meditation where his mind could work without interference from the body.

It was harder than it used to be. There were too many emotions now, too many memories hiding inside, ambushing him at unexpected moments. Memories of his son, clutching his leg or curled up asleep next to him. Memories of Satsuki, of her voice, her touch, the taste of her skin.

They have her. The Masks. They have her, they are hurting her. The knowledge threatened to overwhelm him completely. *I could just ride away, hunt and kill every Mask until I find her…*

No, I cannot. No matter how much I want to. The Monastery had bound his soul in iron chains of Duty, and now he was the High Lord, responsible for tens of thousands of samurai and hundreds of thousands of peasants. For the whole Empire, if he managed to claim the Throne.

He found the void at last, the empty darkness where his mind could work without the distractions of flesh. A timeless moment passed before he opened his eyes. Kitaro and his men were waiting, attentive but without impatience – they were accustomed to his mannerisms by now – and they straightened unconsciously as he focused on them once more.

"Honorable Kitaro. Extend the scouting range forward past the Kiirokusa Plain." That would send them fifty miles and more ahead of the army; the Kiirokusa was the most significant open land between here and the strategic crossroads at Shinku. "If the Jade Dragons approach the Kiirokusa before us, bring up the main cavalry force and delay them."

Kitaro nodded, some of his enthusiasm turning to thoughtful focus as he considered what Akira was asking of him. "I understand, honorable High Lord."

And he does understand, Akira knew. It had taken years to get loyal and trustworthy men into command of his armies, but he had them now. He could give orders and be confident they would be properly obeyed. That was a more valuable asset than ten thousand men, as the great spymaster Sada Sakaguchi had written in his memoirs.

Kitaro bowed again, imitated by his men, and together the four of them kicked their horses back into motion – down the hill and back across the fields, toward the cavalry forces that lurked beyond the forests to the west.

Akira nudged his own horse, walking it down the hill to rejoin the marching column, his guards and bannerman following him. The troops on the road were different now, wearing armor that was mainly black and red, with gray edgings. The banners flying above their heads showed a wolf's paw in a black circle underneath the Wolf Clan's own snarling sigil – the newly chosen crest of Hajime Soto, who Akira had assigned to the rule of Castle Shinshiro last autumn after the death of the previous Lord, Katsura Motosuke. Soto had been a mere lieutenant in Akira's first army four years ago; now he was a Lord, ruling a province. Many of the soldiers marching under his banner had previously been sworn to Motosuke, but had willingly changed their allegiance when the alternative was to be reduced to homeless sellswords. *A samurai must eat, just like a peasant,* the Third Emperor had written. These men might not love their new Lord, but they were practical enough to recognize their options. The ones fanatically dedicated to the late Motosuke had already killed themselves, joining their former ruler in honorable death.

There were many soldiers like these in Akira's armies now. In the last five years the Wolf Clan had been purged of seven major noble bloodlines, an unprecedented wave of slaughter. His father had started it by wiping out the Toride at the end of their brief failed rebellion, while later that same year Akira had personally killed Lord Watsuki and his family when they were on the brink of betraying the Clan to the Jade Dragons. The Konatsu family had betrayed the Clan the following year, but Akira had let his seneschal Amano persuade him to follow tradition and allow the family line to continue in exchange for the ritual suicide of the ruling Lord. His reward for that had been the Konatsu joining the rebellion against his rule the following year.

Akira had won the civil war that resulted, and he had made sure not to repeat his earlier mistake. The Konatsu had been exterminated, along with the Makoto, the Kashibe, and the Akabe – four ancient bloodlines, many claiming lineage back into the early days of the Emperors, all wiped from the earth. Thousands of their samurai had perished with them, unavoidably. In theory that reduced the Clans' military power, but unreliable men were weakness, not strength.

And last winter the Katsura line had perished as well… though that had been Kaede's doing.

Akira's thoughts stuttered for a moment. He didn't know what to do about Kaede. Half the time she seemed to be his enemy, but she was Basho's mother and their marriage was the only thing holding the Wolf Clan together. She had betrayed him with at least two men, but she wanted to have another child to secure their bloodline. She had ordered the Katsura family killed in his name and without his knowledge, leaving him no choice but to back her decision… but the spy reports clearly showed Katsura Suwa had been behind the assassination attempt last year.

He shut his eyes again, reciting the old mantras of calm and focus that the Monks had drilled into him. Slowly his emotions eased enough for him to regain his focus. He reopened his eyes and looked at the marching soldiers again, measuring their pace.

Three days, he thought. *Three days to get the army through to the Kiirokusa Plain, reunited and supplied by the river. How fast will the Jade Dragons react?*

⛩ ⛩ ⛩

THE MAN'S GRUNTS OF LUST turned into a whining gasp as Tomoe slid the knife into his neck. Blood poured out and covered her face, her mouth, and the salt-iron taste of it was intense, delicious. She laughed into his face, licking her lips and watching as his eyes went wide with terror and then slowly dulled, the soul within winking out like a candle.

"Great Chosen of Dakkurru, you needed."

The former swordswoman jolted back to the present. She was sitting cross-legged in one of the Dakkurru army's round conical-roofed tents. Her mouth still tingled with the remembered taste of her father's blood.

The army, while vast, had brought only a few such tents – enough for the priests, the tribal and clan chiefs, and a few specially privileged individuals. The innumerable ordinary warriors and their camp-followers slept on the open ground or in the ruins of enemy structures, warming themselves with fires or with bundled animal furs.

The Lords of Dakkurru knew that in the past the tribal armies had brought many more tents, whose bulk – even when disassembled and folded – each filled one of the army's simple four-wheeled supply wagons. That was back when the wagons were pulled by the thick-furred, horn-headed herd-beasts that the northern peoples relied on for meat, drink, and clothing. Years of war, against rebellious tribes and then against the Empire, had badly thinned the herds, so badly that they would soon die out altogether, knowledge which pleased the Lords. These days most of the wagons were towed by captive men and women. In some ways that method was actually better than the beasts, since the prisoners could be used for ritual sacrifices as well as for food. And the wagons carried mainly war-supplies – arrows, bowstrings, leather and iron for patching armor and repairing weapons. And endless skins of the tribefolk's drink, a beverage fermented from the milk of their herd-beasts; they guzzled it day and night. Food could be found anywhere there were living creatures, or looted from conquest, but drink was more challenging.

"Great Chosen one?"

"Be silent," Tomoe ordered, and the masked tribal priest who had been speaking withdrew instantly, the tent-flap falling closed and leaving her in the buff-toned semi-darkness where she had spent the last few hours. She did not sleep anymore, not in any way a human would recognize as sleep, but when the Lords and the army did not have need of her she would lose herself in memories of past revenges and visions of future ones – of when the Lords would give her the Wolf Lord and Kenji and all their friends. Often the visions would last for many hours, ending only when the unavoidable demands of the body forced her to action. She no longer found any pleasure in food or drink for themselves, but her flesh still needed at least some fuel even with the power of Dakkurru coursing through it.

Tomoe unfolded her legs and rose to her feet. Her muscles moved smoothly despite her long immobility. She picked up the sheathed sword that lay nearby; she had little need for it anymore, and sometimes sensed that the Lords would prefer she not carry it at all, but there was always the chance that some idiot samurai could ambush her. The thought that a random fool might kill her before she got to confront Kenji was… infuriating. So the Lords had not pressed the matter. Not yet.

She slid the sheathed blade under her belt – a leather belt, she wore the tribefolk garments of fur and leather now rather than the Empire's linen and silk – and stepped out of the tent. It was midafternoon, the hated False Light dipping westward in a sky clear except for a few scattered patches of gray-white cloud along the eastern horizon. The tent was pitched alongside several others on a bare hilltop that had previously been home to one of the Empire's shrines. The ruins of that structure, all smashed rocks and blackened timbers and smoldering ash, were visible off to her right, past the tent where the *other* Chosen stayed, the one who had been called Satsuki in her former life.

Tribesmen had torn the shrine apart last night, smashing the statues and artworks, then dragged in two captive Priestesses and tied them to the corner pillars. The naked women had been in the warriors' hands for several days, and they stared blankly, nothing left behind their eyes but animal pain. Still, they had screamed well enough when the tribesmen lit the fire and it consumed them along with the shrine itself. The Lords had watched and listened through Tomoe's eyes and ears, and she had felt the pulse of their hate in time with her own.

Tomoe realized the shaman was standing next to her, waiting. Whatever he had come to her about must not be crucially important, then. He wore a ragged cloak of tanned skins, human and animal; there were stretched and distorted limbs visible in its shape, finger-shapes trailing from the bottom edge. A short staff in one hand was topped with a yellowed bare skull, small enough to be a child or a young woman, held to the staff by tight-wound leather strips. The mask covering his face was an oversized oval of flat wood, fringed with tangles of dark hair, the skin of a child's face stretched flat across the front. There was no visible way for him to see her, but he moved and turned his head as though his eyes' vision was clear.

"What is needed?" she finally asked, feeling the Lords stirring in the back of her mind, taking notice.

"Prisoner," the shaman said. His voice was low, the Empire's speech crude but oddly musical in his mouth. "Samurai."

Ah, Tomoe thought with a sudden surge of inner glee. *This will be pleasant. And... this is why he came for me, not for Satsuki,* she realized. The Lords' other vessel seemed to be more powerful than Tomoe, or at least to be able to channel more of Dakkurru's annihilating power through her flesh, which Tomoe found... irritating. But she was a puppet that could not act without the Lords yanking her strings. Tomoe had been a bounty-hunter, a specialist in hunting and interrogating, in the long-ago time before she had accepted the Lords into her soul; the skills still lurked in the memories she retained.

"Show me," she commanded, and the shaman turned without a word and led her down the hill.

The land below had been farms interspersed with patches of forest. Now it was a trampled muddy wasteland, the army sprawling across it in a jumble of tribesmen and prisoners and occasional animals, clustering around vast campfires built from hacked-down trees, men quarreling over piles of loot, here and there the supply wagons parked in circles with prisoners chained nearby, or with small herds of the shaggy herd-beasts gnawing disconsolately at what grass survived. The whole thing spreading for miles in every direction, a nightmare of disorder that would make a samurai tear out his topknot just to look at it. A stench hung over it all, a compound of ashes and mud, sweat and blood and excrement. That would have bothered the woman Tomoe had been; now it was as meaningless as the rest of the trivialities of mortal existence.

If a bunch of samurai showed up just now, with horses and bows and spears, they could cut this army t'ribbons, a distant corner of Tomoe's thinking mind noted. But that would not happen, because this was merely the heart of the army, not its entirety. Thousands of tribesmen were scattered out in every direction for miles uncounted, in tribal bands or smaller groups, the most distant ones all led by shamans who were guided by Dakkurru's power. Ravaging undefended towns, spying on enemy troops, seizing loot and prisoners, and... ambushing samurai.

She followed the shaman through the camp, mud and ashes squishing and puffing under her leather boots, tribesmen averting their eyes and shrinking back, lowering their heads in submission as she passed. Mutters spread behind her, a low chorus of awe: "Ezen Dakkurru …du kooloi… khu chadal…" *The Voice of the Lords, the Power of the Lords.* Tomoe felt her mouth stretching into a grin. *Always I was at t'bottom, gettin' pissed on by all t'great lords. Now I'm at t'top.*

She raised her feet to step across the burnt shards of a fence, probably the enclosure of a peasant's garden judging from the smoldering ruins of a cottage nearby. Beyond, a group of tribesmen waited with their prisoner; they all cowered to their knees and pressed their faces into the dirt as she approached, while the kneeling prisoner looked around and then peered at her with narrowed, attentive eyes.

He was middle-aged, his top-knotted hair still mostly black but with the first hints of gray in the stubble on his chin and chest and growing in on the shaved parts of his scalp. He was stripped to the waist, his torso covered in ugly bruises, a crudely-bandaged wound on the left side; his wrists were tied and his arms held in place by a stick thrust between elbows and back. His leggings were filthy and bloodstained but looked to have been of high quality, and that combined with his age marked him as someone of higher rank than a mere foot-soldier.

The shaman lifted his staff and began to shake it, the skull rattling from the finger-bones inside, his voice going low and droningly guttural as he recited an invocation. The tribesmen bobbed their heads in time to the chant, growling ritual responses.

Tomoe ignored all of that. It mattered nothing, what the vermin believed and chanted; it mattered only that they obeyed. She walked up to the prisoner and squatted in front of him, looking directly into his face, her own head turned slightly to one side. The man looked back, his gaze steady despite the lines of pain and exhaustion grooved into his face. *Been a prisoner for a couple of days, from t'bruises changin' color and t'hair growing back,* Tomoe judged. *And still got spirit, from t'way he's lookin' at me. And he looked around for a chance t'run when t'guard all bowed.*

She set one hand on his bare shoulder, feeling the tension in his stone-tight muscles, and grinned. "So what's your name, old man?"

The mundane nature of the question combined with her use of the Empire's speech caught him off-guard. His expression went slack with surprise, and without thinking he answered, "I am honorable Captain Tora Shigematsu."

Ah, Tomoe thought, feeling a rush of greedy interest from the Lords watching through her eyes. *So he's from t'rulin' family here, and has some rank.* "A captain, *neh*? So tell me, *captain*, about what's between us and Castle Mouko."

"You are of the Empire's people," Shigematsu said. He was trying to regain his earlier firmness of expression but not quite getting there. "Why are you helping these filthy barbarians?"

"What, you think I should help you samurai instead? Your world's excrement, and it spit on me for my whole life. And then you tossed me a few coins t'hunt for criminals you brave samurai couldn't be bothered t'catch." Tomoe laughed, the Lords laughing with her, through her, the sound like many voices overlapping, louder than should have been possible from a human throat. The shaman broke off his chant in a wild shriek, shaking his staff with blurring speed.

The samurai blanched and dropped his head, shying away from her hand and hunching his shoulders, his arms knotting as he tried to free his hands to cover his ears. "I will not tell you of our troop movements!" he rasped, his voice gone weak and shaky.

Tomoe released his shoulder and tapped his forehead with one finger, feeling a rush of euphoric glee that was better than the best wine. "Oh, we know where your armies are," she said, grinning until it felt like her face would split open. "These fellows who caught you, there's thousands like 'em out there, lookin' everywhere, and what they see... *we* see." She felt the Lords right behind her eyes then, looking out at the samurai, and the man's face went slack as terror overrode self-control. She smelled a rank thick stench as he lost control of his bladder.

"We know where you are. We just need to know t'rest of it. How many men you have, how much food. All that war-fightin' stuff." She brought her hand down and gripped his chin, pulling it up so she – and the Lords – could look directly into his eyes. "And you're goin' t'tell me."

"Amatsu preserve me," he whimpered, and then she slid her finger down across his lips and sealed them, locking the muscles as firmly as she had once been locked into stocks for beating.

"The False Light's far away, old man," Tomoe whispered. "Not that t'bitch ever did anything for anyone." She tapped the side of his jaw and watched his eyes bulge as the first waves of agony went through his flesh. "There's no one here but you... and *us*."

⛩ ⛩ ⛩

"HONORABLE FATHER. WE HAVE RECEIVED... a message."

Lord Kiyogama Heisuke looked up from his writing desk, noting immediately the tightly-controlled boiling anger in his son Daihachi's posture and voice. It was to the young man's credit, Heisuke reflected, that he was guarding his temper so well. Not well enough to conceal it, to be sure, the young always had difficulty keeping their face. But well enough not to be controlled by it, which was the first step toward true adulthood.

Kiyogama's concubine, Aoi, had been playing a three-string lute. Now she stopped and laid it aside, setting the plectrum beside it. Kiyogama set down his writing brush with similar care, laying it across the ceramic ink-tray so the wet bristles would not stain the smooth-planed wood of the table. "A message from the High Lord?"

"Yes," Kiyogama Daihachi replied stiffly. He was in armor, his helmet tucked under one arm; his official position at Castle Kigi was as the commander of its garrison. "Delivered to our gates."

"And you received it?"

"I did. The... the messengers are in the upper courtyard, awaiting your response."

Kiyogama stroked his face where his moustaches had been. It was a habit he had developed to avoid reacting too quickly in conversations, and the instinct was still there even though he had shaved his facial hair to help escape Castle Hokori. It was important to appear calm, self-collected, both for the benefit of his vassals and to teach his son how to behave in like circumstances.

Finally he rose from his cross-legged pose and held out his arms while Aoi tightened the sash of his robe. She finished and slid aside, prostrating herself, and he picked up his swords from the stand against the wall, sliding them beneath the now properly-snug sash. He was a broad-shouldered man with only a slight paunch despite his advancing age, and the hair tied back in his formal topknot was still entirely black; wearing swords projected strength, confidence in his own health and skill, and such things were important – especially now, when the castle and the whole province was rife with rumors of impending danger.

Rumors soon to be intensified by these visitors, unless I miss my guess.

He and his son left the room, Aoi bowing again to their departing backs, and descended the steep, almost ladder-like stairs within the western keep of Castle Kigi. The wooden steps were smooth under their sock-clad feet, requiring them to move deliberately and without hurry to avoid slipping. That was a consistent design feature in the Empire's castles, and Lord Kiyogama half-suspected it had originated as a way to ensure that samurai at home moved with the same calm and dignity as they were expected to show in public.

Castle Kigi had two keeps, east and west, nested atop several levels of walls and courtyards within the irregular circuit of the outer fortifications hundreds of feet below. Each courtyard and open ramp was enlivened by the trees that the wife of a previous Lord Kiyogama had loved – maples, oaks, pines, fruit trees of all kinds, even camphors.

The upper courtyard, located between the two pagoda towers that were the heart of the castle, was also the smallest, no more than forty paces on a side, and made smaller by the maple trees growing at its corners and edges. Their foliage, now in full eruption with the arrival of spring, made the courtyard almost private, its stone flagging visible only from the windows of the towers on either side.

A suitable place for meeting with emissaries of... questionable honor.

The visitors waited silently, a trio of younger men in high-shouldered woven overcoats, baggy shirts, and knee-snugged leggings – the garments of soldiers without armor. A half-squadron of Kiyogama house guards stood on either side, but the visitors still wore their swords – it would have been insulting to demand they surrender them. A wooden box rested on the paving-stones in front of them, but Lord Kiyogama did not look at that immediately; instead he examined the three visitors, noting the crests on their coats.

He smiled inwardly. "Honorable Konatsu Sabato. It has been some time since the Battle of Nagai Kyukai, *neh*?"

The center man of the three made a stiff bow, hiding the glower that started to cloud his face. His two companions did the same. "Honorable Lord Kiyogama. I bring you a message, and a gift, from High Lord Noboru."

Konatsu Sabato had led two thousand Wolf Clan cavalry to the Battle of Nagai Kyukai Plain, then switched sides at the moment the battle was due to start, a betrayal timed to coincide with the assassination of the Wolf Clan's High Lord Okaro. It was the sort of devastating blow that High Lord Ryu Akurai had specialized in, crushing an enemy before the battle truly started. But in this case it had not worked. Some manner of Divine visitation had occurred – Kiyogama preferred not to think too closely about that – and the Wolf Clan had won the battle. Subsequent reports confirmed that Sabato's father, Lord Konatsu Hojo had died for his treason, and more recently that the rest of the family had followed him into death, leaving young Sabato as the sole scion of a bloodline hundreds of years old. He and his cavalry were now samurai without a Lord, living as the dependents of the Clan which had lured them into treason.

And High Lord Noboru sends this man to visit us. Interesting. "I will hear your message," he said aloud, still not looking at the box.

He could see the younger man clench his teeth – the flex in his jaw muscles was unmistakable. A distant part of Kiyogama's mind felt a sort of abstract sympathy for young Sabato's situation – it was, after all, the sort of risk any samurai took when he played both sides of a conflict. *As I have done more than once.* But the Konatsu family had played that game and lost, and there was little room in the samurai world for mercy to the defeated. *Even less now than before, in fact.*

"The most honorable High Lord Ryu Noboru sends you this gift as a reminder of the consequences for betrayal," Sabato recited, staring straight ahead. "Lord Noboru commands you to bring your armies to serve him in the field as honor and your sworn oaths require. If that is done, you may be permitted to slit your belly and pass your lands on to your… remaining son."

"*Ah so*," Kiyogama murmured. He took a step forward and looked down into the box. The face of his younger son Goichi stared up at him.

The head was mounted to a spike in the bottom of the box, the traditional way of displaying such trophies. Its expression was distorted, both by the pain of whatever agonizing death Goichi had suffered and by the effects of more than a few days of decay. A distant corner of Lord Kiyogama's mind reflected on how crude High Lord Noboru's provocations were compared to the surgical mercilessness of his late father, Lord Akurai. That man had won a war by torturing an enemy nobleman's son to death, provoking the father into suicidal rage. This clumsy gesture, while speaking of personal savagery, lacked any manipulative finesse.

Kiyogama Heisuke straightened up, expressionless, and made a small gesture to Daihachi. The younger man, visibly struggling with his own self-control, picked up the box that contained his brother's head. He bowed once to Lord Kiyogama, very sharply, and retreated back to the keep. He would secure the head and summon a mortician to have it cremated for burial.

Konatsu Sabato and his two companions were looking straight ahead, faces set, sweat beading on their foreheads despite the relative cool of the spring weather. *Waiting to be executed*, Kiyogama knew. That was why Noboru had sent them on this errand; he needed someone of sufficient rank to be allowed to convey the message, but couldn't risk any other noble's bloodline, not when the Clan's unity was already so fragile. It showed a certain crude cunning, Kiyogama supposed, though again nothing comparable to what his father had displayed.

"I thank the High Lord for his message, and his gift," Kiyogama said. He deliberately spoke in a way that did not directly address the messengers. "I will consider it with the utmost gravity."

A subtle shift went through the three men as they realized they would live. Almost a deflation, tight-wound muscles relaxing and held breaths slipping out. After a moment Sabato recovered his balance and seemed almost to smirk as he bowed. "I will convey your words, honorable Lord Kiyogama."

Ah, now he thinks I am preparing to submit, Heisuke thought, outwardly ignoring the younger man and instead speaking to his own guards. "I am finished here. Escort these strangers to the gate."

The guards stepped forward and bowed politely, gesturing toward the ramp that descended to the next level. Konatsu Sabato glowered, his earlier fear now turned to rage that Kiyogama was not directly acknowledging him. Heisuke smiled like a predator inside, though his external face remained blandly expressionless while the three men left, followed by the guards.

Alone, Lord Kiyogama clasped his hands behind his back, staring at nothing while he organized his thoughts. After a minute a scuff of sandals on stone and the faint sound of tightly-controlled breathing told him his son had returned. He waited for the younger man to calm down, in the meantime half-idly noting the health of the trees, their three-spined leaves bright green with spring. *Let's see, these would be... eighteen years old?* The tops were over twenty feet above him, but he could remember his wife overseeing their planting when they were saplings only an arm's length in height. She had taken up her ancestor's enthusiasm for trees, though not so fervently. The memory brought a wave of bittersweet melancholy. *She is gone now, ephemeral and brief as all mortal lives. How long will the trees outlive her, I wonder?*

"An interesting message," he said finally.

Daihachi drew a breath. His face was still tight with rigid self-control, but it *was* controlled, which was good. Impressive, in fact, given that he had just received confirmation that his younger brother had died cruelly. That was the second of his siblings to perish at the hands of High Lord Noboru; his sister Chiyu, the High Lord's wife, had been executed last winter after unsuccessfully trying to flee Castle Hokori with her child. "Will you accept the High Lord's offer?"

Straight to the point. Well, the young are often in a hurry, Heisuke reflected. "It does seem tempting, from a certain point of view," he noted. "Not all that different from the offer his father gave to the Sada and Oyama, at the end of the unfortunate rebellion two years ago."

It was the traditional way to handle such things, whether ending a rebellion or absorbing a defeated foe. Even High Lord Akurai, as ruthless as he often could be, had recognized the value of undercutting fanatical resistance by offering a way for nobles to preserve their families if not themselves. It was not really surprising that Lord Noboru was trying the same tack, albeit with crude ineptness.

"Lord Noboru knows you are not loyal – he arrested Lord Wakita." The Lord of Castle Kujira, a minor stronghold on the southern coast of the Empire, had joined Kiyogama and several others last year to discuss their High Lord's increasingly erratic nature. "And he is... he killed Chiyu and Gohachi, he cannot possibly believe you will forgive that. I believe this is a trap, a lie to try to lure you out of Castle Kigi with our army."

"Perhaps so. What if I refuse?"

Daihachi fell silent for a time, thinking. "A siege? No, wait... he said we must support him in the field. Does that mean the Wolf are attacking?"

Kiyogama nodded, pleased at his son's perceptiveness. "Indeed, the command was... very specific, was it not?"

He unclasped his hands and took a leaf between two fingers, admiring the delicate tracery of spines and veins within it. *Interesting. I would have expected the Wolf Clan to wait a year or two, to properly recover from their own internal conflict. Such a delay would benefit them more than us. But there can be no other reason for High Lord Noboru to make that specific demand. Perhaps the Wolf Clan's young High Lord has succumbed to the impatience of youth?*

"The High Lord cannot besiege us immediately, if the Wolf are attacking. But if he wins without us, he will certainly do so afterward, and there would be no mercy then." Daihachi was speaking slowly, as though feeling his way reluctantly to a conclusion he did not like. "So we must either support him now, with no assurance he will keep his word, or…"

Kiyogama released the leaf and watched it spring back from him. "Or?"

"Or we can take the field against him. But we do not have sufficient strength, he will simply crush us. So we… we wait, and hope that Lord Noboru loses. But then we would have to negotiate with the Wolf ruler, this Lord Akira. I have heard that he exterminated all the rebels he defeated last year, down to the wives and children." Daihachi's voice went slightly uneven with embarrassment. "I… apologies, honorable father, I cannot see a good path for us."

Kiyogama turned and met his son's gaze then, and smiled inside his own mind. *The boy is trying his best, and I should not be needlessly cruel.* "I do not blame you, my son. My own assessment would be the same as yours… except for one thing. I received a letter yesterday."

"A letter…?"

"Yes, a letter." Kiyogama allowed the smile to reach his lips. "From Lord Akira's wife."

⛩ ⛩ ⛩

SHE FLOATED IN AN INFINITE darkness that was also infinite pain.

She was not alone. *They* were with her, always. Their incomprehensible words flowed through her, agony and madness, through her and beyond, elsewhere. To a place she could not touch.

Sometimes, just sometimes, when They spoke the darkness would change. She would see things, hear things, faint and distorted as though they came to her through a great distance.

Voices, shouts, screams.

A churning mass of bipedal shapes, topped with the glitter of blades.

A massive object – a castle, she somehow knew, though she no longer remembered what that meant. It distorted and erupted, flying into ruin, shattered like she was shattered.

Then the darkness returned, the pain, all-consuming.

Sometimes she dreamed she had lived in that other place. That there had been a name, her name. That she had been something other than Their tool, Their vessel.

That she had been Satsuki.

The dreams vanished into nothing whenever They spoke. The darkness, and Those within it, were the only real things, the only truth.

They were real. Satsuki was only a dream.

CHAPTER 4

"MAMA! MAMA, LOOK!"

Ookami Kaede smiled, feeling a warmth that went beyond anything supplied by the spring Sunshine. Her son Basho run back and forth through Castle Ookami's garden, yelling with delight at the birds and winged insects that rose before him. He had a thin bamboo stick clutched in one chubby hand, the end of it mounting a wooden caricature of a wolf-head painted bright red. A ball of the same color hung from a cord out of the wolf's mouth. The toy had been a gift from Miyako before she left to take up her new married life; the accepted use for it was to toss the ball into the air and then try to catch it in the wolf's mouth, but Basho found that level of self-control far too difficult and preferred to simply wave it wildly about, the red ball jerking as erratically as the butterflies it stirred into flight.

A serving-maid trailed nervously after Basho, hovering protectively whenever he got close to any of the three carp ponds. Castle Ookami's gardens were not so grand as those in Castle Hokori, or the ancient Winter Castle that had been the pride of Kaede's old Clan before her marriage to Akira had merged the Black Wolf and Gray Wolf back into one. They were impressive nonetheless, two acres of carefully tended beauty tucked in next to the castle's main keep, surrounded by a low wall that shut out the inharmonious sight of the castle's military parade ground. Trimmed shrubs sprouting from fields of gravel raked into pleasing patterns, cherry trees now erupting into the pale white-pink blossoming splendor of spring, flowers artfully planted to seem natural yet in harmony and balance with each other, glittering streams linking the carp ponds, benches arranged in cleared areas to facilitate pleasant conversation and artistic performances... In the evenings the gardens were nearly always busy, crowded with courtiers seeking anything from artistic inspiration to romantic assignations. That would be especially true now, with cherry-blossom season at hand, revered as the most beautiful time of year ever since the early Emperors.

Now, an hour after breakfast, the garden would have been empty even if Kaede had not claimed it for a private visit. Partly she had done that because watching Basho play was a joy she did not get to indulge very often, and partly because she herself felt a deep craving for open air and Sunlight after a long winter inside the castle, and partly...

And partly because I've started feeling queasy after breakfast, and I don't want anyone noticing yet.

She had persuaded Akira late last winter that they needed to have another child to secure the dynasty, and he had been... dutiful, as he had been before. She did not delude herself that he felt any affection for her. It was, at least, a far better experience than it had been when they were first married.

Kaede had known two lovers, one highly skilled and one clumsy and amateurish – the Katsura brothers, Suwa and Motosuke, both now dead. Akira would never thrill her as Suwa had done. But he was no longer anywhere close to so bad as Motosuke had been.

That's because he had a lover of his own, a small petty voice whispered in the back of Kaede's mind. The Satsuki woman was gone, but she felt sure that Akira still mourned her. *None of that matters anymore,* she told herself, though it was often hard to believe it. *What matters is the future.*

Kaede's moon-cycle was two months late, but the morning illness was a more concrete sign that their child-making efforts had succeeded. So far, thanks be to Amatsu's Compassion, the nausea had been mild, closer to what she had experienced with Basho three years ago than her misery last year with the lost child. *No doubt Priestess Ritsuko would tell me I don't deserve to do better this time,* she thought with a momentary twinge of anger, but she immediately cut it off. The old Priestess had not visited since Akira had marched out to war, and Kaede saw no need to encourage that to change. *Look at me, imagining that thinking about her will summon her into my presence like some evil spirit from a folk-tale!*

Normally by this hour of the morning she would be overseeing the castle's court chamber, which meant listening to speeches, receiving petitions, and watching the assembled courtiers for hints of the latest political trends. But showing illness in front of the court would be the perfect way to undermine Clan unity at the start of a war, so she had delayed court until after the Noon prayers. It was early enough in the spring that the chamber would still be reasonably pleasant even then. *And this gives me an extra chance to review my correspondence,* she reflected, picking up the stack of papers on the bench beside her. Lately there never seemed to be enough time for that.

Basho tripped and went sprawling, his stick flying and the red ball briefly flashing in the Sunlight as it described a wild arc overhead and then landed in a shrub. Kaede half-rose from her seat in the gazebo, her hands clutching the papers tightly enough for them to crinkle loudly. She watched as the fretting maidservant descended on her son like a stooping hawk, lifting him to his feet and brushing leaves and dirt off his simple robe. Basho laughed and pulled free, chasing down his fallen toy.

Kaede relaxed and sat down again. She smoothed out the papers on her knee and allowed herself to focus on them, keeping the sounds of Basho's play in her peripheral senses.

Some of the letters were from her own personal network of correspondents, the allies and contacts she had slowly built up over the last four years – with abundant help from Miyako and her parents, to be sure. She read them quickly, making mental notes on which ones needed an immediate reply. After those came the latest letters and freshly decoded spy reports for her husband, delivered to her quarters so late last night that she had been too sleepy to read them. She needed to review those today, since they would be forwarded to Akira no later than tomorrow.

In truth, she was pushing the limits of her own position as High Lady to insist on reading the reports before they went on to Akira. She had maneuvered herself into being able to read them when the Clan spymaster, Seneschal Ookami Amano, left last winter on a mission to the Aelfynn lands. And whatever Akira might think of her, he had not forced her to stop.

The spy reports were, as usual, a muddle of random information, especially since she was reading the originals rather than Amano's neatly-organized summaries. What did it mean that the River of Black Ice was full of dead fish? That was the sort of thing peasants would declare a bad omen, but it didn't seem important otherwise. Unless that meant the peasant unrest in the Jade Dragon lands would get even worse? Peasants and clergy had been fleeing across the border from that Clan's territory since last summer, and she supposed that might represent some sort of advantage to the Wolf Clan – after all, without peasants there would be no rice for samurai to eat.

Two different reports from the north, both of them merchants. One claiming that the Bear Clan was suddenly stockpiling food as though it was planning to march its armies, the other passing on a rumor that a Tiger Clan castle, Castle Dangai, had fallen to the northern barbarians. Kaede frowned to herself. She did not know the geography of the northern Clans – it had taken her years just to get a handle on the Wolf Clan's territory. Was that castle important? How had mere barbarians managed to capture a castle held by honorable samurai?

A spy in WaterCity reported the Nightingale were receiving foreign ships in their ports again. That was probably very important to their young ruler, Lady Naichin Miyu, who was now on her way back to her own lands after spending the winter as a guest of the Wolf Clan. The Nightingale depended on trade with the foreigners for their wealth, and after the events of the last four years – conquest by the Jade Dragon Clan, then a liberation by the Wolf that left them little more than a protectorate – it was the only real strength they had. Wealth flowing in would strengthen Lady Miyu against any ambitious or treacherous nobles within her Clan. The announcement of her betrothal to Kado Kitaro, one of Akira's chief vassals, would also have that effect. *And they both seem happy with the arrangement,* Kaede thought, feeling an undeniable pride in her own part in that winter negotiation… but also an undercurrent of bitter jealousy at those who the Lady blessed with a happy marriage.

She shook her head very slightly. *I really need to learn not to let my feelings run away with me, even in private. Otherwise I'll end up like Lady Yumiko.* Her stepmother-in-law had died last year, leading the failed rebellion against Akira.

She made herself watch Basho for a few minutes, listen to his laughter. When her mind was settled she turned back to the documents, moving from the spy reports to the letters.

A report from Tokaze Kondo, one of Akira's commanders, something about troop movements. Kaede knew him only vaguely: one of the young men who hovered near Akira during the winter, often with a barely-controlled worshipful expression on his face. Kaede still found that irritating, though she had finally realized it was not entirely unjustified. Everyone seemed to agree that Akira was a brilliant general, no matter how strange he might be in other ways. *I suppose a soldier would find that… quite admirable.*

A letter written on paper of pale yellow, scented with something that Kaede finally recognized as sunflowers. She unfolded it, raising her eyebrows at the elegant calligraphy – clearly the work of someone refined and highly educated, writing with a masculine style and characters. The actual content of the letter was mundane, almost oddly so, discussing matters of family and trade. The second half was a lengthy discussion of a tragic familial death, mixed with fervent and pious hopes that further loss might be averted.

Kaede wondered if the letter was written in code, the way the spies' letters were, but then shook her head; if there was a code Amano's secretary Zenjiro would have known and decoded the letter. She squinted at the unfamiliar crest stamped at the bottom: an insect's face surrounded by a sunflower blossom. The calligraphy atop the crest could be read a couple of different ways, but after a moment she realized it was Kiyogama. *Ah,* she thought, feeling a sense of pieces fitting together inside her head. There was a sort of pleasure in that, in recognizing what she was really seeing. *Lord Kiyogama, he's a major provincial Lord in the Jade Dragon lands,* she recalled. *He's dropped hints before that he might be dissatisfied with the Ryu, I remember Akira and Seneschal Amano talking about that a couple of times. Sending this letter now...* She tapped her chin with one fingertip, thinking. *All that talk about family tragedy and trying to avoid more. He's looking for a way out.*

She set the letter aside, re-stacking the rest. They would be sent on to her husband later today, but this... *Akira won't know how to respond to this, but I do.*

⛩ ⛩ ⛩

TOKAZE KONDO REGARDED THE CITY in front of him with an inward scowl that threatened to leak onto his external face. GreenTown was one of the two largest cities in the Wolf Clan, a sprawling trade center that straddled the River of Lengthy Travel for miles to both east and west. Kondo thought it might actually be larger than WolfTown itself, though the flat landscape and lack of a higher vantage point made it difficult to judge. Much of the trade in the Empire's eastern half passed through the city at one point or another, and even from a mile away Kondo could see the masts of countless ships rising above the city skyline. Some of those same ships would soon carry him and his escort would take north to Lord Tamiya's beleaguered province.

The taxes on the city's trade had made its rulers – the Haruto under the Black Wolves, and later the Katsura under the Gray Wolves – rich and influential. *And now the Katsura are gone and we are... back to the Haruto, maybe?* The situation here was uncertain, had been so since the mid-winter assassination of Lord Katsura. The written orders from High Lord Akira, currently folded and tucked under his sash, did not offer a solution. That seemed risky to Kondo, but Lord Akira's orders had never been wrong before and he was not about to believe they would be this time.

Kondo had first met the High Lord in the Nightingale lands four years ago, when his father – the High Lord Okaro – had sent Akira with a tiny army, barely over a thousand men, to support the Nightingale against the Jade Dragon Clan. Kondo had been a mere lieutenant in that army, serving under his older cousin Tokaze Daichi; a young man eager for glory, frustrated to be serving a commander who seemed to be an imbecile at best, at worst half-insane.

And now I am Lord Akira's sworn vassal and command an army of thousands of men. And he might rise into the nobility before it was all said and done – his comrade Hajime Soto from Akira's old army had already been named to the rule of Castle Shinshiro and its surrounding lands, and another companion, Kado Kitaro, was somehow betrothed to the High Lady of the Nightingale

Clan. Kondo wasn't quite sure what to think about such things. If he were to gain a similar appointment, it would be an astonishing rise in station for a man barely twenty-five years old, the son of a minor landholder in the Ookami territory... but after watching Lord Akira wrestle with the rule of the Wolf Clan for the last three years Kondo was not at all sure he wanted more responsibilities than he already had.

I certainly don't think I would ever want to try to rule this *place, no matter how rich and powerful it would make me,* Kondo reflected. The city was numbingly huge, a charcoal-hazed sprawl that ran all across the northern horizon.

Ojima Katsuji cleared his throat. The older man, his chin swathed in a neatly-trimmed beard, commanded a thousand of Lord Shinsen's vassals on the northern border. He had brought them north at the end of summer, arriving just in time to stabilize the crumbling defenses. "Looks like someone's waiting for us, honorable Kondo," he murmured.

Kondo squinted at the mile-distant waystation on the city's edge and nodded. There was a pavilion set up there, with banners fluttering at the corners and a small group waiting in front of it. Too far to make out the crests on the banners, but the predominant color was Wolf gray, which was an obvious attempt to project loyalty. "Well, I'm sure they've had plenty of warning we were coming."

The escort that filled the Wolf's Pace Road behind him was modest – only about a hundred men, infantry except for a single squadron of cavalry, and thirty servants, enough to properly dignify a senior officer who was a direct vassal of the High Lord, and to deter any bandits who might be otherwise be tempted to attack. It was not enough to save them if a local Lord decided to turn traitor, but the odds of that happening now, after Lord Akira had crushed everyone who betrayed him, were very low indeed.

Low, but not impossible, Kondo reminded himself. *Revenge has a value in itself, and there are men who will die to attain it.*

They were closer now, close enough to recognize the crests on the banners flying by the open-sided pavilion. Wolf at the top, and below... *A coiled blue serpent against red?* Kondo was fairly sure that was the Haruto crest, which made sense given what he knew.

The crowd around and under the pavilion appeared to be mostly servants, although he could see at least a few samurai with swords through their belts. None of them armored, which was a good sign. Of course, there were armored men in the waystation just up the road if they were needed.

"Ah, here they come," Katsuji murmured.

Two men had emerged from under the pavilion and walked to the center of the road, waiting. Kondo looked them over as he closed the distance, keeping his horse at a steady walk. The man in the lead was dressed like a courtier, not a soldier – small black hat atop precisely-groomed hair, wide-hipped silk pants, a loose silk shirt embroidered with colorful imagery, a wide-shouldered vest over the shirt that displayed the crests of the Haruto family, the Wolf Clan, and a Magistrate's fan. Kondo noted that here too the Wolf crest had been placed above the other two, as was proper. The man's smooth face and shaved-back temples showed not even a hint of bristle except for a very modest and precisely trimmed goatee, making Kondo wonder if the fellow shaved multiple times a day to keep himself looking that way.

Kondo drew up a few paces away and dismounted, Katsuji doing likewise. The lead man immediately bowed, politely low. "I am honorable Magistrate Haruto Toji, loyal servant of the Wolf Clan and… apologies, but at least for the moment… senior governing authority in GreenTown." He straightened and regarded Kondo with a mild, attentive smile, his eyebrows slightly raised as though to invite a question. When none was forthcoming, he gestured with his folded fan at the samurai riding on his right, who bowed in turn. "This is my kinsman, Haruto Kihachi, currently serving as my ally in maintaining order here and overseeing the military security of the province."

That's a soldier, Kondo thought, noting the shape of muscles under the younger Haruto's more practical-looking shirt and pleated leggings, the twin swords worn prominently at the waist, the hard attentiveness of the narrowed eyes. *But he's in a subordinate position*. He cleared his throat and returned their bows, slightly less deeply – he was, after all, here as a direct representative of the High Lord. "I am honorable commander Tokaze Kondo, sworn vassal to the most honorable High Lord Ookami Akira. My companion is Ojima Katsuji, sworn vassal of the honorable Lord Shinsen. The High Lord has sent us here to request troops from GreenTown for the defense of the Empire."

"My honorable cousin and I are certainly eager to assist the High Lord in such a noble goal," Magistrate Haruto replied smoothly. He gestured toward the pavilion. "Perhaps we might enjoy some tea while we discuss the matter?"

Kondo suppressed a sigh and nodded. He and Katsuji followed the two Haruto samurai into the pavilion. There was a small table there along with several backless chairs, all built lightly to be easily folded and transported. They were not much different in basic design from what Kondo brought with him on campaign, but the designs here were refined and elegant, almost delicate, rather than the simple practicality of camp gear. Servants had set up a charcoal brazier and were boiling tea atop it, and the delicate, slightly floral scent of the tea mingled with the odor of burning charcoal and the background smells of spring grass, human and horse sweat, and the unpleasant underlying tang of the nearby city and river.

A pair of bowing servant-women handed out cups and poured tea, then retreated silently. The two Haruto slowly sipped their tea, savoring the taste and smell, and Kondo did the same, not really tasting it but careful not to lose face by showing impatience. *I wish Lord Akira had sent a courtier along to handle this,* he thought briefly, and then felt embarrassed at the thought. Who among the simpering, whispering, gossiping samurai-in-name-only who inhabited Castle Ookami could have been trusted here? Just the memory of those people from his time in the castle last winter set Kondo's sword-hand itching. The only one who seemed competent was the old Seneschal, and Lord Akira had sent him away to deal with the Aelfynn.

"At the orders of the most honorable High Lord, I am rejoining my army in the lands of Lord Tamiya, to defend the northern border against the threat from the barbarians. He has sent orders for you to assist in this effort." Kondo pulled a sheet of paper from his sleeve and handed it over. Behind his face he thought: *No need to mention that he also ordered me to give up everything north of Castle Yamako if necessary.*

Haruto Toji accepted the precisely-folded light gray paper with a smile, but did not unfold it. "I am sure you already know what is in this letter, honorable Kondo. Our High Lord does not strike me as the sort of man who conceals his intentions from his allies, only from his enemies."

Kondo was tempted to laugh out loud at that. Lord Akira was notorious even among his closest followers for his caginess, always concealing his true intentions until the critical moment. *But he tells us what we need to know to play our part,* he reflected. *I suppose that would look to an outsider as though he is open and clear to us.* Aloud he replied to the Magistrate's unspoken question: "Lord Akira wishes you to send troops with me to the north. At least a thousand men, preferably two thousand or more if you have them."

"If I have them... an interesting phrasing." Toji the letter over in his hands, looking at it as though fascinated by the precise folds and smooth light gray color. Kondo couldn't help noticing the man's fingers were almost as slim and delicate as a woman's, and with nails just as well-kept. "The situation here is... complex, I'm afraid," he continued, tapping the edge of the folded letter against the opposite wrist. "The... execution... of the late Lord Katsura left the city and surrounding territory without an officially sanctioned ruler. A significant number of Katsura samurai remain hostile to us, although we have managed to secure Lord Katsura's remaining child, his daughter, as a hostage. We have thus far received no direction from the High Lord as to what should be her fate, or who shall replace the Katsura as rulers of GreenTown."

"That is not my concern," Kondo said shortly, irritated at the courtier's changing of the subject. Katsuji stirred, aware that Kondo was being deliberately rude. "I am here to fulfill the High Lord's orders."

The other Haruto samurai, who had taken the High Lord's letter from Toji but had not yet opened it, let out a snort. "Honorable cousin. This man is a soldier."

Kondo recognized layers of meaning beneath that, though he could not perceive what all of them might be. He exchanged a look with Katsuji, who returned it with a faint half-smile. A ghost of expression that seemed to say: *We know what it is to be a samurai on the battlefield, even if this fine fellow does not.*

Memories lurked, of the battles that had defined Kondo's life for the last four years. The desperate impossible campaign in the Nightingale lands, fighting always outnumbered. The battle at Nagai Kyukai Plain, charging wildly amid the blazing Divine light. The grim fighting in the north last year, thousands of screaming barbarians swarming like ants, and only last-second reinforcements had prevented them from overrunning him...

"Ah," Toji murmured. His smile changed, becoming self-deprecating. "I apologize, honorable Kondo. I really should know better after the experiences of the last half-year, but a lifetime of habits is difficult to break. And our situation... the situation of the Haruto family, of myself and my cousin and our vassals and relatives... is rather precarious right now, you understand."

"Because you killed Lord Katsura," Kondo nodded.

The man looked elegantly pained, like a gourmet disappointed by his meal, and raised a finger of one hand in a gesture that Kondo vaguely remembered seeing a few times back at Castle Ookami. Growing up in the country, he had never learned the subtleties of courtly behavior – his father, who often seemed more comfortable overseeing the rice-farmers in their paddies than speaking to other samurai, had viewed any education beyond literacy, history, and religion as needless indulgence. Kondo, as the younger son who could not inherit the landholding, would have had little option outside of a military career even if he had not desired one.

Haruto Kihachi leaned forward slightly, a cue that Haruto Toji accepted with a slight backward movement in turn. "Apologies, but with your permission, honorable Kondo, I will speak plainly."

Kondo nodded, granting what Kihachi had asked. Speaking plainly between samurai was generally considered uncouth anywhere but on the battlefield or when drunk.

"My honorable cousin Toji and I acted on orders from the most honorable High Lord to execute Lord Katsura and his son for treason. However, we have received no further orders since then, and we have been forced to continue on our own in an... unstable situation."

Kondo felt as though he was swimming in deep waters. Lord Akira's orders had warned him that the situation in GreenTown was politically unstable and the loyalty of the Haruto was not entirely certain, but they had offered no guidance on resolving local problems. Although, now that he thought about it, requisitioning troops could be a way of doing just that…

They seemed to expect him to reply in some way. He tried to grasp for what seemed to lie underneath their words, remembering that they had agreed to speak plainly. "Are you saying you are unable to comply with the High Lord's order?"

Haruto Toji's pained expression made another appearance. Kihachi grunted and nodded slightly. "Honorable Kondo, the Haruto men under our direct command do not number more than a thousand in total, and these are performing many duties in the city. The Katsura samurai here actually outnumber us, but thankfully they are mainly sworn to the Matsuda vassal family, whose leader Lord Matsuda Kenshin has only recently returned from spending the winter in Castle Ookami."

He paused then, and Kondo wondered what sort of response he expected. Not knowing what to say, he remained silent. He had noticed over the last four years that when Lord Akira remained silent rather than making the sort of polite remarks others expected, it often forced the others to speak more honestly. Of course, Lord Akira had the rank to behave in that way without consequence…

After a pause long enough that Katsuji made a very subtle motion of discomfort, Kihachi continued: "This has not been a fatal problem thus far. Some of the remaining Katsura samurai have accepted the High Lord's judgment, at least publicly. Those who did not choose to slit their bellies and join their late Lord in death have… generally… obeyed whatever requests we have made, though we have been careful to keep those requests within… reasonable bounds. However, others have continued to proclaim their loyalty to the Katsura – in particular, some of those directly sworn to the Katsura line. They regard us as traitors and usurpers."

Toji chose that moment to return to the conversation. "Perhaps you may recognize, honorable Kondo, that such an accusation carries more weight in the absence of any official statement from the High Lord."

I don't know if this is a subtle attempt to cast blame on Lord Akira or a subtle plea for help, Kondo thought irritably.

Kihachi did not directly acknowledge what his cousin had said, but went on after a brief pause: "Thankfully, these unwavering followers have largely retreated to the Katsura ancestral stronghold, Castle Seihin. We believe there are now at least several hundred of them holed up there, possibly over a thousand."

Kondo fought down an urge to grimace openly. He had actually heard some rumors about the castle during the march from Castle Ookami, since the Wolf's Pace Road took him within ten miles of it. He had been tempted to send a few horsemen to check on it, although he had held back when he reflected that even if he knew, there was nothing he could do about it with the men he had. "It is not my current duty to besiege a rebellious castle," he said aloud.

"Of course," Magistrate Haruto said, making a fluttering gesture with the fingers of one hand. Kondo found himself irrationally wishing Lord Akira's wife was there. Lady Kaede's loyalty was... questionable... but at least she understood all this sort of courtly nonsense. "Nothing could have been further from our minds! But perhaps now you understand why obeying Lord Akira's request will be... challenging." Toji retrieved the still-folded letter from his cousin and regarded it meditatively. "Honorable Kondo, I am sure a man such as you can recognize that the... health... of the Haruto family is a matter of great concern, not just to us personally but to all the samurai who serve us, including our close in who hold positions of command under us. Those men risked their honor and station to obey the order we received from the High Lord."

Kondo clenched his teeth. *They are going to refuse*, he thought. *They'll say they cannot risk sending troops so long as Castle Seihin defies them. And then what? I do not have the strength here to force them to obedience. But if I allow them to disobey, I lose face, Lord Akira loses face, we are both dishonored and my mission to reinforce the Tamiya lands will be a failure.* Briefly the thought came to him that he could slit his belly to protest their insult to his honor, which would force them to either obey or do the same... but no, Lord Akira had not given him permission to do such a thing. *But then what can I do?*

Ojima Katsuji cleared his throat. "With your permission, honorable Kondo... Perhaps if, as honorable Haruto says, Lord Matsuda and his men here in GreenTown are being cooperative, they might be the ones to accompany us to the northern border in obedience to the honorable High Lord's command. I do not imagine they would be so foolish as to disobey."

Thank you, Kondo thought fervently, noting how Haruto Kihachi immediately relaxed slightly. Perhaps Haruto Toji did as well, though all the courtier did outwardly was to tap a finger and thumb on his right hand together. His polite smile remained wholly unchanged. *And honorable Katsuji's right, if these men haven't killed themselves and haven't yet openly rebelled, they're looking for a way out, a way to show they are loyal even if their Lord wasn't.*

Katsuji must have noticed the reactions as well, but he continued in the same deferential tone: "And of course your next report to High Lord Akira will discuss all of these matters. No doubt he will be interested to hear about the current situation in GreenTown and Castle Seihin."

Even Kondo could see that put the two Haruto back on their heels a little, though neither of them showed much. But the Magistrate responded smoothly enough. "Of course, as honorable servants of the High Lord we wish for him to be fully informed. And we will be grateful for any wisdom he can offer us with regard to the problem of Castle Seihin."

Kondo allowed himself to scowl, and not just at the Magistrate's continual use of courtly language. *Those men in Castle Seihin... The Matsuda family... Why is anyone still playing these sorts of games? Do they not care about what is happening elsewhere?* "The men in Castle Seihin can obey the High Lord now, or they can accept their fate and perish when Lord Akira returns from war this fall." He said the last part with absolute certainty. He might as well have said, *When the Sun sets in the West.*

There was a brief silence. Then Haruto Toji raised his eyebrows very slightly. "Well, that settles the matter, I believe," he said, and made a small gesture at the servants. "Perhaps some wine now, so that we may toast honorable Kondo and the High Lord."

Kondo sighed. He didn't like wine this early in the day, but it would a needless insult to refuse.

⛩ ⛩ ⛩

PRIESTESS REI MURMURED THE EVENING prayer to herself, keeping her eyes open to watch the last glowing edge of the Sun as it slowly sank below the horizon. Her prayer staff chimed softly as she moved it back and forth – the evening ritual, performed as the Blessed Lady departed for the night, was traditionally quieter and shorter than the others. Many Priestesses skipped it altogether; even Jun, the most pious woman Rei had ever known, had not always done it.

> *With great respect, from the depths of our hearts*
> *We say farewell to the Divine Lady*
> *Amatsu, supreme Goddess*
> *Monarch of Heaven*
> *Until dawn brings Your blessings to us once more*

The sky was a tangle of colors, purples and reds to the west where the Sun was setting, turning to dark blue-gray of clouds overhead, deepening to black in the north where the clouds had been gathering all day. The air had a damp thick smell that warned of impending rain.

Finished with the traditional mantra, Rei hesitated and then, acting on impulse, switched to the prayer for the dead:

> *Judge these souls with Compassion and Honesty*
> *May they be worthy of Your merciful embrace*

For Priestess Jun, for my mother, and... for my father too, Blessed Lady, I beg You to judge them with Your divine Compassion, to offer Your forgiveness... Her thoughts faltered briefly, and then she made herself finish the recitation: *Offer Your forgiveness, as I offer my own.*

Her father had taken her to the Temple School when she was seven years old, and she had run away from the School almost at once, trying and failing to find her way back to her family's farm, surviving for a few months on begging and theft. That was where Priestess Himeko had found her and persuaded her to return to the School. *Father abandoned me. If she had not found me, I would have starved in a ditch or died as a streetwalker.*

After a couple of years at the School she had no longer thought about her parents. For a long time she had not even tried to remember them, or anything else from before she became a Priestess. She did not know if they were alive or dead, nor did she care – and given the difficulty of a peasant's life, they were more than likely to have departed to the Lady's judgment.

And then the Lady's relentless Light had spilled across the Aelfynn city, brighter than ever before. And brought back all the memories, and all the grief and bitterness that rode with them.

How can She expect me to forgive them? Her Compassion is infinite, but mine is only human.

But She made me remember. So I must try.

Rei breathed in deeply and then let it out slow, centering herself as she had been taught to do after prayers. She had seen samurai do something similar after fighting or training, though Kenji never seemed to bother.

The last glowing sliver of Sun dropped out of sight, and the landscape in her sight went quickly from orange-red to purple-black, the stark details of distant rice paddies and treelines turning vague and shapeless as the light faded. Where Rei stood, next to a road that skirted the edge of a rocky hillside, the light had not completely vanished, but below her all the land faded into darkness broken by only a few distant sparks of firelight from peasant huts.

She turned and climbed the grassy verge back to the road. Kenji was there, seated cross-legged on a large boulder, staring at the glowing horizon. Rei got a sense that he had been watching her but had switched quickly to watching the Sunset when she turned back. Three years ago, the knowledge that he had been staring at her while her back was turned would have made her blood run cold. Now she found it... almost comforting.

When did I stop being afraid of him? Was it when I slapped him, on that bridge in the Imperial City? No, it must have been before then, or I never would have done it.

The swordsman did not look quite so desperately tattered as he had when they left the Aelfynn lands a few weeks ago. He had replaced the rags of his previous garments with clothing from samurai who had died in the catastrophe that overtook the foreign spirits. She supposed was stealing, but three years of traveling in his company had somewhat inured her to Kenji's tendency to equip himself from others' deaths. His loose hair, not even tied back these days, hung across his shoulders in a greasy tangle that never seemed to improve even when she managed to get him to bathe regularly. The new wounds – the terrible stab in his stomach from the instant before he had disappeared, the other strange cuts and slashes that had been there when she found him again – had all healed, leaving in their wake fresh scars to join the older ones creasing his lean limbs and torso. There was even a new notch at the corner of his cheek that merged with the older scar running vertically down the right side of his face. She had never learned how he had gotten that terrible facial scar, or any of the other old scars that covered him. He had added dozens more in the time she had known him. How many times would he have died, if the Lady's power did not protect him?

The scar tended to draw one's gaze to his eyes, with their singular pale color. They seemed oddly brighter these days, as though they caught all the light around them. They shifted now to look at her, and she felt a strange warm prickle run through her. That often happened now, and she wondered if it was an aspect of how the Lady's power seemed to have grown stronger within him since… since whatever had happened in the Aelfynn city. He had never spoken of it, and she had not yet nerved herself to ask.

He rose and hopped off the boulder in a single movement that might have been called graceful from a more civilized-looking man. "You ready to move along?" His speech was rough but without the harsh edge of barely-suppressed hatred it used to have. At least with her, it wasn't – he sounded more like the old Kenji when he spoke to others. "Gettin' dark and I don't feel like sleeping in a damned ditch."

"I am ready, Kenji," she replied equably. "Thank you for waiting."

He grunted and shrugged uncomfortably, and she let the deepening twilight hide her smile as she went on. "How close are we to the others, do you think?"

Kenji shrugged again, more irritably. He had not wanted to try to rejoin the Wolf samurai after they left to deal with the Masks in Aotouki Village – the Masks whose presence he had somehow sensed from two days' travel away. Fortunately, now that they were back in the Tiger lands they and the Wolf men seemed to be traveling in more or less the same direction, so it had not been necessary to have a fight with Kenji about the topic.

Rei changed the subject. "I'm not sure how far it is to the next village. There is a settlement a couple of miles that way," she gestured toward the Sunset, "if you want to find a resting-place now."

He shook his head, the motion visible more from the fading light glinting on his tossing hair than anything else. "We need to go east. That's where that scum's friends are."

She didn't question it further. Whatever the Lady had shown him in the Aelfynn lands had... *changed* him in some way. It had led him to that village, Aotouki, and the pack of Demon-worshippers there. Now the same sense, or voice, or whatever it was, led him east, and she was not about to try to dissuade him. Not after all that had happened.

Not after the Lady Herself had led her back to Kenji.

The road scratched and scuffed beneath her well-worn wooden sandals and the equally worn base of her staff, the set of prayer-rings chiming softly as she walked. Kenji was a dark shape on her right, moving with a loose-limbed casual stride that she could sense without seeing it.

I heard Her voice. The knowledge sang within her whenever she remembered. Rei had spent much of her short life praying desperately for Lady Amatsu to bless her with guidance. All the more so after she had been apprenticed to old Priestess Jun, who *did* hear the Lady's words occasionally, if only in brief and enigmatic fragments. But until last month she had never been closer than a distant glimpse of flickering light in the deepest moments of her prayers.

Let me be worthy of Your guidance, Blessed Lady.

The air grew damper, almost heavy-feeling, and she wondered how much longer it would be until the rain started. The thick clouds had long since blotted out the stars, the Moon was shrouded too deeply to be more than a faint paleness in the northeastern sky, and the last of the Sunset was now fast disappearing, the horizon darkening from purple to black. They were following the road as much by hearing and feel as by sight now, and she squinted into the darkness, hoping to spot a light somewhere ahead. She could hear trees on either side of the road, their branches and leaves rustling in the occasional damp gusts of wind. *Yes, there was a forest to the north, so we'll have to pass through it to reach any sort of village... but how far does it go?* She remembered reading in the Temple School that in the days of the Emperors forests had mostly been confined to mountains and steep hills where common folk could not get at them easily. Those in the lowlands had been tightly regulated by the nobles to keep the peasants from chopping them all down for charcoal and farmlands. But four centuries without an Emperor had allowed trees to spread far more widely.

A spattering of cold water hit them. "Excrement," Kenji muttered.

The rain built rapidly to a thick downpour. The tree branches overhead scattered some of it, but Rei could feel drops beating on her head and shoulders, soaking through her robes. She squinted, wiping her eyes with her free hand, and called out: "I see a light!"

They ran as quickly as darkness and rain-wet sandals would allow, and the faint light Rei had spotted – greasy and vague through the intervening rain – resolved into a lantern glowing within an open-sided shrine, set back from the road a few paces and partially masked by trees and undergrowth. Kenji paused, muttering something about wanting a proper place to sleep, but Rei pushed past him and up the handful of rough stone steps. They were clear of leaves, which combined with the lantern meant this shrine was at least somewhat cared-for. She hunched her shoulders as she passed under the eaves; rain-water was already sluicing off the tile roof of the structure, pouring down in multiple streams, and one of them struck the back of her bare head, excruciatingly cold on the shaved skin, and ran down the back of her robes in an icy flood. She let out an involuntary squeak and hopped forward into the shrine, shaking herself violently, then remembered where she was and dropped to her knees in front of the modest statue in the center, pressing her palms together in front of her bowed head. "Apologies for our ill-mannered intrusion, please let us shelter here for a time."

The statue of old smooth-polished stone was only about four feet tall. It was the Divine Mikoto, Lord Moon, in his most typical aspect – a robe-cloaked figure with a hood half-obscuring its face, showing only the sternly frowning mouth. Rei felt another shiver run through her and wished it had been a shrine to the Lady instead. Not that Lord Moon was *bad*, really. He was the other half of the Divine harmony that ruled over earth and Heaven, but there was a reason why those who sought Heaven's forgiveness invoked the Lady instead…

"Excrement," Kenji muttered again, shaking himself disgustedly. "Guess it's better than nothing, but it'll be a damn cold night if we stay here." Water showered off him onto the old wooden planks of the shrine's floor, puddling around his feet. He looked at Rei casually and then more sharply, something changing in his expression.

"What?" The Priestess had laid her staff next to the statue and was trying to wipe off her chilled scalp with the sleeves of her robes.

Kenji said nothing, just stared at her for and then abruptly looked away, walking to the far side of the shrine and sitting down cross-legged. He called back at her without turning his head: "We got any food left?"

Now what is that all about? He was staring and then he got almost… embarrassed? Rei looked down at herself. *Oh.* Her soaking-wet robes were clinging to her body, showing the shapes and curves they normally concealed. She felt her face flame with the sudden heat of her own embarrassment, far stronger than his. Mingled with it was an uncomfortable realization of what his expression had been before he turned away.

She turned her own back, shaking the robes with both hands to try to air them enough to pull free of her limbs. "I, ah, I think I still have a rice-ball left from this morning," she called, glancing back at him nervously. He hadn't moved, which was a relief… although that relief mingled with another emotion that she could not quite define. For a moment she had an odd and unpleasant memory of the Aelfynn city and the strange sensations she had felt when the creature – Eoien, that was what it called itself – had lured her into the woods.

Rei shook her head at herself. *Stop being foolish and focus yourself! You're in a sacred place!*

After a few minutes she was able to nerve herself into opening her traveling pack and digging around inside. Sure enough, there was still one rice-ball left from the meal they had purchased that morning, and a few slices of white radish as well. She knelt by Kenji – not too close, that seemed unwise right now for reasons she did not examine – and split the meager portions in half. He took his share with a wordless grumble and chewed loudly.

I need to get my mind off… off… Rei flushed with mingled shame and frustration. She made herself stare out of the shrine, into the raining darkness. The nearest raindrops were catching the light from the lantern, making a constantly changing pattern of yellow-white streaks that combined with the rushing sound of water hitting ground and trees and shrine roof; it was oddly calming. Presently she felt relaxed enough to ask something that would distract them both: "So, going east… Do you think there are more groups like that one in the village? Packs of Mask cultists?"

"Dunno. Just… ever since She…" Kenji broke off, coughed, looked deliberately away from her. "I can see the shadows now, the Demons' shadows. Even when I'm not… you know. There's a big mass of them away east and north, so many… the whole horizon that way is like a… I dunno, like there's a storm rising up from the ground." He sounded defensive, as though she was doubting him.

Despite herself Rei felt a stirring of awe at what he was saying. *Something really did change, back in the Aelfynn lands.* "So that's where the Lady wants you to be?"

His voice rose slightly. "How in damnation should I know? I ain't the one She sends Her cute little messages to, like you and Jun."

And just like that, the confusing warmth in her stomach was gone, replaced by a familiar irritated disgust. *He's still the same Kenji, after all, even if he forgets sometimes.* The old memories came back: the stories he had told of his past crimes, the drunken rampages, the men he challenged and killed out of malicious enjoyment or sheer boredom.

She rose to her feet. "I believe it is time for me to get some rest," she said coldly, offering a minimal polite bow.

Kenji looked around at her, blinking. "What's gotten under your sandals?"

Rei turned away, ignoring his sputter of expletives, and marched to the far side of the shrine, placing Lord Moon's glowering statue between her and the swordsman. She stretched out on the shrine floor, using her small pack as a pillow, and was instantly conscious of how cold she really was, her damp clothes driving the chill into her limbs. She shivered and curled up, and her mind treacherously thought: *You could ask Kenji to sleep back-to-back with you. He probably wouldn't try anything… and if he did he'd probably stop if you told him to stop…* With a sharp sigh she cut off the perilous notions, reciting a mantra of purification until, slowly, weariness began to overcome discomfort and she drifted toward sleep.

The last thing she consciously knew was Kenji muttering, just loudly enough to be heard: "Crazy woman. What does she want anyway?"

CHAPTER 5

KADO KITARO REINED IN his horse, taking in the view to his south, and felt an exultant laugh bubble in his chest, trying to break free. He managed to control it, but he couldn't stop himself from smiling broadly. Which might appear undignified to some of his men, but to the Seven Demons with that – this was something to glory in!

From his position atop a very gentle hill – really just a roll in the landscape – he could see almost three miles south and east. The distant glitter of lacquered steel and the fluttering of banners were unmistakable even in the fading light of a cloudy evening. Lord Akira's portion of the Wolf Clan army was pouring onto the Kiirokusa Plain, emerging from the narrow forest-bound roads that had confined it for the last week of anxious marching. The chance for the Jade Dragons to trap the army on those roads and destroy it was gone.

He kicked his horse into motion and the company gathered behind him did the same, a hundred-odd cavalry trotting southeast with banners raised overhead. The thick grass of the Kiirokusa Plain rustled and crunched under their hooves, clouds of insects springing up around each animal, whirling in air that smelled of spring warmth and damp ground and the sweet scent of broken stalks.

The front ranks of the army briefly halted as he approached, then resumed as they recognized the red-and-gray colors of the cavalry's armor and the snarling wolf's-dead crest on the banners. An officer with several escorts galloped out from between the formations, displaying a banner with a black wolf's paw in a circle of red. Closer, the officer was recognizable as a noble from the decorations on his armor and the prominent gold-plated crest affixed to his conoidal helmet, but the clean-shaven face underneath was youthful and showing the same involuntary smile of excitement as Kitaro's own. The man reined in his horse in a spray of dirt and loose grass, and made a brief bow in the saddle. "Honorable Kado Kitaro! Do you have news for our most honorable High Lord?"

"Honorable Soto!" Kitaro returned the same bow. Technically he should have shown greater deference, since Hajime Soto was now the Lord of Castle Shinshiro, but both of them had been lowly officers in Lord Akira's first army and that shared experience permitted a familiarity that would have been offensive otherwise. "I do bring news."

"The High Lord will be eager to hear it." Soto escorted Kitaro back though the front ranks of the army. "It is a good omen to see you now, as we leave those forest roads behind. The men were on edge every day and night."

Which, Kitaro knew, was a polite way of admitting that *Soto* had been on edge. *Well, it's understandable, even with Lord Akira leading us there was some risk.* He had not shared their fear. The last four years had convinced him that such fears meant nothing when Lord Akira was in command.

They rode together, threading between the slow-moving infantry formations, then parting to follow their separate duties. Kitaro trotted past the waves of advancing soldiers, the men slowing their march as they spread from columns into lines and spread across the plain. From long experience Kitaro could tell they would be pitching camp soon – probably as soon as the entire force made it out into open ground where they could be properly secure against ambush. *Not that there's any danger of an ambush, but Lord Akira never lets his forces get sloppy.*

He found the High Lord on the southern side of the plain, watching his army from horseback. Or rather, appearing to watch – when Kitaro approached, he saw that Akira's eyes were closed. *He is thinking, making plans,* Kitaro knew. It was one of Lord Akira's many oddities, the way he would close his eyes and simply go away, departing into himself. In the early days many of his officers had thought he was insulting them or that he was simple-minded. These days they just accepted it, in the same way they accepted the High Lord's blank expression and lack of social graces.

Kitaro reined in and waited, exchanging a brief bow with the guards and escorts who surrounded the High Lord. They stood closer than was strictly necessary, perhaps in part because Akira was wearing no helmet and only a basic set of light armor rather than the elaborate full suit of ancestral gear. He always preferred to minimize his armor unless there was a battle about to take place, which was... unconventional, for a High Lord. By now the guards, many of whom came from Akira's original army of four years ago, were also well accustomed to the High Lord's oddities, even to the point of taking a sort of pride in them.

As Kitaro had said to his father, four years before: *He may be a madman, but he is* our *madman.*

He looks… tired, Kitaro thought. That was not unusual – it was how Akira always looked when they were on campaign – but it seemed more acute than he remembered. There was a stripped-down leanness to his face, hollows below his cheekbones, pockets of shadow under his eyes. Kitaro wasn't sure, but he thought the white streaks in the young man's hair might have grown since last year.

Akira opened his eyes. "Honorable Kitaro."

Kitaro bowed. "Honorable High Lord! I have brought you my officers' reports." He pulled a small bundle of folded and knotted papers from under the greave on his left arm and handed it over. "There are no signs of the enemy within a day's march of here, other than at Castle Kosaten." That castle sat astride the juncture of the River of Blue Silk and the River of Many Faces, controlling travel on both. "Our farthest scouts report that the Jade Dragon Clan is assembling its main army at Shinku." Which was a crossroads and former castle site, located nearly three days' march west.

Akira took the papers and handed them to one of his escorts. He would read them later, Kitaro knew. "How much strength at Shinku?"

The full answer was in the reports, but Akira always asked for an immediate summary. Kitaro had read all the reports himself as they came in, of course, and had written some of them. He had been rehearsing his words for hours. "About eighteen thousand assembled thus far. We saw banners from all the Ryu themselves and from all the major noble houses except the Kiyogama, Oyama, Mugai, and Goda. However a number of the noble contingents were quite small. The…" He searched his memory, proud that doing so only forced him to hesitate briefly. "The Furuta, Sada, Onaga, and Yoshida were all less than a thousand men each, and the Tsuchiya only about two thousand. Oh, and…" Contempt crept into his voice, "I also saw a banner for the Konatsu, with about a thousand cavalry." That was the last remnant of the forces who had betrayed the Wolf Clan at the Battle of Nagai Kyukai three years ago.

Akira did not react to the mention of the traitors, whose bloodline within the Wolf Clan he had exterminated last year. Instead he asked, "None of the Goda at Shinku. They are all at Castle Kosaten?"

Kitaro nodded. "Yes, my Lord, as far as we can tell they have their entire strength there. At least three thousand men, perhaps four thousand, all within the castle. A troublesome obstacle for Lord Toshiwara if he advances." Lord Toshiwara Ryohei commanded nearly a third of the Wolf Clan army, and was moving up the southern bank of the River of Blue Silk. He was drawing supply from the river, but would not be able to do for much longer unless he disposed of Castle Kosaten. A siege would be… difficult, even with Toshiwara's greatly superior numbers, against a strong garrison with a secure supply line.

Akira made no response to that other than to close his eyes again, silently thinking. Kitaro waited, allowing himself to wonder about the information he had just conveyed. The small forces from the Sada and Yoshida made some sense, since they had been on the losing side of the Jade Dragons' civil war two years ago and the Sada also garrisoned Castle Ryu in the west. But the absence of the Kiyogama surely meant something – they were among the strongest families in that Clan. Not for the first time he wondered what information the High Lord got from his spy network.

Of course, if the rumors are true, his wife is running the spies now. Thinking about Lord Akira's faithless wife – well, previously faithless, but someone who broke their word once would do it again – was always an uncomfortable topic, even if she had played an important role in Kitaro's own betrothal to High Lady Naichin Miyu. He recited a quick mantra under his breath to center himself.

Around them the steady rumble of marching feet went on even as the late afternoon light began to fade. To the west and southwest Kitaro could see the lights of cookfires being lit and the pale shapes of tents going up, the lead formations making camp as he had expected.

Akira reopened his eyes. "Keep watch on the forces at Shinku and send reports of any change."

Kitaro bowed. "Already done, my Lord," he said proudly.

Akira was silent for a brief instant – which was as close as he got to acknowledging that he was pleased with something – and then went on: "Put scouts north of Castle Kosaten along the River of Many Faces, and on the Nagai Kyukai Plain. Watch all the roads to the north."

Kitaro blinked. The Nagai Kyukai Plain, where the Wolf and Jade Dragon had clashed three years ago, was a good four days' march back to the east. The River of Many Faces was even farther to the north, though at least there the men would not be completely alone – there was still a Wolf Clan garrison at the ruins of Castle Yanagi, captured from the Jade Dragons last year.

But he knew by now that there was no reason to doubt orders simply because he did not understand them. "As you order, High Lord, so it shall be."

⛩ ⛩ ⛩

"MOST HONORABLE HIGH LADY! A privilege to greet you here!"

Ookami Kaede smiled warmly as she emerged from her palanquin. Not just at the welcome but at the clear sincerity of the one proclaiming it.

Kuroi Miyako was a short, round-faced young woman, her features plain and undistinguished. Her hair – her best feature, inheriting the length and glossy sheen of her mother Aya – was now worn loose down her back, while the tie in her sash was to the front, both as befitted her status as a married woman. Her robe, a simple one-piece garment with wide sleeves and a hem so low that the toes of her sock-clad feet barely peeked out, was dyed in the dark blue and gray colors favored by the family she had married into, embroidered in red thread in patterns of stalking wolves and mountain peaks. The servants arrayed behind her, bowing low, wore robes in the same color without the decorations.

Kaede straightened up, enjoying her escape from the palanquin's tight confines, and made a more restrained bow of her own: a superior's polite acknowledgement of loyalty. She waited while her own serving-maids quietly made a few subtle tugs to her robes, shaking out the wrinkles from the day-long ride in the cramped wooden box, fanning her to dry the faint sheen of sweat on her forehead. A palanquin was stuffy at the best of times, and the spring Sunshine beating down all day had made it unpleasantly warm. While that was happening Kaede watched her son emerge from his own palanquin and spot Miyako, his eyes going wide. "Mi-*chan*!" Basho shouted and rushed to her, arms open, his assigned maidservant trailing after him and mumbling apologies. Basho was still young enough – not yet four years old – that such behavior was endearing rather than inappropriate; Miyako laughed delightedly and hugged him, the huge sleeves of her robe briefly enfolding him like wings.

Kaede felt a lurch of intense feeling in her chest, happiness and love so strong that her eyes stung with the urge to shed tears. She made herself look away, checking on the rest of her procession.

It was no simple matter for the High Lady of the Wolf Clan to travel to visit her old handmaiden, especially during wartime. Besides the score of servants – chiefly maids and palanquin bearers – there were also nearly a hundred samurai, their armor glittering in the sun, and four ox-drawn wagons full of supplies. All for a two-week journey within the heart of the Wolf Clan's territory. Kaede supposed she should be used to it by now.

I just couldn't stay in Castle Ookami another day, listening to those courtiers repeat all the same gossip over and over, posturing in front of each other while we all desperately wait for news. She had justified this escape from the castle as a way of showing favor to those she would visit during the trip, and to attend a notable shrine in Lord Musume's lands for the impending Planting Festival, but the real purpose of the whole thing was to visit her only true friend. She had planned the journey carefully so she would be able to spend the night as Miyako's guest.

She couldn't afford to spend too long on the trip, though. Castle Ookami's court was full of schemers, and they would perceive a prolonged absence as weakness. Kaede hid an inner grimace and turned back to Miyako. Her former handmaiden had finished greeting Basho and had returned him to the care of his personal servant, and now she bowed again to Kaede. "Please, most honored High Lady, be welcomed to our humble house. I apologize that my honorable husband cannot be here to greet you as well."

"I am honored to be your guest," Kaede recited, starting up the path from the road. "There is no need to apologize. Your honorable husband is serving the Clan in war." Behind her, most of the servants and guards followed a secondary path downhill – there was a cluster of buildings there, residences for commoners and samurai retainers, where they would spend the night. A few picked guards and personal servants followed Kaede.

"Nonetheless, I apologize," Miyako repeated, falling into step beside Kaede as they approached the gate to her estate. "It is a shame on our family that we are not both here when the High Lady honors us with her presence."

Neither of them meant a word of it, of course. *But if we don't say these things, and say them sincerely, the guards and servants will notice, and wonder why, and spread tales of our poor etiquette,* Kaede thought sourly. Then, as they passed beneath the archway in the estate wall, she looked up and let out a slight involuntary breath. "Oh, lovely," she murmured.

Kuroi Matsuki's estate was on the out-thrust shoulder of a thickly wooded hill, maple and oak and camphor trees growing both inside and outside the estate's tile-topped wooden wall. Overhead was only glimpses of blue sky through the layers of bright green spring foliage, laying a dappled pattern across the clean-raked bare earth, the smooth-packed gravel paths, the large bean-shaped carp pond, and the house itself – a sprawling single-story building, wood and framed paper, encircled by a covered porch. Beyond the house, Kaede could see open sky and bare rock – the outer wall did not extend to the back of the estate, the house abutting the hill's sheer western slope.

"It is a mere simple country estate," Miyako murmured, rejecting Kaede's compliment as etiquette required. "Hardly worthy of such praise."

Basho came through the gate, let out a delighted yell, and broke away from the path, running with arms out to circle around one massive tree-trunk and then another, the servant once again trailing haplessly behind. Kaede and Miyako chuckled together, formality monetarily set aside as they enjoyed the boy's happiness. Miyako had done as much as Kaede – *no, more than me if I am as honest as the Goddess demands* – to care for the boy in his first years.

"A modest country estate is exactly what I need, to rest after a long day's travel," Kaede said, resuming the ritual exchange. "I trust my presence will not be too much of a burden."

It went on from there, the formalized dance of phrases that tradition required, while the two samurai women and their serving-maids strolled through the garden and into the house, two of the palanquin bearers following with Kaede's luggage on their backs. More ritual followed: touring the interior, viewing the rooms assigned to her and Basho, and paying respects to Miyako's mother-in-law, Dowager Lady Kotone, who was debilitated by age and preferred to remain in her room issuing dictates via her equally aged handmaiden. Then a formal dinner that lasted over an hour despite having only four dishes: miso soup with bean curd, rice, a plate of precisely-sliced vegetables – mostly pickled, but with a few spring onions mixed in – and thin-sliced wild boar in soy sauce. The meal's elegance was somewhat diminished by Lady Kotone's relentless biting criticisms of the food and of Miyako's management of her servants and household. Kaede suspected the old woman also wanted to complain about Basho, who was loudly cheerful throughout the meal, but didn't dare speak openly against the Clan's heir.

Once the meal ended, servants took Lady Kotone and Basho alike away to their respective quarters to rest, while other servants slid open the house's exterior panels to let in the cool evening air and refresh the house. Kaede and Miyako went out to the back, where the covered porch led to a rocky drop-off. It was twilight, the remnants of a vivid Sunset staining the western horizon. Some of the servants had already placed a woven mat on the largest and flattest of the stone outcrops, and as the two noblewomen strolled toward it they added two flat kneeling-cushions and a tea-set, a thin curl of steam rising from the spout of the pot.

Kaede knelt on one of the cushions and spent a few minutes enjoying the view. From here she could see for miles, all the way to the castle where she had spent last night as a guest of a higher-ranking vassal of the Tokaze family. The servants poured the tea and then retired inside, bowing as they went.

Miyako picked up her cup and sipped. "It is good to see you again, my Lady." Her voice lost its formality, became relaxed and friendly.

"And you as well," Kaede agreed, holding her own cup but not drinking from it yet. "Though I could have done without seeing your honored husband's mother."

Miyako sipped her tea quietly for a moment, and then she giggled. "She is… oh, so *very* traditional, isn't she? She wants to complain constantly, but it's rather hard to complain too much about a daughter-in-law who has the High Lady's friendship."

"That must be terribly frustrating for her," Kaede agreed, joining Miyako's laughter. She thought back over the conversation at dinner and her laughter gave way to a frown. "I think she was making some implications about you, though. Miyako-*chan*, are you expecting?"

She thought the other woman blushed, though the fading light made it difficult to be sure. "I am, my Lady. I should deliver my honorable husband an heir by the autumn." Another laugh, this time more of a chuckle. "You're right about her making implications, though. She dredged up something about honorable Hyobe, probably through correspondence – she writes an astonishing number of letters for someone who is all but bedridden – and she's been trying to hold it over my head ever since."

"Ah," Kaede murmured. Miyako and Kadomaro Hyobe had been lovers when they were both part of Kaede's small early circle of political allies. Neither had been married at the time, and Miyako had carefully avoided any long-term consequences from the affair. A woman of the samurai class was not strictly expected to be virginal at marriage... but she was very much expected not to have given birth to any illegitimate children.

Miyako sipped her tea. "It is... no great matter, my Lady." Her voice was even, but Kaede could hear the careful self-control in it. "My honored husband and I have a perfectly harmonious marriage, regardless of Lady Kotone. And she is an old woman. Amatsu will gather her in for judgment soon enough, and then nothing she says will matter. Not even—" She broke off, frowning.

Kaede had known Miyako for four years, had spent more time with her than anyone else in her life save possibly her son. She recognized that her friend was reluctant to speak because it involved Kaede, not herself. "Not even about me?"

Miyako sighed. She looked past Kaede, still sipping her tea. Finally she murmured, "She repeats the worst sort of gossip when Matsuki is not around to force her to behave. Such as about what happened to you last year."

"Ah," Kaede repeated. She had miscarried disastrously a little over a year ago, spending many days thereafter in a fever, clinging to life. The child had been dead in the womb. "About the parentage, I would assume." She knew that rumors about her affairs with the now-dead Katsura brothers were still circulating, in the court at Castle Ookami and doubtless through the Clan, though none dared speak them too openly.

Miyako nodded. After a silence she asked simply, "Is it true?"

"I don't know," Kaede answered. Making that admission in private, to a trusted friend and ally, was no loss of face. And it was actually a relief to say it aloud, to speak the truth that had to always be hidden lest it tear the Clan apart. Her affair with Katsura Motosuke had brought him onto Akira's side during the civil war's decisive battle at Yotsukado, and victory against the rebels had saved not just her own life but, infinitely more important, Basho's life. She would do the same thing again, given the same options... but that did not make the memories less humiliating.

She cleared her throat and set one hand over the tie in her sash where it rested above her waist. "But there is no doubt about the parentage of *this* child."

""Oh, that is wonderful, my Lady!" Miyako set down her teacup and clasped her hands. Then she turned thoughtful. "And perhaps it is all the more fortunate that the Katsura are now dead."

"Yes, well... It is also most fortunate that I am still able to bear children, as Priestess Ritsuko has reminded me several times."

"Oh my." Miyako's serious tone gave way to a chuckle that almost became another giggle. "She is still just as dreadful as ever, is she?"

"I am afraid so," Kaede nodded, sharing the laugh more ruefully. Why Akira had chosen to keep Priestess Ritsuko as his spiritual advisor rather than the much more reasonable Priestess Aoi was just one more mystery of his behavior. "Though I am pleased to say that since he departed to war she has spent most of her time praying in the castle shrine. I think she is angry he didn't take her along with him, the way honorable Lord Okaro used to do with Priestess Jun."

"Well, Jun was his personal advisor for many years," Miyako noted. Then she smiled and changed the subject. "Whatever Ritsuko may think, my Lady, the Goddess has blessed your marriage with another child. That is cause for celebration. And from what I hear, you have been doing your own part to forge harmonious marriages, and between Clans at that!"

"It was no great matter, Lady Miyu knew what she wished and I merely facilitated," Kaede murmured, being properly self-deprecating. In truth she was more than a little proud of that accomplishment, especially since she had done it on her own without Miyako to help her. The betrothal between the High Lady of the Nightingale and Kado Kitaro, one of Akira's chief retainers, would keep the Nightingale Clan firmly aligned with the Wolf Clan even if Akira went ahead with his apparent intention of seizing the Imperial City. "They do both seem happy with the arrangement."

She thought she had done a good job of keeping a hint of bitterness out of her voice, but Miyako knew her too well. "Are things no better with the honorable High Lord?"

"Actually..." Kaede hesitated, sipping tea and watching the Moon peek over the horizon, a pale sliver. "It is... tolerable. He accepts my help in the courts, in diplomacy."

"And you are expecting again," Miyako pointed out, picking up her tea and sipping it again with a pointedly innocent smile.

Kaede sighed, but then she chuckled and nodded, acknowledging Miyako's point. Bedding her husband had been a grim duty in the first years of their marriage. These days it was... pleasant, sometimes more than pleasant. It helped, of course, that Akira had not said anything about his Nightingale lover since last summer.

And Miyako can see that I am happier than I was. I do miss her help and advice...

It was tempting, so tempting to ask Miyako to return to the court, to be her handmaiden and chief agent once more. *And I could do it,* she knew. She was the High Lady, second only to her husband in rank within the Wolf Clan. If she gave the order, Miyako would have no choice but to obey or commit suicide in protest.

But Miyako was a wife now, the head of her household, managing this estate for her husband. To force her to give this up would be to dishonor her and her husband alike.

They sipped their tea together. Kaede would not ask, and Miyako knew she would not and was grateful for it. No words needed to be said.

⛩ ⛩ ⛩

AH, I... I REMEMBER THIS place, High Lord Noboru thought. *I was here before, when I was still... just myself.*

Castle Shinku had been the seat of the Red Salamander Clan until his father had conquered and razed it close to a decade ago. Now it was a featureless plain of grass and stone and scattered saplings, uninhabited except for a few small fishing villages perched on the banks of the River of Slow Turning a mile to the west. It would have been utterly unimportant save that it remained the meeting-place of five major roads. That feature had led his father to assemble his armies here four years ago, before marching to unexpected defeat at the Battle of Nagai Kyukai. Now Noboru was using it for the same military reason... though he had other motives as well.

The servants had built a wooden platform for him on one of the plain's few pieces of higher ground, a bare-earth hill that had once been the foundation of the Red Salamander castle. Silk walls embroidered with the Jade Dragon Clan's dragon-head crest, green against a pale gold background, lined the back and sides of the platform, and Noboru sat on a folding chair at the front edge, shaded by the thirty-foot-high Clan banner. By tradition the army's nobles and senior officers would gather here tonight to drink toasts and pledge their loyalty, a custom going back hundreds of years. An elaborate lie, like so many other samurai traditions – most of the men hated and feared Noboru, as much or more as they had hated and feared his father.

But it does not matter so long as their fear outweighs their hate. The thought did not quite carry the usual freight of glee. The Jade Dragon Clan was not the overwhelming military power it had been four years ago. Lord Akurai, his father, had marched to battle with seventy-three thousand men under his banners, and with the knowledge that men in his enemy's army would change sides when the battle began. Over a third of that strength had been lost at Nagai Kyukai, and the subsequent civil war and reprisals had cost the Clan as many or more again. Although every Lord had been busily trying to recruit fresh samurai ever since then, the army assembling here numbered only twenty-four thousand by the most generous count. To be sure, not every Lord had yet arrived – and that was the second purpose of this gathering, to get a final count of which nobles were still loyal.

That was not the sole source of his unease. There was also the persistent lack of guidance from the power of Selfishness, the power that had guided his steps ever since he first put on the featureless white mask that now rested in the sleeve of his robes. Even in the best times there were things the Lords' Voices could not see, could not know. They could not sense those who were warded by the False Light, or by the feeble little creatures from the west who had stolen some of that power. A veil lay across the Wolf army, perhaps from devout clergy like those hateful Monks he had slaughtered last year, or perhaps the slave called Kenji, the most hated enemy of all, was there. There was no telling where that one might wander, shrouded in layers of spirit.

Regardless, Noboru was being forced to rely for this campaign on spies, just like his father or any other Lord at war relied on them. It was immensely frustrating. Even a spymaster as skilled as Mugai Soto was weak, limited, like all things of flesh.

Someone was climbed the steps of the platform, wooden planks thunking hollowly beneath sandals. A young man in the elaborate armor of a nobleman, his helmet lacquered green with yellow edging and a crest of a mountain peak in a yellow half-circle embossed on his breastplate, advanced to within five paces and then bowed low. "Most honorable High Lord! The honorable Oyama family brings you eighteen hundred men to serve the needs of the Clan!"

The most honorable traitors, he means, Noboru thought, though the arrival of the Oyama was a comfort nonetheless, another accession to his strength. They had not dared to stay away. Relief and malignance combined into a giggle that bubbled up through his chest and emerged past his wet lips.

The Oyama had joined the rebellion by his younger brother Kioshi, and this young man – Oyama Hiroyuki – was the only surviving scion of the family, permitted to survive after the rest of them slit their bellies to atone for treason. "Welcome, young Hiroyuki," he burbled aloud, smiling over his shoulder at the nobleman. "A pity you could not bring more men, but that is fate, *neh*?" *A handsome fellow, if a bit old for my tastes,* he thought, and felt drool spill past his lower lip and stain the front of his multi-layered silk robes. *Perhaps soon I can try to... break... this man to my service, as I did Lord Sada.*

Hiroyuki blanched, and Noboru thought he might be physically ill. But the nobleman managed to turn his momentary retching into another low bow, hiding his loss of face. "I live to serve, High Lord!" he barked at the wooden planks before his feet, then backed away, bowing once more. "With your permission, I will see to my soldiers' camp."

Noboru toyed briefly with the notion of denying the rote request and forcing the young Lord Oyama to remain here, but the lurking uncertainty beneath his confidence drained away some of his enthusiasm. He made a languid dismissive gesture with one hand and turned back to watching his army. His hand crept into the sleeve of his robe and stroked the greasy-smooth surface of the mask, seeking its comfort.

I cannot see the Wolf troops... and now something has changed in the Tiger domains. Noboru did not know what had happened to the Aelfynn, or why their power had suddenly faded – all but vanished, in fact, like a lantern blown out by a gust of wind. But even without the all-devouring certainty of Selfishness' guidance, he knew what it meant for the future. *In another year, the Tiger will be gone, and all our Brothers from the north will join with me, along with those already gathering in my domain. And we will feast all across this land, all the way to the shores of the Great Sea.* The thought of it made his mouth flood with saliva and his thighs tremble with lustful energy. Then the surge of anticipation weakened. *Why didn't the Wolf wait a year? Just one year. They lost so many soldiers and nobles last year, why didn't they wait, stay on the defense as they used to?* The question gnawed at him, and Mugai Soto had no answers.

"Most honorable High Lord," the guards called. "Honorable Kuma Joji wishes audience."

That brought Noboru back to himself with a start; he gulped, coughed, clutched the mask inside his sleeve. *Calm down, this is important*, he told himself. Finally he rose and turned, trying to look confident and serene. "Honorable Kuma."

The younger man was already prostrated on the bare planks; he sat back on his heels, speaking toward Noboru's feet. "Honorable High Lord. I have received a letter from my honorable father."

Ah, Noboru thought, his pulse suddenly quickening. It was a tremendous effort not to step forward eagerly, to continue affecting detachment. "I am sure I will be pleased with his answer," he said, struggling not to drool in the midst of the words.

Joji swallowed and spoke carefully. "My most honorable father assures you that his army is now fully assembled and will march to your support, Lord Noboru." He did not lift his head, continuing to speak toward Noboru's feet. Which showed admirable humility for a High Lord's son, though Noboru felt sure the real reason was to conceal his fear and make it harder for Noboru to judge his sincerity.

Noboru felt a loosening within, a wash of relief that brought with it anger that he should feel any fear at all. *And I am sure the letter from his father was not very polite at all,* he thought with sudden viciousness, feeling his mouth twist with a carnivorous urge. *The Bear Lord hated my father, and no doubt hates me even more. There will come a time when I… when* we *can punish him for that, when he will grovel before me, before* us, *and beg for death…*

But not right now. Noboru took a breath and got his face back under control. "I am pleased with your honorable father's decision," he said, his voice slightly uneven. "How soon may I expect his army to reach Castle Kosaten?"

"He stated his intent to march on the day he dispatched his letter," Joji replied. "And said he should reach the River of Many Faces by the tenth day of the Month of the Grasshopper."

Twenty days from now, Noboru thought, his anxiety now entirely swept away by warm exultant anticipation. *I will dispatch orders to Lord Goda at once, to prepare for the Bear army's arrival. And once those forces are united, they can crush the Wolf troops near them and then join with me to defeat this High Lord Akira.* That he could do on his own, he was sure, without Selfishness' power to guide him.

And once the Wolf are broken… the feast will truly begin.

CHAPTER 6

KAEDE WATCHED THE TRIO of Priestesses approach, and thought: *I really need to stop thinking about Priestess Ritsuko whenever I see a woman of the clergy.* When she was sixteen her father had assigned the venomous old Priestess as her spiritual advisor, but Ritsuko's advice had mostly consisted of telling Kaede endlessly what a complete disappointment she was to the Goddess, her family, and the world. *And she still does that whenever she gets the chance.*

Kaede shook her head minutely. *Enough. Ritsuko's back at Castle Ookami praying for Akira to win the war, so she's actually being useful for once. Focus on the duty at hand.*

The Priestesses bowed low. "Welcome to Okujou Shrine, most honored High Lady," one of them proclaimed. "We are grateful for the honor of your visit on this sacred festival day. I am honorable Priestess Chiaki, the Abbess of the shrine, and these are my assistants Priestess Eriko and Priestess Misato."

I will never remember these names, Kaede knew. Priestesses' identical robes and shaven heads meant that most of them were difficult to tell apart, especially once they reached middle-age as these three had done. The only one who seemed notably different – *Priestess Misato, I think* – appeared to be a bit older than the others, and the graven lines of her face conveyed sorrow and pain.

"I am honored to meet you, and to be permitted to celebrate the Planting Festival in your revered shrine," Kaede replied aloud, bowing a bit lower than she would ordinarily have done for the clergy. It was good to show piety in public, especially in dangerous times, and Priestesses who weren't Ritsuko were deserving of reverence.

Okujou Shrine loomed above them, a gold-tiled pagoda perched three hundred paces up on a craggy summit that was all steep exposed rock-face, here and there a tree clinging to a crevice where roots could find purchase. Where Kaede stood, the rocks gave way to thick grass as the crag broadened out into a hill that descended smoothly but quite steeply down to the farmlands below. The hill's broadest and lowest expanse was thickly wooded, forming an additional barrier separating the shrine from the civilized lands below. A trail of bare hard-packed earth emerged from the woods and circled up the slope, passing beneath a series of red-lacquered archways, and it was this trail that Kaede and her entourage had ascended to reach this point. From here it went up the side of the crag, mostly as stairs, with more sacred arches marking out its progress.

The ascent this far had already left Kaede somewhat out of breath, and she was grateful for the meeting with the Priestesses giving her a chance to rest. They were now greeting her companion, Musume Keppai, and the young nobleman – really a boy, despite that he was in an adult samurai's formal robes and pleated silk leggings and high-shouldered overcoat, his temples shaved and his hair tied back and pinned down in a proper topknot – was bowing and expressing pious sentiments with the nervous air of someone reciting a memorized speech. *Well, he can't be more than fifteen,* Kaede thought. *And he can be forgiven for being nervous, under the circumstances.*

The Musume family had initially sided with the rebels during the Clan's civil war last year, largely because they were surrounded by the lands of other rebellious Lords and felt they had no chance of survival if they remained loyal to Akira. *And it didn't help that Akira had no idea how to deal with the politics, and I didn't have the confidence yet, or the support, to act in his place.* After the rebels had lost the decisive battle of Yotsukado, she had intervened to save the Musume, persuading them to not only switch sides but to prove their sincerity by destroying the rebel Akabe family. The Musume heir and his wife now lived in Castle Ookami as hostages, while Lord Musume himself and his second-eldest son Chobyo were both in the field with Akira. Young Keppai was the only male of the bloodline permitted to remain at home, and thus the duty of hosting the High Lady's visit fell to him.

Finished with the ritual exchanges, the boy turned and bowed to Kaede. "Shall we proceed, most honored High Lady?" His voice wobbled a little but he kept his expression well-controlled for someone of such youth; the only other evidence of nerves was the pulse in his neck, which was fluttering so strongly that Kaede could see it from four paces away.

He's probably terrified of getting something wrong and somehow dooming the whole family, Kaede thought with a twinge of sympathy. She smiled at him – a proper court smile, but she put warmth into it. "I am most pleased to do so, honorable Keppai." He actually blushed in response, though he still managed to – barely – keep his face impassive.

The Priestesses bowed again, rang their prayer staffs, and led their two guests beneath another wooden arch to the steep, rough-carved stairs that circled and zig-zagged up the crag toward the shrine. Kaede climbed the steps slowly and carefully, placing her wooden walking-sandals with care, breathing heavily and trying not to show it. *I was right to leave Basho back at the village with the escort,* she thought. *I would lose my mind in fear if he went bounding up this crumbling old staircase.* She had to stop every minute or so to catch her breath, using the successive archways as waypoints and pretending each time that she was pausing the admire the view. *Mustn't strain myself too much,* she justified it, thinking of her pregnancy – nowhere close to showing yet, much of the time she didn't even think about, but it couldn't hurt to be careful after what happened last year. Her self-consciousness over her slow pace was somewhat assuaged by noticing that Keppai, climbing ahead of her, had initially forged ahead but then slowed down and was actually panting, though he kept trying to conceal it when he looked back to check on her.

The view was impressive, and became more so the higher she climbed. Those who had built this shrine so long ago – legend claimed it actually dated back to the time of the First Emperor – had chosen the highest peak in the region; she could see lower hills and forests and fields and winding streams spreading out in every direction, the thin pale lines of roads and tiny regular shapes of buildings occasionally interrupting the natural patterns. To the east the landscape gradually sloped up and, in the far distance, merged into the vertical gray-white crags of the Great East Wall Mountains, while to the west she could just make out the Sun-reflecting curve of the River of Lengthy Travel and, close by it, the distinctive shape of a castle – the Musume family's Castle Kage.

It's like the view from the Winter Castle, but in every direction, and the higher I go the farther I can see.

Below, the village of Shiawase where her entourage waited was spread out like a map, and she could see the moving dots of hundreds of people. *Everyone's out to celebrate the Festival,* she knew. *And at least some of them are surely looking up here… I wonder if Basho is watching, trying to spot me against the rocks?*

She lifted her gaze, looking at the sky – thin streamers of cloud scudding across the Sun – and then into the north, where the distance-flattened landscape faded into the formless blue-green haze of the horizon with the barest white-edged hint of the Great East Wall Mountains. When the stairs circled back to the east side of the crag, those mountains were much more clearly visible, only about ten miles away; when the path went around to the southwest, she could catch a visual hint of lower, more rugged peaks which must be the Mountains of the Sun.

I am glad I chose this place, Kaede thought suddenly. She glanced sidelong at Musume Keppai, five paces up the stairs, who had an almost worshipful expression on his face. *And not just because the politics has worked, though that is good.*

When Kaede had set out on this trip her chief intention was simply to visit Miyako; honoring a shrine with her presence during the Planting Festival had merely been the justifying excuse. But when she had learned about the Okujou Shrine, she'd known at once it was the best choice for her destination – not only because choosing it would help solidify the Musume family's return to loyalty, but also because a visit to such a place would become a story, a legend spreading among the people of the Wolf Clan. The story of the day High Lady Kaede climbed into the sky to venerate the Heavens.

It took nearly an hour for her to complete the ascent, and by then she was high up enough that the air had gone cold and the wind – strong enough to whip her ankle-length hair and tug at the golden pins holding it in place – was chilling her even through her three layers of robes. A final extra-large arch, its lacquered upward-curving crescent fifteen feet overhead and bedecked with strings of prayer-tassels, gave onto a narrow almost-flat space, a few gnarled trees clinging to the edges while most of the area was taken up by the shrine itself.

Okujou Shrine itself seemed at first glance almost unimpressive after the long climb to reach it: a simple two-story pagoda, the front open to the short flight of broad flat steps that ascended from the final archway. Small statues of guardian lions, so old that their features were worn into near-shapelessness, crouched on either side of the entrance. The three Priestesses were waiting in between the statues, their staffs chiming softly as the wind spun the dangling prayer-rings. They bowed as Kaede and Musume Keppai approached, then stood aside to allow a clear path to the interior.

The shrine had a recessed area inside the entrance for pilgrims to leave their shoes and ritually cleanse themselves, with a bowl of water on the right side for that purpose. Kaede let out a tiny sigh of relief at being out of the sharp wind, and while she stepped out of her sandals and wetted her hands she used the pause to let her eyes adjust to the relatively dark interior.

The Shrine was a single rectangular space, two stories high, the second level an open space criss-crossed with support beams. The only light came through the slats of narrow windows, some on each level, throwing thin bright lines on the walls and floor. A heavy stone slab rested in the center of the chamber, and atop it stood the gray stone statues of the two Divine beings – the Goddess in her traditional pose of compassionate welcome, her arms open at her sides, the stern-faced God upright with his hands pressed together in prayer. Kaede wondered if the statues had originally been plated with precious metals, as was common in the great Temples elsewhere in the Empire; if so, there was no sign of it now. There was actually an offering box in front of the statues, made of wood so old it had become almost black.

Kaede knelt before the statues and dropped the expected coin through the narrow slots atop the box. She suppressed a smile as Keppai gulped and muttered an oath under his breath. *He forgot to bring an offering... He'll probably be embarrassed for years, remembering this.*

"It is no great matter," she murmured, just loud enough for him to hear, and he relaxed a little and muttered gratitude.

Behind them the Priestesses began to chant, softly at first and then with increasing volume, ringing their staffs in rhythm with the mantra. Kaede pressed her own palms together and recited the prayer, hearing Keppai's clear young voice join in on the second verse:

Supreme rulers of Heaven and Earth
Bring order and tranquility to our land
So we shall prosper under Divine protection
And the land know peace and fertility

Doing the ritual here feels more... more real *than in a city temple with hundreds of people watching.* Kaede felt a chill run through her that had nothing to do with the wind. *As though a place like this really does get us closer to Heaven.* She felt almost puzzled at how strongly it affected her. She had always considered herself pious, but it wasn't something she dwelt on – it was just part of how she lived, like bathing or taking off her shoes indoors or following proper etiquette.

The ritual ended, the Priestesses ringing their staffs one last time and then going silent. Kaede remained kneeling a little longer, fighting a sudden urge to recite the prayer for expecting women. *That's only for the Festival right before the baby comes,* she reminded herself. *Which won't be until autumn.* She rose slowly, thinking about the cold wind outside and the long hike back down the stairs.

The Priestesses again stood aside, waiting patiently while their guests cleansed their hands once more and put their sandals back on. Kaede took her time, still reluctant to leave the shelter of the entrance, and noticed as she did that the nearest Priestess was weeping silently, tears running down her creased face.

It's the one I noticed before, the one who looked sad, Kaede thought. "Is there something wrong, honored Priestess?"

The Priestess looked momentarily confused, and then she put her free hand to her face and blinked. "Apologies, most honored Lady Kaede," she murmured, brushing at her cheeks. "Apologies, my loss of face shames both of us. It is… it is just that I am so honored… so grateful to finally be in the domain of those who truly revere the Heavens."

Something about the way she said that made Kaede's senses prickle up. Musume Keppai had already gone outside, but she delayed, smoothing the worst of the wind-driven wrinkles out of her robes to give herself a reason. She kept her voice neutral. "Surely all of us revere the Heavens, honorable Priestess."

The older woman shook her head, her motions jerky. "I pray that this will one day be true again, honorable High Lady. In the lands of the Jade Dragon it is becoming dangerous to serve the Divine Amatsu and Mikoto."

Ah so, Kaede realized. Peasants and clergy had been fleeing the Jade Dragon territories since early last year, and Akira had actually toured the border and spoken with some of them. *Wasn't there a story of Lord Noboru destroying a monastery?* "I have heard that the new High Lord of that Clan is lacking in piety," she said aloud. "A tragedy, when a ruler turns away from the guidance of Heaven."

Something shifted in the Priestess' face. "Lord Noboru has not merely… turned away," she said softly. "He has taken the path of Heaven's enemies. This is why I pray each day, each hour, for your honorable husband to prevail in this war."

Kaede almost stared before she caught herself. *Heaven's enemies? Does that mean what I think..?*

The Priestess shook herself, her staff clanging. "Apologies, I should not trouble you with such distasteful things, honored Lady. Thank you for honoring our humble shrine with your presence." She bowed again and turned back into the shrine, ending the conversation.

Kaede looked after her for a moment, wondering if she should follow the Priestess and continue the conversation. *Does she really mean that Lord Noboru is a Demon-worshipper, like the Mask cultists or the northern barbarians?* It seemed like an impossible notion.

And yet… *Hasn't Akira been telling his men that he has to fight the Jade Dragons and take the Imperial City because of the threat from the Demon worshippers? Or something like that…* For the first time in her life Kaede found herself wishing she had paid closer attention to what her husband did and said.

Then she mentally frowned at herself. *Enough delaying, time to go out in the cold, girl!* Musume Keppai was standing by the archway by the head of the stairs, ready to begin the long descent. *And Basho is waiting for me below.*

⛩ ⛩ ⛩

"DRINK UP, SAMURAI! NO FROWNING tonight!"

Satoshi's glum face didn't change, but he accepted the bottle the drunken celebrant shoved at him. That seemed to satisfy the commoner, who wobbled away singing something wordless and off-key. Satoshi set the bottle on the bench where they both sat and regarded Mitsui with raised eyebrows.

"Festivals seem to be slightly different in the Bear lands," he said, then bit into the rice-ball he'd been about to start before the interruption.

"They do seem quite exuberant," Mitsui agreed, chewing his own rice-ball.

The bench they had chosen to eat their meager evening meal was perched on the outer side of a road that cut along the side of a low rugged mountain, supported by walls of tight-fitted stone upslope and down; it afforded a fine view. Houses and shops, packed so tightly together that they shared walls, lined the uphill side of the road. Most of the shops were closed at this late hour, but the teahouses and restaurants were open and packed with guests, people spilling in and out of every establishment and wandering up and down the street. Although the Sun had set hours ago, the town was bright -- colored lanterns hung from the corners of every roof and glowed from inside stone lantern-posts located along the street's outer edges.

Almost all the celebrants were commoners, Mitsui saw, which was not all that surprising. The Planting Festival, celebrating the end of planting season, coincided with the Clans sending their armies to wage war through the warmer months, leaving this festival to be dominated by common folk; that had been true even back at HillTown.

HillTown had been downright level, though, compared to Futeki Village, which climbed the mountain's steep lower slopes in a series of narrow terraces connected by ramps and staircases. Almost all the buildings were two or three stories high, although it was often hard to tell because of their steeply tilted roofs. A mountain stream came down through the levels in a deep crevasse, crossed by arced bridges. Below, the water fed into a series of shallower terraces completely covered in rice paddies, descending into a narrow valley. Above, the town's ascent of the mountain culminated in a five-story pagoda-roofed keep, its imposing height turned festive tonight by scores of the same bright-colored festival lanterns.

A surf-wave of noise came up the street. Mitsui turned and watched a group of celebrants, stripped to their loincloths and wearing headbands decorated with religious symbols, come up the street in a half-trot, half-dance, chanting a mantra to keep the pace. They carried a flat wooden palanquin on their shoulders, and effigies of the Lord and Lady rode atop it, the light reflecting on their lacquered surfaces. The crowds parted, people squeezing against the buildings and the outer edge of the road, clasping their hands in prayer and bowing their heads as the Divine symbols passed by. Behind the sacred palanquin, other celebrants followed with hand-drums and flutes, along with several Priestesses chanting and ringing their prayer-staffs.

It was the second time the procession had made its way through the town since Mitsui and Satoshi had arrived. As it moved on and the crowds spread out once more, Mitsui finished his rice and stood. "I think the fireworks should be starting soon."

Satoshi plucked the wine bottle from the bench and followed him.

They trailed the procession up two more levels of the town, passing street entertainers, food vendors, musicians, families with children dressed in the colorful festival robes they only brought out a few times a year. Mitsui felt a sudden lump in his throat, his eyes stinging. He and Yukari had taken Taro to the Harvest Festival a couple of weeks before he left on that cursed mission to LowTown...

The line of buildings briefly opened on their right, into a small square set with an array of a dozen wooden stocks. Braziers atop man-high iron tripods threw light on the blocky shapes, three of which were occupied – two men and a woman in commoner garb, slumped against the frames that held their heads and wrists in place. Passersby mostly ignored them, except for a few who paused to throw refuse at their heads.

Mitsui paused, his nostalgic mood shifting as old Magistrate instincts rose to the surface. *Let's see... the men are here for drunkenness, I think.* Beating and the stocks was the standard punishment for drunkards who could not pay for the damage they caused, and both of the men had the vacant stares and puffy faces of habitual drunks. *There'll probably be quite a few more such men here tomorrow, after the festival.*

The woman... *No, not a drunk.* Her head was up and she stared with sullen blankness at the passing crowds. *Since she's dressed plainly, she's not a prostitute either, so... most likely just petty theft. Or perhaps not so petty, but the local Magistrate showed mercy.* Theft beyond a mere pickpocketing usually put the criminal directly into the hangman's noose, but women who pled for mercy could sometimes get lesser punishment.

If so, that may not have been wise of the Magistrate. Underneath her expressionless stoicism the woman's face had a hard edge that reminded Mitsui of gang members he had dealt with.

His mind was briefly crowded with memories of old cases, the ordinary investigations into ordinary crimes that had occupied his life for a decade. *I wonder how things are in HillTown these days? I suppose Lord Kaneda must have appointed a replacement for me...*

Enough, he told himself, shaking his head slightly. He turned away from the stocks and rejoined the flow of the crowd, Satoshi following.

Futeki Village's Temple was located on the town's uppermost and widest terrace, an oval space with stone lanterns all along its outer curve. The walls of the castle loomed above, with a steep staircase ascending along the side of one wall to the gate. The Temple was tucked in next to the castle's foundations; its pagoda-tower was six stories high, impressive for a community of this size, the upper floors and pointed roof actually rising above the level of the castle's front gate. A huge crowd had gathered in the stone-flagged open space, densest in front the Temple but spreading onto the streets in either direction and even up the Temple's and castle's stairs, though they made sure to leave an opening for the arriving statues.

Mitsui and Satoshi stayed closer to the outer edge where the crowd was thinner. It wasn't just the inherent samurai unease at close contact with strangers – Mitsui kept imagining an assassin slipping through the crowd with a knife. *Unlikely*, he told himself. *A Demon-worshipper would not find this a comfortable place.* The energy of the festival was palpable, enough to send prickles up his back. *Are people just more pious in the Bear lands?*

The celebrants carried the effigies to the base of the Temple steps and set the platform down there, then danced around it, their motions ritual and yet wild, chanting mantras with their arms flung high. The Priestesses – now joined by others emerging from the Temple – rang the chimes on their prayer-staffs in counterpoint.

A sharp *whoosh* sound made Mitsui look around. An instant later, a blossom of green and red flame erupted overhead, accompanied by a thunderclap. The crowd let out a collective gasp of delight.

A quartet of men in peasant garb, long baggy coats and tight-fitting white leggings, crouched by the platform's outer edge, between the stone lanterns. One of them had a burning taper while the other three wrestled with what appeared to be brown cylinders of… paper?

Fireworks, Mitsui realized. *I've never been close enough before to see them being set off.*

The other three men moved back, leaving a trio of the objects sitting on the paving-stones, facing upward. The man with the taper stepped forward and touched it to each of the three cylinders in turn, then jumped away. An instant later there was another rushing sound as fire and smoke shot skyward; an instant after that, and a trio of thunderclaps sounded overhead, the sky filling with blazing color. Mitsui's ears rang and he inadvertently took a step back – he wasn't used to being quite so close when the foreign things exploded.

He looked around for Satoshi and was momentarily at a loss – the older samurai was no longer at his side. His earlier unease returned. *The Masks have a way of finding us over and over…*

Finally he spotted his companion. Satoshi was speaking to one of the men setting off the fireworks. As Mitsui watched, they exchanged bows, the commoner smiling broadly. Satoshi retreated to Mitsui's side as the next wave of fireworks launched and exploded.

"What was that about?"

Satoshi held out a small brown cylinder. "Seeing the colors overhead reminded me of... what happened in GreenTown. It occurred to me that having some green fire of our own might not be a bad idea."

Mitsui opened his mouth to reply, but then had to wait through the next set of explosions. "How much did it cost you?" Their money was limited and the only way to get more would be to pawn their belongings or resort to thievery.

"Oh, nothing. I traded him the wine bottle that fellow gave us at dinner."

Despite himself Mitsui laughed aloud. After a moment he regained his face and asked, "Did you ask him how to use it?"

Satoshi shrugged. "It seems simple enough. Apply fire and run."

CHAPTER 7

KENJI DREAMED.

He was in the pit once more, the Masks' pit. He had always been in the pit.

Darkness and stench and pain surrounded him, and his stomach ached with hunger. By feel he sucked the last bit of water from a bamboo canteen, his hands trembling as he struggled not to spill anything.

A ghost of a whisper, behind him: "Ken-*chan*... thirsty..."

He hunched his shoulders, trying not to hear. But now he could *feel* it, feel the agonizing pain of his sister Yuki's parched throat and cracked lips, feel her fear and grief at his betrayal.

She knew he had water.

Kenji woke, strangling the scream that tried to burst from his throat. His face was wet. He sat up, scrubbing angrily at his eyes with the heels of his hands, breathing heavily, trying to force the dream away even as the darkness and his own disorientation made him wonder if he had woken up at all. Then he became aware of the smooth-planed wooden floor under him, of the faint red glow of banked coals below to his right, of the barely-sensed gray light seeping through the vertical lines of walls. *That's right. I'm in a peasant hut. Rei talked 'em into letting us sleep here.*

She had done that during their previous trips as well, laboriously convincing the peasants to overcome their instinctive fear of an unknown swordsman. It was strange for him to stand back and let another take care of such things, stranger yet for it to generally turn out well, rather the peasants trying to kill him or drive him away at the first opportunity.

His eyes had adjusted enough to show the interior of the hut. He was lying on one side of the square firepit, and he could see Rei sleeping on the other side, her robes just light enough to stand out against the darkness. Other, darker shapes marked the peasant and his wife and their children, emitting the occasional grunt or snore.

...thirsty, Ken-chan...

He let out a sound of his own, a grunt that was almost a whimper, and stood up. Instinctively he grabbed the sheathed swords that lay on the floor beside him, then groped his way to the door. It was a wooden panel, plain and functional, with a few cracks between the boards; he slid it open and went through, stepping down the two feet to the ground and shoving his feet into the sandals waiting there atop a wide flat rock.

The outside air was cool and slightly damp, smelling of earth and dew and charcoal smoke, with an underlying stink from the excrement used to fertilize the rice paddies. The sky was a dark gray, stars hiding behind clouds, except for a paleness to the east. It was about an hour until dawn, he judged.

Some of the dreams, the ones filled with chains, had ended when he freed the Lady from the Aelfynn prison. But the dreams of the pit still came, not every night but close enough, and now the memories no longer stayed hidden in his waking hours. Wine didn't seem to dull them anymore, when he could even get wine.

I killed my sister. I killed my friends. The Masks put us in the pit, but they didn't kill them. They waited for me to do it.

And I did.

He stared at the distant pallor that marked where the Sun would rise, and his hands clenched around his sword-sheaths until the wood creaked and his palms ached. The darkness was there, the corruption of spirit, flickering behind the wall of reality, impossible for him *not* to see ever since he had left the Lady's presence.

Kill me, he had begged the Sun Goddess. And She had refused.

Rei talks about forgiveness, about the Lady's Compassion. What kind of damned Compassion makes me stay alive with this? It ain't like I can get forgiveness from Yuki, from the people I killed – they're all dead! They're out of this damned world, on to their next life, and I'm stuck here. For what?

The Lady's voice, terrible in its purity, rang through his memory: YOU STILL HAVE MUCH TO DO.

The darkness roiled, and somehow he could tell that part of it was closer than it had been yesterday. *Whatever's there, we're getting closer to it, or it's getting closer to us. And when I reach it...*

There was one thing he could still hope for: Revenge. Revenge on the Masks, and on the Demons they served.

I didn't ask to be Your damned Sword, he yelled inside his head. *But if You want me to kill Masks, I'll kill them to the end of time. Every damned one of them. Just make the dreams go away!*

The sky had grown subtly lighter, and Kenji frowned and squinted. There were a half-dozen tiny pillars of blackness rising along the horizon to the east and north.

That ain't me seeing spirits, that's smoke, fires. Castles or villages, burning.

He grimaced and started to slide his swords under his belt, then realized the sash had gotten loose overnight and was nearly falling off his hips. A time of clumsy fumbling and muttered curses followed, until he finally had it re-wrapped and his leggings re-tied as well. By then the light had grown enough to see the whole landscape around him, albeit in colorless grays.

"Up already, honored guest?"

Kenji looked around sharply. The peasant stood just outside of the outhouse ten paces from the hut, shuffling his feet and adjusting his loincloth. Kenji felt annoyed that he hadn't noticed the man coming outside. *I must really be going soft… or just going crazy.*

The peasant finished and let his knee-length robe drop back into place. The simple gray-brown linen garment was the only thing he wore, which Kenji knew was typical for common folk in warm weather. From the age of the children in the hut, this peasant was probably only in his thirties, but he looked much older, his skin roughened and tanned by weather, his hair – tied back with a headband – already showing hints of gray.

"Had a bad dream," Kenji said, and then wondered why he'd bothered. It wasn't like he had to explain himself to some random peasant.

Even if he'd been born a peasant himself.

The man nodded judiciously as he walked back past his vegetable garden. "Even samurai have bad dreams, *neh*? Sometimes it's just a dream, sometimes it's an omen. When I was fifteen I had a nightmare, right before we got a locust swarm ate half our crop…" He gestured ahead toward the hut. "There's cold rice if you want it, and t'wife's boiling tea."

Kenji hesitated, then shrugged and climbed the steps back inside the hut, kicking off his sandals behind him as he stepped through. The hut was built atop thick base-beams, holding it two feet above the ground, and the steps were more like a short ladder than a typical staircase.

The peasant's plain-faced wife was indeed tending the fire and a teapot that she had hung above it on a bamboo post; the children crowded together sleepily, eating rice from small bowls. The woman picked up two more bowls, filled them and handed them to Kenji. "One for t'honored Priestess. She's gone out back t'wash up."

Typical, Kenji grumbled, glancing at the now-open back door of the hut. Rei's staff leaned against the wall next to it. The Priestess had bathed and shaved her head last night, but she never seemed to be satisfied – when they had stayed in the Imperial City two years ago, and then again in GreenTown last year with that Magistrate and his gang, she had washed at least twice a day and sometimes more. *And she always scolds me if I go more than a day without it!* He sat down cross-legged, snatching up one of the sets of simple wood chopsticks stacked on the edge of the cooking pit. As he dug into the clumped rice, Rei came inside, wiping down her head with a piece of linen. She looked past Kenji, toward the front door. "Honorable Bunta? Are you all right?"

Of course she knows the fellow's name, Kenji thought irritably. Her face and scalp were smooth and clear, and somehow that made him uncomfortable, though his mind had at least stopped trying to paint a streetwalker's hair onto her. He made himself follow her gaze, looking back over his shoulder.

The peasant was standing in the door, looking out into the distance. His posture had changed, his shoulders hunching, almost as though he was shrinking into himself.

Rei went to stand behind him, peering outside. "Oh, that's… a lot of fires," she murmured. "I don't remember seeing those yesterday, Kenji, do you?"

"No," Kenji muttered, chewing rice more rapidly. *Time to fill up.*

"Amatsu's mercy," the peasant – Bunta? – muttered. He looked over at his wife. "Reckon I better talk t'the neighbors, wife."

The woman's broad tanned face creased into worry-lines. "Right now?"

"Think so, yes. Apologies, honored guests." The man bobbed a half-bow and climbed down out of the hut. A moment later Kenji glimpsed him hurrying away down the dirt track that paralleled the rice paddies.

Rei looked from the peasant to Kenji. He handed her the second rice-bowl, chopsticks pinned across the top with his thumb. "Better eat up. We're leavin' too."

She took the bowl, frowning slightly. "A lot of that smoke is to the east. I thought that's where we were going?"

"It's still where we're going," Kenji growled. "Now eat. No telling when we'll get another chance."

Rei's frown deepened, but she didn't argue further. It was only a few minutes before they were both climbing out of the hut, though Rei paused to recite a mantra of blessing over the family, ringing her staff in time to the rhythmic words.

The farms here were built in a lowland, crowding on either side of a broad but shallow stream; Kenji could tell the whole area likely went underwater during heavy rains, which explained why the widely-scattered huts were all built several feet off the ground. There wasn't really a village here, just individual farms spreading for miles alongside the water. A mile downstream from Bunta's farm, they passed a small building – barely more than a shack – perched between the dirt road and the water; it appeared to be a teahouse, but the door and windows were shut and a circle of men were standing outside it, speaking in low voices and looking uneasily toward the spirals of black smoke on the horizon. Kenji recognized the farmer among them, and felt his lip curl in a sneer of disgust. *A few smart ones will run now, and the rest… They'll stand around here talking forever, until the Masks show up and kill them all and take their children.*

He dismissed the peasants from his mind and walked on, his pace swift enough to be almost a trot. It was full daylight now, the Sun well above the horizon, though one of the pillars of smoke was close enough to give the light an unpleasant orange tone that made the green rice-fields and the distant trees look unhealthy. He barely noticed; his attention was on the layers of darkness coiling and shifting behind the horizon. Without knowing how he could tell that most of it was still far away, though closer than it had been yesterday. But there were smaller coils and flickers much closer. He focused on the closest of them and stepped up his pace.

"Kenji," Rei's voice came from behind him, panting heavily, her staff clanging. "Where are you going?"

He drew up on the top of a berm between two rice paddies, squinting against the rising Sun. "That way," he growled, pointing a little south of the orange orb. The lowlands ended there in a line of forested hills, low ones at the edge of the farms and higher jagged peaks behind. There was no smoke there… yet. "Some of 'em are there. A few miles, I think."

"Some of who?" Rei drew up alongside him, breathing heavily and leaning on her staff. "Masks?"

"Them or something like 'em." He shrugged. "Doesn't matter what they call themselves. And a whole lot more behind them, all that way." He gestured broadly, taking in the smoky horizon.

"The Tiger say the barbarians are Demon-worshippers," Rei said, her thoughtful expression at odds with her panting and the dust on her feet. "But I thought the barbarians were far away to the north."

Kenji shook his head. "Doesn't matter. Whoever they are, I'll kill 'em."

ĦĦĦ

CAPTAIN TOKAGE REINED IN HIS horse and peered ahead, scowling behind an impassive expression. It was easier to keep his face immobile after a week of baths and decent meals and proper sleep, and he could sense the same relief and renewed energy in the men marching along the road beside him. Even the simple fact of traveling on a proper road rather than shouldering through unkempt wilderness helped everyone relax. If there was worry about what might happen when they reached the Tiger Clan's capital, no one showed it.

For that matter Tokage himself found it more difficult to worry now that he was back in civilized territory and dealing with things he understood. The events in the Aelfynn lands receded into memory, so strange that he half-wondered how much of it had really happened and how much was a demented dream, like the visions of a fever.

Well, some of it definitely happened, he reflected, glancing aside at the small group of Tiger samurai marching alongside his own men. They did not show the same recovery of spirit, despite now being clean and shaved and properly dressed. The additional Tiger samurai who had joined them as escorts from Lord Handen's castle looked perfectly normal, but kept themselves apart from the survivors of Tora Saneda's troops as though dishonor might be contagious. Their commander, a gaunt older sergeant named Ryuma, rode with his gaze set rigidly forward, not looking at either the shamed men marching behind him or the Wolf Clan samurai walking alongside and ahead.

Can't really blame him, he's been thrown into a difficult situation, Tokage thought sympathetically. In three decades of service to the Ookami he had known his own share of such duties, though thankfully fewer since Lord Okaro had honored him with the appointment as Captain of the Guard. Ryuma was doing his best to maintain face and fulfill his duty without shaming himself or his own men, and with no knowledge of the larger political ramifications of the situation he was holding himself apart from the Wolf samurai as much as possible.

Not that I have much better idea of the politics than he does. That was the duty of Seneschal Amano, currently riding on a wagon at the back of the column to rest his travel-damaged thighs. Still, it did seem most likely that the political consequences of the events in the Aelfynn lands would be bad.

They'd had a foretaste of that after their arrival at Lord Handen's stronghold. Even the final approach to Daitouki Village had been unsettling; the River of Black Ice was in the midst of an unpleasant spring flood, the muddy water full of dead bodies – not just animals but human bodies – that had bumped against the sides of the boats that ferried Tokage and his companions across the water. That had struck Tokage as a very bad omen indeed, and later questioning among the locals had confirmed that it was not at all normal for spring floods to be filled with corpses. Rumors had been circulating through the town of war in the north, of the barbarians advancing, of castles burning. Wealthy people were said to be quietly leaving town, fleeing south under the excuse of trade or travel.

Lord Handen had been desperately unhappy at having to deal with the news they brought. The man had not impressed Tokage during their earlier visit, striking him as the sort of Lord who preferred to ignore problems outside his own lands. However, when Amano had politely suggested it might be best for the Wolf samurai to return immediately to their own lands – "to remove any unfortunate reminders of the tragedy which has befallen the Tora bloodline" – he had nervously insisted that would not do.

"You must convey this news to High Lord Iesada," he had muttered, tugging the front of his robes as though he could pull out his fear along with the wrinkles. "For it to be delivered by anyone of lesser stature would be an unbearable insult."

Tokage had reflected that Lord Handen himself would be of more than sufficient rank to deliver the news. But of course the matter of rank was merely an excuse; the truth was that Handen wanted to protect himself by ensuring the Wolf outsiders would deliver the bad news and thus be the ones in danger of the High Lord's anger. Not to mention getting them out of his lands and beyond his responsibility as quickly as possible. It was an entirely understandable bit of self-defense, if lacking in honor, and Sergeant Ryuma was now trapped by it.

Well, he won't be trapped much longer, one way or the other. Another couple of days and we'll be at Castle Mouko. And that crazy swordsman and his Priestess companion – if that's all she really was, I have my doubts – haven't rejoined us, which at least eliminates one potential problem. Tokage shrugged inside. *Of course, lose one problem and you find another...* He looked north, where the road curved past the last of the hills, and felt his inner frown breaking through his face. Something there had drawn his attention, and now he was sure of his suspicions: a column of smoke was rising from somewhere beyond the wooded hilltops, a smudge of gray-brown against the pale blue-and-white of the sky.

And not the first one I've seen today. The others had also been to the north, but far more distant, enough to not to be directly threatening.

The road they followed – it was a secondary route that was supposed to eventually connect to the Road of Dancing Foxes, the main north-south road to Castle Mouko – wound back and forth across the shoulders of a series of low hills, clumps of trees on the crests to the west, farms covering the flatlands to the east and north. Far off to the east, Sunlight glittered on the rectangles of rice paddies and the winding line of a stream that irrigated them. He could see a cluster of buildings there, the village whose residents worked these fields; the farmers themselves were doll-tiny with distance, sowing the seedlings in the rice paddies in a rhythm of steady rise-and-fall-and-step motion. The tap of a hand-drum drifted in the air, barely audible from over a mile away, setting the pace for the relentless labor. The closer fields were all bare churned earth; some of those would already be planted, with millet and buckwheat and soybeans, and others would be seeded later once the rice was in the paddies. All the endless labor that kept the Empire fed…

"Honorable Captain!" A soldier was trotting back down the column toward him, coughing a little as he passed through the dust stirred by the men's marching feet.

Tokage wiped his frown away – samurai expected their commanders to be imperturbable – and nudged his horse forward. The beast responded readily enough, having regained much of its strength since they had gotten back to the Empire and it had been able to supplement its grazing with grain. A few moments brought him to the approaching samurai, and that was enough time for Tokage to recognize him. "What is it, honorable Seijin?"

"Honorable Captain!" The man snapped off a quick bow. "Honorable Lieutenant Arima sent me back to inform you… that fire, honorable Captain. It appears to be a shrine."

Tokage looked over at Sergeant Ryuma. The Tiger samurai might be aging but there was nothing wrong with his hearing; his grizzled head snapped up and he moved his own horse out of the column. His voice was high-pitched but clear, directed at Seijin rather than Tokage. "A shrine? Do they need help?"

"Many apologies, I do not know, honorable Ryuma." The Wolf soldier's shame at being unable to clearly answer the Tiger samurai was palpable. "It is on a side-path beyond some prayer-arches… We could just see the top of the roof from the road, all wrapped up in fire and smoke."

Tokage raised his eyebrows. "A bandit attack, perhaps? Bandits have no honor, they will not hesitate to attack a sacred site."

Ryuuma nodded agreement. "As you say, honorable Tokage."

A pause, and Tokage knew the Tiger was considering the numbers of his own soldiers – a mere reinforced squadron, sent as representatives of Lord Handen rather than as actual guards. However, it would shame him to ask for help with a threat in his own lands.

"Honorable Ryuma, I am sure your men can deal with this problem, but our own piety calls on us to assist the servants of Heaven. I hope it would not be offensive for my men to support you."

Ryuma nodded and bowed in the saddle, gratitude evident in the subtle relaxation in his face and posture. "It would be no insult at all, honorable Captain Tokage." He straightened and made a gesture to his men. "I trust you will not be insulted that we take the lead."

"Of course not. These are your lands, and we are mere guests." Tokage called a halt to his own men, who shifted to one side of the road so the Tiger samurai – including the handful of Tora Saneda's survivors – could move past them. While he waited he sent a messenger back to the rear of his column, to let Seneschal Amano know there might be a delay to their journey.

⛩ ⛩ ⛩

"AH, THERE YOU ARE, YOU scum," Kenji muttered to himself.

He was well up on a forested slope, half-trotting and half-climbing as he angled downward, catching tree-trunks in his hand to slow himself when his speed threatened to get out of control. Dead leaves fountained up from his feet as he slid and jumped and slid again in what was almost a controlled fall.

The hike up the far side of the hill had been punishingly difficult, especially at the end of three hours' hard travel from the farm where they had spent the night; Rei had already been lagging behind, and he'd lost sight of her halfway up, though he could still occasionally hear her calling plaintively for him to slow down. He might have done so, normally – her distress bothered him, and the fact that it bothered him made him inexplicably angry. But right now the shadows were so close, just over the hill, and the desperate call of vengeance overrode all else. *Besides, she's in no danger. The enemy's ahead, not back with her.*

He could hear them in the valley down below, hear the screams and war-cries, and smell a sharp note of burning. The crowded tree-trunks and intermittent boulders allowed him only brief glimpses of buildings, especially a multi-story pagoda which was probably some kind of temple or shrine. The screams sounded feminine, though it was hard to be sure – men could shriek like girls when agony overwhelmed them.

He slid down another ten paces, brown leaves spraying up around him, the slope even steeper as he got closer to the bottom. He cursed and stopped himself with one sandaled foot against a moss-greened boulder, the jolt making his teeth click. The huge rocks were all over the slope, more frequent and larger higher up – some of those were as big as peasant houses. This one was the size of a horse, still large enough that he had to skirt around it before he could look downslope again.

A glitter of light showed water at the bottom of the slope, still a good fifty paces below him. Beyond it he glimpsed a shape in bright yellow-orange robes, flickering between the trees as it ran. Dark figures pursued, indistinct at this distance but he could see the *shadows* within them, layered behind them, like light behind a puppet-show. Another scream floated up, this one unmistakably a woman.

Kenji muttered something obscene. He skirted the edge of the boulder to the left, circling down and to the side, trying to ride the slope at an angle to keep his descent under control. He could only snatch a few more glances downslope, trying to gauge whether he was catching up with the fleeing

Priestess and her pursuers. Another boulder loomed before him; he palm-slapped it and shoved himself off farther downhill. Abruptly the slope was too steep and he half-jumped, half-fell five paces, landing on his rump with a jolt that drove a curse past clenched teeth. He slid a half-dozen more paces, cursing again as he crashed through a tangle of brush, twigs and leaves slashing at his arms and face.

Amid the chaos a distant corner of his mind whispered, *How is Rei going to get down this slope?*

But then he could see through a larger gap in the trees. The Priestess was running along the far side of the water – a stream, full of rocks – and the pursuers were right behind her, leaping and shouting in guttural voices. A sword flashed and she tumbled forward, the bright robes suddenly dark with blood.

Kenji was still sliding, the slope now so steep that he had no control, and he realized the hillside in front of him turned into a sheer dropoff, the stream shining below. He slammed his hands down on either side and shoved himself upright and forward, both legs uncoiling, and he leapt between the last trees and over the stream, suddenly out of the trees' shadow and into bright daylight. The stream fountained away from him in a spray of white, the gravel riverbed slamming into his feet and momentum driving him down, both hands hitting the gravel an instant later, jolts of pain in feet and palms, legs and arms—

And it didn't matter because the enemy was *there*, right in front of him, gathered around the fallen Priestess, looking up at him in surprise. Strange-looking men, short and swarthy, their greasy hair tied back in odd-shaped topknots or hanging loose, their bodies clad in garments of leather and fur. *They aren't Masks,* Kenji realized, but it didn't matter, the darkness within them screamed at him, and the pain in his limbs vanished as he sprang out of the stream-bed, smashing through the fountain of spray still rising from his impact, and his long sword was in his hand as though it had always been there.

⛩ ⛩ ⛩

THE TIGER SAMURAI WERE IN the lead, the squadron formed into three-man ranks and advancing at a quick trot. Captain Tokage's own troops, forty-odd men not counting the servants at the back with Amano, followed at the same speed, watching to either side of the road for an ambush.

The road curved over the shoulder of the next hill, passing through a brief belt of trees that merged overhead and turned the route into a green-lit tunnel, the embankment on the upper slope covered with layers of brown fallen leaves. Beyond the trees they descended into a broad open area, not farmland but perhaps farmed at one time, crossing a narrow but deep stream on a flat wooden bridge with stone supports so old that they were green with layers of moss and vines. The plain beyond was covered in thick grass and scattered bushes, stretching a mile or more to the next forested hillside. A short distance beyond the bridge, Lieutenant Arima and his half-squadron waited where two smaller paths broke off from the main road. One led off to the right in a long curve that took it out around the forested hill's lowest extent and out of sight – Tokage suspected that led to the village he had noticed earlier. The other path headed left, fairly straight, into a narrower side-valley and passing beneath a huge prayer-arch whose lacquer had long since flaked away. The smoke rose from that direction, much thicker and more imposing from this closer view, a pillar trying to climb into the sky but instead falling away eastward.

"*Ah so*," Tokage murmured. Yes, he could see the upper floors of a temple's pagoda-tower rising above the trees, orange flames billowing through the windows and slurping up from under the eaves, mingling with the churning smoke that mounted higher and higher.

Sergeant Ryuma shouted an order and drew his long sword, slashing it forward. The Tiger samurai roared and went up the path at a near-run. Tokage grimaced and shouted orders to his own men, then kneed his horse to a half-gallop to follow close behind the Tiger. Behind him he heard Arima lead the men in the ancient mantra that was the ritual cheer of every samurai army: "The Lady with us!"

Wooded hills rose on all sides, steeper as they advanced into the small valley. The stream they had crossed earlier ran along the southern edge of the valley, while to the north the trees encroached from the hillside into the narrow valley floor, though the clergy who lived here had kept the ground beneath them clear of fallen leaves. The path went through a whole series of prayer arches, these smaller and better-kept than the ancient one by the road, lacquered in yellow-orange to mark this as a place dedicated to the Goddess. Fresh prayer-ribbons fluttered from some of the pillars.

They emerged from the tunnel of the archways and could finally see the shrine properly. The stream broadened out into large pond, almost a lake, fifty paces across and studded artistically with boulders, another huge prayer-arch rising in the midst of it. The shrine structures were adjacent to the pond: the huge four-story pagoda-tower flanked by smaller buildings, some of them adjacent and others spaced out along the banks of the pond, everything linked with covered walkways. The road curved through a space of smooth-raked open ground to the broad staircase that ascended five feet to the covered porch that encircled the temple at ground level; an open double-door led into the central shrine chamber. The whole was lit oddly by the flames rising from the upper floors of the tower; Tokage could see they were spreading relentlessly down into the main floor.

Arrows stuck in the walls, Tokage thought, feeling a cold focus descend. *And bodies everywhere.*

The ragged lumps scattered on the lawn and porch were clearly Priestesses, their light-yellow and saffron robes unmistakable even when stained with blood. He could see arrows sticking from some of them as well. The Tiger samurai had reached the nearest ones and hurried between them to see if any still lived.

"Check for enemies," Tokage snapped. His men fanned out, weapons drawn; a half-squad remained with him. He dismounted, moving carefully – it was a tricky business, getting off and on a horse with only one arm – and followed the Tiger samurai.

The Priestesses had died while trying to flee, cut down or shot in the back. He murmured a prayer beneath his breath as he passed them, watching for movement – the wounds looked dire but a lifetime of war had taught him that the human body could survive an astonishing amount of punishment. The steps of the shrine creaked under his sandals as he climbed up to the covered porch, glancing left and right at the walkways that led to secondary buildings. No enemies in sight. The fire overhead roared greedily, visibly growing and working its way lower on the structure. *Started with fire-arrows,* he realized, noting the shafts still visible projecting from the walls of the upper floors.

Several Priestesses lay dead around the shrine's open front doors; these had been killed from the front, cut down with blades, and Tokage felt his chilly focus deepen into anger. *They opened the doors to flee the fires, and those who attacked them were waiting outside.*

He stepped carefully past the bodies and into the shrine's main chamber, murmuring a prayer for the minor blasphemy of doing so without removing his sandals or cleansing his hands. The huge interior was lit oddly, daylight from the high windows merging with flickering firelight from above; flecks of glowing ash drifted down like unnatural snowflakes. The great statue of the Lady had been toppled over, the gold-plated stone form broken in pieces by the impact, precious metal flickering with reflections of the fire above. Tokage could see at least two other Priestesses lying there. Someone behind him let out an oath, then muttered an apology for their loss of face. Tokage decided he would let the brief lapse go, for he shared the man's shock and confusion. *What sort of bandits slaughter Priestesses but leave the loot?*

One of the Priestesses moved.

Tokage hazarded a single look upward at the yellow-orange flames wreathing the thick beams and pillars that supported the upper floors. *It will collapse soon,* he knew, and in that knowledge made his decision. "Come with me!" he shouted, and ran forward. A clatter of sandals on the wooden floor told him his men were following.

The fire was louder out in the center of the room, louder and much hotter, the air almost painful as Tokage gasped for breath. He saw the Priestess move again, stirring faintly, and pointed with his one hand; two of his men caught her under the arms and dragged her back toward the entrance, her head rolling back and forth and a faint moan emerging from her mouth, barely audible over the greedy roaring of the flames. Tokage and his remaining men hurriedly checked the other fallen Priestesses – there were two more, one of them half-hidden behind the ruined statue. *Dead, or close enough I can't tell the difference,* he thought grimly, and then flinched as a beam snapped overhead, loud as a thunderclap, and burning fragments rained down. He swung his arm in a broad gesture and they ran back to the entrance, batting at smoldering bits on their heads and shoulders.

The outside air was a shock of cold purity, and Tokage doubled over coughing, resting his hand on his knee. By the time he straightened and wiped the tears from his eyes, the rest of his escort column had arrived. Seneschal Amano was standing up in his wagon, watching the scene with an expression of refined courtly horror.

The Priestess lay on her back, gasping and moaning in pain. The men around her looked uncertain – some of them probably knew a little basic field medicine, most samurai did if only to try to keep their wounded alive until a Priestess could tend to them. But a lifelong education in Courtesy made it all but impossible for them to strip and treat a wounded Priestess.

Tokage knelt carefully next to the woman, trying to assess her wounds without violating her modesty. For the first time he found himself regretting that the swordsman and his Priestess companion had left them behind – despite her youth, Priestess Rei had done much to help their injured survive and recover back in the Aelfynn lands. *A lot of blood, and some of it fresh,* he thought grimly. "Honored Priestess? Can you hear me?"

The woman's eyelids fluttered and lifted. She croaked something, and Tokage gestured for the men to give her water. She sipped carefully from the offered canteen, then laid her head back and murmured a mantra of thankfulness. Others gathered around, Wolf and Tiger alike waiting for her to speak. Seneschal Amano had arrived on his wagon, and leaned forward attentively as well.

"I am honorable Ookami Tokage. Honored Priestess, can you tell us what happened here?"

The Priestess' eyes reopened. They were clear now, but with a glittery weakness in the pupils that Tokage recognized as a mark of fading life. Judging from her skin he thought she was middle-aged, though the absence of hair on her scalp made it difficult to be sure. She licked her smoke-cracked lips and whispered, "Barbarians, honorable samurai. Foreign men, in furs and leathers."

A mutter of oaths from the watching Tiger samurai. Amano and Tokage exchanged a look. "Can the barbarians be this far south?" the old courtier asked.

"Is that who these scum are?"

Tokage felt a jolt of mingled surprise and resignation. He straightened and looked around, waving his men to calm when they drew weapons.

The swordsman – *Kenji, that's his name* – strolled across the thin grass beneath the trees, his motions cat-smooth. His garments were somehow even more ragged and dirty than when Tokage had last seen him, now covered with rips and tangled with leaves and broken twigs; the same detritus was snared in the man's long filthy hair. He was stained in fresh blood, spatters on clothes and skin that Tokage recognize as the patterns of a fight, and more blood coated the drawn long sword he carried casually in his right hand, dripping off the point where it hovered a few inches off the ground. In his left hand he held two severed heads by their tangled hair. He saw the prickling hostility of Tokage's men and grinned at it, then tossed the two heads underhand. They bounced and rolled across the ground, stopping near the Priestess' body.

"I thought they were Masks. They have the shadow on 'em. But I've never seen people like this before, not even in that filthy spirit-place." Kenji's voice, casual and amused, turned harsh in that brief mention of the Aelfynn realm, and for a moment Tokage swore the man's strange pale eyes were lit from within. Only a moment, and then the amused crudeness returned: "They died as easy as Masks, though."

Tokage deliberately looked away from the swordsman and back to the fallen Priestess. Her eyes had shut again, and he could see the bloodstains on her robes had grown since they had brought her out of the shrine. Hesitation, and then he knelt, muttered an apology, and set one hand on her chest to feel her heartbeat. *Weak*, he thought. *She is fading.* "Lady judge you with Compassion, honored Priestess," he murmured.

"Who is this?"

Tokage looked up again and saw Sergeant Ryuma approaching, now on foot, followed by several of his men and a Priestess. The old Tiger samurai looked from Kenji to the severed heads, and his face went gray, making him look not just experience but aged. He toed one of the heads over with the heel of his sandal, carefully not touching it with his sock-clad toes, and let out a long breath. "I served on the northern border, many years ago. The Demon-worshipping barbarians… I could never forget them." He picked up an arrow from the ground and turned it over in his hands, nodding. "Yes, I remember these too. Their arrows."

Tokage nodded slowly, sharing another look with the Seneschal, pondering what it could all mean.

Ryuma gestured toward his returning men. "We found this Priestess in the woods, but she says she is not from this shrine."

Of course, Tokage thought. *If that swordsman is here, of course she is as well.*

The young Priestess looked little better than Kenji, her robes dirty and covered in the detritus of the forest, limping and leaning on her staff. The Tiger samurai escorted her with a solicitous air, but stopped in confusion when she suddenly hurried toward the swordsman Kenji. She was glaring like an angry housewife, and in response the bloodsoaked killer shuffled his feet and looked around like a boy caught at mischief. The scene was so bewildering that Tokage made himself deliberately look away, stepping aside and placing himself closer to Ryuma.

"These barbarians," he said, speaking low, conversationally, not looking directly at the older man. "Are there more than he killed? Are we in danger?"

"Danger? I… don't know." The sergeant suddenly tossed the arrow away as though its touch disgusted him. "There were more, they left a trail north of here. Twenty or so, I think. That fellow must have caught a few wandering stragglers, the scum aren't disciplined like proper soldiers. I think they…" He broke off and drew a breath. "They should not be here. The border is a hundred miles and more to the north."

Tokage felt a chill run through him. *Does that mean the border has been overrun? We were sent here to negotiate an alliance, and the Tiger said they needed help against the barbarians. But surely a few primitives cannot defeat a Clan's samurai…* Aloud he offered, "I am sure your High Lord will wish to know of this."

Ryuma nodded, took another breath. "As you say." He looked bleakly at the burning shrine, now steadily transforming into a gigantic pyre as the flames continued to spread downward. A rumbling crash announced the pagoda collapsing inward, followed by a thick cloud of smoke and ash billowing out of the open front door. The grooves on the older man's face seemed to grow a little deeper. "There is nothing more we can do here, save to pray for the dead."

CHAPTER 8

THE SUNFLOWER CROP LOOKS *to be a strong one this year,* Lord Kiyogama thought, sipping his tea and savoring the soft-bitter flavor of Green Peaks.

It was early yet, of course, the plants only put into the ground a month ago. The sloping fields visible from his gazebo were carpeted with fresh green sprouts, their tops just starting to swell with the buds that would become the distinctive circular blossoms. It would be months until they were ready to be harvested, the seeds rendered for oil, the blossoms fermented into the rich red dye used in art and cosmetics. Storms or drought could ruin the crop before then... *All in the hands of Fate and the Lady's Compassion,* he reflected.

Kiyogama set his teacup on the low table to his right, position between himself and his son Daihachi. At a minute nod, a serving-maid scurried forward, her sock-clad feet silent on the gazebo's wooden floor, and filled both teacups. Steam rose in a soft cloud as she poured with deft precision, then set the teapot on the table in between the cups. Finished, she bowed low and retreated to the gazebo's exit, descending the steps to where the other servants waited in the spring Sunshine.

A few minutes of silence passed while father and son sipped their tea, holding the cups in both hands and savoring the delicate flavors. In summer, drinking tea outdoors would be unpleasant, the heat of the drink and the weather combining to overwhelm the senses – unless it was barley tea, of course. But in the mild warmth of spring it was an enjoyable experience.

Kiyogama waited. This meeting was as close to a private one as he and his son could have, only a few servants present and none of them within earshot. It was difficult to arrange such meetings without drawing the attention of spies, but viewing their family's important and valuable sunflower crop was a fine excuse, especially since Kiyogama regularly hosted other guests here for the same purpose.

A line of farmers made their way slowly across the fields, backs stooped as they dug out weeds. The men and women worked in separate groups, the women in simple knee-length robes and with their hair under tied kerchiefs, the men in vests and chest-wrappings and loincloths with headbands to keep hair out of their eyes, all of them barefoot. Occasionally one or two would stand up to stretch their back or clean the caked dirt off their wooden hoes, and when that happened they would also bow toward the distant gazebo. Even if Kiyogama had not posted his personal banner alongside it, they knew that anyone in that structure was of the nobility, entitled to proper respect.

Daihachi finally set down his teacup. Kiyogama picked up the teapot and refilled it.

"Honorable father, apologies, I have questions," the young man ventured.

"I am sure you do," Lord Kiyogama agreed, smiling and lifting his hand to acknowledge the bows from the commoners.

Daihachi nodded toward the field as though commenting on the crops. "We are going to war together, and taking nearly all of our soldiers, leaving only the most token guard behind."

He said nothing further, but nothing else needed to be said. They both knew that for generations now, ever since the Peacock and Ox Clans had been wrecked in the first century after the Dread Eclipse, Lords did not take their whole strength into the field when their High Lord summoned them to war, nor did they take their only heir to fight at their side. Any Lord who wished to preserve his position and bloodline held back enough strength to protect their holdings and an heir who could keep the family intact in the event of defeat.

He understands all of this, and knows I understand as well and that I am acting with purpose nonetheless, Kiyogama thought, feeling pleased. *He is fierce and proud, in the way of a young man, but he is not foolish. I am fortunate.* One of the problems that troubled every noble bloodline was raising a suitably capable heir; all too many bloodlines had failed when a foolish or inexperienced son frittered away what his father had built. *As Lord Noboru is doing right now...*

He lifted his teacup again, sipping from it carefully. *He still needs to learn more patience, as all young men must,* he knew, sensing the young man's emotions through his outward face. *But if this gambit succeeds, there will be time enough for it... and if not, a passionate spirit will be his best weapon.*

He set the cup back on the tray, allowed Daihachi to refill it. "A lord must be prudent, and cautious, and always have as many options available as he can make for himself and his bloodline," he said slowly. Instinctively he raised one hand to stroke his moustaches, as he often did when thinking, only to remember that he had shaved his face to aid his escape from Castle Hokori in late winter. "This is well known. But there are times, just a few rare times, when the only viable option is to throw everything you have into one great blow. And if you hesitate at those rare times, you and all you have built are doomed."

Daihachi set down the pot and lifted his own cup, trying to imitate his father's deliberation and almost succeeding. "And how does one know that such a time has come?"

Ah, very good, he did not waste time asking if I believed we had reached such a time. If the boy had insisted on asking that despite all the evidence, it would have been a troubling sign of foolishness. "One can never be absolutely sure," he said aloud. "That is the difficulty, of course. Our darkened Empire is a place of confusion and fear. A Lord must be cautious... right up to the moment he *cannot* be cautious. One must understand the situation as much as possible, and make the best judgment one can. Or fail, and perish."

Daihachi rested the teacup in the lap of his folded legs. He was still looking at the sunflower field, but his eyes were focused far away. "If we hold back from the war and Lord Noboru wins, he will crush us afterward." He spoke slowly, feeling his way through the problem, but without any sort of questioning tone, which was good. If he made it sound like a question, it would mean he was more interested in his father's approval than in finding the correct answer. "If we join his army now..." He shook his head. "Lord Akurai might have accepted that. Lord Noboru will not. If he wins, he will turn on us afterward."

A flock of birds swooped across the field, then switched direction abruptly when one of the peasants rose and spun a noisemaker – a pair of small boards on ropes, making a buzzing clatter as they whirled over his head. Kiyogama watched the birds go, his thoughts suddenly filled with the ephemeral nature of life. After a moment he murmured:

Flights of dark wings
Vanishing into infinite distance
So too our souls

I am turning pious and sentimental in my old age, he thought with an inner smile. Aloud he said, "I agree. Lord Akurai was cruel, but also wise. Lord Noboru is cruel, but also foolish." *Or simply mad,* his mind added, but there was no need to say that. "Thus we are left with only one choice for our own survival."

"Could we not stay out of the war altogether? The Wolf Clan's leader, this Ookami Akira… by all accounts he is a formidable general. We could await his victory, then swear fealty."

"Tempting," Kiyogama agreed. "That was my first plan."

His son was silent for a long moment. Finally he confessed, "I fear my knowledge is insufficient, honored father."

"Humility is the first step to wisdom," Kiyogama replied, quoting the famous Priestess Akari from the reign of the fourteenth Emperor. Inwardly he added, *And I was unfair, because I know you do not have all the information I do. But you were willing to admit it rather than bluster or lie, which is good. Lie to others, show them only your outer face… but within your own family there must be Honesty.* "Last year, High Lord Akira defeated a rebellion. He exterminated nearly all the rebellious nobles. Completely, down to their last heirs."

Daihachi opened his mouth, shut it, covered his lapse of face by taking another sip of tea. "He did that to his own nobles? Even Lord Akurai…" He broke off. They both knew Lord Akurai had wiped out the ruling line of the Red Salamander Clan and their most loyal nobility when he finally defeated that Clan seven years ago, but nobles who had switched sides in time, such as the Kagami and the Jinno, had been allowed to swear fealty as vassals to Jade Dragon Lords.

And they both knew their own family had originally been part of the Grasshopper Clan, escaping to the Jade Dragon after that Clan had collapsed into bankruptcy and defeat.

"Yes, precisely. And so… we have no choice but to take sides against Lord Noboru now, with all our strength, if we are to survive." Kiyogama spread his hands, smiling as though he was presenting a work of art. "In the end, the decision is simple, is it not?"

⛩ ⛩ ⛩

LORD TOSHIWARA RYOHEI PAUSED ATOP a heap of raw earth, waiting for the five men following him to finish climbing from the siege trench. Momentarily alone, he contemplated the distant walls of Castle Kosaten and the military challenge they presented. He was an older man, lean and spare and precisely dignified, with a carefully trimmed gray-white goatee beard. His affectation was to wear his mostly-white hair bound in a long ponytail that hung two feet down his back rather than the conventional topknot. Inwardly, he enjoyed the way that one unconventional aspect of his appearance could distract conversationalists, much like how an ostentatious feint could throw an enemy formation into confusion.

The High Lord has never seemed to notice, though. Fitting.

His companions finally caught up, and he stepped off the pile of spoil and continued on to his destination, a wooden observation tower. The tower was a typical wartime makeshift: a crude twelve-foot-high structure built from raw-cut lumber hastily bound together with ropes and pegs. Toshiwara climbed the ladder on the east side, wary of splinters – no time for careful planing to glossy smoothness here. He felt a quiet pride that he could still climb a ladder in full armor without becoming winded. At the top he paused to brush his hands free of bits of wood, doing it by feel because with age his eyesight was no longer very good up close – if he looked at his palms, he would see only a flesh-colored blur.

But Fate has two sides. He might be unable to make out the details of his wife's embroidery, but he could see better than ever over great distances. Toshiwara circled the tower's small platform, looking in each direction in turn, starting with the castle.

Castle Kosaten squatted in the narrow wedge of land between the merging of the River of Many Faces and the River of Blue Silk. A modest-sized fortress, its outer walls abutting directly on the water of both rivers, it had been built long ago – originally by the Salamander Clan – specifically to control traffic on both rivers. The central keep was only four stories high, barely visible over the outer walls, which by contrast were unusually high, over thirty feet. Toshiwara could see the gleam of helmets on the tops of those walls, part of the three-thousand-odd men of Lord Goda who held the place.

The army Toshiwara commanded was much larger, almost fourteen thousand infantry and five hundred cavalry. It was encamped primarily on the south bank of the River of Blue Silk; the land there was now a sprawl of thousands of tents, intermingled with hastily-built structures – horse stables and ox enclosures, latrines, smithies, kitchens, bath-houses, and observation towers like the one Toshiwara stood on. An outer ring of crude stockade walls and ditches served as defense if an enemy somehow got close enough to mount a raid. A haze of smoke drifted over the camp, coiling up in thin spirals from hundreds of cooking fires and from the bath-houses heating water. A forest two miles south had been largely swept away by the army's relentless appetite for wood, leaving a wasteland of stumps and bare earth. The sight brought a very slight frown to Toshiwara's mouth, disgust at the way crude necessity so often crushed beauty.

Of course, the siege lines were even uglier. The tower where Toshiwara stood was nearly at the center of them, an ugly cross-hatching of ditches and arrow-shields and temporary stockades that zig-zagged across the half-mile peninsula between the two rivers, sealing Castle Kosaten inside. Soldiers and peasant volunteers, all stripped down to loincloths and headbands, worked in the ditches, hacking at the earth with wooden mattocks to inch the lines closer to the distant castle walls. Other samurai in full armor waited in reserve in case the castle garrison tried a sortie. Toshiwara had almost a third of his strength here, forty-five hundred men – enough to ensure that any such sortie would be defeated.

Boats large and small shuttled back and forth across both rivers, carrying troops and supplies from the main camp to the siege lines and to an additional smaller camp north the River of Many Faces. A thick line of warships flying the Wolf banner was anchored downstream from them, guarding against any sortie from the eleven Jade Dragon vessels anchored underneath the walls of Castle Kosaten, and more ships were moored upstream, ready to trade out with the picket line or to reinforce it if needed. They were mainly ships from the Ookami river-fleet based in WolfTown, but also including a handful of ships from Toshiwara's own resources. In total there were almost thirty vessels, comprising the majority of the Wolf Clan's naval strength, and more than enough to crush any misguided aggression from Lord Goda's fleet.

Even with naval superiority, Toshiwara was not entirely comfortable with having his strength divided in three parts by the rivers; in fact it was the kind of situation that would have desperately alarmed him in former years, a recipe for having his separated forces crushed by a focused counterattack. The history of warfare in the Empire was full of stories about generals and Lords who pulled off spectacular victories in just that sort of situation. But...

Toshiwara looked north, across the River of Many Faces. After a couple of minutes he spotted a squadron of horsemen, dot-tiny with distance but their motion unmistakable, trotting through the farmlands. *Kitaro's horsemen are my real defense, not the stockades or the rivers. They will warn me if anything goes wrong, if any enemy troops get within a day's march.*

A wry smile briefly touched his lips. *Folk in the courts like to tell stories about how Lord Akira must be guided by the Heavens, or the Demons, to be able to win so many battles. But it isn't magic. It's just a new way of using horsemen.*

Then he looked at the walls of Kosaten again and suppressed a sigh. All his superior knowledge of enemy movements could not make the walls of the castle vanish, and the Wolf Clan's river fleet could not force passage on the water. Any attack on the Jade Dragon ships would face a devastating barrage of fire-arrows from the castle walls above them. And while the River of Blue Silk was wide enough that vessels could, in theory, sail past the castle without entering that lethal archery zone, Goda's fleet could swoop out from the castle to strike in overwhelming force at any such passing ships. In practical terms, the castle controlled the rivers and no maritime traffic was possible without its permission – which meant that no Wolf army could be supplied by water west of the castle.

It also meant that trade on the river was at a standstill until the siege ended. These rivers formed one of the two largest trade routes in the Empire, and Toshiwara could see almost a score of trade ships anchored upstream from his fleet, their cargoes rendered worthless by immobility. The merchants are not happy about that, Toshiwara knew. He had been forced to endure a petition a few nights ago from a trio of Wolf Clan merchants – soft-faced, well-groomed men in dark coats of thick, high-grade silk that doubtless had elaborate embroidery on the inside where the sight of it would not insult any samurai. They had been respectful, submissive, but also extremely persistent, endlessly repeating how much it was costing the Clan – they couched everything in terms of the Clan, not their own interests – to keep the river closed.

There were Lords, generally of the more traditional sort who ruled over smaller territories, who refused to deal with merchants at all, considering them so lowly and grasping that their mere presence contaminated the honor of a samurai. Toshiwara's family had learned long ago that a wise Lord did not indulge in such notions, since trade created the prosperity that was needed to fill treasuries with taxes that would fund troops and castles. Still, there were times when merchants' single-minded obsession with money above all else could become nigh-unbearable. The men had not seemed to grasp that the Wolf Clan was entering a death-grapple with the Jade Dragons, and Toshiwara was not going to end the siege of a crucial enemy castle just because they were in danger of defaulting on loans.

Ryohei shook his head minutely. *If they were wise, those merchants would be finding ways to help us win the war quickly… well, war is the domain of samurai, not of common folk.* He shaded his eyes and peered at the distant walls of the castle. *Yes, there are plenty of men on the parapets, and at least some of them are officers… that fancy helmet might even be Lord Goda himself. Excellent, it is time for me to do my part to make this war end more quickly.*

Lord Toshiwara went to the edge of the tower and looked down at the men who had waited patiently for his word. "Come up," he called.

The five samurai slowly climbed the tower. One had brought a folding chair, while another had a furled banner, so large that he had to pass it up to the first man before ascending the ladder. After setting up the chair, the two men positioned themselves at the back edge of the tower, raising the banner between them. The Ookami crest snarled out from the fluttering vertical rectangle of gray silk. Two other men deployed themselves to either side of the platform, adopting the rigid upright postures of bodyguards.

The fifth man was dressed in a bulky full suit of armor, ancient and splendid, lacquered entirely in Ookami gray and red. The massive helmet mounted a cluster of feathers and a steel-carved wolf's head mounted between two inward-curving crescent moons. The man's face, framed by the helmet, was almost completely concealed by an iron war-mask in the shape of a snarling wolf's jaws.

The ancestral armor of the Ookami line. Toshiwara had seen it on many occasions, but this was the first time he had seen it worn by someone other than the Clan's High Lord. It gave him an almost physical sense of inappropriateness, nearly of blasphemy, as though he was seeing a Priestess strip off her clothes or a peasant carrying a long sword.

It is not my place to question Lord Akira's orders, Lord Toshiwara told himself firmly. *This is a deception of war, not some indulgence of madness.*

He knelt and prostrated himself to the armored figure as though it was the High Lord himself.

⛩ ⛩ ⛩

CAPTAIN TOKAGE FROWNED AT THE sky, then turned his horse and kicked it into a fast trot. It took only a few moments for him the reach the back of the little column.

Seneschal Amano was riding today, finally recovering from the stresses of their earlier journey. As Tokage drew up he nodded toward the northern horizon, a motion exaggerated by the black courtier's cap he had resumed wearing once they had returned to the Empire. "That cannot just be a single burning temple, honorable Tokage."

The road they followed ran east along the side of a forested hill, affording glimpses of farmlands through the foliage on the right-hand downslope side, the left-hand upslope a near-impenetrable wall of trees. Even though those intervening trees, though, it was impossible to miss the spirals of black smoke that lined the horizon in an arc stretching from northeast to northwest. The light wind that stirred the leaves carried a faint but inescapable harshness of ash.

"Indeed it cannot," Tokage nodded grimly. "Honorable Sergeant Ryuma reports we are within a few hours of Castle Mouko, but in light of the situation, I wish to know if you still intend to proceed." Unspoken, but understood by both men, was that their primary duty was to the Wolf Clan and High Lord Akira. If the alliance with the Tiger was already hopeless, delivering word of a barbarian invasion would be far more important than speaking to the High Lord of the Tiger.

Amano stroked his goatee beard in thought. "I have already dispatched more than one letter to the High Lord, including one after our unfortunate encounter at that shrine," he noted. "If there is still a chance of forging an alliance with the Tiger Clan, the current situation makes it all the more important that we seek it out."

"As you say, honorable Seneschal." Tokage bowed in the saddle and returned to the head of the little column, the men shifting aside on the narrow road to make room for his passage. He was not sure if Amano was right, but it was not his place to question such things. Akira had entrusted the mission to the Seneschal, and Tokage's duty was simply to try to get the old man to his destination and back safely. Which, so far, he had managed to do in spite of some extraordinary obstacles.

Still…that many fires, the invading force must be vast indeed. He sighed. *Regret is a Sin, a form of Selfishness, but all the same I will regret it very much if I cannot see Aya or my sons or our dear Miyako*-chan *once more.* He recited a mantra under his breath. *Blessed Amatsu, show Compassion for my sinful weakness.*

"Honorable Captain?"

The young Priestess looked much cleaner and more respectable today than she had when she staggered out of the forest two days ago, although her swordsman companion was little improved. Tokage could not deny he was unhappy that Kenji had found his way back to them, but the Priestess had been a vital help after the disaster in the Aelfynn lands – and besides, Tokage and his family had always been pious. Not to mention that she seemed to be angry with Kenji right now, which improved Tokage's opinion of her judgment. He nodded to her respectfully. "Yes, honored Priestess?"

She pointed downslope. "There are people down there, heading the other direction. Should we be worried about that?"

Tokage squinted after her gesture. He could just make out a narrower track about fifty paces down the slope, probably a hunting trail worn by foot traffic. It was indeed full of people, mostly on foot but with some two-wheeled carts mixed in. Common folk, the men dressed in baggy jackets and tight-fitting white leggings or merely loincloths, their heads bare or with headbands to keep their hair back from their faces, the women in simple one-piece robes that ended just below their knees, kerchiefs tied over their heads. All of them burdened with thick bundles, often held in place on wooden frames tied to their backs.

Kenji was looking as well, and now he laughed, a sour bitter noise. "Those are the smart ones, gettin' out while they can," he said.

He is right, Tokage thought, frowning enough that some of it crept onto his face. *Those are refugees, avoiding the main roads and the samurai they might meet on them.* Peasants were supposed to be tied to the land and the Lords who ruled that land, and traveling without permission was a crime… though one seldom enforced so long as the numbers of those leaving stayed low and the crops got planted.

"They're fleeing the fires?" Rei looked visibly distressed. Tokage felt a brief stab of envy at the reminder that Priestesses were not expected to be nearly so stoic and self-controlled as samurai. "Can we help them, do something for them?"

Kenji laughed again, the same unpleasant sound, and Tokage wondered how much pain it was hiding. *This man seems like he could have been born a peasant, even if he's learned to talk – mostly – with the samurai forms.* "Do what? Give 'em our coin? We don't have enough for more than a few of them." The swordsman spat at the ground. "Damnation to this, damnation to them. We keep on moving east. We're gettin' close, I can tell."

And what does that mean? Not for the first time, Tokage thought back to the events at the Aelfynn city, to Kenji's strange behaviors before the disaster struck. And to the odd things Priestess Rei had said afterward. *Kenji is the sword… what was that supposed to mean?*

With an effort of will he refocused himself. *Enough. You have a duty, to get Seneschal Amano safely to Castle Mouko. Focus on that.*

CHAPTER 9

"AMATSU PRESERVE US," CAPTAIN Tokage whispered.

It had been midday by the time his little column of samurai passed the shoulder of the long line of forested hills and descended toward the farmlands below. As they emerged from the treeline, marching downward in a back-and-forth pattern on the embankments between terraced rice paddies, they had finally gotten an unimpeded view eastward. Castle Mouko, the seat of the Tiger Clan, lay two miles away, surrounded on all sides by an endless patchwork of Sun-reflecting rice paddies and rich green fields of grain and soybeans, sliced through by the pale tan-white lines of roads.

Just as important, they finally got a clear view of what lay to the north.

A thousand spirals of brown-black smoke rose at the limit of sight, spiraling and twining into larger columns of darkness, all of it merging together into a great gray smudge that blotted out a quarter part of the sky, the top of it thinning and slowly drifting eastward with the prevailing winds. Tokage had seen great fires before, forests ignited by thunderstorms, castles burning to the ground. They had never approached the magnitude of this.

Despite samurai self-discipline, more than one of his men let out a gasp or a muttered oath. The young Priestess, Rei, began to recite a prayer to the Goddess, ringing her staff in the intervals. The swordsman next to her just stood with his hands on his hips, his pale eyes distant and unfocused, as though he wasn't even looking at what the rest of them saw.

Tokage exchanged an expressionless look with Seneschal Amano, then toed his horse over to where Sergeant Ryuma sat stock-still on his own mount, staring wide-eyed. The Tiger looked at him as he approached, and the older man's face was haunted. "This cannot be," he muttered. "Has the whole north fallen?"

"Not quite yet, I think," Tokage replied. He pointed.

At the edge of sight, banners fluttered and metal glittered in the Sunlight that shone from the south. *An army in the field, and a large one,* Tokage thought. A Tiger army, though it was too far away to make out anything beyond a general sheen of color in which orange was the strongest tone.

Closer than the army, but still far distant, he could see roads clotted with dark lines and blotches that resolved into the countless tiny shapes of people – common folk fleeing south, toward Castle Mouko.

Kenji was right, the smarter ones got out first. Now the flood comes.

"Get moving," he called, waiting for his men to pass him and then swinging in next to Seneschal Amano. *If we're going to get inside the castle, we'll have to reach it before the refugees do,* he thought grimly. He could already see crowds starting to form on the city's northern side.

Castle Mouko's primary keep was only five stories high, but it sat atop a tower-like foundation three times that height, the whole adjacent to a much larger structure, an artificial hill comprising an overlapping tangle of different levels, each the size of a small town and crowded with buildings – barracks, shrines, residences, gardens, and towers. Trees tall enough to date back to the days of the Emperors rose within the larger spaces. Walled and bridges and fortified ramps interconnected the levels and the adjacent keep in maze-like patterns, finally descending in sloping ramps and staircases and gatehouses and moats to ground level and the walled city that surrounded the castle on all sides. In turn, a larger moat surrounded the outer walls of the city, crossed by bridges on the west, north, and south sides.

"Formidable," Tokage murmured. He felt sure there were also hidden basement floors within the massive citadel and the smaller tower that mounted the keep, probably many levels of them. Even Castle Ookami, of far more conventional design, had three levels in the foundation below the keep. "Beautiful as well. Reminds me of paintings I've seen of the old Imperial Palace, before the earthquake."

"Indeed," Amano agreed. "If I recall my histories correctly, that is not an accident. This castle was originally ordered built by the Seventeenth Emperor. He intended it as a stronghold and administrative center for his servants to oversee the northern half of the Empire, because the great distance from the Imperial City meant the Clans here often quarreled and fought on their own. It was still incomplete at the time of the Dread Eclipse, and soon afterward the

Tiger Clan took possession and proclaimed it as their seat of power. Which gave them a considerable advantage over the White Fox Clan, their chief rival at the time."

So much was ruined by the fall of the Emperors, Tokage thought. *And how much more will be lost?* Embarrassed by such sentimental maundering, he looked for something mundane to say. "The city is rather modest, though. Almost more of a large town, compared to a place like WolfTown."

Amano nodded. "The Tiger have a lower population than we do, but it is still a touch surprising. Of course, there is no navigable river here to facilitate trade."

The land here had abundant moisture – their road crossed three different small bridges in the two miles leading up to the western gate – but none of the streams were more than a few feet deep. Tokage reflected that this was probably part of why the Tiger Clan had endured for so long when so many other Clans had been destroyed – there was no river offering a convenient supply route for an assault on their core territories. Now, though, it also meant there was no easy way for refugees to flee – he could see crowds choking the roads at each bridge as they came southward. *At least it means we will reach the city ahead of them. But what then?*

As they approached the western side of the city, the fortress looming higher and higher as they closed the final distance, they began to pass groups of people and occasional clusters of wagons along the road. *Merchants and laborers, waiting to see if they can get inside,* Tokage recognized. Some of those waiting seemed quite calm, squatting in little circles to eat or throw dice or smoke pipes, while others milled about talking and peering anxiously northward. They all moved aside and bowed as the samurai marched past; a few of them prostrated and recited mantras as Priestess Rei passed them, and she kept pausing to bow in return and recite the replies to the prayers, to the annoyance of Kenji.

"Surprising how calm they are," Amano murmured.

Tokage felt an inner scowl and managed to keep most of it off his face. *The man's never been to war,* he reminded himself. "They don't really believe it's happening yet," he said aloud. "They'll stay calm… until they don't. Best we be inside the gates when that happens."

The Tiger had a small gatehouse on the near side of the moat, and there the line of people waiting to enter the city became a milling and noisy swarm. Still, even here they moved aside for the approaching samurai. The harried guards did not seem to know quite what to do about Tokage's group, but the presence of Sergeant Ryuma and his Tiger was enough for them to wave them all through.

The moat beyond the gatehouse had steep-sloped sides of fitted stone; the water at the bottom was stagnant and green-tinged, the smell noticeable even from thirty feet above. The bridge which crossed it to the city's walls was forty paces of thick wooden planks on a structure of support pillars each a foot square, sunk into stone foundations in the slimy water. *Strong defense,* Tokage thought, glancing up and noting the archer slits along the wall's upper edges, then observing the thickness of the wall itself as they passed through the darkened tunnel of the main gate. *But a bit old-fashioned. Interesting that they've not allowed the city to grow beyond its walls the way WolfTown has.*

From the city's outer walls to the keep at the top of Castle Mouko's citadel took them from late morning into late afternoon, interrupted by the Noon ritual. Each layer of walls and ramps, each ascent to a higher level, entailed a delay while the guards reviewed listened to their story, asked questions, and waited for word from their officers. They left their mounts at a stable on one of the multi-acre intermediate levels – almost a town in itself, complete with a smaller keep watching over it. Ryuma and the rest of Lord Handen's men broke off around that time, satisfied with having delivered the Wolf samurai here safely, but the little group of survivors from Tora Saneda's escort continued on with them.

It was the Hour of the Peacock when they reached the uppermost of the citadel's many sub-complexes, at the same level as the keep on its isolated tower. At this height there was no longer a fortified wall around the sprawling rectangular space, just a waist-high railing to keep people from falling the hundred-odd feet to the next level down. Here their escorts assigned them housing in a barracks building, thankfully with an attached bathhouse.

Tokage knew this was as far as most of his men would be permitted to go; no High Lord would allow more than the most token of an honor guard to enter his seat of power. He spent some time making sure his men all had food and places to sleep before he permitted himself to wash. The Tora men were already gone, no doubt to cleanse themselves before holding vigil for their impending ritual suicides.

The Sun was lowering in the western sky, its light dimmed unpleasantly by the haze of smoke from the north, when Tokage finally emerged from the bath-house, washed and shaved and dressed. The Tiger had given him fresh pleated leggings, shirt, and overcoat, and even showed the consideration of making sure they were in Wolf Clan red and gray, though with no crests or markings. Seneschal Amano, likewise cleansed and with his hair carefully tied and pinned into a flat topknot, wore the set of elaborate formal clothing he had carted all the way from Castle Ookami but had donned only a few times on the entire trip. Tokage had to admit the old man still looked the part of a true courtier, his aged frame all but invisible within the layers of silk robes, pants, and coat, his hands folded inside the huge sleeves, his feet concealed beneath the wide-bottomed leggings that just brushed the ground. *Not quite as impractical as the old Imperial Court get-ups, but close enough,* Tokage thought with an inner snort. He'd seen silk paintings of the Imperial era in Castle Ookami, and they always gave him a chuckle – robes so long that the men wearing them had to move on their knees, with servants walking behind them to hold up the rest of the silk and keep it from dragging on the ground.

An armored Tiger samurai met them outside the bathhouse, bowing low. "Honorable Seneschal Ookami Amano. The High Lord has graciously permitted you and your escort, the honorable Ookami Tokage, to attend him in court this evening."

Faster than I expected, Tokage thought behind the concealment of his own acknowledging bow. From the raised eyebrow that Amano offered him, he suspected the old Seneschal was equally surprised. Normally a High Lord would wait at least a day before granting an audience to someone of their rank; longer, sometimes much longer, if he wished to frustrate them or to ostentatiously display his power and rank.

On the other hand, he restricted it to just the two of us, with no other guards, which is definitely a reminder of his authority. Instinctively Tokage glanced around for the swordsman and his Priestess – it would not do for those two to cause any trouble – but they were nowhere in sight. *Hopefully still bathing or eating, not picking a fight. The fellow dueled Lord Akira himself, there's no telling what he could do. .*

He and Amano together crossed the thirty-pace bridge that arched from the citadel's platform to the isolated keep. Tokage glanced over the side and noted several other bridges crossing below, joining with ramps and walkways that traced along the sides of both the citadel and the keep's tower; far below, light glinted on water, a moat occupying the bottom of the gap.

Reaching the keep, they passed through a final gatehouse, then climbed a walled ramp that circled two sides of the keep to the exterior door on its second level. Here too they passed other ramps that descended the keep toward lower levels of the complex. *This place is a maze even compared to Castle Ookami,* Tokage thought. *It would be a nightmare to try to capture it by assault.*

The view from the circling ramp was impressive, even better than from the level they'd left behind, stretching for miles even with the smoke blurring the distance. To the east Tokage could just make out the jagged gray-green-white line of the Bear Mountains on the horizon. Southward and westward the white lines of roads snaked through a rich landscape of woodlands and farms and rice-paddies reflecting orange in the late-afternoon smoky Sunlight, and northward...

Northward the distant sparkle and fluttering motion of a great army, and beyond it the smoke of a thousand fires.

Ah, of course, that's why they're seeing us so quickly, he thought.

ĦĦĦ

THEY ARE HERE, LOOKING THROUGH me.

Tomoe sensed the Lords of Dakkurru as a vast pressure within herself, a prickling eagerness in every part of her body, an anticipation so intense she could not stand still. She stalked back and forth, her hands twitching, the muscles in her face tightening like twisting ropes to the point of agony and then releasing suddenly. Her left hand started to tap on the hilt of her sword where it projected past her hip; she lifted the twitching hand and stared at it for a moment, wondering why it had done that. The faint curiosity shriveled under the weight of the Lords' all-consuming presence.

The army of Dakkurru sprawled across a three-mile arc of open land, a mixture of farmlands and open fields. The warriors were in tribal groups, clustering around their leaders. Burning peasant huts interspersed the lines, orange-yellow beacons with spirals of blackness rising up to drift eastward, merging with the vastly greater clouds of the great burning underway where the army had already passed. Somewhere back there, isolated pockets of samurai huddled in smaller castles and walled towns, left behind when the forces of Dakkurru swept through and cut them off.

Samurai are so stupidly arrogant, a corner of Tomoe's mind gloated. *They expect wars t'be fought on their schedule, accordin' to their rules.*

The rest of her, and the Lords within her, merely exulted at the sight of all that burning, at the overwhelming stench of smoke and burnt flesh, at the unseen destruction the smoke-clouds marked out. *A thousand villages and farms turned t'ash.* It brought a rush of choking glee that momentarily held her still, her muscles locking in a rictus of inhuman ecstasy. The shamans and priests who clustered around her shrank back, whimpering and groveling and pressing their masks into the trampled grass. The only one not to react was the one who had been named Satsuki, who Tomoe had taken to labeling as simply the Other. *She* merely stood, face pale and unmoving beneath her hood, her one working eye staring fixedly at the enemy army to the south.

They're watchin' through her as well as though me, Tomoe knew. *But she can't… enjoy it, as I can.* The other woman was no longer a person at all, really – merely a puppet of meat and bone.

The Lords within her turned her attention south, toward the enemy army, but where she stood all she could see was an endless sea of tribesmen, heads of lank black hair greased with rancid butter, dark-stained leathers and furs, here and there the pennants of chieftains raised on spears. The banners of Dakkurru were on the ground, not yet raised, not yet adorned.

She crossed the smoldering ashes of a peasant hut, cinders crunching under the soft soles of her leather boots. In the space between four farmhouses, one of them still burning, a three-posted tower rose twenty feet into the air, with a metal plate hanging from a cross-piece atop it. An alarm for warning neighbors of danger, though it had done them little good when the scouts of Dakkurru's army swept through. Tomoe climbed the ladder to the top, gripping one of the posts and leaning out to scan the landscape ahead. She felt again the Lords within her, using her senses, a painful *pressure* as though her body was struggling to contain something far vaster than its flesh. Tomoe's eyes had always been good, but now she could see farther, better, the Lords forcibly wrenching a performance from her flesh that she could never have evoked on her own.

Beyond the farmlands where the army of Dakkurru had camped, the land became green rolling plans, speckled with the brighter colors of flowers and pampas grass, here and there a few trees. The open terrain stretched southward for several miles; just on the edge of vision she could make out the shape of a castle and city silhouetted against the sky, a smudge of charcoal smoke above it like a banner. To the east she could see the line of the Bear Mountains stalking the horizon, while to the west the land became rugged and wooded. The plain here was probably the largest piece of open ground in the northern Tiger lands, which made it inevitable as the site of battle.

Ah, there, she thought, with a sense of greedy, all-devouring anticipation. The Tiger army, all of it they had been able to assemble, spread across a mile and more of the rolling landscape. Twelve thousand men, divided into a score of rectangular formations at staggered intervals. Back-banners made a continual flutter above the ranks, supplemented by the glitter of upright spears, their foot-long razor-edged heads reflecting orange-yellow Sunlight. Larger family and officer banners rose from the centers of each formation, and a cluster of them at the center, at the crest of one of the low slopes, marked the position of the commander and his entourage. Tomoe felt her free hand clench and grasp, as if she could reach out and wipe that distant cluster of nobles from the world… *No, too far, even for t'Other,* she knew, feeling a frustration that could have been her own or the Lords' in equal measure. *That'll have t'come later, when their army is crushed and I can get close.*

She slid back down the ladder and turned to the waiting shamans. "The Lords proclaim, time for battle. Begin t'ritual."

The chant began, low at first, spreading from one tribal gathering to the next. "Dakkurru! Dakkurru! Dakkurru!"

The shamans shouted orders, their voices guttural with eagerness, and tribesmen brought forward their prisoners. Women and children, dressed in the torn and bloody remnants of their clothes, their faces battered into swollen ugliness. They stared blankly, misery and despair mingled in their eyes. The women's hands and heads were locked in crude wooden stocks laid across their shoulders; the children were simply held by a tribesman's iron-hard grasp on an arm or a shoulder.

Mostly peasants, Tomoe saw, *but those two are samurai-class.* The two young women were dressed in now-tattered silk robes, the sleeves dangling in shreds from their arms, the lower hems torn up the sides. Delicate embroidery was still half-visible beneath stains of blood and ash and dirt. A flicker of awareness showed in their dazed expressions, sheer bewilderment foremost, and Tomoe felt a laugh brewing inside her at the sight. *A few days ago you were sittin' in your garden, playin' with flowers and waitin' for your servants t'bring you dinner. Now everything's turned upside down… And t'best is yet t'come,* neh?

One of the children looked to be of the samurai class as well, judging from his half-shaved head and the quality of the tattered coat he wore. Tomoe thought there was a family resemblance between him and one of the women, and that made the laugh grow stronger, like a great bubble swelling in her throat.

The shamans raised their hands overhead and shouted in unison: "Akal her Dakkurru!" They joined the army's chant, their voices deep and droning, the rhythmic sound spreading outward like ripples in a pond.

The Mask priests among them also chanted, in the Empire's tongue, though there was almost no one here to understand them – a few of the Brothers and Sisters had joined the army since it crossed the border, but most of them were traveling south to the lands ruled by the Voice of Selfishness, spreading chaos as they went.

The tribesmen pushed the women to their knees, ten of them in a long row, the stocks banging and bumping against each other. A few of the victims let out cries or whimpers; the rest stared blankly. Shamans and robed cultists came forward with bowls, holding them alongside the waiting sacrifices. Others dragged the children to the great banners that waited on the ground, to the hooks that were black with dried blood.

Some of the women did react then, shrieking in horror, or squeezing their eyes shut and shaking their heads. The samurai woman let out a howl of negation as the cultists placed her son on the waiting hooks. Tomoe met the woman's suddenly wide-open stare with her own, and the laugh erupted from her throat, raucous uncontrollable glee. The woman shrieked uncontrollably, her eyes wide and fixed.

The chanting rose into a crescendo, echoing across the fields.

"DAKKURRU! DAKKURRU! DAKKURRU!"

The woman's screams were inaudible now, drowned within the invocation of the Lords, and Tomoe could not hear the scream turn to a wheezing gurgle as the sacrificial knife went across her throat and her blood poured into the waiting bowl. The banners swung up, four men raising each of them hand over hand until they swayed above the crowd, the huge triangular red cloths fluttering wildly, the small figures pinioned on them twitching and wailing. The army's chant briefly became a roaring wordless howl of triumph.

The bowls were full now, and they passed from one shaman to the next. Tomoe set one to her lips and drank, the salt-iron taste more intoxicating than wine, hot fluid spilling from the corners of her mouth and dripping from her chin. The Other drank as well, the blood garish on her pale face, but showed no more reaction to it than to anything else. That made Tomoe grin, more blood spilling from her own mouth. *Just a puppet now. And soon t'Wolf Lord will know you're* our *puppet.*

Tomoe passed the bowl to the next tribesman, the sacrificial blood cycling outward to the chieftains and family elders who surrounded the shamans, and from there to their closest followers. The chant continued, deafening-loud, a physical pressure on Tomoe's body that matched the spiritual pressure within, the Lords exulting in the annihilation of life. Above them the sacrifices writhed on the banners, their agony adding to the strength of the ritual.

The chieftains shouted, inaudible amid the chanting, and the banners shifted forward, men carrying them toward the enemy. The army responded, an organic motion that acquired structure as it continued, thousands moving as one. Flowing toward the distant Tiger army, and the castle beyond.

⛩ ⛩ ⛩

CAPTAIN TOKAGE KEPT HIS FACE properly impassive, but inwardly he felt forced to admit the truth: *Castle Mouko's court chamber is impressive.* Then loyalty made him add: *Though not so impressive as Castle Ookami!*

The ramps outside had brought them in through a pair of heavy oak doors – both valves open, but with armored guards posted just inside. *Ready to close it at a moment's notice,* Tokage had known, and had noticed also the careful looks they gave to his swords. It would be an insult to ask a guest's escorting guard to go unarmed, but they were clearly uncomfortable with the weapons nonetheless, which told volumes about the tension here.

An unctuously bowing courtier had met them inside the doors, shown them where to leave their sandals, and then led them to a waiting room, small but beautifully paneled in cedar, with silk paintings on the walls and a tea-set in blue-glazed ceramic on a low table. A female servant poured the tea and then knelt by the door, patiently waiting in case they needed their cups refilled.

Amano had politely sipped once before sitting on his heels to wait. *Hurry up to get us inside, and then make us wait again,* Tokage had thought irritably, kneeling in the proper place slightly behind Amano and to his right. He knew such conventions were important, part of the intricate dance of precedence and face and etiquette that maintained order and civilization – his wife and daughter understood that world and thrived in it. Still, there were times when he almost sympathized with High Lord Akira's blundering disrespect for such customs...

It was almost an hour before the courtier had finally returned and led them through a brief maze of interior corridors – about half solid wood, the rest paper or silk partitions that could be moved and rearranged – and down a staircase to the main court chamber on the castle's second floor.

It was physically smaller than the same chamber in Castle Ookami, but like the latter it was two stories, with a balcony on the second level for an audience to observe. Huge wooden pillars ascended on both the left and right sides of the room, each of them larger around than a man's arms could reach and polished to a high sheen. The huge cylinders of cypress rose from below the floor and ascended through the ceiling two stories above, and Tokage was sure they were set into the castle's basement and rose all the way to the upper floors. *Trees of that size can't be found these days, at least not anywhere they could be harvested,* he thought. Such massive central pillars had been a feature of ancient castle design, but had faded in modern days as the supply of sufficiently large trees grew sparse.

The rest of the large room was more restrained in its design, but gave off the same air of ancient splendor – the surfaces all highly-polished wood that had darkened with the centuries, the floor mirror-smooth from the tracks of countless thousands of sock-clad feet. Banners hung from the balconies above, each displaying the Tiger and Tora crests at the top in huge embroidered circles, each with a different noble bloodline's crest below.

Some direct Sunlight – orang-tinged by late afternoon and the distant smoke – was coming in to the upper level, probably through open windows in adjacent rooms, but the main floor was only dimly illuminated by light filtering through multiple layers of paper-frame walls. Lanterns hung throughout the chamber, works of art with panels of yellow silk set in frames of gold-embossed wood. The room smelled faintly of wax and sandalwood, more strongly of the fear-intensified sweat of the courtiers who crowded the floor, as well as incense and something else unpleasant that Tokage could not identify. No one would comment on the unfortunate odors, of course.

Seneschal Amano crossed the room toward the dais at the required stately pace, silent and eyes downcast. At a distance of five paces he stopped, sank to his knees, and bowed deeply – not quite a full prostration, since he was the direct emissary of another High Lord, but close to it. Tokage stopped five paces behind Amano and bowed as well, then sat back and looked over the scene while Amano recited a lengthy ritual greeting.

The High Lord of the Tiger Clan was dressed in the full court garb expected of a man of his rank in a formal setting: oversized leggings and shirt that hid his hands and feet within them, all made of fine-spun pale orange silk embroidered in thread of slightly darker orange with images of tigers, flowers, and trees – the embroidery almost invisible until one looked closely. The wide-shouldered vest-coat he wore atop the other clothing had shoulders that projected out like wings, and was done in shades of black and near-black dark gray, except for the brightly visible crests – Tiger Clan and Tora family – embroidered on both sides at chest height. The man within the clothing seemed shrunken, like a stick-figure puppet draped with silk; his face showed the same, with sunken cheeks and eyes deep in their sockets under thick eyebrows, the shaved temples of his scalp showing age-spotting. The hair tied back in a carefully-arranged topknot behind the shaved temples was as much gray as black. Tora Saneda had been a fit man in his forties; if Tokage had not known better he would have assumed his brother Iesada was in his seventh decade.

The woman kneeling in the wife's place to his side was, by contrast, an elegant and well-preserved lady, clearly in her forties, though her makeup could not conceal the narrow pinched unattractiveness of her face. The young man and young woman behind her, both with high foreheads and narrow mouths, surely the High Lord's children; Tokage vaguely remembered the man as having visited Castle Ookami years before, though he could not recall his name. The family resemblance was plain enough.

Ah, and there's honorable Saneda's son, Tokage thought sadly. Tora Arinobu stood alone on the far edge of the dais. He was in armor, in sharp contrast to everyone else in the room, and had a warrior's stony-hard eyes in a heavily scarred face. He looked at the Wolf Clan visitors with open hostility.

His uncle Iesada waited out Amano's lengthy speech impassively. The High Lord's expression was a blank scowl, as though time had worn the skin and muscles into that expression and he could make no other. When Amano finished he did not speak at once, instead slowly pushing one hand with a folded fan out of its bulky sleeve. He made a slight gesture with it.

In apparent response a pair of servants emerged from behind the crowd of courtiers. They carried a small rectangular wooden platter between them; something lay atop it, along with a bowl holding a smoldering stick of incense. They laid the platter on the floor between Amano and the dais, then prostrated themselves and backed away. A soft murmur went through the room, courtiers speaking behind fans or smothering disgusted exclamations.

Ah so, Tokage thought, nodding inwardly.

The thing on the platter, its outlines slightly blurred by the smoke spiraling up from the burning incense, was one of the Aelfynn – no, one of the bizarre creatures the Aelfynn had become after whatever had happened in their now-destroyed city. It was a tiny, hairy, spiky thing, bone-skinny limbs sprawled away from a rotund body covered in yellow-brown fur, its triangular head mounting a face that resembled a shriveled old man with no chin. Death had exaggerated the thing's inhuman nature, bloating the stomach and shrinking the flesh of limbs and face; a rancid smell rose from the corpse despite the incense's efforts to blot it out.

Lord Iesada pointed his fan at the small grotesque corpse, but did not look at it – instead he stared at Amano. "This is... this *was* the noble Third Tier Speaker to Strangers Seaic, who led the delegation of our honorable Aelfynn allies at Castle Dangai," he said. His voice quivered slightly, and Tokage noted a subtle shift in his son's stance, a protective tension. "Before the enemy attack, they all became… like this, and the northern barbarians unleashed foul sorcery such as none had ever seen. Our castle fell, with great loss of life, and now the barbarians march through the heart of our lands."

A second round of noise went through the room, this time louder, and the universal smell of sweat intensified. Tokage was no great master at reading faces, but even he could see the tension in the powdered face of the High Lord's wife, the quivering barely-contained emotions of her children. *Everyone here is afraid,* he thought. *Though they're hiding it well, for courtiers.*

Amano, after a brief initial glance, did not look at the corpse either. "It is precisely to discuss these matters that I have come to your court, most honorable High Lord Tora Iesada, rather than return to our own lands." *Ah, clever, making it sound like we had a choice and took the more honorable path,* Tokage noted approvingly. His wife was adept at those sorts of rhetorical maneuvers, even in their family arguments. "With the barbarian threat growing, our discussions can only acquire greater urgency."

The High Lord opened his fan with a sharp flick of his wrist. The fan made an angry *snap* noise that was shockingly loud in the anxious near-silence of the court, revealing yellow-dyed paper painted in an elaborate image and calligraphy. "There is no time for word-games now, honorable Amano. I must know what happened to my brother, to our allies. For two decades now the Aelfynn have stood beside us, lent their strength to ours. Now they are… gone. And the barbarians are upon us like an unstoppable flood." The old man's thick eyebrows pressed down, the lines in his face deepening. "You went into their lands, with our permission and support, escorted by my honorable brother Tora Saneda, whose son now stands here awaiting him." He gestured at Arinobu. "My brother traveled with you, so that we all might join together against this threat. And now you return… *without* my brother, and the Aelfynn have…" He broke off, cleared his throat and slowly folded up his fan. "Explain this."

The Seneschal bowed low once again and settled back on his heels, the motion as smooth as ever. Tokage felt an undeniable respect for the old courtier. *It surely hurts him bitterly each time, kneeling like that at his age, but you'd never know it from looking at him. Perfect Discipline and Courtesy.*

"I can only report what I saw," Amano said, his voice clear and unwavering. "Soon after our arrival in the Aelfynn's land, a catastrophe fell upon them. Their land was torn asunder by earthquake, and their powers seemed to depart them. Those which we saw afterward were… lessened, in the same manner as this one."

A shift went through the room, not quite a noise this time but a perceptible reaction nonetheless. The High Lady briefly looked sidelong at her husband. *This is confirming what they already feared,* Tokage realized.

The High Lord himself did not react except to say, "And my honorable brother?"

Amano bowed a third time. "The most honorable Tora Saneda took his own life."

This time the reaction was audible. Tora Arinobu clenched his fists and lowered his head, hiding his reaction. The High Lord's son rose to his feet, his pinched face gone loose with anger he could no longer control. "You expect us to believe my honorable uncle would kill himself without my most honorable father's permission?"

"Apologies, but I can only report what I saw," Amano repeated, his voice unwavering. "I cannot say what honorable Tora Saneda's reasons were, for he did not tell them to us."

The Tiger heir's face flushed, his voice rising almost to a shout. "Do you take us for children or simpletons?"

The High Lord lifted his fan slightly. "Enough, Giichi."

The rebuke was enough to make his son's face go from red to white. Tora Giichi gulped and bowed. "I apologize for my terrible manners. I allowed my grief to overcome my Honor."

"I offer my apologies as well," Amano replied smoothly. "I have no wish for my words to cause offense or distress, most honorable Tora. What happened is as much a mystery to us as to you."

"If you cannot explain this, why are you here?"

Tokage smothered a laugh, proud that he showed nothing save a tightening of his face. *As if we could just leave! Your Lord Handen would probably have arrested us, and you surely know it. Though… the people here might* not *realize that,* he reflected, looking sidelong at the courtiers in their floor-length robes and powdered faces and precise poses. *Not nearly so many of them as there would be in Castle Ookami,* he admitted grudgingly. In fact, now that he paid attention, he realized the number of people in attendance was actually rather low for the size of the chamber. *How many have already fled?*

Amano answered without hesitation. "Our High Lord devoutly shares your hope of an alliance against the barbarians. With that threat now even greater than before, it would be wholly dishonorable for us to abandon the task he set us." He paused, and when the High Lord did not immediately speak into the gap he continued: "Is it permitted to ask more about the barbarian threat? We encountered some of their atrocious raids during our journey here, but we have no other information."

Nicely done, turning the conversation, Tokage thought. *Now the High Lord will be answering us, instead of the other way around.*

Lord Iesada had realized it as well, his mouth tightening with irritation. Before he could speak, however, the doors that had slid shut behind Amano and Tokage opened once more. A soft rustle went through the room as all the courtiers shifted, trying to see who was entering without actually doing anything so undignified as craning their necks.

The man who came in was in light armor, a small banner tied to the backplate displaying the crests of the Tiger and of one of their noble houses – Tokage recognized it as one he'd seen on some of the courtiers in the hall. He hurried forward, panting hard but trying to control it; although he had removed his sandals like everyone else, his armor and calf-snugged leggings showed dust and dirt, some of it sprinkling on the floor-mats, and Tokage suddenly found himself imaging some servant in a far corner flinching at the desecration.

The newcomer dropped to his knees, pressing one fist to the floor. The body language of a soldier in the field reporting to his commander, rather than a petitioner in court. "Most honorable High Lord! I beg your forgiveness for this intrusion! I bring a message from Lord Matsuba!"

The High Lord nodded, his face now altogether still. "Speak."

The man gulped, took a breath. "The battle has been joined!"

⛩ ⛩ ⛩

TOMOE TROTTED ACROSS A CARPET of bodies, her lips skinned back from her teeth in a predator's grin. The sight of each body, the feel of the corpses' flesh under the soles of her boots, sent jolts of warmth through her. She knew some of that was the Lords, glorying through her senses in the destruction they had unleashed, pulsating with glee at seeing so many lives ended in pain and squalor. But her own feral joy mingled with theirs until they could not be told apart.

She came to the crest of a swell in the landscape, walking through torn and trampled grass, grass that was stained with blood and sprouted arrows in massive clumps. An irregular line of corpses lay on and beyond the crest – samurai bodies, skewered with a dozen or more arrows apiece. A few tribesmen were scuttling around pulling arrows from the ground and the bodies with uncaring equality, stuffing the usable shafts back into their quivers; they broke off staring as she passed them, then groveled and whimpered as they sensed the Lords' power within her.

Tomoe did not have any escort with her, no banners or chieftains or shamans. Those were moving forward in small groups, each pushing one of the major tribes ahead of them with the sacred banners of Dakkurru. Those banners and their writhing decorations whipping the warriors back into frenzy whenever their advance faltered. Tomoe knew the Other was with one of those groups, probably the one with most of the Empire-born Mask sorcerers. Ready for the Lord to use her whenever needed, but so far that had not been necessary – the sheer numbers of the tribesmen, and their eagerness to both kill and die, had been enough to drive the samurai army back.

And now the scum aren't just fallin' back, they're breakin'. Tomoe had never been at a battle, knew nothing of how they were fought, but even she could see that the distant lines of samurai were no longer a cohesive army. Some large blocks of soldiers remained intact, throwing off flashing reflections from swords and spear-heads as they clashed with attacking tribesmen, or spewing waves of white-fletched arrows at more distant enemies. But the gaps between the formations were larger, and her sight – sharpened by the Lords who used it – picked out the flutter of orange-black back-banners on hundreds of men running away, the vaunted samurai courage breaking under the weight of defeat.

The heart of the Tiger army was still intact, though, crouched on a low hill a mile away. A larger banner rose there, a great vertical rectangle of orange silk with a snarling Tiger's face above the calligraphy for "Tora" and, below that, a symbol made by three triangles joined at their corners to make a larger triangle. *Some Lord's symbol, probably t'commander,* Tomoe thought, feeling a surge of hatred and contempt that was not wholly born from Dakkurru. *T'nobles in their castles, lookin' down on all of us like we're vermin.*

The old Wolf Lord, his face expressionless: *Let her be beaten, and placed into stocks.*

Some of the Tiger army was rallying to their commander, groups of men shifting left or right to join the core who were probably the Lord's personal retainers. Other formations continued to fall back, retreating toward the distant castle. *It's a delayin' action,* Tomoe suddenly knew, the understanding imposed on her thoughts by those who used her eyes. *The Lord is standin' ground t'draw t'tribesmen on himself, so t'rest of t'army can withdraw to their damned castle.* And it was working, too; the tribesmen's natural aggression combined with the battle-frenzy imposed by Dakkurru made them concentrate on visible opposition, and they swarmed toward that defiant banner. Even the chieftains and shamans were heading toward it, driven to rage by the continued samurai resistance.

Tomoe felt the same rage, but overriding it was a sense of furious impatience, the fury of Dakkurru at humanity itself, at the endless thwarting stupidity of even the most loyal servants. The castle of the Tiger lay before them, the stronghold of the Clan that had withstood the tribesmen for decades, and mortal idiocy would hold them back from it yet again...

She quickened her pace, stepping lightly over the scattered bodies, closing the distance toward that insolently fluttering banner. She could hear the sounds now, the ring and screech of steel, the ripping-cloth sound of hundreds of arrows in flight, the roar of men shouting in rage and fear, the shrieks of the wounded. The air reeked of blood and voided bowels.

Arrows rippled down out of the sky, the white eagle feathers flashing red in the smoke-darkened afternoon Sunlight. Tomoe broke into a sprint, her long sword in her left hand and slashing blinding-swift at the arrows that fell too closely. That was a trick she had seen a few sellswords pull off as entertainment, earning a few coins from gawkers on the street, but she had never imagined it was a real thing that could be done in a real fight; now she did it without thinking, her body moving with the superhuman speed the Lords had granted her even before she became their vessel.

The arrow-barrage had stalled the latest attack from the tribesmen, their battle-fury momentarily overwhelmed by the shock of sudden casualties. She ran past them, vaulting over the still-writhing bodies they had left behind when they recoiled, and now she was all alone between the lines. In front of her was an unbroken line of samurai, their orange-black lacquered armor gleaming even through the dust and blood-splatter of battle. Spear-points thrust toward her, foot-long razor edged blades on eight-foot shafts, half of them blood-soaked; behind the forest of edged metal she could see scores of faces, clenched and bestial in the absolute intensity of combat. She felt the Lords within her, seething with hatred and disgust for all of miserable, crawling, breeding, excreting humanity, and her own hatred burned along with theirs, a hatred that could never be quenched.

Tomoe flung her left hand forward, and Dakkurru's hatred boiled out, an arcing blaze of blue-green fire, greater than before, as great as the Other could do, agonizing and glorious as it coursed through her flesh, the pain rising until she thought her body would be torn apart. Men screamed as their eyeballs melted and their armor fused into their flesh. Burning bodies tumbled into the grass, igniting it in puffs of yellow-orange light and black smoke. Tomoe screamed and laughed, wild and shrill, then choked on the smoke and staggered to a halt, coughing and weeping and laughing, still laughing, as the green flames finally guttered out. For a moment she did not want to look at her hand, convinced it had been torn apart by the power forced though her flesh, but then the thought vanished from her mind so completely she did not remember having it. She laughed again, more ragged now, and walked through the smoking ruins of the Tiger's front line, flames from the burning landscape licking at her boots and leggings, blackened flesh crunching beneath her feet to release blood that steamed into vapor.

The great banner still stood, though drunkenly slanted, and armored men clustered around its base. *Just far enough away t'fire didn't reach 'em,* Tomoe thought, and the thought mingled anger with gleeful anticipation. *There you are, samurai lord, in your fancy armor. Can't help showin' yourselves off,* neh*?*

The nobleman was unmistakable, his elaborate armor a display of station that was also a challenge to any foe who might approach. Huge plates projected from his shoulders and hips, and the front of his breastplate was embossed with a brightly-colored snarling Tiger's face. A similar snarl was on the iron war-mask that covered the lower half of his face, while the top of his helmet displayed a pair of upward-curving horns with a flat disk mounted between them, decorated with the same triple-triangle crest as on the banner above.

He still had a few guards around him, two of them trying to hold up the banner – the original bannermen lay writing in the half-scorched grass – and a third man with a long-bladed spear, looking around for threats. He spotted Tomoe and his eyes widened. "My Lord, beware!" His voice wavered slightly, and Tomoe knew he was afraid of her… but infuriatingly, he did not run, instead positioning himself between her and his liege, both hands tight on the haft of his spear. The long, slightly-curved blade angled up toward her.

"Out of my way, excrement," Tomoe called. She lifted her sword in a loose grip and let it wobble back and forth, shifting her wrist each time it threatened to overbalance. "I'm here for t'big man, not you. Run away and maybe you'll live out t'day." She laughed. "I know you want to!"

"I do not fear to die for my Lord!" the man shouted, his voice high and almost shrill. The nobleman stepped up alongside him, drawing his own long sword, his dark eyes steady. The two samurai shared a brief glance, an exchange of resolve between Lord and vassal.

The sight infuriated her, her and those within her, and she felt one of the Lords rise above the others, focusing its hatred through her flesh. Her mouth moved, forming words, though she did not know what they would be until she spoke them.

"YOU… WILL… SUBMIT."

She gagged and staggered, her throat burning, her head suddenly throbbing as though she had drunk ten bottles of wine. The two men let out screams as they dropped to their knees, their swords thumping into the grass, dropped from strengthless fingers. Tomoe straightened up, her grin returning as the shock of pain retreated and gave way to hot joy. She stepped forward casually, flexing her fingers around her sword-hilt and then lifting the blade to rest its blunt back edge on her shoulder.

"Scary not t'be on top of things, *neh*? Not so much fun without your pet spirits t'slow us down." Her voice rasped in her ravaged throat, but she didn't care. The helpless terror in their staring eyes was better than any wine.

She flicked the sword down in a sharp arc and the soldier's head came off, spinning away in a spray of blood as his body toppled sideways and lay twitching and voiding in the grass. The nobleman's eyes, now weak with tears, flickered from the fallen corpse to Tomoe's face, and his mouth worked wordlessly, trying to ask: *What are you?*

Tomoe slid the point of her blade into his throat, slowly, watching the blood well up in his mouth and then spill out and down, watching his body shake and his eyes roll back. "Ah," she sighed. *And that's fine, and it'll be more fine when I do it t'the Wolf Lord, and t'Kenji,* she thought, for once the thoughts entirely her own. *But I'll take more time with them.* She whipped the sword free and the noble toppled forward, the helmet's elaborate horns brushing the side of her leg.

Tomoe looked around and felt her grin return. The nobleman's force had been shattered by the impact of Dakkurru's power, the solid line broken into isolated fragments, clusters of men trying desperately to stay alive as the tribesmen overran them. The more distant formations were in full retreat, trying to stay ahead of pursuit until they could reach the distant castle.

And t'castle won't help 'em, she thought hungrily, starting forward once more but then flinching and stumbling as a fresh wave of pain went through her body. Her grin turned into a tooth-gritting grimace of anger – not her own anger but that of Dakkurru, angry at the limitations of her feeble mortal body. They would have to rely on the Other when they attacked the castle, she knew, while her body recovered from the strain of channeling so much of their power.

CHAPTER 10

PRIESTESS REI COUGHED AND wiped at her eyes, blinking against the painful tang of the smoke, then lifted one tattered sleeve-end and tried to blot them clear, her other hand clutching her staff for balance. The smoke in the north had grown worse all day as they had trudged eastward with the rest of the Wolf samurai, but now the air itself had acquired a hazy note and the Sun was an ugly orange as it descended in the west. The individual columns of smoke rising on the horizon were no longer distinguishable from each other, reducing the whole skyline to a churning gray-black that gradually smeared into muddy blue overhead. Rei wasn't sure, but she thought the smoke might actually be worse up here in the great castle's upper levels than it had been down at ground level.

She would have preferred to be inside the barracks where the rest of the Wolf samurai and servants had been quartered, but Kenji had insisted on coming out here as soon as they finished the simple meal of rice and vegetables and bean-curd. He wanted to see what was happening north of the city.

He stood now by the northern-most corner of the village-sized rectangular platform, leaning forward and bracing himself with one hand on the six-foot-tall carved stone tiger mounted on the corner itself. Rei thought there was a resemblance between the granite beast's snarling face and Kenji's own tooth-clenched glare. The smoke didn't seem to bother him much, aside from the occasional cough; he stayed unmoving, staring fixedly into the distance.

Rei had positioned herself a few paces back, next to one of the trees – this one a fir – that dotted the castle, sprouting from between the paving flagstones. The foliage seemed to cut a little of the smoke, and putting her back to the Sun-warmed bark felt somehow comforting in this place of ancient stone and armored men. *It must have been a great deal of work to bring trees up here and replant them… no, wait, I'm being foolish, they must have planted little saplings when they first built this place long ago.* She was no expert on such things, but even her limited knowledge from her days in the Temple School and the Imperial City told her the stonework of this castle dated back to the time of the Emperors.

"Kenji," she called, raising her voice a little more than she needed to because he seemed so focused. He glanced at her briefly, then turned back north. "What do you see?"

"It's a battle," he said. "Not just samurai, though. The other side, they're different… must be like those foreigners we fought at the shrine."

"The barbarians." She said the words uncertainly, as though trying out how they sounded. The Temple School had spent countless hours teaching the young acolytes about the history of the Empire, but barely mentioned the primitive tribes who lived beyond the northern border. She did recall that they were supposedly Demon-worshippers, which was only to be expected of such backwards people. How could they be here, inside the Empire, and in such numbers? "Is that where the… the darkness is?"

Kenji nodded. "It's… it's strong," he muttered. "Stronger than anything I've ever…" He broke off and shook his head. "Samurai're losing. They're falling back, see?" He swung out one arm to point.

Rei squinted. Yes, she could see lines and clumps of men coming closer, up the roads and across the fields. And down below, where the wall and moat marked the edge of the city…

"Oh, Amatsu have mercy," she whispered, and started to recite a mantra.

When she and the rest of the Wolf Clan party had arrived at midday there had already been hundreds of refugees outside the city's north side, with smaller numbers trickling around to the other gates or past the city toward the south. Now there were thousands, the land black with them, clustering not only at the northern gate but also the western one. *And probably the southern gate as well, if I could see it.* Word of the army's defeat must have just arrived, because the clotted masses of people had gone into chaotic motion. Some rushed forward, desperate to get inside, and she could see tiny black shapes tumbling off the edges of the moat and bridge. Others sought with equal desperation to flee, sending shockwaves left and right through the crowds. Rei thought she could hear them even at this height, a cacophony of fear and rage and despair.

"It'll get worse when the samurai get here," Kenji said, his tone almost observational. "They'll cut through that crowd to get to the gate... if the enemy doesn't catch up with 'em." He shaded his eyes, then muttered a curse and wiped them on his sleeve. "Damned smoke... Some of 'em are already close, see there?"

Rei looked where he pointed, but she couldn't understand what she was seeing. Everywhere was now motion, ant-tiny people, flowing toward the city or away from it. "What happens when the enemies reach here?"

"Dunno... I guess they try to break in?" Kenji grinned suddenly, rolling his shoulders and opening and closing his hands. "And then I get to kill 'em. Which is what I came here for, *neh*?" He glanced at her and scowled. "What? That's what your damned Lady wants me to do, or She wouldn't be showing me where they are."

He's not really a samurai, Rei reminded herself. *He doesn't even know much about war.* Not that she knew much either, but even her limited education in the Temple School had talked about sieges and how often they figured in wars. *We'll be trapped in here, and there won't be enough food, especially if they let a lot of those poor people inside, and...* Her chest tightened until she thought she would choke. *Fear is a sin,* she reminded herself, trying to imagine Priestess Jun's voice saying the words. *And if I die here, the Lady will surely find my soul worthy of Her compassion after all that has happened... surely?*

The Sun sank toward the horizon, throwing strange garish hues into the smoke-shrouded sky. A terrible chaos now reigned at the gate, blocks of samurai forcing their way into the crowd just as Kenji had predicted, others forming lines behind them to hold off the enemy. She could see the difference now: the samurai in their bright armor, moving in a way that seemed familiar even from this height and distance, the barbarians a disordered brown-black clutter that ebbed and flowed like water. Orange flicks in the air marked arrows catching the Sun as they flew back and forth, hundreds of arrows, making it look like a great swarm of fireflies hovered above the clashing armies.

She glanced at Kenji, who was still leaning out over the edge of the platform, gripping the statue for balance. "Should you... I mean, you could go down there?"

"You think I could get close? I'd have to go through a dozen gates between here and the city, and these stupid damned samurai... Cats, Tigers, whatever they are... won't let anyone in or out now, not with everything going wrong." He gave Rei a half-accusing look. "We should've just ditched these stupid Wolf samurai once we got here and headed out on our own."

Trying to make it my fault, Rei thought resentfully. *He really is just like a child sometimes.* She frowned, trying to find words to express an uncertain thought. "Kenji… if you showed them the Lady's Light, surely they'd do whatever you wished."

He scowled at her. "You think it's that easy? Like pouring a drink?"

She felt her face flushing and looked away, gripping her staff more tightly. *Why does he still upset me so easily? Why was I so angry that he ran ahead to fight those barbarians? I should be used to all his nonsense by now.* The worst of it was that he was right, she did not understand how his… power, gift, whatever it was… actually worked. "Apologies, I should not have spoken out of ignorance," she said tightly, keeping her gaze turned resolutely toward the Sunset.

By apologizing so completely she had shifted the burden of shame onto him, and even someone as crude and ill-mannered as Kenji understood that. He cleared his throat, sounding uncomfortable, and she waited to see if for once he might actually apologize.

Instead he let out a sharp grunt. "Excrement!"

In the same instant something flickered in the corner of her eye, painfully bright. *Lightning*, she thought, and then in confusion: *But it's not storming, and the light was* below *me!*

She looked down at the city gate and let out a gasp.

The gate was gone. In its place was an expanding cloud of gray smoke, shot through with dark spots and flickers of blue-green light. It bubbled into the city, rolling across streets and houses, tiled roofs and window-panels smashing as it swept over them.

It took her a moment to realize the darker blots tumbling through the air were human bodies, wooden beams, and man-sized pieces of stone.

A wave of air slammed into her, making her step back, squint her eyes, and clutch her staff with both hands. With it came a thunderclap so loud it felt like a physical blow on her ears. Her head rang and her vision went blurry. A sickening sense of nausea churned in her belly.

When she could see clearly again, the smoke-cloud was drifting away to the east and the last of the debris was falling, hundreds of paces away in the city. She thought everything had gone silent, and then Kenji swore again and she realized her ears were deafened; his voice came to her as though through ten layers of silk, mushy and formless.

The samurai on the outside of the gate were gone as though they had never been. All she could see was a solid wave of brown-black foreigners, sweeping across the bridge and through the smoldering gap where the gate and towers had stood.

Kenji caught her arm and jerked her back from the edge of the parapet. His mouth moved, and she puzzled out his shouted words through the ringing in her ears. "City's lost. This place too, if they do that again."

She groped for words. Her own voice sounded strange, faint and hollow, as though it was echoing inside her head. "What… what was that?"

"It's them. The Demons." He was dragging her across the stone-flagged parade ground toward the gate that led down to the lower city. With his head turned away she could barely make out his words. "Come on, we gotta get you out of here. Can't fight if I have to worry about you."

A part of Rei's mind was responding to his words as she had been taught: *My life is not important, I live only for others, as the Goddess' Compassion demands.* Another part was trying to process his words: *The first thing he thought about was to protect me. So why did he leave me behind in the woods?*

She shook off the welter of emotions and pulled up short, her unexpected resistance momentarily halting him as well. *I am a Priestess, I must remember my duty.* "We have to get the others," she declared. "Honorable Tokage and his men."

He stared back at her. "Those scum? Why?"

The reversion to his usual selfishness swept away her momentary confusion and replaced it with disgusted outrage. She yanked her arm free of his grip and took hold of her staff with both hands once more, shaking it at him. "Because they are honorable men, and I did not work to save their wounded back in the Aelfynn lands just to see them be killed by Demons here!"

He glared at her, then threw up his hands. "Fine! Don't blame me if you end up dead for them!"

⛩ ⛩ ⛩

SOMETHING IS HAPPENING, OOKAMI AKIRA thought. He could feel it, a prickling all along his nerves, as though he was standing in the midst of a thunderstorm.

The actual weather was warm, the evening sky clear except for a few thin streaks of cloud. The Sunset was startlingly colorful, the western horizon turning a rich golden-red that dyed those few narrow clouds in a mingling of orange and purple. The light lent that same garish tone to the thousands of tents that spread across the Kiirokusa Plain to the limits of sight, and to the thin spirals of smoke rising from hundreds of cooking fires. The air smelled of burning charcoal and boiling rice, of human and animal sweat, of dung from horses and oxen, and faintly of human excrement from the latrine ditches on the southern edge of the plain. All the odors of an army in the field.

His army had been encamped on the plain for five days, collecting stragglers and bringing in supply convoys from Lord Toshiwara's position astride the River of Blue Silk twenty miles to the northeast. In that time the Jade Dragon army at Shinku, forty miles to the west, had not moved. Kitaro's scouts confirmed that it was still gaining reinforcements.

Akira knew Kitaro was surprised they had waited here rather than immediately advancing on the enemy. It went against Akira's demonstrated style of campaigning, especially since the Jade Dragon army was continuing to grow in strength while they waited.

Though no reinforcements flying the Kiyogama crest, Kitaro's scouts had confirmed. And they had also delivered another message this afternoon, one Akira had been awaiting ever since he ordered Kitaro to send men north of the River of Blue Silk.

Which made it time to deliver fresh orders.

Akira looked to his left, at the silk-walled pavilion where his officers were gathering. Servants had lit braziers and hung lanterns from bamboo poles within, and in the gathering twilight the silk already glowed with their illumination. Most of the commanders would already be there, but Akira was waiting for the arrival of Lord Toshiwara and his companions, riding down from their position astride the river. He wanted everyone present before he spoke. And in the meantime...

Something is happening, Akira thought again. *Does it have to do with Lord Noboru?* He was sure by now that the High Lord of the Jade Dragon was allied with the Demon-worshippers, both the Cult of the Mask here in the Empire and the barbarians assailing the northern frontier. *No, it feels... too strong, but distant. It feels like...*

Like that night I dreamed about Satsuki.

For a terrible moment his mind was unraveling, a festering knot of suppressed rage and grief breaking loose with irresistible force. He shut his eyes, reciting the mantras the Monks of War had drilled into him in his youth, seeking the void of meditation. Slowly, slowly he fought his way back to control, bound the emotions once more in the chains of duty and discipline.

Noise intruded on his senses: the whinny and hoof-clopping of horses, a brabble of cheerful voices. He opened his eyes and saw men dismounting by the pavilion, walking inside to be greeted and toasted by the others awaiting them. The light showed him armor of dull red and pale gray, and the triple-crosshatch crest of the Toshiwara family. *Time to begin,* he thought, cold and self-controlled once more, as a commander had to be.

His manservant Kaito was waiting next to the pavilion, holding a tray stacked with folded papers. He bowed silently as Akira approached, then fell in behind to follow him inside. Kaito had been with him since the campaign in the Nightingale lands four years before; the old man knew Akira better than anyone else.

The pavilion did not have the traditional table set up down the middle, nor the drinks that were usually supplied for the men to offer endless toasts. Akira had halted that nightly ritual during the campaign against the rebels last summer, using supply shortages as his excuse, and then simply not resumed it. *They can drink after we win a victory*, he thought. The Third Emperor had written about that: *Men will accept the harshest discipline before battle, or as punishment for failure. But success must be rewarded, or soldiers' hearts will turn sour and they will abandon Honor for bitterness.*

The men sat on folding camp-stools, or cross-legged on mats laid on the grass. Lord Toshiwara and his companions had just chosen their own places but were not yet seated, still shaking out the cramps of their long ride from their limbs. Servants passed around the pavilion, offering tea and rice-balls. They spotted Akira first, pausing in their labors to bow low; a moment later all the officers and nobles were doing the same.

Lord Toshiwara Ryohei had been the first among the older generation of Wolf Clan nobles to demonstrate the same loyalty to Akira as to his late father, High Lord Okaro; that loyalty had won him admission to Akira's inner circle of followers, trusted to independently command the one-third of the army currently besieging Castle Kosaten and holding the head of the supply line at the River of Blue Silk. In former times, such favor to a particular Lord might have bred resentment and dissension, but Akira had killed most of the noblemen who behaved in such ways and cowed the rest into submission.

Two of those present were in that latter category. Lord Musume Noriyuki, Lord of Castle Kage, had joined the rebellion last year – albeit reluctantly, or so he claimed – and had saved himself only by switching sides again and then mercilessly exterminating the rebel Akabe family. Even so, his eldest son and only grandchildren were back in Castle Ookami as hostages to his good behavior. His face was impassive behind his long beard, watching and listening quietly.

Lord Ito Kyogo was the young leader of a Makoto vassal family that held lands south of the now-razed Castle Jushin. His father Tsuguru had saved the family from extermination by turning on the Makoto, killing his own superiors within the Ito, and handing over the lead of Akira's stepsister Oroko as proof of their sincerity. His own family, and those of most senior men in the Ito family, were still hostages in Castle Ookami even today.

Akira had never been able to do the meaningless introductory talk that samurai, especially noblemen, used to start every conversation; his feeble attempts had only drawn mockery. He began abruptly: "Tomorrow I will accompany Lord Toshiwara on his return to the northern force." Men blinked or went wide-eyed, a few of them physically shifting as though they'd been struck. He ignored that and forged ahead: "These are your written orders." Old Kaito began walking down the length of the pavilion, bowing low and presenting a folded paper to each of the senior commanders.

He watched while they unfolded and read the papers, watched some among them as he would watch an opponent in a duel, looking for hesitations, for the subtle weakness that would mark fear or deceit. He was not concerned about the men he had appointed, and only mildly attentive to Lord Shinsen, who had proven himself reliable in the last two years and showed no disquiet now. His focus was on those who remained from the older noble lines of the Clan – Lord Musume, Lord Shinsen, Lord Kuroi, and their subordinates from the major vassal families like the Ojima and Fuse.

As he'd expected, all of them gave off subtle hints of unhappiness, but none showed dangerous signs – at least not that he could detect. *Lord Katsura always was unreadable,* Akira remembered. *Maybe it was for the best that Kaede had him assassinated.* That thought was… unsettling, and he mentally shook himself and continued: "Until I return, the army here will be commanded by honorable General Chujitsuna Nomi."

Chujitsuna Nomi slowly bowed acknowledgement of the order slowly, his lined face calm but shifting his shoulders like a man preparing to lift a heavy weight. "As you command, honorable High Lord, it shall be done." He was the oldest man in the pavilion, his jowls gray despite obviously being freshly shaved, a crippled arm tied to his chest. A minor landholder in a vassal family, he had been a mere captain in Akira's first army four years ago, but had proven himself as reliable as the Sunrise. He stood next to two of his chief subordinates, Tokaze Seikichi and Fuwa Hiroshige, themselves both promoted from even lower ranks in that same army.

Akira continued to watch the nobles. They were surprised and somewhat offended by his choice of commander, but hid it well. Men of ancient lineage would not be accustomed to serving under the command of an ordinary samurai like Nomi, no matter what appointed rank he might possess.

A brief silence then, all the men still coming to terms with his announcements. Akira's men, accustomed by now to him giving strange orders, looked calm and confident; the rest seemed uneasy. After a moment Lord Kuroi Hisahiro glanced around, cleared his throat, rose and bowed respectfully. "Most honorable High Lord. We will of course obey your orders. However… I do not see anything here about what we are to do if the Jade Dragon should advance on us."

Akira could see that even some of his own loyalists had been wondering the same thing. "High Lord Noboru is currently outnumbered. It would be very unwise for him to advance."

Lord Shinsen chuckled. "In other words, if he's stupid enough to attack us now, we don't need the honorable High Lord to hold our hands while we crush him."

Laughter echoed through the pavilion, and then Kado Kitaro jumped up and shouted: "The Lady with us!" They all joined in repeating the cheer the traditional three times, even the doubtful men shouting as loud as the rest... except one.

The odd man out sat alone in the far corner of the pavilion, sipping from a teacup. He was a short, bandy-legged fellow with a smooth-shaven head and skin that showed the dark tone of a weather-roughened peasant, though his muscles and thick wrists and the callouses on his hands marked him as a swordsman. He watched the scene with a thoughtful, slightly bemused expression, as though he did not quite believe what was happening.

Akira looked directly at him. "Honorable General Akiyama. Do you have anything to add?"

The others had been carefully ignoring the former Jade Dragon up until now, and several of them looked briefly startled that Akira was drawing attention to him, then schooled their features back into proper calm.

The former general's eyes widened and he let out a snorted half-laugh. He was not so skilled at hiding his emotions as men who had been samurai their whole laughs. "You think I can give you advice? Amatsu's mercy, boy, you beat us when we had you outnumbered. You don't need my help to beat us when we're on the short end of the stick."

"You were a leader of the Jade Dragon Clan's military forces," Akira reminded him. "You may know things we do not, see things we cannot."

Akiyama looked into his teacup. "And you expect me to just tell you..."

Someone muttered angrily, low enough to avoid losing face. Akira's voice remained flat. "You already betrayed Lord Noboru. Your only hope now is my own victory."

The former general threw back the tea, swallowed, shrugged. "There's not much to say that you haven't already. I'd guess that Lord Noboru is holding position at Shinku because he's waiting for the Bear Clan to come to his assistance."

That brought a response, a round of murmurs and shifting postures, hastily stilled.

Akiyama smirked, then continued: "Also, maybe, to see if any of his recalcitrant Lords finally give in and join him. The longer he waits, the more pressure on them. Especially once the Bear arrive."

"Honorable Akiyama's assessment is the same as my own," Akira declared. "Honorable Nomi, so long as the Jade Dragon remain at Shinku, you will hold position and use honorable Kitaro's cavalry to maintain observation of them. Notify me at once if Lord Noboru receives any reinforcements."

Nomi cleared his throat. "I shall, my Lord. If it is permitted to ask... How long do you expect to be with Lord Toshiwara's forces?"

Which was as close as anyone would dare get to asking why Akira was leaving and what he planned to do.

"I do not know. At least a week, possibly more." Akira waited a beat, then looked around the pavilion once more, focusing on each man in turn. *They will obey,* he thought. *Some are unhappy, but none are enemies. Not this night.* He had learned the hard way that such assessments were only temporary, at least among the old nobility… and if the books at the Monastery of War were accurate, it had always been thus. Even the Emperors had faced disloyalty.

Kitaro had been rereading his orders while the others talked. "Honorable High Lord, you are talking over half the cavalry with you. Honorable Shungo is a brave and capable man, but, apologies, he has never commanded so large a force…" He trailed off, oddly uncertain.

Akira had already considered the question, of course. Tamashiro Shungo had been one of Kitaro's subordinates during the civil war last year, and currently led the relatively small forces patrolling north of the River of Blue Silk. It was true he had never commanded more than a thousand men, but…

"Honorable Shungo will be operating under my direct supervision," he said. "I do not anticipate a problem."

Kitaro seemed almost to flinch, covering it with a low bow. "Of course, honorable High Lord. Forgive me for questioning your orders." Akira wondered why he was reacting this way. There was no hint of disloyalty in him, but it was unusual for him to ask such a question.

"Relax, honorable Kitaro," Lord Hajime Soto called from across the row of chairs. "Honorable Lady Miyu won't break off the betrothal just because Shungo wins the glory this time rather than you!"

A gust of companionable male laughter went around the pavilion. Kitaro smiled while flushing with embarrassment. "At least I've found a wife, honorable Soto," he replied. "You're a Lord with your own castle and still don't have one!"

Soto shrugged, holding out his cup to the nearest servant with a teapot. "Plenty of time for that after we've crushed the Jade Dragons. Maybe one of those high-and-mighty Lords will want to save his bloodline with a marriage, *neh*?" More laughter, the tone of the meeting shifting as men sensed that the serious business was over.

They may end up doing toasts after all, Akira thought, feeling suddenly tired.

General Akiyama stood, holding out his own teacup for a refill. "Honorable Lord Akira, since you permitted questions… I have one."

The jovial atmosphere drained away, all of the Wolf Clan men looking at the defector with cool hostility. He ignored it, which spoke well of his courage.

Akira considered denying him, and then wondered if that would make him look weak. Akiyama took his silence as assent. "You don't need me to tell you Lord Noboru's intentions. Why am I really here?"

An almost subvocal mutter from the others, a soft rumble of anger at the former Jade Dragon samurai's disrespect. Akira looked at Akiyama measuringly, trying to sense if there was a malign purpose behind the question. *He is a capable man. As he should be, to have risen so high from such humble beginnings.* The histories he had studied so intently at the Monastery of War had contained a handful of stories about such men, individuals of such drive and skill and cunning that they could overcome the massive barriers of the Empire's class system. They were not always admirable men, but they were always formidable ones.

If I answer him, I have to tell the others. Is it time? He shut his eyes, focusing himself inward, letting the void of meditation take over while his mind processed the meeting, weighed and measured each man's words and spirit. It was harder than it usually was, because the distraction was still there, lurking beneath thought, the buzzing uneasy certainty that *something is happening...*

He opened his eyes and looked at Kaito. "The map."

The manservant bowed and hurried out of the pavilion. Akira turned back to the general. "Honorable Akiyama. You are here to take command of the Jade Dragon troops after Lord Noboru is dead."

Akiyama blinked, opened his mouth, almost laughed aloud but stopped himself.

Lord Toshiwara nodded slowly. "Lords may swear allegiance to a new liege after their Clan is destroyed – it has happened before. But such families often do not find a comfortable home in their new Clan. Their loyalty is suspect, even after generations have passed, like the Toride." The Toride family had originally been from the Hawk Clan before joining the Wolf. Four years ago they had rebelled against the reunification of the Black and Gray Wolves, and Akira's father Lord Okaro had been forced to wage an expensive campaign to crush them.

Akira could see the confusion on his own men's faces, even his trusted inner circle, the questions boiling underneath their barely-controlled faces. Several of them looked sidelong at Lord Musume. *They wonder why I would show mercy to an enemy Clan after crushing Lady Yumiko's rebels,* Akira knew. And in truth, he knew that if this was just a war between samurai he would be as ruthless with the Jade Dragon as he was with those rebels.

Kaito returned, holding a rolled-up paper and a folding table. He set up the table in between the rows of chairs and rolled out the map atop it. A few of Akira's inner circle – Kitaro, Soto, Nomi – let out soft grunts as they recognized it: a map of the Empire they had used to plan campaigns, back in the sub-basement records chamber of Castle Ookami.

Akira looked down at it for a moment. "Lord Noboru is our enemy, but he is not the true enemy, just an ally of that enemy." He pointed north, to the

Tiger lands, to Lord Tamiya's province of his own Clan. "The barbarians, the Demon worshippers."

"Ah!" Kado Kitaro exclaimed. "That is why you sent Kondo back north, with those orders." Soto and Nomi nodded in understanding. The old comrades had spent the winter together, and Kondo had spoken at length about the barbarian attacks on the borderlands.

"The barbarians have already overrun the northern Tiger lands." Half-smothered exclamations from some of the men in the room – none of them knew that secret, which the Tiger emissaries had shared last winter in strictest confidence. "The Empire is weak, broken. The barbarians will destroy us if we remain so."

Toshiwara's face changed slowly, realization dawning. "You knew this last winter. That is why you spoke of the Imperial City..."

That drew actual exclamations from the majority there who did not yet know his intentions – Shinsen, Musume, the Kuroi, Kaneda. The middle-aged Kuroi Hisahiro and young Lord Kaneda were so shocked that samurai self-control altogether failed, leaving them briefly open-mouthed and staring. Lord Shinsen smiled after a pause, nodding to himself. Lord Musume tugged at his beard, trying to rebuild his face.

"That is why we will march on the Imperial City after Noboru is defeated!" Kitaro said exultantly, his eyes shining.

Soto interjected caution. "But we have to defeat Noboru... and the Bear Clan combined."

"Do you think we cannot, with Lord Akira leading us?"

A fresh roar of cheers went around the pavilion, men putting down their teacups and calling for wine.

Akira had watched Akiyama through the whole discussion. He could see the thoughts churning behind the general's narrowed eyes, though he could not guess what those thoughts were.

Finally Akiyama nodded, as if to himself. "Yes, I see." He tipped back his teacup, swallowed, and set it on the servant's tray. A faint crooked smile touched his mouth. "I had thought Lord Akurai was the only man strong and cunning and ruthless enough to reunite the Empire. But it seems... perhaps I was wrong."

⛩ ⛩ ⛩

CAPTAIN TOKAGE THOUGHT THE TIGER court had acquired an almost dreamlike atmosphere. The sense of unreality was only made worse by the deepening gloom of evening that turned the upper level of the chamber a dusty orange-red while the main floor dimmed into twilight. Servants went around the walls, lighting candles and setting them inside carved wooden lanterns with yellow-dyed paper panels.

Samurai came in regularly, covered in dust and sweat, while the splendidly dressed and scrupulously clean courtiers watched from behind their fans. The men brought messages from the battle outside the castle – written ones now, rather than shouted aloud, which they conveyed by hurrying to the foot of the High Lord's dais, kneeling, and presenting them in both lands like men offering gifts. Tora Giichi, the High Lord's son, took each letter, read it, and passed it to his father. The High Lord would then apologize to Seneschal Amano, break off their conversation, and read the letter himself before handing it back to his son.

I suppose I should be glad that we're all behaving like a normal court now, instead of the High Lord seeming like he's looking for a chance to execute us. The distracting news of the battle seemed to have drained away much of Tora Iesada's anger, or perhaps simply overwhelmed it with tension and carefully-hidden fear, leaving him to fall back on the comfort of ritual for his discussions with the Wolf Clan Seneschal. Amano, for his part, had taken advantage of this to move the conversation into diplomacy, talking about a potential alliance in the carefully indirect language of the court, all mannered suggestion and unspoken assumptions. The contrast between that and the incoming military couriers grew more jarring with each new arrival.

Unable to do more than vaguely follow the meandering thread of Amano and Iesada's repeatedly interrupted conversation, Tokage focused on not letting his legs cramp up from kneeling for so long and on trying to figure out how the battle outside was progressing. The High Lord himself was maintaining his face well enough now not to give anything away, but his son – in the way of most young men – was having a harder time. From the set of his muscles and the way his face tightened with each message, it was clear the news was bad. The courtiers were picking up on it as well, a subtle tension growing in the air, fans fluttering more often, the smell of nervous sweat becoming more noticeable. No one was going to leave so long as the High Lord remained – to depart without his permission would be an unforgiveable breach of etiquette, the sort of thing that ended with slit bellies – but Tokage suspected many of them desperately wanted to.

For his own part he still found it bewildering that mere barbarians, uncivilized people who did not even bathe, could defeat samurai armies. High Lord Iesada had spoken of "sorcery," but Tokage had no idea what that might mean. *Something like the power the Aelfynn used, before… whatever it was that happened to them? I suppose that would explain why the Tiger relied on the spirits to protect them.* He started to frown, but managed to suppress it. *I thought Lord Akira wanted an alliance with the Tiger to fight the Jade Dragons and to try to make a play for the Throne, but... he did mention the threat from the barbarians, Lady Kaede told us that. Aya and I shrugged that off at the time, but... perhaps he saw farther, more clearly than any of us?*

That was an odd thought, and an unsettling one. Lord Akira was a capable general, but he was a madman, or so everyone said. *Even Lady Kaede said so, and she is his wife!*

Another messenger came in, bowing and hurrying forward, and this time the courtiers could not stop themselves from murmuring aloud. Tokage glanced at the man sidelong and felt a knot of tension grow in his chest. The samurai was not just sweaty and dirty but had bloodstains on his armor, and at least two broken-off arrow-stubs projected from the lacquered plates as well. As soon as Lord Iesada acknowledged him, he rose and hurried forward – no written message this time, he dropped to his knees at the front of the dais and spoke in a low voice, forcing the High Lord and his son to lean forward. Even so, the man was loud enough for the nearest courtiers to catch much of what he said – and Tokage as well, though he was careful not to look like he was eavesdropping.

"—Lord Matsuba pledges his life to buy time for our men to reach the gates—"

Excrement, Tokage thought, with vehemence. He looked sidelong at Seneschal Amano and saw the old man had caught the words as well. A wordless moment of agreement passed between them, and then Amano bowed low – not quite a prostration, but as close as another High Lord's representative would get. "Most honorable High Lord," he said, clear but not too loud. "Perhaps it would be best if this meeting were postponed—"

A thunderclap echoed through the castle, rattling door-panels in their frames, shaking dust from the ceiling. The courtiers murmured and shuffled, one or two of them letting out inadvertent and hastily smothered screams. The messenger fell silent, looking around with an expression that, Tokage realized, mingled fear with grim realization. For his own part Tokage felt only confusion. *The sky was clear when we came in... well, clear except for the smoke. Where did the thunder come from?*

Tora Iesada rose to his feet abruptly. "This court is ended," he announced, taking one sharp stride forward and then pausing as his bulky, confining robes threatened to trip him. Amano rose and bowed smoothly, which Tokage had to admit was impressive after kneeling for so long; his own legs protested bitterly as he stood up, pushing his one hand against his knee in an embarrassing admission of weakness. Fortunately no one was paying attention, the courtiers now all in motion, some leaving the room, others clustering together to discuss what was happening.

"Honorable High Lord," Amano repeated. "Shall we resume this discussion at a later time? We are at your disposal."

Lord Iesada looked at him blankly, then made a sharp gesture with his fan. "Come with me." Another gesture, this time at his family. "You also." He hitched up his robes and strode out of the court chamber as quickly as they allowed, sacrificing dignity for speed; his family crowded close behind him, his wife and daughter hitching up their robes in the same way. Tokage, following with Amano, noted immediately that they took a different and narrower staircase turn than the one for guests coming in, and noted also the escort of servants and guards that rapidly coalesced around them as they ascended to the third floor and then the fourth. The whole castle was suddenly full of moving people, every corridor crowded with tight-faced samurai and panicked servants.

This is what the beginning of a catastrophe looks like, Tokage realized. *This may be the day my life ends.* His lips moved in a silent prayer. *Amatsu, watch over me, and if it is time for me to go to Your judgment, let me die with Honor…*

Servants hurried ahead and knelt to slide open a pair of wooden panels, admitting a wave of outside air heavy with smoke. Beyond was a balcony that stretched around the castle, a three-foot-high wooden railing separating it from the steep slope of the third floor's dark-tiled roof. From here Tokage had a clear view down at the main citadel's village-sized top platform, where he and Amano had eaten and bathed. He noted with half-idle curiosity that there seemed to be an altercation at the entrance to the bridge that connected that level to the keep.

The High Lord turned right, circling around to the north side of the castle, and the rest of them followed. There he stopped, looking down silently. Tokage followed his gaze, frowning as he tried to see through the clouds of smoke and dust roiling across the city. It took him a few moments to realize what he was seeing.

Amatsu have mercy.

There was a huge gap in the city's northern wall, the stone on either side splintered and broken. Arcs of destruction cut through the city within, buildings flattened and on fire. Human shapes poured across the external bridge, through the gap and into the city in an endless dark flood, here and there with banners overhead that flickered with a strange crest Tokage did not recognize. The roar from them had a shape, a rhythm, and after a moment he recognized it:

"Dakkurru! Dakkurru! Dakkurru!"

Amano spoke, and for once his voice had no smooth elegance – it was quavering, uncertain. "Honorable High Lord… What is happening here?"

Tora Iesada did not answer, but his son Giichi spoke, pointing lower. "They've broken the Gate of Flowers. That must have been the second thunderclap."

Tokage followed the pointing arm. One of the ground-level gates into the castle complex was below them, only two hundred paces away but more than twice than distance downward. It too had been smashed, flames shooting up from the broken towers on either side, and he could see the orange-red glitter of metal on blades as hundreds of the barbarians flowed up the switchback ramp beyond. The air hazed with bright streaks above them – arrows, raining down from the defenders in the walls.

"Yes, I see it," Iesada replied bleakly. He straightened and looked down at the fan in his right hand. Tokage was close enough now to see that the fan was painted with an image that entwined the Tora calligraphy with a stylized depiction of one of the western spirits.

"If they were still here…" the High Lord murmured, and then grimaced. With a sharp motion he tossed the fan over the balcony; it flickered once, catching the Sunlight as it passed the edge of the tile roof, and dropped out of sight. Iesada shared a look with his wife, who nodded very slightly. He let out a long breath and turned to the crowd of escorts who had followed him. "Fetch our armor. My son and I shall join the battle against the enemy. And you—" He turned sharply on Arinobu, who had opened his mouth to speak. "You will leave here, and take my daughter Sumiya and grandson Enji with you."

The young man stared stricken, his face going chalk-pale and the scars standing out livid. Then he dropped to his knees, pressing his forehead down between flattened hands. "Honorable uncle, I beg you not to shame me. Let me fight alongside you and honorable Giichi. Let me—"

"Be silent," Lord Iesada snapped, and his nephew's words broke off in a strangled gasp. "You will endure the shame, because while the bloodline lives, the Tiger Clan lives." Without another word he strode past them, around the corner of the keep and back inside. His wife and son followed, not even pausing to speak to their daughter, who stood with a stunned, blank look on her face. Arinobu remained prostrate, forehead pressed to the smooth floorboards of the balcony.

Amano and Tokage shared a look. Tokage cleared his throat. "Honorable Amano, we should go find our men."

Before the Seneschal could reply, a rough voice shouted from below. "*Oi*, you Wolf fellows!"

A young woman's clear voice added more tentatively: "Honorable Captain Tokage?"

What in Amatsu's name…? Tokage circled back to the west side of the castle. Below, the swordsman and his Priestess companion had crossed the bridge and stood just outside the keep's gate; behind them the rest of Tokage's men were gathering on the open ground outside the barracks where they'd been housed. Several men in Tiger armor stood on either side of Kenji with weapons out, shuffling back and forth but unwilling to press an attack home; Kenji had both of his swords in hand, half-casually gesturing with them at the samurai. At the sight of Tokage two levels above, he grinned and called: "Front gate's gone, we better get out of here while there's still a way t'get out. I'd already be gone, but this damned soft-heart," he jerked his head at the Priestess, "said we had t'warn you fellows."

The Priestess glowered at him, then called: "Please, honorable Tokage, the barbarians are inside the city. Surely there would be no shame in departing?"

Ah, clever of her to put it that way, Tokage thought with an inner smile. He looked at Amano, who was now walking alongside young Tora Arinobu as they came around the keep and headed inside. "Honorable Amano?"

The Seneschal looked up and nodded. "Honorable Tora Arinobu is going to fetch his nephew. We will help escort them out of the castle. Assemble our men at once, honorable Tokage."

CHAPTER 11

TOMOE PICKED HER WAY across the bridge, laughing as bodies twitched and groaned beneath her boots. Many of them were tribesmen, but her laughter did not grow any less for that. *You're all excrement on two legs, just like me,* she thought, and beneath that thought coiled the roaring hatred of Dakkurru, hatred for all things that lived. Her body ached with the residual pain of channeling so much of their power, her left arm throbbing from shoulder to fingertips with a pain that reminded her of burns, though when she looked it seemed unharmed on the outside.

The Sun was setting, the vile False Light departing at last, staining the western sky in dark red and orange behind the purple-black haze of distant smoke. The lurid half-light reflected from the surface of the moat on either side of the bridge, showing hundreds of floating corpses and a few men still feebly struggling. The blood which coated the bridge planks, glistening black in the fading light, stuck tackily to her boot-soles. She enjoyed the sensation.

Beneath her enjoyment an unease lurked, a sense of lurking threat too subtle for Dakkurru to care about. She wondered if one of the false spirits had managed to hold onto enough of their stolen power for her to feel it. If so, it would be pleasant to hunt the scum down.

Tribesmen raced past her, scores at a time crossing the bridge to push on into the city, mostly silent save for their panting breath. They shied away from her, so she crossed the bridge alone despite their presence. One of the tribal shamans – she did not know or care which one, they were all interchangeable weapons – trailed behind her, muttering invocations in his own language and rattling his skull-topped staff.

Jagged stone rose on either side – the city walls, shattered like pottery when the Other had unleashed Dakkurru's fire on the gate and the fortification that guarded it. Beyond, flames licked up from the shells of buildings knocked flat by the blast, the light of the fires brighter than the fading Sunlight. Bodies were more widely scattered here, all of them samurai or common folk – many reduced to mangled remnants by the destruction of the gate, others lying where they were cut down or shot by the tribesmen pouring through the gap.

Tomoe paused, no longer laughing but her face still locked in a wide grin, while the endless stream of tribesmen flowed by and scattered deeper into the city, following one or another of the streets that were not blocked by fire and wreckage. Some distant corner of her mind was flinching from the sight of a burning city, remembering fire alarms and panicked crowds in a hundred cities and towns and villages – fire was the great fear in a land where almost all buildings were made of wood and paper. The memories, the weakness they represented, annoyed her, and as she realized that she stopped remembering them at all.

Castle Mouko loomed above the burning city, a multi-leveled citadel connected by ramps and bridges, the keep itself highest of all but closest to her. The walls – sloped rather than straight up, but steep enough that no man could hope to climb them – were bright yellow on their lower levels where they caught the light of the city fires, fading to a dull orange-red higher up where only the fading Sunset touched them. She knew the Other had blasted open one of the gates at the foot of the citadel, and was leading the most aggressive and fanatical of the tribesmen up through the defenses. *She can channel enough power t'do it twice again, and maybe more times yet*, Tomoe knew, with a sense of mingled envy and subtle relief.

She began to walk toward the citadel, ignoring the majority of the tribesman and Brothers ravaging the city. The suffering of the city's thousands of commoners was pleasing, but the torment and death of the samurai in that fortress high above would be far more delicious, and she wanted to be there. Besides, there was still that subtle, uneasy awareness of a lurking threat, a sense that now felt more localized to the citadel itself.

It feels... familiar, she thought suddenly. *Why does it feel familiar?*

THEY WILL NOT ESCAPE.

Her puzzlement was wiped away by the surge of rage that was not her own. Identity and perception vanished beneath the overriding demands of Dakkurru's will.

When she could perceive herself again, she was trotting along a narrow street close to the base of the citadel wall, followed by the shaman, two of the black-robed Mask cultists, and a score of tribesmen with nocked arrows. Here there were no fires, no flattened wreckage, no fighting at all – she had left all of that behind. The citadel was black above her, a dark sky-filling silhouette against the fading light of Sunset, which meant she was on its east side. The buildings along the street were mostly two-story wooden structures with tile roofs, the ground floors all narrow little shops with wood-grill windows. Door-panels and shutters slammed shut as she passed, commoners out in the street fled shrieking, but she ignored it all – they were dust to be swept away later. Now, at this moment, all that mattered was where she was going; the knowledge lay in the center of her mind like a stone placed in an open field.

Tomoe emerged from the street into a slightly wider route and turned left, toward the looming wall of the citadel, now so close that she could not see the keep above without craning her head back. She speeded her pace, driven by the pulsating rage within her thoughts; the small part of her that could still think was aware that the Other was being driven forward by the same raging demand. *The Tiger Lord's family's tryin' t'escape, and some of t'Wolf Lord's people with 'em.* That made her lips skin back from her teeth in a snarl of hate that rivaled the pulsating, inhuman fury channeling through her body. At the same time a question lurked briefly below the rage: *If the Lords can see 'em tryin' t'flee, why do they need me and t'Other both? Couldn't they just guide her t'the right place?*

A nagging flicker of doubt mingled unpleasantly with her own earlier discomfort: *It's like something is blockin' 'em. One of t'Aelfynn bastards or... something else..?*

The thoughts cut off as though sliced by a blade as she emerged from another street and turned alongside a twenty-foot-high stone wall topped by sloped tile. It was dark enough now that colors were no longer visible except where light leaked from houses or shone from lanterns on the wall's far side – the latter, widely spaced, showed the green of trees growing in an elevated space the wall enclosed. She sprinted along it, the driving need to find and kill overriding all remaining hesitation. Ahead the wall was interrupted by a gate – nothing elaborate here, just a built-out stone frame around a double-door of thick oak timbers, opening inward so the bar would be on the far side. There was a tile-roofed guard room built above the gate, probably accessed by ladders from inside the enclosure; its window-shutters were closed, but lamplight glowed inside and Tomoe could see motion.

She felt the Lords force their power through her stressed body once more, and flung out her left hand with a scream that forced its way past gritted teeth. Green fire seared out, piercing the middle of the door and shifting both valves back as it blasted a three-foot hole through them and through the thick bar on the other side. Tomoe clenched her hand shut and the agonizing hate stopped flowing; she staggered to a halt, gasping in short breaths. Tribesmen rushed past her to shove open the broken gates. The shutters of the guard room slammed open, samurai armor and helmets throwing off reflections from the city's distant fires as the men leaned out with their bows to fire on their attackers. The two Masks held up pale hands, fingers clawing at the air, and the samurai let out strangled grunts and moans as their muscles locked. Even in the midst of her pain Tomoe laughed at that, wild and shrill. She stumbled through the gate and stopped on the far side, shoulders heaving as she panted for breath. Tribesmen swarmed up the ladders to either side, into the guard room with blades drawn, and the samurai's groans turned briefly to desperate whistling squeals as their throats were slit.

Beyond the gate, a set of shallow stone steps climbed up to a garden area – there was a carp pond with a pair of stone lantern-posts next to it, oil-wicks already burning within their open chambers. Paths of smooth-packed gravel snaked away into the trees which covered much of the space. The not-quite-sheer wall of the citadel rose beyond, featureless black. *Clever,* she thought grudgingly. *No way t'tell from here that there's a way up to t'keep from here.* "Come on," she rasped aloud, her body lurching forward in spite of the pain, driven by Dakkurru's demands. The others followed, the tribesman casually knocking over the stone lanterns as they passed, laughing as the carefully-carved pieces broke and scattered.

On through the engulfing darkness of the trees, a few other lanterns casting light dimly between the trunks, the tribesmen panting and muttering, the shaman rattling his staff, the gravel of the path crunching beneath their feet. Tomoe did not think about where she was trying to go, she just let the Lords' force within her drive her forward.

The path ended at the base of a narrow stone staircase built into the side of the citadel. There were no lights, no carvings or statues or tile, nothing that would make it stand out against the wall it climbed – just a steep ascent with a plain two-foot-high guardwall on its outer edge. Tomoe stumbled at the first step, wheezing for breath, then started up, slapping at the upper steps with her hands to keep her balance.

The stair rounded a corner on the outer wall and changed to a ramp, just as narrow but shallower, and up ahead she could see the keep rising on its own massive stone pillar. The route she was on connected to a larger ramp and then to a bridge, the lowest of four visible bridges that vaulted across the thirty-pace gap to the keep's smaller but still massive foundation. Tomoe could see light on the highest ramps, the yellow glow of lanterns and the glints of reflections on lacquered armor; far below, in the gap between the keep and the main citadel, the lights reflected in the water of an interior moat.

Blue-green lightning flared, bathing the lower of two platforms that circled the wall of the main citadel, and in that brief unnatural glare of destruction

Tomoe glimpsed a tower shattering, men and chunks of stone tumbling out and down to hit the water in pale fountains two heartbeats later.

At the same moment her eyes caught movement against the keep's lower levels, a group of men hurrying down a staircase toward the third of the four bridges. They were moving without lights, trying not to draw attention. *No good,* she thought exultantly. *Maybe you have an Aelfynn t'hide you from Dakkurru's gaze, but you can't hide from a bounty hunter's eyes... And now we* all *see you, t'Other will see you too, and she'll get t'you, and if you slip past her somehow, you'll come straight t'me.* She licked her lips, hungering for the taste of blood... but her unease, the prickling sense of something wrong, was stronger than ever. *Do they really have an Aelfynn over there?* She squinted against the deepening twilight, trying to make out more details in the tiny dark shapes three hundred paces away.

And something *shone* on that distant staircase, like a star come to earth.

Tomoe felt her mind lock up like a jammed waterwheel.

Him. It's him. *Kenji's here. T'slave of t'False Light. He's* here.

She started to run forward again, heedless of the pain from her strained flesh, her companions trailing after her in confusion.

He's here. Her right hand closed on the hilt of her sword.

⛩ ⛩ ⛩

CAPTAIN TOKAGE GRUNTED INVOLUNTARILY AS armored men jostled him. For a moment he stumbled, feeling a stab of fear at the thought of falling and being trampled in the tight-packed corridor. The only light came from single candles mounted at the corners where the passage turned; people might not even realize he had fallen until it was too late. He caught the shoulder of the man beside him with his only hand, using that to steady himself without slowing down.

The low-roofed passage, stone except for the ancient support-beams that braced the walls and ceiling every ten paces, echoed with the sounds of shuffling sandals, the clank and rattle of armor, and the panting breaths of a hundred people trying to squeeze ahead as quickly as possible. Somewhere far back in the passage a metallic chiming marked the presence of the Priestess. Tokage could faintly hear whimpering sounds from back there as well, which probably came from the servants – the Priestess had insisted on bringing them as well, and with time at a premium Tokage had not tried to argue.

And we do have a responsibility, after bringing them all the way from Castle Ookami to the Aelfynn lands and back. Commoners' lives were not on the same level as a samurai's, but Honor, Duty, and Compassion all required they be protected nonetheless.

There were a few Tiger servants back there as well, the entourage of the High Lord's daughter Tora Sumiya, carrying her clothes and effects in wooden crates tied to their backs. She had wanted to bring everything, two dozen servants and all her belongings, but thankfully her cousin had overridden her. Still, it had all taken time, time to assemble everyone and get organized, time for all the samurai to get back into the armor they had removed when they arrived earlier that day – *is it really still the same day?* – time to decide on an order of march through the narrow passages of Castle Mouko's lower levels. And all the while samurai kept rushing in and out of the castle, shouting reports of disaster, and the unnatural thunderclaps sounded twice more, each time closer.

Midway through the whole process, Lord Tora Iesada had descended from the keep's upper levels clad in an elaborate full armor, all ancient steel lacquered in yellow and brown and black, the helmet a steel tiger's snarling face with the fanged lower jaw represented by the face mask. His wife had accompanied him upstairs but did not return, and Tokage half-wondered if she had already taken her own life in ritual suicide, or was waiting for the outcome of the battle. Iesada spoke briefly with his nephew Tora Arinobu, their voices too low to be heard, and then marched out the front of the keep with his son Giichi at his side while Arinobu had bowed at his retreating back. Tokage had heard the young man choking back sobs, and had looked away rather than witness the loss of face.

This is how a Clan dies, he had thought, his own emotions threatening to take control. That had almost been the Wolf Clan, after Ookami Basho died and Lord Okaro led an unreliable army out to face the Jade Dragon at Nagai Kyukai Plain...

They rounded another corner, the candleflame wavering in the wind of their passage, and ahead of them the corridor ended in a heavy wooden door, almost a miniature gate, barred from the inside. "The exit," Tora Arinobu grunted – they were the first words he'd spoken since they descended into the castle's lower levels – and then barked an order. Two of his men pushed past Tokage, armor scraping on the walls. They lifted the bar down and pulled the door open; it protested, wood grinding against the frame. A gust of fresh air blew in, cooler and cleaner than the stuffy closeness of the passage but smelling of distant smoke.

Tokage stepped out and moved aside, setting his back against the stone of the keep's exterior to make room for the many others following him out. After a moment Seneschal Amano joined him, panting heavily and leaning against the wall for support. They looked around, trying to orient themselves.

The door had opened onto a railed wooden platform built into the side of the keep's two-hundred-pace-high foundation tower. Tokage could see it was actually one of several such platforms built into the walls – some of them wooden like this one, set atop support posts projecting out of the stonework, while others were built into the stone of the tower itself. Interconnected ramps and staircases snaked around the upper half of the keep's foundation, and bridges spanned out to connect to similar ramps on the wall of the main citadel. Those extended off to left and right, variously flat or descending, until they passed around the corners of the greater structure. The military side of Tokage's mind was noting how this maze was challenging to navigate but also meant the castle had many different access points rather than a single route through layered defenses. *This place was built in the days of the Emperors,* he reminded himself. *Defense against a siege was probably not so important then.*

Looking up, Tokage could see the silhouette of the larger bridge he and Amano had crossed into the keep a few hours earlier: a black shape fifty paces above, silhouetted against the darkening twilight of the sky. The Sunset was a fading glow behind the citadel. A lesser light, yellow-orange but erratic, came from below – parts of the city were on fire, though it looked like it was still confined to the north side.

So there's still time for us to get out of here. He spotted Taro Arinobu and called: "Honorable Arinobu! Where do we go from here?"

Before the other man could answer, a flare of blue-green light stabbed at Tokage's eyes, followed an instant later by a thunderclap. People around him screamed – he was sure even a few of the samurai did – and then screamed again as a hard wind buffeted them all, trying to shove them back against the keep's wall.

Kenji snarled something and ran to the edge of the platform. Tokage followed, staring.

A cloud of dust expanded from halfway down the northern corner of the main citadel, five hundred paces distant. Tokage glimpsed rocks and men tumbling off into the darkness below, white clouds of splashes as they hit the inner moat. Distance-tiny men emerged from the dust, some fighting, others running ahead toward a staircase that ascended to the lowest of the four connecting bridges. *Barbarians,* Tokage realized, seeing how they moved and catching hints of their alien clothing in their silhouettes.

"There, that's the one," Kenji snarled, pointing. Tokage squinted, the poor light reducing the distant people to stick-dolls. One of them who seemed to be wearing a loose-flowing robe moved through the chaos in a bubble of open space, the others all staying back as though repelled by an invisible wall.

"They are trying to reach the lower bridge," Tora Arinobu snapped, pointing. "We must move, get across before they can reach us."

"If they reach us, I'll kill 'em all," Kenji snarled.

Arinobu and Tokage ignored the sellsword's bluster and hurried back to the rest of the group, the Tiger nobleman already shouting orders to his men. Tokage made his way to Amano, who was now speaking with Lady Tora Sumiya. A young boy with his hair in a samurai topknot huddled against her legs, doubtless the grandson Enji who Lord Iesada had mentioned; servants waited nearby in an anxious huddle that had expanded to include the Wolf servants as they emerged from the basement passage. The Priestess was there as well, reciting a prayer within a growing circle of the servants, ringing her staff softly in time to the words. Tokage noticed a few of his own samurai quietly joining into the words.

"Honorable Amano, we need to move at once. The enemy is drawing close."

The old man nodded, bowing politely to the wide-eyed young woman beside him. Lady Sumiya seemed to draw some strength from that gesture of civilized formality; she bowed in return, then spoke to the elderly servant waiting next to her. That gray-haired woman clapped her hands at the crowd. "*Yosh*, sluggards, no more time to rest! The honorable samurai are moving and we must keep up. Hop to it!"

The whole group – samurai and servants intermingled – flowed along the platform and up a switchback staircase, likewise of wood, to a stone platform ten paces above them that headed back in the opposite direction. The railings on the outer edges were low, only two feet high, and Tokage saw several people get squeezed against them and nearly go over; he shouted for his men to control themselves.

Back across the higher platform, and ahead Tokage saw the bridge projecting out to his left, a slightly arched wooden structure that crossed thirty paces of open space. He turned onto it, panting, the thick beams echoing hollowly under the tread of his own sandals and dozens of others. He kept turning his head left and right, trying to keep track of where everyone was. There was Seneschal Amano, walking briskly enough despite obvious weariness, and there was Lady Sumiya limping – had she twisted her ankle? The old servant was supporting her with an arm around her shoulders, another servant following holding the little boy by the hand. Taro Arinobu was up ahead, leading the way – he had already reached the far side of the bridge and was swinging his arm sharply, turning everyone left onto another stone ramp that sloped down across the face of the citadel.

Arrows slashed past Tokage, angling up from the right. A samurai ahead of him grunted and staggered as two shafts struck him, one lodging harmlessly in his armor's shoulder-plate but the other piercing the narrow gap between his back and breast plates; he clutched the arrow and nearly fell, and Tokage caught him with his one good hand and kept him stumbling forward. More arrows whipped past; somewhere behind him a woman screamed, and the thought *Please don't let that be Lady Sumiya* flitted through his mind. A quick glance to the right showed him the barbarians were much closer now, crowding along a ramp less than forty paces away and half that distance down. Some of them were volleying arrows while others with drawn swords fought their way up a staircase against a dwindling group of Tiger samurai. One of the barbarians had some sort of mask or helmet covering his head; he followed the swordsmen up the stairs, waving his arms and chanting incomprehensible foreign words.

Tokage reached the far side of the bridge and found Lieutenant Arima there alongside Tora Arinobu. "They'll be here in a minute, we'll have to buy time and then do a fighting withdrawal," he shouted, and Arinobu nodded grimly, drawing his sword and calling orders to pull men out of the flow of retreat. The barbarian arrows continued to arc in; the angle was awkward, they were firing upward at targets half-concealed by the bridge's structure, but they were scoring some hits. He saw a servant-woman take an arrow through the head and drop like a bale of rice, those around her screaming in horror.

Tokage drew his own long sword, awkwardly as always, and took a deep breath to center himself. *A minute, maybe two at best, until they finish off those Tiger,* he thought, frowning uneasily at how quickly the samurai were falling. The barbarians were all chanting now, and at this distance he could make out the rhythm of the words: "Dakkurru! Dakkurru! Dakkurru!"

We'll move forward to the top of that staircase, force them to keep fighting uphill. There were at least fifty of the barbarians, but the ramps compressed the fighting front and made it hard for their numbers to tell. *We can hold them long enough for Amano and the Tora to get away, I think.*

The robed figure was at the bottom of the staircase, standing apart from the archers, and Tokage blinked as he realized it was a woman – the long hair and pale angular face were unmistakable.

A ringing sound to his right, the glint of distant light on metal. The Priestess had just crossed the bridge, Kenji following a dozen paces behind. The swordsman had his long sword out and held low, and he was moving slowly, glaring down at the enemy. The Priestess turned and called at him to hurry; even as she spoke an arrow flashed at him and he whipped his long sword up, the dark streak of the missile turning into two pieces tumbling harmlessly past.

Tokage blinked, taking an instant to process what he had just seen. *Arrow-cutting… I've seen masters do it in the training hall, but never on a battlefield. How can a thug like him…?*

Blue-green light stabbed at the corner of Tokage's eye. His head snapped around and he caught a frozen glimpse of the robed woman holding up one glowing hand, the light flaring as though she held a sickly star in her palm.

Then she thrust out her hand and the light whipped forward in a hellish spiraling line, crossing the distance to the bridge in less than an instant.

Kenji leapt forward – had somehow *already* leapt forward – and the glaring flame slashed through the bridge behind him. The structure shattered, erupted, twenty-foot beams tumbling away end over end, flailing bodies wreathed in fire as they tumbled out and down. A hurricane wind slammed into Tokage and he nearly fell; some of the men around him did go down, yelling. The Priestess, standing at the near end of the bridge, was knocked flat, her staff clanging as it tumbled past her and bounced off the citadel wall.

Burning wreckage plunged into the moat below, the dark surface of the water erupting with spumes of white steam.

Kenji landed on the shattered, smoking stub of the bridge, but instead of tumbling helplessly he rolled and then sprang upright next to the Priestess, snatching at her arm with his left hand and pulling her up in a single wrenching motion. For an instant Tokage swore that the man's eyes glowed yellow-white.

Then the fading screams of those who had fallen from the shattered bridge caught up with him. *Who did we lose?* He looked around frantically. There was Lady Sumiya, still being helped by her servant. And *there* was Seneschal Amano, Amatsu be praised, already a good two hundred paces down the ramp… but then he felt his heart clench. Distance-tiny figures were coming around the corner of the citadel three hundred paces away, on a lower-level ramp but it connected to this one, and he could see they were not samurai. *They got ahead of us somehow, we're trapped—*

The terrible blue-green light flickered again, the robed woman now standing on the very edge of the lower platform, lifting her glowing hand to strike once more. The barbarians were chanting louder than ever. *What is happening, what is this? Amatsu preserve us—*

Tokage heard an old childhood prayer running through his head:

Amatsu, sacred Lady of Heaven, protect me
Mikoto, divine Lord of the night, protect me
Lay your sheltering robes over me…

Kenji let out a wordless howl of rage and sprang onto the railing of the shattered bridge, both swords drawn now. Then his legs coiled and flexed and he leapt into open space, his swords held out like wings, soaring out and down toward the woman a hundred feet away.

Tokage just stared, his mouth hanging open, all face lost.

"Kenji!" the Priestess shrieked, and amid his horror and confusion Tokage found himself incongruously thinking: *She sounds like a woman in fear for her lover.*

The pale robed woman swung her hand and the green fire lanced out toward Kenji, a line of reality-denying agony connecting her to him, and then—

Light.

⛩ ⛩ ⛩

THE DARKNESS ECHOED WITH DISTANT noise, the clamor of battle.

Her flesh moved swiftly, running up a long slope and then a staircase, a castle looming high overhead. The names of these things moved through her awareness and vanished, swept away by the infinite dark and Those who held her within it.

Pain, immeasurable pain as They sent power through her. Somewhere far away, stone burned and exploded. People and wreckage tumbled away into nothingness.

It meant nothing, was nothing, as she was nothing.

Light.

A sliver of light before her, flickering like the whisk of a fox's tail.

A fox. What was a fox?

Something she had dreamed once, long ago. A man had shot a fox, and she had fallen from a horse…

The darkness seized her with crushing force, forcing the dream away.

But the light was still there, flickering on the edge of the darkness, a blaze of purity that hurt worse than all other pains she had known.

For the briefest instant the light saw her, knew her, and just for that same fleeting instant she knew:

I am Satsuki.

⛩ ⛩ ⛩

THE BLAZING POWER OF THE Demons swept at Kenji, six lines of hatred that spiraled out of nothing and sliced through reality like candleflame through paper. He clenched his teeth, reaching for the flicker of Her within himself, and instantly it was *there*, the Light flooding through him in unbearable purity, straining his mortal pattern to its limit.

The Demons' fire washed over him, deflecting away from the Light, spinning outward in a hundred searing tendrils like smoking cinders cast off a burning log. Stone shattered around him, chunks the size of men's heads blowing out of the wall of the citadel and the bridge's foundations as the blue-green lines scoured across them.

The Demons' hollow woman-shaped shell sprang back as he descended on her with swords raised overhead, and he landed on the stone platform where she had stood and it *dimpled*, a circle the size of a house sinking and buckling, shattered pieces spraying out and meeting the still-coruscating green fire exploding into powdered fragments. Barbarians tumbled away from him like flung dolls, screaming as they plummeted over the side of the ramp or caught the deflected fires and burst like overripe fruits, blood fusing instantly to steam and smoke. One shape in a furred robe with a strange mask over its face lay convulsing amid the rubble; Kenji stepped past, his swords flicking absently, sending the man's soul snapping away as the blade severed it from the corrupted pattern of his flesh.

The one-eyed woman in the robe was a horror of non-light, six spiraling coils that wound through every inch of her and spun away into an infinite distance of time and reality. Fragments of darkness clung to the cloak itself, a tangle of agony-broken patterns. Somewhere in the midst of all that chaos was the pale red thread of whatever soul had once ruled her body, now a remnant just enough to keep its flesh alive.

The power of six Demons pulsed through the layers of reality, flooding into this flesh they were using, stretching the limits of what it could bear, erupting through the outstretched hand to flay him. Her *Light* caught their power, warped and scattered it, but not all, not nearly all – some got through, agony great enough that he felt it even amid the exultance of Her embrace. But pain was nothing now because he was *whole* again, his useless life given meaning.

Kenji leapt forward, swords raised like thunderbolts to strike down this flesh-puppet, but the Demons' power hammered at him like the winds of a hurricane and the leap became a stagger, one lurching step after another, pushing forward through the storm of their hatred and the lances of pain as needles of their power touched him.

All six of them, he thought blurrily, *too much, it won't—*

The woman's hand trembled. In the midst of the coiling void of madness within her, the red sliver of her soul flickered briefly, like an ember stirred by breath. For an instant the hurricane of power faltered.

In that instant he took one long step forward and brought his swords down, a shockwave of Light striking with them into the chaos of the Demons' intermingled hatred and scattering it, leaving the human body open to his next attack. The Demons screeched in fury and frustration but not in fear—

Something flashed in the corner of his eye. Swordsman's instinct wrenched his long sword around, driven by the Light faster than muscle alone could move, deflecting a sword-blow in a shower of green-white sparks. His short sword struck the one-eyed woman a glancing blow, tangling in the corrupted patterns of her cloak, and knocked her sideways off the ramp. She tumbled end over end down toward the moat below, never making a sound. The green fire lanced out from her once more, slashing across the walls of the citadel and the keep in alternating arcs, unleashing a rain of shattered stone that turned the whole surface of the moat to churning foam.

The second attacker was a woman too, the Demons were in *her* too but her own soul-thread was stronger than the other's near-emptiness. Their power swelled within her flesh until its pattern stretched and blurred under the strain, trying to rend apart. She was screaming, raving at him, some incoherent jumble of words that meant nothing—

"—Big Taro and Pretty-Boy, had me beaten in stocks, the Wolf Lord—"

He fell back across broken rock, shards of stone shifting around and beneath him, his limbs blurring as his interweaving blades warded off a dozen blows in half as many seconds, sparks of burning reality flying off from each deflection. His swords would have broken if they were just swords, but the Light within him suffused them, making their patterns continually whole. Pain mounted to agony as his own body strained under the burden of the Light, and he felt a sudden rage that he could not simply cut this woman down – *she's not that crazy Lord Akira, what's she doing standing up to me in a sword-fight?* – and then he recognized her, the human face and voice warped by the forces within but still the bounty hunter who had captured him, captured him *twice*.

Hate erupted from her flesh, the Demons forcing their power through even as it frayed her beyond the breaking-point. Slashes of pain across his arms and legs and chest as fragments of the blue-green fire touched him. *Damnation, I'm fighting all of 'em twice over!*

She screamed, wordless agony as her existence started to unravel, and he could feel his own pattern crumbling from the combined burden of the Lady's power and the Demons' relentless attack. The deflected green-blue blasphemy sprayed out in every direction. The ramp beneath his feet and the wall beside him erupted for fifty paces, and then the whole side of the citadel gave way, sagging and collapsing with ponderous finality.

The world became a chaos of tumbling stones each larger than a man. Kenji leaped upward through it, blurring from one falling boulder to another, his consciousness fading as his body passed its limits. Briefly he saw the swordswoman far below him, bouncing limply off a beam of the shattered bridge as she fell into the moat, and then his own strength broke and he lost control of his limbs, the Light slipping away from him, rocks battering him as he fell.

Amid gathering darkness he glimpsed a Priestess' shining staff and a fear-etched face beneath it, and with his last strength he hurled himself toward them.

CHAPTER 12

TERROR AND PAIN AND wonder blazed unbearably through Ookami Tokage. The world heaved beneath his feet and he staggered, lurching against the wall, feeling shockwaves run through the solid stone like ripples through a pond. He tried to focus, to see what was happening, but the light, the *Light*, swept through him irresistibly, showing him… himself, in all his unbearable weakness.

Somehow he got to his feet, his limbs trembling as another shockwave washed across him. Tora Arinobu was huddled on the half-shattered stone ramp next to him. Tokage groped wildly with his one hand and managed to catch the other man by the shoulder-plate of his armor. "Get everyone moving! We must flee!"

For a moment Arinobu just stared blankly at him, *through* him, seeing something altogether different than the world around them. Tokage shook him again, shouting his name, and finally the younger man gasped and nodded, his eyes spilling tears. He lurched upright and started down the ramp, away from the terrible light, away from the thunderclap impacts of incomprehensible forces.

Tokage caught two of his own men the same way, pushing them down the ramp, away from the bridge. He almost didn't see the Priestess. She was on her knees, groping blindly, sobbing, and then her hands closed on her staff. "Kenji, Kenji, blessed Goddess protect us," she cried wildly. He caught her under the shoulder and half-dragged her with him, along the ramp and down, his heart pounding, the stone trembling and shifting like mud under his feet. After a dozen paces she finally got her own feet under her, staggering forward half-blind.

Someone caught Tokage's groping arm. With an effort he recognized Lieutenant Arima, the man's face contorted with grief but his eyes open. "There's enemies farther down, honorable Tokage! What should we do?"

"Fight them," Tokage rasped, and then realized he had lost his sword back at the bridge. A stab of shame amid all the other terrible emotions; that sword had been an heirloom from his wife's family, passed down from her great-grandfather. *No time for shame,* he told himself harshly, pushing the younger samurai ahead of him. They were passing other people now, servants and samurai alike huddled against the wall of the citadel, sobbing, wailing, a few crawling or staggering forward. "Get moving," Tokage shouted hoarsely. "Don't stay here, get moving."

Another thunderclap, and the blazing, flickering light behind them brightened immensely, like a fire given fresh fuel. Tokage kept his eyes averted, squinting against the glare.

Ahead the ramp split, one half angling shallowly up toward the top of the citadel, the other becoming a staircase that descended. Tora Arinobu knelt on one knee by the head of the stairs, not blank-faced now but staring down bewildered.

Men knelt or sprawled all the way down the stairs, men in the strange fur-and-leather of the barbarians. Some of them gazed vacantly into nothing, others clutched themselves or beat fists on their own heads. Two figures in black robes flopped like gutted fish, clawing at their own eyes and mouths with bloody hands; Tokage saw a broken white mask lying next to one of them, and felt a wave of fear that chilled him even through the crushing emotions of the moment. *A white mask… the Cult, the Demon worshippers? What are they doing here with the barbarians?*

Lieutenant Arima had his sword out, but he did not seem to know what do with it. "What… what's happened to them?"

Before Tokage could answer, another thunderclap echoed through the passage between the keep and the citadel. The light flared once more and then abruptly faded, like a quenched lantern, and the sound changed to a rumble of tortured stone. He forced himself to look back.

The air was full of stone, pieces small and large and incomprehensibly huge rising outward amid a cloud of boiling dust like a stormfront, black in the sudden near-darkness. The front wave was already past the ruined bridge and rolling across the lagging ranks of Tokage's people, rocks dropping out of the cloud with ponderous finality to smash into the ramps and bounce off the walls above and below. Light flickered once more within the cloud, brief and piercingly bright, and then went out.

The dust-cloud roared across Tokage and he threw up his arm to shield his face. Wind slammed him against the wall and fragments rattled on his armor and drove pin-pricks of agony into his skin. Something hit nearby with a rending crash of stone on stone, voices screaming in panic and pain.

And then a vast empty silence, save for the gasps and moans of the survivors.

Tokage lowered his arm, blinking hard to shake dust out of his eyelids. The cloud was still settling, now turning a dull red as it sank into the city below and absorbed the firelight. People rose slowly to their feet around him, filthy with powdered rock, their eyes and teeth shocking white against crusted dust. Tora Arinobu was stepping drunkenly down the stairs, wiping at his face with his free hand, stabbing awkwardly at each of the insensate barbarians as he passed them.

"Who's alive, who's hurt?" Tokage said – or tried to say, then coughed and spat gray-black. He began to work his way back up the line of survivors, looking for recognizable faces. Yes, there was Seneschal Amano, praise be to Amatsu, his fine robes all torn and filthy but still alive and blinking to try to clear his eyes. Here was Lady Sumiya as well, weeping through the dust on her face, cradled in the arms of her old servant, who seemed to be unconscious. He bowed to the young noblewoman, then continued on, marking out his men as he spotted them and sending them down the ramp. *Don't think about what just happened here. Focus on your Duty. We can still get out of the city, if we move quickly...*

Tokage pulled up short, his breath catching in his throat. "Honored... honored Priestess?"

Priestess Rei knelt on the edge of a circular crater torn out of – no, perhaps *beaten into* the citadel wall. A tattered, bloodstained man lay unmoving in the crater; somehow she had managed to drag him half-out so that his head and shoulders rested in her lap. She was slowly wiping the blood and filth off his face with the sleeve of her robe.

She looked up and met Tokage's eyes. "Kenji's alive," she said, her voice a hoarse whisper. "But I will need your help to carry him."

⛩ ⛩ ⛩

SOMETHING *HAPPENED.*

A jolt that ran through Ryu Noboru's whole body, not the pleasure of the Lords' power coursing within him but something else, an incoherent sense of rage and bafflement and almost a sort of pain. He was suddenly trembling, his hands shaking, and he could not hear the toasts his nobles were calling, could not taste the wine in his mouth. He dropped his wine-cup and shoved his right hand in his left sleeve, frantically gripping the mask inside.

The nobles were staring, their evening revelry paused. That did not matter, nothing mattered but the misery coursing through his body, misery he suddenly knew had to be afflicting every Voice. He rose from the table and stumbled to the edge of the platform, the rough-planed boards of the low balcony scraping against the silk that covered his legs. His eyes were pointed toward the army, his army, gathered on the evening-darkened plains before him, but he did not see it. His mind was consumed with only one thought.

What is happening? What is so important that Selfishness will not speak? The warm lustful certainty he had wallowed in for the last three years was gone, and with its absence he suddenly saw himself as though from the outside: a pale bloated thing that hunched sluglike, flushed lips dangling pendulous and slobbery, the guards at the back of the platform watching him with disgust and contempt beneath their stone-still faces.

For a brief moment he was on another wooden platform, cowering and pissing himself as the terrible, merciless Light swept across the field of Nagai Kyukai...

Noboru clutching the mask so tightly that his fingers ached, his left hand gripping the opposite elbow with equal force. Finally, finally he sensed a flicker of renewed attention from the Lord whose will he Voiced, and with it a wave of self-abnegating warmth that swept away the worst of the painful mental images.

Noboru sensed the unease and confusion of the nobles behind him, and knew danger in it. I must not let them sense weakness. He let out a long breath, licked his lips, and made himself turn back to the table. "A new toast," he called, angry that his voice wobbled. "And more wine, at once!"

⛩ ⛩ ⛩

A DOOR BANGED IN ITS frame. "Well, how good of you to make time for me!"

Ookami Kaede looked up sharply.

Priestess Ritsuko stood in the entrance of her sleeping chamber, leaning on her staff with both gnarled hands. The old woman's bald scalp had a leprous aspect, all dark spots and flaking scabs, sharply at odds with the purity of the yellow-and-orange religious robes she wore and the polished gleam of her prayer staff. Her head was thrust forward inquisitively, and that combined with her unusually large nose gave her a raptor-like aspect. The fading Sunset coming through the exterior window only enhanced the impression, throwing long shadows that emphasized Ritsuko's gaunt frame and cadaverous face.

The serving-maid kneeling by the door would normally have been the one to open it in response to the arrival of a visitor. She was bowing to Kaede in apologetic consternation.

Kaede had been combing her hair, watching herself in the mirror as she slowly ran the long black strands through the lacquered wooden comb's tines; now she set the comb on the table with a precise motion, looking at Ritsuko in the mirror's reflection rather than face-to-face. "I sent for Priestess Aoi," she said, proud of how even she kept her voice.

"Yes, of course you did. She's the sort of Priestess who can be counted on never to tell anyone an unpleasant truth," Ritsuko agreed. Her voice was harsh, almost raucous. "Unfortunately for you, Priestess Aoi is with your honorable husband's army, seeing to their spiritual and medical needs. So when your request arrived at the Temple, I generously volunteered to take her place!" She laughed, a rasping cackle. "You can't send me back now without insulting the Abbess, you realize."

Which was true, Kaede knew. Not that it would be a Clan-wrecking crisis if she insulted the head of the city's temple, but it would be a problem – an Abbess who was insulted could find all sorts of ways to make trouble for the local nobility, from failing to provide medical assistance for armies to stirring up unrest among the common people. A wise leader avoided such needless trouble, especially during wartime.

Being a wise leader seems to consist mainly in doing unpleasant things, Kaede thought sourly. *But I can't risk undoing all the goodwill I built with my trip during the Planting Festival.* She turned her head slightly and addressed the servant. "Priestess Ritsuko will be seeing to my health. Go and prepare my bath for afterward."

"Yes, honorable High Lady." The young woman prostrated herself, retreated out of the door, then knelt once more and slid it shut behind her, all the motions as smooth and practiced as a dance.

Ritsuko watched the door close with a smirk. "Privacy, eh? Don't trust your servants?"

Kaede made no reply, instead carefully putting her comb back in its case and rising to her feet. In truth, Ritsuko was right – she did not entirely trust her servants. She knew some of them had spied on her for Lady Yumiko, Akira's stepmother, before that woman had led a rebellion against the Clan. She had never been able to learn which ones. The only one she was confident wasn't a spy was the woman called Koko who had joined the household last summer, and there were others reasons Kaede didn't want to deal with that particular servant more than necessary.

Ritsuko stumped forward, peering beadily. "Well, I suspected what this might be about the moment the request came in, but it's obvious seeing you in person."

That startled Kaede into looking at the old woman directly. "Is it?" She knew her belly was starting to show when she was in the bath, but she'd been confident it wasn't noticeable while she was fully dressed – the concealing bulk of her robes and sash concealed the change in her figure.

The old Priestess snorted, then coughed heavily. "There's more to carrying a child than having a swollen belly," she said finally. "Anyone with experience can see it in your face, your posture... There's probably rumors going around the castle already. Including gossip about who fathered the child, no doubt. Is Akira actually the father this time?"

Kaede felt a prickling of humiliated rage wash over her skin, her face tightening and heating. "Of course my honorable husband is the father," she snapped.

Ritsuko cackled more loudly. "Oh, 'of course' is it? After you spent two years spreading your legs for any man who told you a few pretty lies? Though I have to admit you cleaned that up nicely by getting them all killed."

Kaede clenched her fists, fighting a childish urge to hit the old woman on her smirking face. *Why does she always say the worst thing possible?* A moment of clarity then, almost of calm. *She enjoys it, doesn't she? She likes making people angry. If I give in to it, I'm proving her right, and that's what she wants.*

She started to untie her sash. "Shall we get on with the examination?"

Ritsuko raised her eyebrows and snorted again, but she set her staff against the wall and began tying back the sleeves of her robes. "Light a candle or two, there's not enough light left in the day."

The examination was no worse than any other. For all her bluster the old Priestess' wrinkled hands were gentle and careful. Finished, she sat back on her heels and let out a thoughtful grunt. "Well, you seem to be doing well enough. Of course you are fortunate to even be able to conceive after what happened last time."

"Yes, so you have often told me," Kaede replied. It was easier to keep herself calm, she noticed, by concentrating on other things – in this case restoring her clothes, a time-consuming process even for the simple two-layered robe she had changed into after her evening meal. "How soon should I expect the birth?"

Ritsuko took hold of her staff and used it to pull herself back to her feet, letting out a theatrical groan. "If nothing goes wrong... probably a month or so after the Harvest Festival. Just like the first time you had a legitimate child, *neh*?"

"I am sure Priestess Aoi will be back by then," Kaede replied through gritted teeth, then immediately turned her head to hide her flush of shame. *I* just told myself *I wouldn't let her make me angry!*

Ritsuko cackled long and loud, her staff clanging discordantly. "And she'll be far more considerate of your delicate noblewoman's aesthetics than this old bitch, is that it?" Her laughter turned into a cough and she hacked something yellow into her palm. "Well, no doubt you're right, the war will be over by then regardless—"

Something *happened*. The two candles on Kaede's table flickered.

The old Priestess' head snapped up, her rheumy eyes going wide. Kaede froze, her hands still on the sash she was knotting. For no reason she could think of she found herself looking toward the window, where the Sunset had faded into a dull red on the western horizon.

A voice wailed, dimly heard through intervening walls. Without thinking Kaede started toward the door, but before she could reach it, it slid open – awkwardly, jamming in the channels halfway – and Basho squeezed through. The boy flung himself into Kaede's arms, sobbing. "Mama, mama, I dream, mama."

Kaede sank down on the floor, holding the boy close and stroking his sleep-tangled hair. *I won't be able to do this much longer, soon he'll be too old and we'll have to keep face even in private,* she thought, and inexplicably she felt tears starting to her eyes. She swallowed hard, trying to control herself.

A servant-woman was in the door, her head bowed in apology. Kaede's discomfort was distracting enough that it took her a moment to recognize Koko. "Apologies for the interruption, most honorable High Lady. He came rushing out of his room and caught us by surprise."

"And why would you ever stop a child from going to his mother?" Ritsuko snapped, looming suddenly over the door and glaring down at the servant.

But to Kaede's surprise the other woman did not flinch, though she kept her head lowered. "Apologies, the honorable High Lady asked not to be disturbed."

Kaede found her voice, harsher than she meant but the appearance of that woman had brought with it a host of suppressed memories. "Go. You may leave Basho with us."

Koko bowed lower and slid the door shut once more.

Ritsuko looked from Kaede to the door and back. "Now you hate servants too. What'd that woman do to you?"

"Nothing," Kaede muttered. She kept smoothing Basho's hair and he started to relax, curling up in her lap. She cleared her throat and spoke more clearly. "Nothing that's her fault."

Ritsuko raised her eyebrows but to Kaede's surprise she didn't pursue the matter. Instead she stumped around the room, staff clanking, describing a half-circle before returning to Kaede's side and looking down narrow-eyed with both hands clasped tight on the staff. "You felt it, didn't you?"

Kaede was silent for a long moment. "I felt… something. Like someone called my name."

The Priestess nodded. "If even *you* felt it, I imagine half the Empire did." She lifted her gaze, staring at nothing, her mouth working. "I don't think it was your husband. The Moon is too subtle, and too mad. So it must have been the other fellow. The Goddess is a mystery to our mortal limits, but even for Her, that choice is hard to comprehend…"

Kaede looked up at the Priestess, for once not angry or humiliated, simply bewildered. "What… what are you talking about?"

Ritsuko snorted, her face falling back into its familiar venomous lines. "You haven't figured it out by now? Well, I've always known you were a fool, but I suppose you never tire of proving that." She stamped across the room to the door. "Take care of the child. And the other one too, once it comes. If you can't do anything else for the world outside yourself, do that much."

Kaede opened her mouth to retort – *you have no idea what I've done for Basho!* – but the old woman was too quick; she slipped through the door and slid it shut behind her. After a furious moment, though, Kaede realized that one thing was different: Ritsuko had not let the door bang in its frame, so Basho had not awakened.

⛩ ⛩ ⛩

"ALL RIGHT, WE'LL REST HERE for a little while."

Priestess Rei let out a long breath and leaned against her prayer staff, gripping it with both hands as her legs wobbled and threatened to let her sink to the ground in undignified exhaustion.

After a moment she straightened up and looked behind her. Castle Mouko was a black shape against a horizon that glowed dull red with distant fires. The sky above that horizon was now night-black, the last of the Sunset gone and the stars hidden behind smoke. Yellow-orange flickers showed the fires burning within the city at the castle's feet, but they were far enough away now that she could no longer hear the sounds of battle and slaughter.

"Honored Priestess?" The man's voice was strained with effort. "Can I set this fellow down? He's almighty heavy, Amatsu bless."

The speaker was one of the male servants from the Wolf traveling party. Kenji was draped across his hunched back; the man had his hands hooked under the swordsman's thighs, while Kenji's arms hung limply over his shoulders, his head lolling back and forth. The servants had been trading off carrying the unconscious man every half-hour or so.

Rei looked around, trying to find a good place to lay Kenji down safely. The Moon was a pale smudge behind the northern smoke, but the sky to the south was clear and the stars offered enough light to make out the general surroundings.

The little column of Wolf and Tiger was spreading out to either side of the narrow trail they had followed since leaving the main road an hour ago. The path curved along the edge of a series of low hills covered in old-growth forest, and they had passed a few even narrower paths climbing into that thickly overgrown domain, probably leading to shrines or hunters' shacks. Opposite from the forest the land sloped shallowly into an overgrown grassland that had probably been rice paddies sometime in the past. Rei led the servant down the short slope and gestured at the thick grass. "Lay him there, please."

The servant squatted, laying Kenji's legs and rump on the grass, and Rei caught his shoulders and helped lay him back. As she did Kenji let out a gasp and stiffened; his hands shot out and caught her by the shoulders, hard enough to bruise. His pale eyes were suddenly open, glowing in the dark, and Rei felt a jolt run through her body – an echo of the impossible grief and exultance that swept through her each time he summoned the Lady's power, mingled with a belly-warming relief that he was awake at last.

"Where—?"

"It's all right, Kenji." She laid down her staff and set her hands atop his, pulling gently. The light in his eyes faded, and he let her loosen his grip. "We're south of the city, well south. There's no danger here."

He looked around sharply, starting to rise and then letting out a hissing breath and sinking back down, setting his hands on the grass to support himself. Through clenched teeth he growled, "Who is *we*? The Wolf fellows?"

"Them and the Tiger who were with us. Most of us got out, thanks to you."

It was true. Kenji's battle with… whoever, whatever, he had fought at Castle Mouko… had taken the wind out of the barbarians' assault on the city. Captain Tokage and the Tiger nobleman – Rei gathered that he was from the Clan's ruling family – had been able to move them all quickly the rest of the way down from the citadel. Once they reached the city, though, things had gotten ugly; the streets were full of panicked commoners, some with pitiful bundles of personal belongings, many with nothing but the clothes on their backs. Hundreds of them had packed into the streets leading to the city's southern gate, desperate to escape the barbarian threat. Tokage had ordered his men to draw their swords and form a wedge…

Rei shuddered, the memories still fresh and ugly. She had emptied her stomach back then, but it still twinged at the mental images and at the feel and scent of blood stuck to her sandals and the hem of her robes and even the base of her staff. The Tiger samurai had not hesitated to carve their way through their own people to get to the gate and escape the city. *What use is it to make Compassion one of the samurai Virtues if they ignore it so easily?* She longed for a bath and a chance to recite the mantras.

Enough, she told herself. *Kenji's awake, you need to focus on that.* "How are you feeling?"

"Like I got trampled by a herd of oxen." He stretched carefully. She couldn't make out any details of his face in the dark, but the tone of his voice told her well enough that he was in pain. He smelled of dried blood and burnt linen. "Damnation. I thought I had that... thing, the one in the samurai woman's body, I got lucky somehow, something changed and I had it beat... but then that other bitch showed up."

The words made no sense to her. "What happened? Were those people Masks?"

He shook his head. "Worse than Masks. Something... something new." He fell silent, still letting out an occasional hissing sound as he slowly moved and tested his limbs. Abruptly he said, "Old Jun talked a lot about the... you know, the Swords, in the old days. But she never said what happened to them."

"They defeated the Demons," Rei said instantly, reciting from her old lessons in the Temple School. "They drove them into the icy wastes, and then the Lady sealed them away—"

"I don't need to hear the same old kid's story," Kenji snapped.

Rei flinched, pulling back from him. "I'm not Jun," she snapped back, angry at him for falling back into the same old cruelty, angry at herself for letting it hurt after so many times.

He huffed out a breath but made no reply.

Footsteps drew her attention. A figure in armor loomed out of the darkness, and she recognized Captain Tokage. His voice was gravelly, exhaustion leaking through samurai stoicism. "Honored Priestess? They said your companion had awakened."

The servants must have told him. I didn't even notice them leaving. Rei felt a surge of shame at her own oblivious selfishness, deepened by her anger at Kenji's behavior. She picked up her staff, rose to her feet, and bowed. "Yes, honorable Captain, he is recovering. Thank you for your concern."

"He ain't—" Kenji started, but she went on boldly, speaking over him with a rudeness she would never have dared in normal circumstances: "Do you have any other wounded I should tend to while we are resting, honorable Captain?"

The samurai made a rusty sound; it took her a moment to realize he was chuckling. "No, honored Priestess, nothing worse than blisters and bruises and sore legs, Amatsu be praised." He paused, and when he spoke again his voice was different, lower and more serious, freighted with emotion. She wondered what his face looked like right now. *It's dark, he can let feelings show without us being able to see them.* "Swordsman Kenji. This Priestess has called you the… the Sword of the Lady."

Kenji grunted. "That's what she says."

"I was not at Nagai Kyukai Plain. But I heard about what happened. And then in the Aelfynn lands, and now…" Tokage broke off, his armor rattling as he shifted his stance. "I saw you fight High Lord Akira in the court last year. Are you our savior, or our doom?"

"If I wanted to kill you, old man, you'd already be dead."

Rei let out a sigh. *Why does he always…*

"I am a samurai," Tokage answered, quietly dignified. "I do not fear the Lady's judgment. And Fate guides our lives as it wills, not as we might wish."

Rei, moved by the palpable sincerity in his voice, felt her anger fade. She murmured the mantra he was quoting.

"I serve the Wolf Clan and High Lord Akira," he continued, still calm. "If you are a weapon against these Demon-worshippers, it is my duty to bring you back to my Lord along with honorable Amano and the others in my care. But if you are a threat to the High Lord, it is my duty to kill you. Or die trying."

Rei's momentary calm dissolved in a rush of outrage. "Kenji *is* the Sword of the Lady, honorable Tokage. There is no need for—"

She broke off as Kenji laughed aloud.

It was a weak, reedy echo of his usual laugh, but there was still a power in it. She felt and heard Tokage take a step back, heard whispers and a few cries from the others, a muttered curse in a voice she recognized as the Tiger nobleman.

Kenji stopped and caught his breath with a thin gasp that told of his lingering injuries. "Calm down, old man. I'm coming back with you, and yeah, your precious High Lord is the only… the only man… who's ever beaten me in a straight-up fight. But right now… right now I'm not *allowed* to fight anyone but those Demon scum and their slaves." A pause, and his voice lowered. "If that old bitch Ritsuko is right about who your precious Lord Akira is, then maybe it's gonna take both of us to beat the Demons. So… I can settle up with him afterward. Deal?"

Tokage was silent for a beat, and then he bowed. "I suppose I cannot ask for more than that." He turned back to his men, calling orders. The Tiger nobleman joined him and they stood together, conversing in low voices.

Kenji started to get up, then sank back with a hiss of discomfort. "Don't suppose anyone brought any wine?" he called.

"There's no wine, Kenji," Rei said in a quelling tone, gripping her staff as she leaned forward and tilted her head, letting the darkness conceal the rudeness of her eavesdropping. "I think we're going to be moving again soon. Will you be able to walk, or should I send for the servants to carry you?"

"What's got into you?" Kenji growled, but there was no heat in it. After a minute he gathered himself and rose, letting out a series of unpleasant clenched-teeth sounds until he was upright, if slightly wobbly. "If there's no wine, at least give me a new sword."

"Oh, I made sure we brought you new ones," Rei said absently.

"You... what?" He fell silent again, and in the dark she found herself imagining a surprised expression on his face. The image swept away her earlier anger, and she actually felt a wholly inappropriate urge to giggle.

Finally he said, "Why'd you do that?"

"Well, you *are* the Lady's Sword. It wouldn't be very useful for you to have no swords, *neh*?" She looked critically at his wavering outline, barely visible in the starlight. "Are you really able to walk? From what honorable Tokage said to that other samurai, I think we'll be pushing on until morning."

"Damned samurai think they're so tough," Kenji muttered, and then louder: "Yes, damnation, I can walk!"

⛩ ⛩ ⛩

"THERE THEY ARE, MY LORD." Tamashiro Shungo pointed, then dropped his hand in embarrassment as he realized Akira could see the distant army as well as he could. He bowed in the saddle, suddenly flushed and red-faced. He was a young man, not yet twenty-five and unmarried, like most of the officers Kado Kitaro had promoted to command in the Wolf Clan's cavalry forces. His face, still clean-shaven despite days in the field, lacked the iron self-control that veteran samurai and nobles developed. Akira's two bodyguards, older men who were veterans of the old Nightingale army – it was considered a privilege of that service to be part of Akira's personal escort, even though casualties were always high – shared a flat-faced look, amused by Shungo's discomfiture but not changing their expressions, which only made the younger man flush harder.

Akira ignored it all. Such byplay was still baffling to him at the best of times. Instead he focused on the distant army Shungo's gesture had noted.

The group of them – Akira and his guards, Shungo with a deputy officer and a trio of mounted couriers – stood their horses atop a low ridgeline, rolling fields covered in blooming pampas grass stretching out ahead and behind. The slope concealed the two hundred cavalry who had accompanied them;

Lord Toshiwara and nine thousand infantry lay ten miles back, moving north from Castle Kosaten at a deliberate pace to avoid stressing horses and oxen. In dry weather there would probably have been dust on the horizon to show its presence, but the sky had been cloudy-gray for the last two days and since last night occasional rain squalls had been sweeping through, drenching everything for a few minutes before blowing away.

One such squall was crossing the fields toward them now, the pale-topped grasses waving as the screen of gray passed through. Beyond, blurred by the drifting rain but impossible to miss, the army of the Bear Clan trudged southward, following the same route it had been on when Akira's scouts had first spotted it.

Once it became obvious Lord Noboru was waiting for the Bear, there had been three routes they could take. The first and most obvious was this one, marching down through the Tiger borderlands the Bear had captured last year, advancing directly to Castle Kosaten to link up with the Jade Dragon forces. The second option had been to strike through the Mizumori, which would have allowed a direct attack at Akira's northern flank. The third option had been to come down the Road of Promises through Fumato Village, which would have allowed the Bear to plunge into the lightly defended heartland of the Wolf Clan and threaten Castle Ookami itself. That was the option Akira himself would have taken, if the roles were reversed, but Lord Noboru was unlikely to trust the Bear to do such a thing even if he thought of it. As for the Mizumori, the Bear were known to be blunt and direct in their approach to warfare; they would not wish to spend many days, perhaps weeks, struggling through the Mizumori's infamous maze of rivers and narrow valleys and small castles.

He had sent scouts to watch all three routes. *Do not assume your enemy will take the most intelligent choice,* Sada Sakaguchi had written.

The rain swept over the crest of the hill, wetting his face and beading his armor with clear droplets. For a few minutes he could see no more than a hundred yards in any direction, the air a haze of gray, the rushing of water drowning out all other sounds. The horses snorted and shook their heads and flicked their tails while their riders properly showed no reaction to such minor physical discomfort.

The rain passed, and now the Bear army could be seen clearly: a dark mass advancing in long rectangular blocks, leaving churned earth behind. The dominant colors of the armor and banners were brown and dark green, giving the army a drab, workmanlike tone in contrast to the exuberant brightness most Clans exhibited in the field. Nor did the individual nobles make much effort to stand apart, confining their personal colors to the crests on their forces' banners. Akira remembered reading that the Kuma family made almost a fetish of plainness, and viewed any noble who violated that tradition as a potential traitor. Even the Ishii family, absorbed long ago from the defunct Ox Clan, had forsaken its ancestral bright blue for a muted tone of that color in its double-arc crest.

Akira counted formations and banners, confirming to himself the reports Shungo and the scouts had delivered. *At least twelve thousand men, at most fourteen thousand.* Which, if his spy reports were accurate, represented a heavy majority of the Bear Clan's active strength in samurai. It was a major risk for the Clan to bring so many soldiers out of its own lands, but the Kuma family's only living male heir was in Lord Noboru's hands, and with the future of the dynasty at stake the Bear High Lord could not risk leaving any of his nobles behind to scheme.

Akira looked at the army, advancing sluggishly through these empty lands toward a battle it did not wish to fight, and thought: *I can defeat them here, before they ever reach Castle Kosaten. They have me outnumbered somewhat, but they have no cavalry at all, not even scouts on foot. Shungo has already confirmed that. Their supply train is at the back of their marching order, barely guarded – they are used to fighting enemies who confront them head-on. I can destroy their supplies with Shungo's horsemen, then pin them in place with a fighting retreat while they starve. In a week at most, hunger will break their discipline and then my men will slaughter them.* He shut his eyes and saw it play out in his mind, as inevitable as an end-game of Stones, the outcome known long before the last piece is laid down.

He opened his eyes and turned to Shungo and his guards. "Wait here."

The young man's eyes widened, and the two guards exchanged another look, this one of confusion, overriding their self-control. Before they could do anything more, Akira kicked his horse into a run, racing down the long slope toward the Bear army, the pampas grasses parting before the horse's legs like water before a boat's prow.

Someone shouted curses behind him, and for a short time he could hear hoofbeats of pursuit, but it was too late for them to catch up – he was already a hundred paces down the slope. His horse jumped a narrow washed-out ditch with brown water chuckling in the bottom, then sped to a full gallop as it reached the flatlands. The Bear army loomed closer with shocking speed, changing from a collective mass of gleaming armor and rain-deadened banners to the distinctive individual shapes of thousands of men, stretching out to either side as he closed the distance. Akira took one brief look back to see what the others had done, and nodded mentally. The guards had recognized the futility of interference and broken off, blocking Tamashiro Shungo when he tried to pursue on his own.

Now some of the Bear had finally noticed him. The nearest formation suddenly dissolved as men broke out of the march and hurriedly formed into squadrons, most of them lowering their spears to form defensive bristles, a few trying to string their bows.

Akira reined in fifty paces away. He waited for the first wave of chaotic motion to subside, for all the soldiers to focus their attention on him. The initial alarm on their faces slowly changed to puzzlement as they realized they were facing a single man.

He raised his voice to the shout the Monks had taught him long ago, a shout that could cut through the noise of a battlefield and compel obedience from men exhausted and terrified: "I wish to speak with honorable Kuma Gotaro!"

CHAPTER 13

MUD SQUISHED UNDER OOKAMI Akira's sandals as he followed his appointed escorts through the Bear army. The march of thousands in damp weather had reduced the grassland to a slough, and now the men stood in ranked formations with their feet sunk ankle-deep in it. They showed no outward discomfort, of course, especially in the presence of an outsider.

It had taken the Bear about an hour to figure out how to respond to his sudden appearance, couriers racing back and forth with their back-banners fluttering and mud spraying up from their heels. Finally the army had reorganized itself into a defensive formation, blocks of infantry in front and on both sides, while servants hastily prepared a meeting-place in the center. They had laid down woven mats in a rectangle about as large as a modest house, with silk barriers along the edges to form an open-ended enclosure. Now the servants knelt silent at the bases of those temporary walls, while armored guards stood behind them, watching Akira with hard-faced attention.

Akira paused at the edge of the mats, noting the neat rows of muddy sandals along the outer edge. After a moment he did the same, stepping out of his sandals and bowing politely before advancing across the mats in his split-toed socks. The mats flexed slightly beneath his feet, pressing into the mud beneath.

Within the silk enclosure, two armored men waited. Their armor's lacquered plates were as drab-colored as the rest of the army, but the excellent quality was unmistakable. The shorter of the two, standing in the center of the enclosure, was clearly High Lord Kuma Gotaro; he had a huge Bear Clan crest embossed on his chest-plate, and wore a helmet with an expansive mane of brown-dyed fur that framed a face mostly hidden behind a war-mask resembling a snarling bear's snout. The taller man standing to Lord Gotaro's right had a thick beard and wore a straightforward warrior's helmet with no decoration beyond a Clan crest on the brow. He looked vaguely familiar, and Akira belatedly recognized him as an emissary who had met with his father years before.

Akira stopped five paces away – any closer would have been a lethal threat with swords at his side – and bowed, then stood waiting.

After a pause the men returned the bow – though only to the most minimal politeness. The older one called out in a gravelly voice turned slightly hollow by his war-mask: "You have requested a meeting, Wolf samurai. We have granted it. What does your Lord wish you to say to me?"

Akira was momentarily silent, bewildered by the question, until he realized: *They don't know who I am.* He was in his usual simple back-and-breast, shin guards, and greaves of undecorated gray and red, the practical gear he wore in the field, not the elaborate Clan armor he had sent to be worn by others at the siege of Castle Kosaten.

Finally he said: "I am Ookami Akira."

Both men stiffened and the older one snorted, smothering a laugh. He pulled loose the ties of his war-mask and let it drop down onto his chest, revealing a creased face framed by a close-cropped graying beard. Deep-set eyes peered narrowly beneath thick eyebrows. "I do not take kindly to mockery, samurai. Am I supposed to believe the High Lord of the Wolf would walk into my army alone?"

Akira stood confounded. He had never considered they would simply not believe him.

The Bear Lord's taller companion suddenly blinked, peering narrow-eyed. Then his eyes widened and he bowed again, much lower than before. "My Lord… I believe this is indeed Ookami Akira."

Lord Gotaro looked sharply at his subordinate. "You recognize him, honorable Hirosada?"

"I… think so, my Lord. He was present when I met with Lord Okaro four years ago... though he was not so thin at that time." A smile peeked through Kuma Hirosada's beard. "He spoke briefly, but plainly."

Akira knew by now that to speak "plainly" would be considered an insult in his own Clan's court – suggesting a person was crude, unimaginative, lacking in manners. Apparently, among the Bear speaking plainly was a compliment.

"*Ah so,*" Lord Gotaro muttered, visibly unsettled. Finally he huffed out a breath, stiffened his posture, and bowed more deeply than before. "Honorable

Lord Akira, welcome. I apologize for my lack of manners. I am honorable Kuma Gotaro, High Lord of the Bear Clan."

He gestured to the side, and several of the kneeling servants rose and scurried forward, deploying a trio of folding camp-chairs. The Bear Lord sat on his, the wood creaking under his weight, and gestured for Hirosada and Akira to take the others.

"I am afraid that under the circumstances I cannot offer you much in the way of hospitality."

"I did not come here for hospitality," Akira replied. Inwardly he was glad they would not have to labor through drinks and toasts and all the other posturing that would normally be expected. "And you cannot receive a formal parlay without violating your alliance with the Jade Dragon Clan."

The two older men blinked, and Lord Gotaro nodded thoughtfully. "Yes, I would have to reject any formal request for a meeting. So you came here… alone? Without any soldiers, any guards?"

Akira said nothing.

Gotaro grunted and nodded to himself again. "Hmm. Yes. So, you are here. I suppose you will ask me to break my alliance with honorable Ryu Noboru."

"Yes." The Bear Lord seemed to expect him to say more, but what more was there to say? Extra words would just be saying the same thing again.

"I cannot, as you well know, no matter what I might wish. My only living son is a hostage of the Jade Dragons, and barely survived their civil war two years ago. I must protect my bloodline."

He did not add that the Bear had one male heir because the older son, Kuma Jubei, had been poisoned three years earlier – almost certainly by the Jade Dragons.

"If you remain allied to the Jade Dragons, we will fight. No matter who wins, Lord Noboru will never let your son return alive." Akira recited the facts with pedantic care, the way he explained military plans to officers he did not know.

The High Lord glared and started to rise to his feet, putting one hand on the hilt of his long sword. Akira sat still, watching him. The man opened his mouth, drawing breath to shout, and then went still, narrowing his eyes. Finally he blew out a long breath and sat back down, gripping his knees tightly.

"You speak plainly indeed, Lord Akira. There is cruelty in such open truths… but also honor." His hands tightened until the greaves on his knees creaked in protest. "What am I to do, then? I have no other heirs. Do I just accept the death of my bloodline, the collapse of my Clan? No Clan can survive the extinguishing of its ruling line. Not even mine."

"You have two daughters."

Gotaro shook his head. "The Bear are not the Nightingale." Akira flinched slightly at that, a reflex he could not control, but if the Bear Lord saw it he made no comment. "My people will not consent to be ruled by a woman – we do not even allow regencies. Any man who marries my daughters will be seen as illegitimate by all his rivals within the Clan, and that will mean civil war."

Akira felt the eternal frustration rise within him. *Lord Gotaro is a prisoner of the same false thinking as Amano was, and all the others too.* "A civil war is a risk. The loss of your son is a certainty. Choose one."

Hirosada let out a grunt of anger. Lord Gotaro surged back to his feet. "What? How dare—" He broke off again, staring, and then suddenly laughed, a deep booming laugh that echoed across the camp. "You are… an extraordinary man, Lord Akira. No other would say such a thing to my face, not even my closest advisors. Not even my wife!" He sat back down heavily, the chair uttering a protesting groan at the impact. "And you come alone into the midst of my army to say this. Are you a madman? Why would you do this thing?"

Akira focused all his attention on the man, boring in on him as he would on an enemy in battle. His mind hummed in the void, the world fading out except for the man – the soul – sitting in front of him. When he spoke his words felt dense, heavy. "The Empire is dying. The barbarians are overrunning the northern border and the Demons are loose from their prison." He paused then, because he had not known he would say that second part. But the moment he spoke the words, he knew they were true.

The Bear Lord sucked in a sharp breath but couldn't seem to say anything. Akira went on, relentless, merciless: "There must be an Emperor before it is too late. And the Emperor will need samurai to fight for him. I must crush the Jade Dragons, because they are allied with the Demons. But you are not."

He sat back and closed his eyes, emerging from the void. *How did I know about the Demons?* But it was true, of course. Now that he had said it, his mind was going back over all the information of the last five years, seeing the patterns, fitting everything together. The Mask cult, the barbarian attacks, Kenji and his powers, Noboru's actions as ruler of the Jade Dragons… *Yes. This is the underlying pattern, what I could only see in fragments until now. Why did I suddenly understand all of it?*

It was almost as though someone… Someone… had spoken through him.

He opened his eyes. Kuma Gotaro and his vassal were staring at him, their mouths half-open, their faces wet with sweat as though they had been fighting. Finally Hirosada coughed and, as though that released them from something, they both straightened their postures and schooled their faces. Lord Gotaro opened his mouth, shut it again, visibly groping for words, blinking as sweat oozed into his eyes. Finally he stood up, cleared his throat.

"Lord Akira. Do you intend to claim the Imperial City?"

Akira stood as well, focused again, alert and utterly calm, ready for violence but showing no outward threat. "I do."

For a long time the High Lord of the Bear stared at him, his expression subtly changing once and then again, while his vassal looked between him and Akira with desperate attention, barely daring to breath.

Then, slowly, the High Lord of the Bear sank to his knees.

⛩ ⛩ ⛩

"HONORABLE LORD NOBORU?" THE SOFT question, barely above a whisper, was accompanied by a scratching on the exterior of the tent-flaps, tied shut since last night..

Ryu Noboru emerged from a waking dream, his stomach and loins pulsating, and opened his eyes. He was sitting cross-legged, his belly resting on his knees, the Mask of Selfishness on his face. For a moment he saw only darkness, then Selfishness overrode his awareness and he could see the layered patterns of the silk-thin illusion which men called 'reality.' On the far side of the tent-flaps a human soul flickered, vibrating with delicious fear. An impulse possessed him to reach through the tent and drag that body inside, revel in its pain, devour its flesh, watch its soul fray and contort… *No*, Noboru reminded himself. *I still need my army, at least for now. I must observe some… limits.*

Rage then, at being thwarted, and he reminded himself – or perhaps Selfishness reminded him: *Soon. Soon it will no longer be necessary to deceive these rancid vessels of flesh, to pretend to care about their absurd customs and fancies.*

Though with that knowledge came another layer of frustration, not his own but the frustration of Selfishness and the others like it. The invasion of the Tiger lands had stalled. One of the Lords' avatars had nearly been destroyed by the slave of the False Light. A setback, unexpected and thus doubly infuriating, that had happened because the Light's creatures could not be *seen* in the manner of other mortals.

Since that day there had been something different about Selfishness' presence, a sense of bitter impatience.

"Honorable Lord Noboru?"

It was an effort to lift his hand to the mask. So much better to keep it on forever, to forever escape from his own flesh, his own confining self-identity…

Selfishness forced his hand to move. *I cannot command this army while wearing the mask,* he thought, or perhaps Selfishness thought it for him.

Noboru pulled the mask off, blinking and feeling momentarily nauseous as his senses blunted and his awareness shrank, as though he was suddenly being crushed into a small cold space. He trembled violently, staring down at the blank inner concave surface of the mask, and he had a sudden inexplicable urge to fling it away.

He tucked it under his futon and rose to his feet. "What is it?"

"Word from a spy, my Lord. The enemy is on the march, and should arrive within a day."

Ah, he thought, feeling a sudden tingle of both anticipation and fear. It was only six days ago he had learned the Wolf army was actually at the Kiirokusa Plain, barely forty miles away. That had come as a bewildering shock after becoming so well accustomed to Selfishness and the other Lords telling him the locations and secrets of his enemies. Instead it had been Mugai Soto's spies who had learned the truth.

But while the enemy army was perilously close it had remained in place, not moving save to send cavalry raiders this way and that. *Is Lord Akira afraid to fight?* That did not seem possible, given the rumors of what the Wolf Clan's ruler had done to his own rebels the year before, but Selfishness could offer no insight on that topic either. The crazed young Wolf lord seemed as much a mystery to Dakkurru as he was to his own people.

"Send for my servants. I will dress for war this day," Noboru said. "Inform my Lords I will meet with them at the usual place, and tell honorable Mugai Soto to meet me there as well." The samurai outside the tent shouted an affirmation and hurried away.

The servants arrived a few minutes later – three young woman and two boys, all of them pale and trembling with barely-contained fear. It was still early enough in the morning that they carried lanterns, and the shaking in their hands threw garishly-dancing shadows on the tent's silk walls. That only made them more afraid, since such an inelegant display was worthy of anger. Their misery made Noboru's mouth flood with saliva, but there was no time to wallow in it; he stood quietly, raising arms and legs as requested, while they stripped off his sleeping-robe and dressed him in pleated leggings, embroidered shirt, wide-shouldered overcoat, and wide silk belt. All the while he was trying to think, his mind as anxious and fretful as a cat, chasing itself in circles.

Why are they marching now, after waiting so long? Is that filthy peasant traitor Akiyama with them, did he tell Lord Akira something? Have they learned about the Bear? Soto had only just confirmed that last night. *Or have they learned about Lord Kiyogama?*

Castle Kigi was actually closer to Shinku than most of the other Jade Dragon provinces, so by now, with even the Sada and Onaga and Mugai troops finally at hand, it was obvious that Lord Kiyogama had rejected his final warning and chosen the path of treason and destruction. However, the knowledge had not brought quite the gleeful anticipation it should have. Noboru no longer had the advice of the treacherous General Akiyama, but even on his own he realized that attacking Castle Kigi at the precise moment when he needed to bring the greatest strength to bear against the Wolf Clan would weaken him far more than the mere absence of Kiyogama's troops. *No, I must deal with the Wolf Clan first,* Noboru knew. *Punishing Kiyogama will be a reward to myself once this campaign is ended.*

The servants finished and retreated in a desperate flurry of bows and barely suppressed whimpers. As soon as they were gone he collected the mask, stroking it anxiously for a few moments before tucking it into the baggy sleeve of his shirt. He did not bother to collect the swords that rested on a travel-stand in one corner of the tent.

He stepped outside and squinted. The Sun was a painfully bright haze on the eastern horizon, hidden behind low-hanging clouds. The sky overhead, on the other hand, was gray and felt close, pressing down and creating a dimness that contrasted oddly with the diffused Sunlight. Noboru instinctively wanted to look eastward – that was where the enemy was coming from – but the light made him feel slightly queasy. Instead he made his way to the observation platform a hundred paces away, slowly climbing the steps and then pausing to breathe heavily before walking to its front railing.

Lord Onaga and Lord Tsuchiya were already there, sitting on folding camp-chairs. They rose and bowed low as he passed, then reclaimed their seats. If they felt any contempt for his poor physical condition, they gave no sign, and he simply ignored them – there was no point speaking with such weak and treacherous men. Tsuchiya Bunta's subordinate Hioka Atsuto had been executed for treason last winter, and Noboru was certain that Bunta had shared his subordinate's disloyalty. Short, baby-faced Lord Onaga Kitsuya had initially sent only a token force to Shinku, pleading that he needed to hold back men to protect his eastern border against the Nightingale. *As if the Nightingale have the strength to invade him!* But unlike Kiyogama he still had a son in Castle Hokori, and so in the end he could not outright refuse Noboru's command. Last week he had finally arrived at the head of another thousand of his samurai. Still not his full strength, but enough that he could at least claim to be serving his High Lord loyally.

Noboru would have enjoyed calling out both men, but he knew it would be unwise to shatter the illusion of unity and loyalty before the war was over and won. So he continued to ignore them, making a show of clasping his plump fingers behind his back and looking out confidently at his army.

Tents stretched out in long rows, each set flying the banners of the Lord who commanded their loyalty; the colors, normally bright, were greyed-out by the poor light. The encampment was stirring, the usual soft rumble from thousands of men talking, eating, bathing, tying on their armor, sharpening weapons. An undercurrent of animal noises, lowing oxen and neighing horses, and a distant ringing from the blacksmiths who had accompanied the army to repair armor and weapons. In a typical samurai army there would also have been the sound of Priestesses welcoming the Sunrise, but of course such were no longer allowed in the Jade Dragon army. Still, Noboru suspected there were many prayers hidden within the general rumble of twenty-four thousand men preparing for the day.

Noise announced the arrival of others on the platform. Noboru turned around, his face settling into its usual droop-lipped smile, and acknowledged the bows of the other senior nobles of the army. Young Lord Oyama smiling nervously, desperate to appear loyal. The Wolf Clan traitor Konatsu Sabato, his face set in lines of bitterness, still displaying the Konatsu yellow peony crest as though it meant something. Lord Furuta Ikuo looking awkward in armor too big for his fifteen years, trying desperately to act like he belonged here despite losing his father, lands, and castle to the Wolf Clan in the last four years. Lord Mugai Hokuto, lean and morose in an oversized suit of gold-lacquered armor with an elaborate helmet displaying a gold-plated dragon.

Mugai had been late to arrive as well, but his tardiness was more forgivable since his lands were the farthest away and his loyalty was not in question. He had brought almost four thousand men, most of his strength, a bold statement given his proximity to the Tiger Clan border. *Of course, the Tiger are no threat anymore,* Noboru thought with a giggle. *But he does not know that. So his gesture is… sincere.* His mind invested the compliment with disgust.

None of the Lords let themselves react to the giggle. Last winter had taught them, at last, to fear Noboru more than they had ever feared his father.

"The Wolf Clan army has finally stirred itself to march," Noboru announced.

He waited expectantly, and after a brief anxious silence the Lords responded as they were expected to respond – with smiles, cheers, boasts. "They march to their deaths!" Lord Mugai declared fiercely, and Lord Tsuchiya asked eagerly, "How soon shall we go forth to face them?"

After the wave of obligatory enthusiasm passed, Lord Onaga cleared his throat and asked a real question: "Do we know how many soldiers the Wolf bring to this fight?"

Everyone already knew, of course. Each Lord had his own spies and correspondents, his own covert sources. They had been calling in favors for weeks to learn what they would be facing.

Still, it was one thing to know the truth in private, and another to discuss it openly. Lord Onaga was showing courage to ask the question, and Noboru felt something bare its teeth inside. *Such courage warns of treason, as Kiyogama shows,* he thought, his temples throbbing, his fingers clutching with a sudden desire to rend and tear. Some of it must have shown in his eyes, because Lord Onaga paled, sweat beading on his soft round face.

"Their numbers are not important," Noboru declared. He waited, tasting the fearful doubt that scurried through the minds of his Lords, and then he lifted his left hand and made a beckoning gesture with his plump fingers.

Mugai Soto climbed the steps onto the platform, stopped, and prostrated himself. "Humble apologies for this interruption, most honored Lords. I have received information which I believe to be of the utmost importance."

"I will forgive your ill manners if this information is truly as important as you say," Noboru giggled.

Soto prostrated himself again. "I am informed that the Bear Clan army is crossing the River of Many Faces, five miles west of Castle Kosaten. Over thirteen thousand men, led by Lord Kuma Gotaro himself. It should be here within two days."

"Two days," Noboru repeated. He smiled beatifically. "Which is also, by singular fate, how long it will take the Wolf Clan army to reach us."

The aspect of the Lords began to change, the tightly-controlled doubts under false bravado giving way to genuine enthusiasm, smiles deepening with sincerity, the tension giving way to a crackling energy of aggression.

Mugai Soto rose and scurried forward, holding out a folded paper in both hands; he knelt and bowed once more, holding up the paper in upturned palms. "Also, I have received this letter from Lord Goda at Castle Kosaten."

Noboru raised his eyebrows. This part he had not known about in advance. He took the letter, tugging the knot out of the paper with clumsy haste, and tore the cool green-gray sheet slightly as he unfolded it. "Ah," he murmured as he scanned hastily down the rows of calligraphy. "It seems the Wolf still have many soldiers besieging Castle Kosaten. And…" A line of drool went down his chin. "It seems Lord Goda has spotted the High Lord of the Wolf in their ranks, with his banner."

A shocked silence. Then someone – it might have been Lord Tsuchiya – murmured, "He has divided his forces."

A madman indeed, Noboru thought, a pulsating hot glee running through stomach and mouth and groin. He swallowed a mouthful of saliva and burbled, "They have marched forth to their doom."

And then all his pleasure curdled as Lord Mugai came to his feet, lifting one fist overhead. "Victory is at hand. The Lady with us! Ryu!"

The cheer repeated the obligatory three times, and Noboru clenched his teeth against nausea and murderous rage.

⛩ ⛩ ⛩

KADO KITARO RODE HIS HORSE through the Noble Waters River, the water churning as the beast swam through the deepest parts, then bursts of spray rising up in a cloud as it reached the shallows. The cascading water joined the thin drizzle that had been misting the air since last night. His escort, an overstrength squadron led by a Lieutenant named Juzo, followed him out of the river, all of their mounts snorting and neighing and shaking their heads resentfully as the water sluiced off their bodies. The current was thankfully not overly strong, but the brown water was deep enough in midstream that an unmounted man would have been under save for his topknot.

A hundred paces to his left a bridge crossed the same river: a flat wooden platform held up by a series of square pillars set in narrow fitted-stone foundations, the whole connecting the higher eastern riverbank with the somewhat lower western side. The bridge's thick planks rumbled and shook under the passage of marching men – thousands of samurai in the colors of the Wolf Clan, moving west as fast as the bridge's constraint allowed.

On the east side of the river the shallows became a series of pools and gravel-banks under a steep earth embankment, creased with occasional grooves of erosion. Kitaro walked his horse along the barrier until he found a shallowed portion of the bank and kicked the beast up the slope, the rest of his men following. At the top was thick grass and scrub trees and clumps of bamboo; Kitaro's group wove through the obstacles and into open ground beyond, finally giving them a clear view of Onbin Village.

It was a large enough settlement that it probably deserved to be called a town rather than merely a village. There was actually a main street lined with two-story and three-story buildings, with a sprawl of farmers' and craftsmens' homes radiating out northward to croplands and rice paddies. Sitting astride the Road of Red Fields which connected Castle Kosaten with Shinku, it was customarily a prosperous place. Now, though, it might as well have been abandoned; the residents had locked themselves inside their homes while the invading army passed through. That army filled the town's main street from one side to the other; additional formations spread across the fields east of the town, waiting their turn to funnel up the street and across the bridge.

Kitaro finally spotted what he was looking for: a group of mounted men, their normally colorful armor turned drab by the hazy weather. They were on a wooded knoll just south of Onbin Village, positioned to have a good view of town and army alike. He kicked his horse into a gallop and closed in rapidly, his voice bubbling with excitement as he called: "Honorable Shungo!"

Tamashiro Shungo's face broke into a smile of recognition. He bowed in the saddle. "Honorable Kado Kitaro. It is good to see you again!"

The words carried an extra weight of meaning. Kitaro and Shungo had both been in Lord Akira's original army, the thousand-odd men who had fought against impossible odds in the Nightingale lands four years ago. Most of the senior officers in the Wolf Clan's cavalry force could boast of that, though there were some – like Lieutenant Juzo, following Kitaro in and exchanging his own bow with Shungo – who had earned their postings from more recent service against Lady Yumiko's rebellion.

"I bring the High Lord news from the main army," Kitaro said. "He is here?"

"Honorable Lord Akira was on the northern side of the town by the shrine when I last saw him," Shungo reported. "I am sure he will be eager to hear your report. Amatsu watch over you, honorable Kitaro!"

"And you, honorable Shungo." Kitaro put his horse back in motion, riding along the back of the town's main-street buildings, weaving between shrubs and fences and garden-plots and outhouses, until he could cut through a gap in the army's marching column and get to the northern side of Onbin Village. His men followed him, Lieutenant Juzo slapping his own horse into enough speed to ride alongside.

Kitaro glanced at him. "Is there something you need, honorable Lieutenant?"

The other man swallowed and bobbed his head in a half-bow. "Apologies, honorable Kitaro. It is simply that I have not met the most honorable High Lord before. In person, I mean."

Ah, Kitaro thought. *He is worried about shaming himself, poor young fellow.* Then he laughed at himself within his mind. *'Young' is it? If I am not mistaken, Juzo is actually a year or two older than I am. Why does he seem younger to me?*

Kobayashi Juzo was the son of a minor landholding family in the lands near HillTown, recruited into the cavalry by Lord Kaneda during the buildup two winters ago. The war last year had been his first. *He's even married, and has a child, if I recall correctly. I'm barely officially betrothed!* Then he had to distract himself, because his mind abruptly started showing him memories of Lady Naichin Miyu, of the way she blushed and lowered her eyes modestly when she smiled, of the delicate curves of her cheeks and lips… *Enough,* he told himself sharply, feeling a pleasant but embarrassing warmth run through his body. *Focus on your duty! Time enough for such things after the war. And besides, I shouldn't be wallowing in thoughts of Lady Miyu while Lord Akira is still mourning the loss of Lady Satsuki.*

That Akira and Satsuki, the now-lost heiress of the Nightingale Clan, had been lovers was an open secret among the old veterans of that campaign.

"Lord Akira is… unusual," he said aloud. "Some find him unsettling. But he is an honorable man and a great general. So long as you fulfill your duties, you need not be concerned."

"Ah so," Juzo nodded, his aspect calming. He pointed ahead. "Is that the shrine honorable Shungo mentioned?"

An eight-foot wall topped with dark gray tile ran alongside the secondary path they were following. They could just see a shrine's pagoda-roof tower, also dark-tiled, rising beyond it. Ahead of them, the wall was interrupted by an open gate; in front of the gate was a massive prayer-arch, twenty feet tall and lacquered entirely in glossy black.

It's a shrine to Lord Moon, Kitaro realized. That was unusual in a town; it was more common for Monks to hide themselves away in Monasteries out in remote corners of the countryside.

A Monk was standing in the gate: a man in pale gray-white robes, his shaven head showing a sheen of moisture in the damp air, one hand holding a black-lacquered staff in a forward-leaning pose as though he was prepared to bar entry to the shrine's grounds.

Opposite from the Monk, on the road by the archway, Lord Akira sat his horse alone. He wore only a plain minimal suit of light armor, the helmet dangling from his saddle-horn, his white-streaked hair beaded with rain. The escort of guards and couriers was several paces back; Kitaro noticed they did not have the huge Ookami banner they normally carried when the army was in the field.

Lord Akira stared at the Monk and the Monk stared back, each of them pale and still and utterly expressionless.

For a moment Kitaro felt as though he was riding through a thunderstorm, his skin prickling and tightening, and his horse snorted and tossed its head uneasily. That must have drawn Lord Akira's attention, because he turned his stare on Kitaro… and then a muddle of expressions went across his face, too fast for any one to be seen clearly.

"Honorable Kitaro," he said, and he was the normal Lord Akira once more. "You have a report?"

Kitaro shivered and made himself straighten up and bow. "I do, most honored High Lord," he said, proud that his voice didn't waver. *What was happening there?* He glanced at the shrine's gate, but apparently the Monk had gone inside. "Honorable Chujitsuna Nomi moved out the army yesterday, as you commanded, west along the Golden Sun Road." That road started at Shinku and ended, over a hundred miles southeast, at Toryu Village and the Mountains of the Sun. "They should be crossing the Noble Waters today."

The Noble Waters River was a secondary tributary to the River of Many Faces, one of many such smaller watercourses. Kitaro knew from the old maps in the basement of Castle Ookami that at some point in the distant past it had been the boundary between the Salamander and Peacock Clans. There were three major bridges; two of those were now in use by the Wolf Clan's armies.

Akira nudged his horse into motion, following the path that paralleled the shrine wall and then zig-zagged between a pair of farms. "Did honorable Nomi have any trouble with the nobles?"

Kitaro had known Akira long enough by now to hear the extra layer of coldness beneath the question, despite that Akira's expressionless face did not change. "No, my Lord," he replied, smiling with a slight coldness of his own.

In point of fact, two of the nobles – Lord Musume and Lord Ito – had wondered aloud why they could not use the bridge at Onbin Village rather than moving all thirty-two thousand men on the Golden Sun Road. Nomi had merely said, "Lord Akira is aware of Onbin Village's bridge," and they had shriveled up and obeyed rather than appear to be doubting the High Lord.

Akira drew rein on a grassy tussock next to the path. From here they could look a quarter-mile southwest and see the bridge, see his army flowing across it relentlessly. "What news of the Jade Dragons?"

"The Jade Dragon army has not moved from its new position." The enemy had reacted to news of Nomi's march by shifting four miles east of Shinku, deploying there on a line of low hills, the Midorisaka, with marshy ground to the south anchoring their right flank. He had sent Akira a letter yesterday by fast courier, reporting the new deployment. "They have continued sending out spies. My scouts have swept up a dozen already, but some of them will probably get through."

Akira nodded. "That is fine as long as they don't get close enough to identify me."

Kitaro fought down a disrespectful chuckle. "If you are dressed like this, my Lord, I doubt any spy could identify you." Akira looked more like a low-status spearman than a noble. "Is that why you're not flying your banner?"

"The banner is back at Castle Kosaten with Lord Toshiwara," Akira said briefly.

He's planning something, Kitaro knew. *Something to do with his trip to Kosaten, and bringing these troops back from there on this route.* The thought brought with it a crackling energy, a surge of confidence almost bordering on arrogance. *Forgive me my sins, blessed Amatsu,* he thought, and followed it with a brief mantra. *And bring me Courage, when the time comes to fight.*

"Keep the scouts out but consolidate all the rest of the cavalry north, behind Nomi's right flank, by tomorrow morning," Akira said, his voice going even more clipped as he issued orders. "Maintain contact through couriers with both Nomi and myself."

Kitaro inwardly steeled himself. The new orders meant he would be in the saddle for the rest of the day and probably most of the night, but such privations were expected of loyal samurai in wartime. *Duty is the greatest Virtue, for a samurai who fulfills his Duty will also fulfill all other Virtues of the Code,* he reminded himself; that was a quote from *Wisdom in Emptiness*, a treatise on the Samurai Code written by the swordsman-philosopher Kiritsume. Kitaro had never been much of a reader, but he had always loved that book.

"Go find Kaito before you leave," Akira continued. That was the name of his manservant, who had been with him as long as Kitaro himself – all the way back to the nightmarish campaign in the Nightingale lands. "He has written orders for you to take back to Nomi." He turned his horse and rode back the way they had come, his escort parting around him and then following.

Most samurai would have been insulted by such an abrupt dismissal, without even a chance to acknowledge the orders and bow in response. Kitaro knew Akira had behaved this way precisely because Kitaro would not be insulted. It was a gesture of absolute trust.

"It shall be as you say, honored High Lord," he murmured at Akira's retreating back, already indistinguishable from the men around him in the gray drizzle.

CHAPTER 14

THE COOK CRACKED OPEN an egg with a flourish, dropping it into the piping-hot broth. "Your meal, honorable customer!"

Kobayashi Mitsui accepted the bowl with both hands, making a polite smile which almost faltered when his shortened finger pressed on the side and twinged sharply. The wound had scabbed over without becoming feverish, thank Amatsu, but the finger was still intensely sensitive.

He stepped back from the counter and went to find Satoshi. The older samurai had already seated himself on one of the two wooden benches next to the noodle-stand and was busily scooping up noodles, onions, and bean-sprouts with his chopsticks, chewing with glum efficiency. Mitsui sat next to him, pulling out his own chopsticks from his travel-pack and wiping them on his sleeve before using them to stir the half-cooked egg into the noodles. He took a long sip of the egg-enriched hot broth before he started on the noodles. *Good*, he thought. *Simple, but good.*

There is so much of life that is simple and good. Why did I never notice before? He chewed the noodles, savoring the textures and tastes, the crunch of the bean-sprouts, the savory-sweetness of the soy-paste broth with the extra richness of the egg. As he ate he looked around, at the lands and the road and the passers-by.

The Road of West Winds ran along the upper bank of a small bean-shaped lake, one of many such modest bodies of mountain-fed water scattered throughout the Bear lands. He had lost count of how many such lakes they had passed since they crested the mountain pass and entered the Clan's home territory weeks ago. The hills rising up from the lake on all sides were covered in terraced rice paddies, intensely green with spring growth, farmers' huts scattered randomly between and among them. From a cursory inspection Mitsui suspected the farmers had built their homes wherever the ground was simply too rocky for growing anything. South from here, where the road passed the end of the lake and followed the stream that drained from it, he could see the haze of charcoal smoke from the large town he and Satoshi had passed through that morning. It wasn't big enough to be a city, and he was starting to suspect the Bear lands didn't have any real cities as he understood the term.

Plenty of people here, but they're not crowded together the way they are in the heart of the Wolf lands. They have to spread out across all these little valleys to grow enough food.

The road was wide enough for trade wagons, and one of those had passed since he sat down, axles creaking and the pair of yoked oxen complaining loudly, the wagon loaded down with crates that most likely held iron or steel. There were plenty of people on foot as well – farmers walking to and from their fields, a pair of woman carting laundry down to wash in the lake, a Priestess with chiming staff, a bean-curd seller with his hand-cart, a trio of slim pale-faced young men with bulky packs on their backs who were probably traveling actors, a woman in makeup and colorful robe who was either a prostitute or an actress, a sellsword with a swaggering gait that reminded him of that strange Kenji fellow…

The noodle-stand, pleasantly shaded by a trio of oak trees sprouting from the hillside behind, was doing a brisk business. After a minute Mitsui had to shift over to make room for another customer on the bench.

No Bear samurai, though. He'd noticed a scarcity of them for many days now. Judging from the gossip in the inns and teahouses, the Bear Clan was going to war – something which the common folk seemed to accept with resigned equanimity.

I suppose that isn't entirely a bad thing. Fewer samurai means fewer people interfering with my investigation. Mitsui suppressed a grimace as the memory of why he was here swept away the momentary serenity of eating lunch. He finished up his food, tucked his chopsticks away, and returned the empty bowl to the shop's countertop. Satoshi had already done so.

The two samurai got back on the road, hard-packed earth and gravel crunching softly under their sandals. They turned north, following the road the rest of the way around the lake to where a wide stream, almost a river, sliced through the hillside in a series of whitewater rapids. The road vaulted over the watercourse on an arched wooden bridge; like much else that Mitsui had seen in the Bear lands, the bridge was overbuilt, almost ostentatiously thick and sturdy, and the planks did not flex or echo at all under the weight of those crossing. Beyond the bridge, the road paralleled the stream, winding through thickly forested, steep-sided hills. Trees crowded close to the road on one side and the stream on the other, shutting out much of the daylight. Smaller roads, barely more than paths, sometimes branched off into the forest; one of them was marked with a prayer-arch, suggesting it led to a religious site, while another led to a charcoal-burners' village just visible from the main road.

They passed several roadside shrines, mostly tucked back into the treeline and almost invisible in the foliage's shadows: wooden shelters with ancient, weather-worn statues of the Lord or the Lady accompanied by smaller carvings of sacred animals, foxes or dragons or lions. They were all clean and well-kept, often with small piles of offerings in front of them, and sometimes Mitsui noticed a traveler kneeling and praying before them. *People do seem more pious here,* Mitsui reflected. *Though if I am right, that has not kept the Masks from getting their claws into this land.*

In late afternoon the road finally broke out of the narrow valley. A tableland with a patchwork of farms stretched off to the right, the farms growing gradually sparser until a distant line of forest denoted the root of the jagged green-gray-white barricade of the Bear Mountains. Mitsui had already noticed how one could seldom escape the view of those peaks for more than a few hours in this land.

To the left where the hills still loomed close, a town clustered along the far side of the river, built up the slopes rather like a fungus creeping up a wall. Roads and wooden staircases zig-zagged up the steep hillside behind the town, ascending through bare earth and old tree-stumps to a treeline much higher up. People wended their way up and down the slope, carrying loads of wood strapped on their backs.

Mitsui could see two bridges crossing the river into the town, and farther upstream what appeared to be a dam with a pair of larger waterwheels turning below it. Pillars of dark smoke rose from a dozen places throughout the town and a scent of burnt wood and hot metal hung in the air, a miasma that left a faint acrid taste on the tongue even from a distance.

"Well, this place seems a likely candidate for a town called Tetsukakka," Satoshi observed. "Burning Iron Village, indeed." He gestured at a wagon approaching them, and the two men stepped onto the rocky edge of the road while it passed. The back of the wagon, like the others they had passed, was tight-packed with wooden crates. "Bear Clan steel is much in demand these days... Do you think our friend Goro's name is painted on those crates?"

"Possibly," Mitsui nodded. "Though I doubt Merchant Goro is the only metal-dealer in this town." He was, however, the only merchant who had smuggled the Cult of the Mask's supplies to the warehouses of Fuse Iemon, the Mask cultist whose house Mitsui had raided back in GreenTown. "Let us find a place to stay, and perhaps see what the local people know of our target."

Tetsukakka Village was a dirty place, unsettlingly so for a samurai. The smell of forges and crucibles intensified as they crossed the river, passing a small patrol station which looked like it housed no more than a squadron and turning north up the town's main street. The buildings crowding on either side, a mix of one and two-story structures with heavy tiled roofs, seemed to mostly be shops and tea-houses, the latter crowded with customers as the afternoon trended toward evening. There was more than one obvious brothel with weary-looking young woman sitting behind wooden-barred windows and waving tepidly at the laborers who passed them. Mitsui also spotted a number of boarding-houses, the sort of crowded dives that catered to day-laborers and other poor folk. *I suppose we can stay at one of those if we have no other choice.*

All the buildings seemed to have a coating of gray, as though the smell in the air had congealed onto them. A long line of men with dark-stained clothing, their skin blackened with mingled charcoal and sweat, waited to enter one larger riverside building that proved to be a bath-house. Every side-street ended in a large structure that belched smoke from vents in its roof – forges and crucibles, turning wood and charcoal, iron ore and bamboo into the famous Bear Clan steel. Wagonloads of dark iron ore clattered up the side-streets, others departing loaded with crates of finished ingots. The whole place hummed with a relentless energy that was very different from the trade-hub cities Mitsui had visited before.

And the noise...! A relentless clangor of metal on metal, the constant brabble of the laborers talking and joking and laughing and grunting with effort; under it all the roar of the town's myriad forge-fires, like a perpetual distant thunderclap.

Mitsui felt an odd sense of relief when he saw a pair of samurai patrolmen walking the streets, even though he knew the presence of local authorities might complicate his own work. He had been half-wondering if the local garrison stayed inside their station, or if they had all left for the rumored war – though he would expect the Bear to leave men to protect such a valuable resource. Still, compared to towns in the Wolf lands their presence here was minimal, and they walked the streets with a casual air that reminded him of sellswords more than of Clan samurai.

He and Satoshi reached the northern side of the town, emerging from the shelter of the half-deforested hills, and a brisk wind hit them from the west, turning the air cooler and cleaner. The ground sloped up as they passed the dam they had seen before, the road turning sideways and ascending the berm. Above the dam, the stream had broadened into a small oblong lake – more of a pond, in truth. Wooded lands lay on the left, with a few pleasant-looking houses scattered among them and a prayer-arch marking the path to a shrine somewhere deeper in the trees.

Satoshi paused, breathing deeply. "Ah, this would be the neighborhood of the local samurai. Nicely free of the town stench."

"And that appears to be what we are looking for," Mitsui added, pointing to their right. Perched alongside the water was a pleasant two-story building with a large walled garden that encircled its front and side; a sizable stable was built to one side of the garden. "A respectable inn."

"We are hardly respectable these days," Satoshi objected. "One of those flophouses back in the working neighborhoods would be more our style, I think. Cheaper, too.... But I suppose adding lice to our trials and indignities might be excessive."

Mitsui actually chuckled, and felt a sense of surprise. *I've not even felt like smiling lately... I suppose no grief lasts forever.* "Sleeping without lice does have value, I agree." He led them through the garden's open gate, starting toward the front door and then stopping as he noticed a man squatting in the garden. "Do you have a room available, honorable innkeeper?"

The man's head was mostly concealed beneath a tattered, fraying basket-shaped straw hat, showing only a frowning mouth and grizzled chin, and he wore a dark brown ankle-length robe; his large hands moved with slow, stolid patience, pulling weeds one at a time. He made no reaction to Mitsui's inquiry.

"Honorable guests!" A thin fellow in overcoat and leggings, his hair tied back in a proper commoner's topknot, hurried out of the inn's front door, hands clasped unctuously. "Welcome, be welcome! I apologize for my gardener, the man is simple-minded, I'm afraid. Welcome, welcome, of course you are in need of rooms!" He managed to usher them toward the door while bowing, smiling, and at the same time looking over their threadbare garments. "We do have a few rooms available, honorable guests, if you believe our humble establishment is suitable..?"

Mitsui held up his money-string. "It is suitable."

The innkeeper's face cleared and he bowed more vigorously, leading them inside.

⛩ ⛩ ⛩

"MOST HONORABLE CAPTAIN, APOLOGIES, THE most honorable Seneschal wishes to speak with you."

Captain Tokage looked up from the bowl of rice-porridge that rested on the porch at his side. The servant who had spoken was now prostrating himself, which looked rather absurd in a dirt street. The chief result was a growing stain of brown earth on his hands, knees, and forehead.

Tokage sighed. "Please inform the honorable Seneschal I will be with him shortly." The servant prostrated once more and hurried away.

Left to himself once more, Tokage picked up his bowl and tilted it back, slurping up the rest of the porridge as best he could – it was difficult to eat quickly with only one hand. Finished, he rose, still chewing, tucked his chopsticks under his belt, and carried the bowl back to the serving-table.

They had stopped yesterday by a large roadside inn, a three-story structure that stood alone alongside the Road of Dancing Foxes. The place was well-kept, the owner – an older woman with three grown children and a newborn grandchild – the sort of respectable, serious commoner who Tokage instinctively liked. She had brought out extra woven mats and linen cloth so the men who could not fit inside the inn could sleep on the covered porch that surrounded the inn's ground floor on three sides; Tokage had joined his men there, leaving the rooms inside the building for those less fit and for the women in their group – servants mainly, but also Lady Sumiya and Priestess Rei.

They'd been bathing in shifts since they arrived, workers hauling endless buckets of water from the inn's well and endless stacks of firewood to heat the water in the bathhouse. Tokage had gotten his chance near midnight, and it had been wonderful to finally scrub and rinse all the lingering ash and rock-dust out of his skin and hair. Not least because it also felt like he was rinsing out some of the unsettling memories of that night.

This morning the innkeeper and her sons had set up tables outside and brought out pots of freshly-boiled porridge and stacks of wooden bowls, enough to feed everyone. Now she smiled and bowed at him as he returned his bowl, and he smiled and nodded back. It was good to be with normal people again, free from the madness of recent days.

Finding Seneschal Amano proved to be more of a challenge than he expected. The old man had slept inside, of course, in an upstairs room, but neither he nor his servants were in that room now. Tokage went back downstairs and then outside, circling widely around the inn.

A wooded hill rose behind the inn, with a well-worn path going up between the trees probably led to some sort of shrine or sacred site. Sure enough, the young Priestess was coming down the path, her staff chiming gently. She smiled and bowed greeting as he passed, and despite himself Tokage stopped and asked her, "Honorable Priestess. How is your, ah, your companion?"

"Kenji is recovered, mostly, honorable Tokage. Well, he's still complaining." She let out an involuntary half-laugh. "But he always complains, I'd be worried if he didn't!"

They bowed again, parting, and he passed around the inn and out from the shade of the forested slope.

In every other direction was open land, sloping gently eastward, much of it divided up into farming fields lush with buckwheat and millet, flax and soybeans. He could see a few farmhouses scattered across the landscape, though there didn't seem to be a true village here. The inn itself was apparently the center of the local community, and he could see farmers coming toward it with hand-drawn wagons – bringing more food and supplies, it appeared.

Two miles away, stark against the horizon, a small castle – little more than a three-story keep – perched atop a single isolated hill. Men had come from there last night, speaking with Tora Arinobu, and he had departed in their company. He was back now, speaking with a circle of his own men on the far side of the road. Tokage noted that Arinobu was back in his armor, unlike everyone else who had kept it off after bathing. *What does that mean?*

And there, at last, was Seneschal Amano, standing by the road with a servant holding a parasol to shade him. That seemed excessive given that the sky was heavily clouded, but Tokage knew better than to say so. He approached and bowed. "You wished to speak with me, honorable Seneschal?"

Up close, Amano looked worn, almost haggard, despite a bath and fresh shave the night before. His face had acquired a certain gauntness in the last few months, and his eyes seemed watery. He was not in full court garb today, merely a robe of Wolf Clan gray-and-red and a black courtier's cap on his balding scalp.

His voice, however, was as smooth and practiced as ever. "Honorable Captain Tokage. I wished to discuss our next steps."

Tokage straightened and put his hands behind him, adopting a posture of attentive focus.

"Honorable Tora Arinobu informs me that he intends to rally the remaining strength of the Tiger Clan, here in these southern provinces, and lead a counterattack to retake Castle Mouko."

Tokage turned his head enough to watch the distant circle of Tiger samurai. Tora Arinobu was speaking quite fiercely, gesturing with both hands. "I do not know enough about the Tiger Clan to say whether that could succeed. But how can he hope to prevail now, after... what we saw?"

It was better, even now, not to speak directly of what had happened. The memories were too sharp-edged.

Amano cleared his throat. "Yes, well... honorable Arinobu spoke with the local samurai here at length. Apparently the barbarian invasion lost its momentum after the battle at Castle Mouko. So perhaps there is some hope of success. Or at least of halting any further advance."

"*Ah so*," Tokage said neutrally. It was admirably honorable and courageous for Tora Arinobu to carry on the fight – especially since he might well be the last adult male of the Tora line – but he wondered how many Tiger samurai had already perished in the fighting north of Castle Mouko, how many could possibly be left for Arinobu to rally. It was not his place to say such things aloud, of course.

Amano nodded, looking off into the distance rather than at Tora Arinobu or anyone else. "Indeed," he said, as though Tokage had agreed with him. "He does recognize the difficulty of the challenge facing him, and I have assured him that High Lord Akira will likely wish to offer whatever assistance is possible."

Which is a very elaborate way of saying nothing at all, while making it sound like you are promising something, Tokage thought irritably. He knew such language was an unavoidable necessity in the world of the nobility – his wife knew how to use it, and she and his daughter had helped Lady Kaede to master it – but his warrior's soul rebelled at such prevarications.

"So…" Amano turned to face Tokage, "He and I have discussed certain matters, and he has agreed to send his sister Lady Sumiya and her nephew Enji to the Wolf lands. We will, of course, provide a safe escort, along with a squadron of Tiger Clan samurai."

Tokage felt his eyebrows go up before he got his face back under control. "As our guests?"

Which was a polite way of saying 'hostage' while maintaining appearances.

Amano smiled thinly. "To protect the Tora bloodline… but he is fully aware of all the potential consequences. The current situation requires a reassessment of our relationship." He cleared his throat again. "I would expect us to depart tomorrow, after we've had time to properly rest and purchase supplies. Do you anticipate any difficulty with this?"

"I do not believe so," Tokage answered carefully. "Should I learn otherwise I will of course inform you at once." He knew and Amano knew where the source of any 'difficulty' would be found, but neither of them would say it aloud. He bowed, the Seneschal returning it less deeply, and retreated to the Inn.

It took only a few minutes to deliver the orders to his men, who were clearly thrilled at the prospect of finally going home, though they limited themselves to smiles and enthusiastic bows. Finished, he went looking for the source of the potential difficulty.

Kenji was seated cross-legged on the Inn's back porch, shoveling rice-porridge in his mouth with crude efficiency. The Priestess was absent, which was unusual enough that Tokage paused and looked around for her.

Kenji's voice was muffled by chewing. "Lookin' for my keeper?"

Tokage opened his mouth to issue a polite denial, then looked at the swordsman's pale eyes – eyes that always seemed to shine slightly, these days – and decided otherwise. Instead he made a brief bow. "Honorable swordsman

Kenji. I wished to notify you that we intend to begin our return to the Wolf lands tomorrow."

"She's in the bath-house," Kenji replied, still eating.

He does enjoy being ill-mannered, even for a sellsword, Tokage thought. *The Priestess said he has a habit of trying to start duels. I suppose I should be grateful he hasn't done too much of that on this journey.* He noted the sheathed swords resting on the porch next to the man. *Are those the same ones he had before? The lacquer on the short sword looks different...*

Thinking about all of that was easier than thinking about other aspects of Kenji's nature, such as the way he seemed to heal terrible injuries almost overnight. The only sign of the bloody ruin he had been when they fled Castle Mouko was a few new scars on his arms, easily visible right now with his shirt-sleeves tied back for the meal.

That and how raw-boned, almost gaunt, he had become. *The man's always been lean, but now he looks like he's practically starving.* Which perhaps explained his refusal to stop eating.

Kenji shoved the last of the porridge into his mouth with his fingers, then sucked the fingers clean one by one before he set the bowl down. "Why're you tellin' me this?"

"You are not under my command. It seemed proper courtesy to notify you of our intentions."

"And make sure I don't cause trouble, *neh*?" The man laughed, though thankfully it was not the awful laugh he unleashed sometimes, just a sour chuckling noise. "Excrement, you ain't got anything to be scared of. All I can kill now is the damned Demon-worshippers, She won't let me do anything else."

Tokage chose not to ask what that meant. He was debating how to ask if the man intended to accompany them, but before he could decide, Kenji went on, his tone almost contemplative.

"I'd be heading south anyway. To talk to your damned High Lord again. Maybe fight him again too, if She'll let me." Another chuckle. He turned his head, looking directly at Tokage for the first time, and the old samurai felt a prickle run through his body, an echo of what he had felt during the battle at Castle Mouko. "So relax, old man. I'll behave myself until we get there."

⛩ ⛩ ⛩

THE TOWN OF TETSUKAKKA DID not seem to truly sleep. Well after nightfall the forge-fires still burned, casting a vague orange-red glow on the walls and rooftops. The throbbing rumble of noise diminished but did not cease. From Kobayashi Mitsui's position in the inn's garden, it felt as though he was gazing into some mythic domain, a place of monsters and evil spirits such as his nursemaid had told him about as a child.

The prospect of going back into that noisy, grimy place was somehow more daunting now, after he'd had his first proper bath in days and had enjoyed a pleasant meal of rice and grilled fish and tea. The innkeeper's wife, a plump woman with a pleasant smile but a formidable way with her servants, was an excellent cook. Mitsui had also changed into his somewhat-cleaner spare shirt and leggings while the innkeeper's servants laundered the other set, though he had no choice but to keep wearing his single overcoat. By habit he patted the breast of it, where tattered embroidery showed his family crest and a few stray threads marked where he had once claimed authority as a Magistrate.

The night-darkened garden was cool without being chilly, lit by the glow from the inn's windows and doors and by a single candle inside a carved stone lantern by the exit to the street. It was typical of the Bear lands, he reflected, that public lanterns were stone mounted on pillars rather than paper hanging from bamboo poles. The candle, like the ones inside, was an expensive luxury – they showed the inn to be high-class but did so subtly, which samurai guests would appreciate.

Mitsui had covertly sniffed the burning wax, making sure it didn't have the odd musky odor of the Mask cult's imported candles.

A scuffing of sandals behind him, and the distinctive lean frame of Tamashiro Satoshi emerged from the inn's front room to stand beside him. "Hmmm, it seems our esteemed host's odd gardener has departed for the evening."

Mitsui nodded to himself. He had glimpsed the silent man several times through the windows earlier in the evening – that huge basket-hat was impossible to miss. *Just as well he's gone,* Mitsui decided; he had no intention of discussing their plans where anyone else could hear, even a mere gardener. The last four years had taught some very harsh lessons.

Satoshi ran a hand over his own freshly-shaved temples. "So what does our solicitous host know about honorable Merchant Goro?"

"He recognized the name," Mitsui replied. "But knows nothing, it seems, save that Merchant Goro is said to a respectable man… as merchants go." The innkeeper had no doubt tailored his response to the fact that Mitsui was a samurai and thus could be expected to despise merchants.

Satoshi nodded. "Naturally. Our honorable host knows better than to gossip about a wealthy merchant with visiting samurai. But as you expected, his employees are less refined." Satoshi had been raised by servants – he had never shared why, and Mitsui had never pried – and that gave him a knack for speaking with common folk that most samurai lacked. It had served their investigation well on more than one occasion. "Merchant Goro has a house and office in the town. Apparently the local Bear samurai do not allow merchants to dirty their fine neighborhood out here."

I suppose even the Bear have their standards, Mitsui reflected. He took a breath, then touched the hilts of his swords where they projected past his hip. "Shall we get to it, then?"

"Well, red-lit noisy darkness seems almost like a familiar friend at this point." Satoshi checked his own swords, tightened his sash. "And the clamor will drown out any screams we might utter."

There was a time when Mitsui would have been confused by that response, or laughed at it. Now he made no reply, simply leading the way out of the garden and down the road into the town.

The teahouses and brothels were twice as busy as they had been during the day, blazing with lantern-light, criers in color-coded overcoats standing outside the doors and calling the virtues of their establishments to passersby. The heavy burnt-metal scent of the town was now made heavier by the reek of spilled wine and a bitter undertone of vomit from drunkards emptying their bellies in the alleys. Mitsui grimaced inwardly, reminded of former days as a Magistrate when he often had to deal with the aftermath of drunken brawls.

"Down here, I believe," Satoshi murmured, and they turned onto a secondary street that ended at one of the forge buildings. The buildings here were close-packed two-story structures, often sharing walls, the ground floors dark inside but lights visible through some of the upper-story shutters. There were no outside lanterns here, most of the illumination coming from the forge building a couple hundred paces away, and Mitsui realized another reason why the town seemed grimmer and more unwelcoming than others he had seen – the construction was much more heavily wooden, with almost none of the paper-frame walls and screens that typified Empire architecture elsewhere. He supposed that was because of all the forges – floating sparks would be far more likely to ignite paper walls than solid wooden ones.

Satoshi counted doors as they passed. "It should be this one, if the servants were truthful with me."

It was a building like the rest of them, a narrow two-story structure, the ground floor dark, light visible from the upstairs window. The front door had a similar construction to the window-shutter: close-set vertical wooden slats in a sliding frame, and almost certainly locked with a blocking-bar on the inside. Mitsui looked back and forth, checking for observers, but the street was empty and agreeably dark; the main road fifty paces away was bright in contrast, full of noise and moving figures. *We're unlikely to be noticed unless we make a truly absurd commotion.* Even then he felt a slight twinge of shame at what he was doing. *I am a Magistrate, dedicated to the law, but everything I have done for the last year has been a crime. Breaking into houses, killing people without trial...*

For a moment he felt Akemi's spirit hovering behind him, wordless.

"Right," he muttered, and kicked the door squarely. Wood splintered and crunched. He yanked his foot clear, grunting in pain as splinters stabbed him through his socks, and thrust his hand in after. It took only a few heartbeats for his groping exploration to find the blocker-bar and pull it aside. Another moment, and the door slammed open and he went through, Satoshi on his heels.

The thick darkness inside blinded him, and he stumbled against a table; then yellow light flashed from above, showing him a very steep staircase climbing up one wall. A querulous voice called down: "Is someone there?"

Mitsui drew his short sword – that was the better choice in close spaces. In the jolting excitement of the moment he barely noticed the pain from his damaged finger. He went up the stairs in a gasping rush, pulling himself upward with his free left hand, and caught a momentary glimpse of a thin-faced man in a night-robe, holding a paper lantern in one hand. The man's eyes went wide and he jumped back, pulling the upstairs door closed. Mitsui lunged and thrust his left arm forward, letting out a grunt as the thin interior door slammed against his bicep; the light spun crazily and then went weak and flickering as the merchant dropped the lantern and tried to pull the door shut with both hands. Mitsui braced himself and pushed farther in, getting his shoulder into the opening, trying not to think about knives or about a sorcerer's power clamping onto his muscles. Satoshi was behind him, pushing on his back, and then he finally got enough leverage and the door slammed open, the merchant letting out a half-scream of fear and outrage as the momentum tumbled him to the floor.

Mitsui stepped past him, looking around for another foe. Satoshi, behind him, set his own foot on the fallen man's chest, pinning him to the floor; the fellow let out a gasping squeal. The fallen lantern was now burning, and Mitsui instinctively stamped on it, grinding out the flames under his sandal.

He could see an open interior door, and beyond it another room – the back half of the upper floor, lit by yellow candlelight. A low table waited there with cups and bowls, and a serving-maid cowered in the far corner.

"Damnation," Mitsui growled. *A witness.* He shot another look at the merchant, now thrashing and twisting under Satoshi's foot, grabbing at the samurai's leg with his skinny hands. "Merchant Goro?"

The writhing man's eyes widened. "How do you know my…" Despite his situation his voice rose in shrill outrage. "How… how dare you! This is my home!"

Satoshi pointed his short sword at the man's face. The merchant broke off yelling and let go of Satoshi's leg, eyes now wider than ever, holding out his hands in a gesture of surrender.

"We have questions," Satoshi told him. "About your connections to Fuse Iemon."

The startled outrage drained out of Goro's voice, leaving it hollow. "I... I don't know what you..."

Mitsui grimaced, still looking back and forth between the prone merchant and the staring maidservant, who had risen uncertainly to her feet. "Please don't waste our time, Merchant Goro. We know what you are. I just need you to tell us one thing."

The man's eyes darted toward Mitsui, then flickered away. His hands were trembling. "What—I don't know—"

"I think you do. Where is the Voice of Treason?"

Goro's face went slack, his eyes losing focus. "I… I can't, he won't let me," he whispered.

Mitsui took a step closer, focusing now wholly on the merchant. "Do you think I cannot make you talk? I have questioned your kind before, that is how I found you. And I am very tired of playing games."

"Games?" The merchant's face suddenly twisted, a rictus grin pulling back the corners of his mouth. His hands slapped together, pinning Satoshi's sword-blade between them. The samurai let out a half-shout of surprise and tried to yank it free, but Goro's hands and arms were locked, the tendons standing out.

The merchant thrust his head and shoulders forward, driving the point of the blade down into his own mouth. Blood spurted. Satoshi shouted in angry disgust.

Prickling instinct made Mitsui look over his shoulder. The maidservant was rushing at him, sock-clad feet all but silent on the smooth wood floor, a kitchen knife gleaming in her upraised hand. Mitsui spun with frantic haste, whipping his short sword in a rising-angle cut that took the young woman across the front from lower hip to upper shoulder. Her rush went stumbling-clumsy and she collapsed against him, her overhand stab losing its strength. The knife-point scored across the thick cloth of his jacket but didn't penetrate. Mitsui gagged against the intense iron-excrement stench and the sensation of hot blood fountaining down his front. He shoved the dead woman off to sprawl bonelessly on the floor, a vast flood of dark crimson spreading around her.

Satoshi finally yanked his sword free with a curse. "Like in the prison," he rasped, panting. "With Hanzu."

Mitsui nodded, shuddering. Hanzu had been a deputy magistrate in LowTown, manipulated and controlled by the Masks. When Mitsui and Satoshi had tried to interrogate him, some outside force had taken control and forced him to attack them.

Goro sprattled and shivered, blood spilling from his mouth, his eyes rolled back in his head. The movements slowed, stopped.

"Damnation," Mitsui whispered again. His last lead had just died out.

CHAPTER 15

THE SUN ROSE, A dull orange-red circle behind fog, and the light gleamed on thousands of spears. Somewhere in the ranks of the Wolf Clan army the cheer began, scattered and soft at first, then rising and spreading: "The Lady is with us! Ookami! *The Lady is with us! Ookami!*"

Kado Kitaro felt a shiver run up his back as the cheer grew and grew, echoing through the damp early-morning air. He shook himself free of its grip, took a bowl from a bowing servant, and stepped forward and to the side, making sure the line at the meal-table kept moving. The men with him were doing the same, moving out of the way before slurping down the soup. It was fermented-soy broth, strengthened with pieces of spring vegetables and dried bean-curd; behind the serving tables a score of servants from the army's baggage-train were busily chopping up ingredients and dumping them into the pots, while others scooped the soy-paste into the broth to boil.

He sipped the hot broth, shutting his eyes to enjoy the savory warmth. Around him thousands of his men did the same, fueling themselves before the battle. The army's far more numerous infantry had already eaten – servants had started carrying pots to the tents two hours before dawn – and now it was the cavalry's turn; unless the enemy suddenly broke and ran, they would not be needed for hours yet.

Six thousand cavalry here, Kitaro thought, opening his eyes to look around. The horses were being brought in from their overnight grazing lines – well away from the main camp so their droppings would not foul the local water

– and they whinnied and snorted and shook their heads and tails, catching the building excitement of the riders brushing down their coats and saddling them. *The enemy can't have more than a thousand horsemen at best, and most of those are the Konatsu traitors.*

It would be good to finally punish those Konatsu men.

Patience, he reminded himself, taking another long drink of the soup. The urge to charge out and confront the enemy was strong, but Lord Akira was counting on him to be sensible. Cavalry could not fight prepared infantry straight-up and hope to prevail, the mounts were simply too vulnerable to the foot troops' spears so long as the infantry kept their nerve. Poorly motivated troops might break and run in the face of a cavalry charge, but for every story of an army defeated in that way there were two stories of foolish cavalry commanders wrecking their forces against impregnable walls of spears. That had been the doom of the White Fox Clan in their last great battle with the Tiger, when they tried to sweep the enemy away in a single massive charge and instead were wiped out almost to the man.

Finished with his breakfast, Kitaro returned the bowl to the servants – they had another group with buckets of soapy water, scrubbing the bowls as fast as they came back – and went in search of his own mount. He found it by his tent, along with all of his command group: Okada Kazomiru, Tamashiro Shungo, several Captains promoted from the old days, Lieutenant Juzo today carrying the banner with the Ookami wolf and Kitaro's personal crest, and a half-dozen couriers to carry orders. He checked the ties on the saddle, then swung into it with practiced ease. The others fell in behind him in a double-line, trotting past their men and on toward the main army.

The infantry force was already deployed, staggered blocks of armored samurai stretching to Kitaro's left for over a mile, the most distant ones little more than vague shapes in the morning mist. As the thunderous cheers finally died down the formations began to move forward at a slow walk. The enemy position was almost two miles away, barely visible as an intermittent glitter of metal atop the chain of low hills, the Midorisaka, they had chosen to anchor their position. They were not moving yet, content to wait for the Wolf to close the distance.

Kitaro turned left and trotted along behind the front line, looking for the command group. He found it quickly enough, the cluster of banners unmistakable. Many of the nobles had already moved out to join their own formations, but Lord Musume, Lord Kuroi, and Hajime Soto remained for now with the commander.

Kitaro reined in and bowed. "A very good morning, honorable Nomi." He bowed more generally to the other senior men present.

Chujitsuna Nomi had been past his prime when he led a company in the thousand-man army Ookami Akira took into the Nightingale lands four years ago. Now he was unmistakably *old*, his face creased with weariness and pain, his crippled arm shriveled and atrophied. His eyes, though, had a fierce energy they had lacked in those former days. That was accentuated by the war-mask covering the lower half of his face, which resembled a warrior's scowling mouth framed by long moustaches. "Honorable Kitaro, welcome," he called. "Has anything changed with the enemy position?"

"No, honorable Nomi." Kitaro's cavalry had been watching it for four days now, and never more intently than last night when the opposing forces were encamped so close together. It was normal for opposing armies to camp within shouting distance of each other while they rested and prepared for the decisive clash – the same had happened at Yotsukado and the Nagai Kyukai Plain, and Kitaro, even with his limited education, knew of a score of battles in the Empire's past where the same thing happened. Still, it would have been unwise not to guard against the possibility of a night ambush.

The Jade Dragons had anchored their right on a slough that extended for several miles south of the hills, while their left flank extended a little beyond the northernmost of the hills and curved back westward, refusing an easy target to the Wolf advance but still offering a welcome to any reinforcements – such as the Bear army – that might arrive from that direction. If Nomi's army had possessed a larger numerical advantage, he could have attacked that flank while maintaining enough strength on its own center and right to deter a counter-strike from the Jade Dragons. As it was, with only a five-to-four edge in infantry strength, a direct assault would have been the only viable tactic even if Lord Akira had not ordered it.

Nomi walked back and forth, watching the advance, his motions accentuated by his broad-flanged helmet. "Honorable Lord Musume, I believe your soldiers will be the first to come within arrow-range. No doubt they will benefit from your presence."

"As you say, honorable Nomi." The bearded nobleman bowed and kicked his horse into motion, trotting toward the three-thousand-man block of his sworn vassals. A trio of escorts followed him.

Kitaro watched them go, then then sidled his horse over to Hajime Soto and spoke in a soft voice. "Any further trouble with them these last two days?"

Soto shook his head, hiding a grin behind the business of tying his own war-mask into place. "Not a bit of it. The old man just had to say Lord Akira's name once and they went quiet as mice." He held out one gauntleted hand and Kitaro slapped his own hand against it, old comrades of the Nightingale campaign together once more. "Amatsu watch over you, honorable Kitaro." He kicked his own horse's flanks and galloped toward his men on the army's left.

Nomi let out a grunt. "Ah, there we go."

Kitaro looked ahead, squinting. *Yes, there.* Pale flickers of arrow-fletching, flights of missiles going back and forth between the front lines and catching the rising Sun at the apogee of their arcs. The Jade Dragons had shifted their formations somewhat, moving their archers in front of their spearmen to have clear fields of fire. When the Wolf frontline got too close, the archers would retreat up the slope past the spearmen, forcing the Wolf samurai to advance uphill.

Nomi nodded – to himself, probably, but the exaggerated motion of the helmet made it noticeable. "I should move a bit closer, I think. Honorable Kitaro, your horsemen?"

"They were eating and readying the horses when I came here," Kitaro replied. "They should be prepared within the hour, but I can order them to speed up if you need...?"

"No, this will likely be a face-to-face fight for quite a while." Nomi's voice carried an impression of a grim smile. "A soldier's fight. Appropriate for an old worn-out fellow like me to command, *neh*?"

"Apologies, honorable Nomi... Old perhaps, but hardly worn-out," Kitaro replied firmly.

Nomi chuckled. "Polite lies are the best ones. Back to your men, honorable Kitaro. I'll see you after the fight."

⛩ ⛩ ⛩

THE FIRST THING RYU NOBORU had done after his army reached the Midorisaka hills was to have the observation platform reassembled on the crest of the left-most hill. That was not actually the tallest of them, but it gave the best view to the north, where the Bear would arrive.

Now, though, he wondered if he should have kept it in the center of the line. Most of the fighting was happening to his right, far enough that he could only get the vaguest sense of what was happening. And Soto's spies had confirmed last night that the Bear army was close, well within a day's march.

They had also told him that Lord Kiyogama had marched forth from Castle Kigi with all his strength. *Probably he expects to arrive here and join whichever side is winning,* Noboru thought, his stomach clenching with rage. *Fool. Too late for that now. I will enjoy his death, and I will make it last a long time, and he will watch while I eat his insides...*

"Ah, splendid!"

Noboru blinked back to himself, suddenly aware of how badly he was drooling. He looked around and saw Lord Oyama Hiroyuki standing by the platform's southeast corner; several lower-ranking men crowded near him, along with Konatsu Sabato, all of them pointing and letting out impressed sounds.

Oyama and Sabato were here, along with Lord Onaga, because their troops were in reserve. Onaga Kitsuya, however, seemed to have little interest in the battle; he was sitting on the northern side of the platform, quietly eating a bowl of rice, leaning forward to keep the drizzle out of it. A pair of vassals stood at the ready for orders, though he ignored them in favor of his meal.

Noboru couldn't decide whether Lord Onaga's deliberate disinterest or the others' performative cheering was more infuriating. *None of them want to be here, they are all frightened to be around me,* he knew. Which was why he insisted they be here until their men went into the fight, of course. *Treacherous scum.*

He swallowed hard and waddled to the eastern side of the platform, his armor clanking, and peered off to the right to see what had Lord Oyama so excited, unconsciously leaning forward and squinting – without wearing Selfishness' mask to boost his senses, it was hard to see details through the fog and drizzle that still hazed the air three hours after dawn. He fumbled under the layers of his belt and stroked the mask hidden there, feeling a warm relaxation and with it a slight sharpening of the world around him – not as good as wearing it, but now it was as though he was looking at a line-drawing rather than messy reality.

Two of the Wolf infantry forces were falling back, abandoning their latest attack on the center-hill positions. The withdrawal looked chaotic, some individual men walking back slowly and facing the enemy, others simply turning their backs and trotting or running. *But it looked that way after the last attack too,* Noboru knew. Samurai formations fell apart in combat, and it was all their commanders could do to convey simple orders like 'advance' or 'withdraw.' Once they got clear of the fight, though, they would reform quickly enough… and yes, as the distance between the lines widened to two hundred paces the scattered Wolf troops began congealing into ordered lines once more.

Konatsu Sabato made a theatrical gesture, slapping one fist into the other palm. "A lost opportunity! A counterattack then could have broken them. Lord Noboru!" He turned and bowed low. "Release my men and when the next Wolf attack fails we will sweep them off the field like fallen leaves!"

Noboru felt a powerful urge to seize the boasting, lying fool and jam his thumbs into his eyes. Instead he giggled and smiled vacuously. "Not just yet, honorable Sabato," he said. "Your chance to prove your loyalty will come soon enough."

He looked at the battle again, frowning inwardly. *If only I could wear the mask right now!* Without the all-encompassing guidance of Selfishness it was difficult to figure out what was really happening. *Are we winning or losing?* The Wolf army was attacking in staggered waves, first one part of its line and then another. While the assault on the center hills had pulled back, infantry were still clashing in front of the northern hill right below Noboru, and when he looked to the right and strained his eyes he could just make out a similar clash happening in front of the lower southern hills near the marsh.

By now all the ground in front of the hills had been churned into bare dark earth by the clashing and shifting armies, and with the air still misting with drizzle that earth was steadily turning into mud. Already the bright armor of the samurai was turning dark and blotchy with it, and the fallen bodies, initially bright and stark against the ground, were slowly vanishing into the squalor. *Fitting*, Noboru thought suddenly, a thought that was not truly his own. *Fitting for the filth to die amid filth.*

The Wolf cavalry had not shown itself save as an ominous hint of motion a mile and more to the northeast, half-obscured by the waves of drizzle that swept across them. Vastly more cavalry than Noboru himself possessed, and there were so many terrible rumors of what it had done against the Wolf Clan rebels last year… That was the real reason why Noboru was holding back so many reserves. If the Wolf cavalry tried to sweep around his northern flank he needed to have men who could parry the move until the Bear could get here.

And why aren't the Bear here yet? I was sure they would have arrived by now… He fumbled for the mask again, suddenly desperate for reassurance. He didn't like battles, had never liked them though his father and brothers all loved them and mocked him for his weakness. Memories suddenly welled up – his father grunting crudely, his big brother Gyukai laughing at him when he tripped while parading in his new armor, his second brother Rokaro sneering and parading his pretty wife like a prize trinket, little Kioshi recoiling in disgust after catching Noboru with a servant-boy…

Well, they are all dead now, he thought fiercely. *No one laughs at me now, no one dares hurt me now.* The Masks had killed Gyukai for him, the final step before he accepted the mantle of Selfishness. Rokaro had been cut down by his precious wife, father had been knifed to death in front of the whole court by Lady Naichin, and Noboru could still remember the taste of Kioshi's blood, the feel of his rending flesh.

The rain had gotten slightly heavier, individual droplets dinging on his helmet and spattering from his shoulder plates, and the clouds were now a solid gray roof overhead, though there were still a few hints of Sunlight trying to slip through in the east.

And when the Wolf are defeated, I can finally be rid of the traitors like Kiyogama, and the brethren from the north will join me. His mouth filled with saliva, his fingers and toes clenching in anticipation. The heat of that anticipation was only slightly dampened by the vague knowledge that something had gone wrong in the Tiger lands. *Whatever it was, it is only a delay, not a defeat,* he told himself, stroking the mask once more.

"My Lord!"

Noboru's head snapped around, sharply enough that his helmet went slightly askew and he had to adjust it. He snatched his hand out of his belt and wiped away the worst of the drool on his chin with his fingertips, wishing he was in court robes so he could blot it with a sleeve.

One of his couriers was on the northern side of the platform, pointing urgently. Lord Onaga, seated nearby, had lifted his head from his rice-bowl and was peering in the same direction thoughtfully, still chewing his last mouthful.

"The Bear have arrived, honored High Lord!"

"Finally," Noboru muttered, his lips curling into a gleeful smile. He scuttled across the viewing platform to the north side, almost tripping over the heavy waist-plates of his armor, just as he had done in front of Gyukai so long ago.

Two miles north of his own position was another low line of hills, the nearest ones bare of trees but growing wooded toward the west. Infantry were spilling over the crests, rows and rows of them, dark armor glittering even through the rain, fluttering back-banners stark against the green of spring grass. Thousands of spearmen, their weapons held upright as they advanced at a steady trot.

Noboru shuffled his feet in a quick dance of triumphant glee, then capered back to the east side of the platform, no danger of tripping now, laughing aloud as he looked down at the armies clashing on the flatland below. "Too late!" he called, still laughing, drops of saliva spraying free. "The more you press forward, the worse it will be. And your precious cavalry are no use now!" And indeed, even as he shouted he could see that great lurking mass of horsemen pulling back, almost recoiling like a spooked animal.

"My lord," Lord Onaga called, his voice oddly flat. "You must see this."

Noboru spun around, opening his mouth to shout in fury. The expression on Onaga's face curdled his rage. The nobleman remained on the north side of the platform, but he was no longer chewing and his round soft face had gone pale.

Most of the Bear army was over the hills now, forming up in the mile of open grassland below them, a bristling front three thousand men wide and four men deep. Perfectly positioned to turn left, anchoring themselves on Noboru's flank, and sweep into the side of the Wolf Clan army.

But another army was coming out of the low valley to the northeast, troops flowing smoothly from marching formations into fighting blocks, deploying on the left of the Bear. Thousands of men in gray and red, some of them with darker red that seemed almost black, the colors muted by the rain but unmistakable.

Konatsu Sabato had come to the north side of the platform as well. "Are those… Wolf troops?" His formerly loud voice had gone soft and weak.

This cannot be right, Noboru thought frantically. *Lord Akira stayed at Castle Kosaten, Lord Goda and the spies both saw his banner there, they even saw* him *in the ancestral armor that no one else ever wears… And Selfishness saw nothing, warned me of nothing…* He started to reach for the mask again but then stopped, conscious of the others' eyes on him.

As the new army finished deploying, company banners went up above the men, and with them the larger banners of the commanders. A hundred Wolf Clan crests snarled at Noboru, along with the bright triple-crosshatch of the Toshiwara and the black wolf's head of the Kuroi.

A half mile to their right, the Bear army waited stolidly, its own dull-brown banners fluttering softly.

"Why aren't the Bear doing anything?" Lord Oyama sounded genuinely puzzled, his voice somehow even more boyish than usual.

Fool, idiot, I should kill you here, Noboru raged behind a vacant drooling stare. He could see the same truth on Lord Onaga and Konatsu Sabato's faces that he had just realized himself. *The Bear have betrayed us somehow.*

Without thinking he seized the man by the war-mask dangling from his helmet, dragging him close -- a violation of etiquette that drew a few gasps even in this intense moment. "Move your men to the north flank at once," he hissed, lines of saliva spewing from his lower lip and spattering the nobleman's breast-plate. "At once, do you understand?"

Lord Oyama nodded frantically and Noboru shoved him away, not even bothering to see if he obeyed, and rounded on the nearest courier. "Go to honorable Mugai Soto at the headquarters tents. Tell him to send word back to Castle Hokori. Kuma Joji must be killed. Tell him now!"

The man bowed low, his face chalk-pale, and raced down the stairs from the platform, passing Lord Oyama and his retinue. The young nobleman was shouting orders to his men in a voice gone shrill with sudden fear.

Lord Onaga was still watching the distant armies. "Who is that?"

A single mounted man rode out in front of the newly arrived Wolf army. A thin, small-framed figure in simple gray armor, riding as though he and the horse were a single creature. He reined in fifty paces out, rearing the beast and turning it in place, and a roaring wordless cheer rose from the Wolf ranks.

Onaga rose to his feet, his rice-bowl forgotten in his hand. "Is that… High Lord Akira?"

Yes, it is, Noboru knew, and felt a chill of strange fear run through his belly and turn his limbs weak. Somehow it was hard to look at the mile-distant High Lord of the Wolf. His eyes didn't want to focus on that doll-tiny figure, his mind locking up whenever he tried. He pawed at his belt, touching the mask without regard for what the others might see.

Selfishness' power flickered through him briefly, but it did not bring the usual comforting warmth of confident lust. Instead, it felt... angry, and distant, and *cold.*

"Yes," Konatsu Sabato said aloud, his voice hollow. "Yes, that is him. I saw him at Nagai Kyukai."

Noboru had forgotten about the useless traitor and his horsemen. "Get to your men, you fool. Be ready to counter any move by their cavalry." The imbecilic man opened his mouth to say something, and Noboru's voice rose to a shrill screech: "*NOW*, or slit your belly where you stand, vermin!"

Sabato fled.

The distant High Lord reared his beast again and shouted at his men, his voice echoing across the field with unnatural clarity. To Noboru it was a lance of ice piercing his head.

"The Lady with us!"

The Wolf army roared the sacred cheer back at their High Lord.

And then the Bear shouted it as well, a deep-chested unified bellow that struck like a thunderclap:

"THE LADY WITH US!"

Their spears came down, a long ripple, and they started forward. South, straight toward the Jade Dragon army's left flank.

⛩ ⛩ ⛩

"HONORABLE KITARO, SHOULD WE—?"

It was Lieutenant Juzo, currently assigned to hold the cavalry's banner. The question was inappropriate, of course, but rather than scold the man Kitaro simply pretended the noise of the rain had drowned it out. After a moment Juzo mumbled an apology for forgetting his place, and Kitaro pretended the rain had drowned that out as well.

The rain turned everything beyond a half-mile's distance into gray vagueness – he could see motion, the back-and-forth shifts of the battle-lines, but that was all. Noise drifted through the air, the unmistakable clamor of battle, an uneven discordance that mingled battle-cries, shouts, screams, the crash of impact and the clang of metal. Thankfully, at this distance and in this weather the scents of the battle did *not* carry; all he could smell was the rain, the damp earth, and the strong but not unpleasant odor of thousands of wet horses.

He glanced up and around, trying to gauge the time. The clouds had thickened enough that he could get only a vague sense of the Sun's location, but if his guess was correct… *Has it only been four hours? It feels so much longer…*

A sound resolved itself from the larger background noise – a thutter of hooves, a man in light armor and back-banner galloping out of the rainy mirk toward them. His banner showed the Ookami wolf alone, marking him as part of Lord Akira's personal retinue.

The man reined in, his horse snorting and throwing off a spray of droplets from its mane. "Honorable Kado Kitaro! The High Lord requests that you move the cavalry to the northwest, to the far end of the Bear army's lines."

Kitaro felt a jolt of excitement, mingled with the hint of fear that always came with imminent battle. "It shall be as the High Lord commands!" he called to the courier. He snatched up his spear from where it rested point-down next to him, tucking it under his right arm, then turned to his own entourage and relayed commands. Men galloped off through the rain, leaving roostertails of spray behind them, and the whole assembled force began to shift and gather itself. Slowly at first, because six thousand men on horseback could not all start moving at once. First the orders had to filter out, to captains and then to lieutenants and down to the squadrons; then the troops in the front ranks had to start forward to open room for the rest to follow. The formation thinned and extended as that began, then gradually thickened up again as the trailing squadrons got moving and closed up the gaps. They advanced at a trot, fast enough to reach their destination quickly but not enough to exhaust the horses or risk injuries on the wet ground.

Kitaro rode with the leading squadrons, blinking as rain splattered his face and bounced off his helmet's brim. They passed to the right of the fighting, close behind the Bear reserve formations, men standing stolidly in ranks with spears held vertical while they waited to move forward. Earlier in the battle they would probably have been serving as archers to support the ground combat, but the rain had put a stop to that. Some of them turned their heads to watch the Wolf cavalry pass, and Kitaro glimpsed a group of men on horseback who watched closely while leaning together to speak. *Is that their High Lord?* They had a large banner with them, but the rain had left it drooping, the crest unreadable.

The cavalry pulled up beyond the right flank of the Bear, spreading out into a broad front a thousand horses wide and six deep. Kitaro positioned himself in the center, where everyone could see his banner and take their cue from it; the captains set themselves at the front of each company. The noise level dropped as the last of the squadrons settled into position, leaving only the hissing rush of the rain and the now-distant mutter of the battle.

From here open grassland extended westward to a belt of low forested hills a couple of miles away, barely discernible through the rain. To the left, in the low ground behind the Midorisaka hills, Kitaro could see the shapes of hundreds of tents – the Jade Dragon camp. There was a sense of activity, of people and animals moving, but he could not make out any details.

"What now, honorable Kitaro?"

This time Kitaro answered the Lieutenant. "Now we wait for Lord Akira."

ℏ ℏ ℏ

RYU NOBORU COULD SEE – could *feel* in the cold clenching terror that radiated through his belly – the situation collapsing around him. And he knew the men around him on the platform could see, could feel the same thing.

On his right, the fighting that had begun at dawn continued unabated, the Wolf troops pressing forward despite rain and mud; his lines there, pinned in place by the attack and no longer able to support themselves with archery, were now slowly giving ground, inching back up the slopes.

In the center, the new Wolf army – the army that was supposed to be at Castle Kosaten! – had overrun the lower slopes of the northernmost of the Midorisaka hills and was within three hundred paces of the observation platform itself.

And on the left, the Bear army – the treacherous, betraying Bear army – was steadily grinding Lord Oyama's men into bloody ruin.

"Most honored High Lord," Lord Onaga Kitsuya said, his voice just audible over the rain.

The rain! He hadn't realized how much that would matter. Bows didn't shoot properly in the rain, could barely shoot at all now, and that weakened his own forces more than the enemy.

"Most honored High Lord," Onaga repeated, slightly louder. He was the only nobleman remaining on the platform, representing the last reserve of Noboru's army. "Do you have orders for me?"

Noboru could just see the enemy cavalry, moving up behind the Bear like a river in flash-flood. *How long until my lines give way and those horsemen ride us all down like grass? Oh, that fool Konatsu Sabato will try to stop them, but what use will that be?*

I'm going to lose, Noboru knew, his mind stuttering, darting about like a mouse chased by a cat. *This can't happen. I killed Gyukai and Kioshi, I outlived father, I'm chosen by Selfishness!*

That thought brought him up short. *That can save me. I don't have to hide it anymore, not if this is the only way out. And if I can get out, the Brothers and Sisters will protect me because I'm a Voice.* His hands dug frantically in his belt, worming through the layers of tight-wrapped silk.

"My Lord?" Lord Onaga was still hovering, waiting. *Miserable fool*, Noboru raged inside his head. *I know he wanted to betray me like Kiyogama, he* would *have betrayed me if I'd given him any chance.* He rounded on the nobleman, spitting to clear away the rain that kept running down his face and into his mouth.

"You and your men will secure the line of retreat," he snarled.

Onaga's eyes widened very slightly. "Retreat, my Lord?"

"Yes, retreat, damnation on you!" Noboru screeched. He lifted his left hand and pointed a shaking finger at the road behind the army's camp, the distant woodline to the west. "Secure that road at any cost. No matter if you and all your men die to do it! You understand?"

The man's expression subtly changed. Noboru could not quite understand it – the subtle relaxing of his face around his eyes. Was he… *happy* to get this order?

Lord Onaga bowed. "Of course, my Lord." He walked quietly down the stairs from the platform, his escorts following.

Noboru looked back at the battle, his right hand now clenching on the mask as he waddled a half-circle around the platform, north to east to south. Everywhere he looked he could see his army edging backward, the lines losing more and more cohesion, individual men drifting to the rear as the knowledge of defeat ate away at samurai courage.

He yanked the mask out and looked at it greedily. The raindrops splashed off of it, water running smoothly down its curves and dripping cleanly off the bottom edge as though it was unwilling to touch the white surface.

One of the guards let out a grunt of shock, his gaze tracking from the mask to Noboru's face and back. "My… my Lord..?"

Noboru slapped the mask onto his face. The world became a monocolored vision, flickering with the pale lights of thousands of souls, flaring and winking out of his perceptions as the bodies they belonged to died and they fled to a realm he could not, would not, perceive.

Somewhere nearby, amid the Wolf army's ranks, something glowed brightly, fierce as a lightning bolt, and he turned his head away from it, away from the knowledge of what it might be.

That swung his face toward the guards. They let out strangled cries, and the one who had spoken before set his hand on his sword.

Hatred filled Noboru, not just his own emotion but the hatred of Selfishness and of the five others to which Selfishness was joined. Endless, insatiable hatred for these useless things of flesh that somehow, impossibly, contained within themselves small pieces of eternity.

He swung his hand up, palm-out and fingers spread, and the hatred boiled free and consumed them.

ᚱᚱᚱ

"MAKE WAY! MAKE WAY FOR the High Lord!"

Kado Kitaro stood in the saddle and looked back for the source of the shout. A quartet of horsemen was approaching at a near-gallop, weaving between the cavalry squadrons, the mounts throwing up fountains of water and mud from their hooves. As they closed the distance to him, he recognized Lord Akira.

The High Lord was covered in blood, the rain sluicing it down to run in pale red showers off his chin and hands, off the lower edges of his helmet and the waist-plates of his armor. Broken-off stubs of arrows projected from his shoulder plates, and a scar of bare metal gleamed through the lacquer of his helmet. The snorting, blowing horse he rode was different than the one he had taken into the battle two hours ago. The three escorts with him looked the same or worse; one of them was missing his helmet and had a blood-soaked bandage wrapped around his head and covering one eye.

Akira reined in next to Kitaro. His voice was clipped, flat, piercingly clear through the noise of rain and combat. "Honorable Kitaro. The cavalry will attack, in this direction." He pointed with his left arm, straight at the distant camp. "I will accompany you."

"It shall be as you say, most honorable High Lord!" Kitaro stood in the saddle and shouted to his men. "Prepare to attack! The Lady with us! Ookami!"

The men roared back, the horses bugling and snorting as they caught the excitement.

"I need a spear," Akira said. Before Kitaro could even speak, Lieutenant Juzo lifted his spear upright and handed it over.

Kitaro sucked in a deep breath and blew it out slowly, centering himself, sweeping out the fluttering weakness in his belly. "Advance," he shouted, and behind him Juzo leaned the banner sharply forward. The front rank stepped off, a walk and then a trot, the others following, the formation coming back together quickly as it built up speed.

Ahead of them shapes emerged from the rain, a line of horsemen, their armor Jade Dragon green but with a yellow peony on the banners overhead. *The Konatsu,* Kitaro thought, laughing exultantly, all earlier nervousness swept away in the joy of battle. *At last, at long last.* "Charge," he called, swinging his spear upright and raising it overhead. "Charge, *charge*!"

The horses went to a gallop, water spraying up in a great blinding cloud. Somewhere off to the left a beast slipped on the wet grass and went down, men and animals screaming and colliding and tumbling, others leaping and swerving to get past the sudden obstacle, but it barely mattered now, the charge was at full speed and the enemy line coming at them was the same, the opposing lines suddenly close. He could see the fixed grimaces of the enemy cavalrymen, the wide eyes and red nostrils of the horses, the raindrops spraying off the foot-long blades of the spears as they came down to the level.

And then a blade was coming at his face, and he tried to simultaneously duck aside and thrust his own spear forward. Impact on his left shoulder plate, a wrenching yank on his shoulders and back and neck as the spear lodged in between the lacquered metal pieces, and then the silk ties gave way and the release of tension flung him in the opposite direction. At the same time a heavy impact jolted up his right arm and shoulder as his own spear slammed into an enemy's belly. The Konatsu horsemen went back off his horse, the spear-point lodged in his stomach, and Kitaro let go of the haft and rode past, briefly glimpsing his foe tumbling on the ground and the spear-shaft snapping.

Kitaro swung his head left and right, trying to see what was happening through the rain slashing his face. The enemy cavalry line had vanished, swept away by the crushing weight of five times its numbers. His own men were still charging forward, most of them at least, though he could no longer see Lieutenant Juzo with the banner. Akira was still on his left, holding a spear whose point sluiced blood, and ahead of them foot-soldiers loomed out of the rain, scores of them, hundreds, some standing to fight while others turned and ran. Kitaro howled wordlessly and swept out his long sword, cutting down again and again, slashing at heads, shoulders, upraised arms. Going uphill now, angling across the slope, and the small thinking part of his mind knew: *We're behind their lines!*

Somehow there was a fire, upslope to his left – something there was burning, orange flames flickering amid the rain. *How did a fire start in the middle of this?*

Akira was suddenly ahead of him, gesturing with his spear at a loose group of armored samurai fifty paces away. They were hurrying downslope and away, and even through the blurring rain Kitaro could see that one of them was in the bulky elaborate armor of a nobleman, while another carried a large banner with the Ryu coiling-dragon crest.

Their High Lord, Kitaro knew with a surge of triumph. He looked around one last time for Lieutenant Juzo, then screamed, "Ookami! Ookami! Onward, *onward*!" and waved his sword over his head, whirling it in a circle and cutting downward as he turned his horse to follow the High Lord. Not all his men heard him – the charge was breaking up into a thousand smaller charges as the horsemen chased the targets on every side – but some of them did, a squadron or more. They bore down on the retreating enemy.

Twenty paces. Abruptly the heavy-armored man stopped and turned, and Kitaro felt a strange icy jolt run through his body. The face within the helmet's frame was a pale blank oval, like an actor's mask with no eyeholes and no paint. *That can't be the High Lord, can it? Why would Lord Noboru be wearing that on his face?*

The masked figure lifted both hands, the palms flickering with a greenish luminescence. A high-pitched voice screeched something from beneath the mask, and the noise made Kitaro's head suddenly throb as though he had been drinking wine for hours. His mouth started to form the words racing through his mind: *Amatsu preserve me, what is that—*

Steam exploded away from Lord Noboru's hands in an expanding ring that flung the rain out in a series of rippling spheres. Rancid green light slashed through the air in a wild arc, striking men and horses. A man's head vanished into the flame, helmet and skull flaring yellow-white and then searing away in another spherical steam-cloud, this one reddish-pink; there was not even time for him to scream.

Without thinking Kitaro ducked down behind his horse's head, and an instant later the flame swept past him and the horse uttered a single shrill scream and pitched forward into the ground, flinging Kitaro off its back. For an instant he hung suspended in the air, water and steam whirling past him, the ground above and the gray sky below his feet, his sword slipping free of nerveless fingers. In that eternal brief heartbeat he saw Lord Akira leap clear of his own horse, leap *forward* as the unnatural green fire passed beneath him and struck the horse like a flaming scythe, the beast coming apart in pieces that spewed a cloud of reddish-black vaporized blood.

The ground slammed into Kitaro like a monstrous sledge, numbness and then a ghastly shock of pain through one arm. He flopped on the ground, helpless, half-blind with tears, wheezing for breath. The air stank of death and terror and burnt meat.

Five paces away, Lord Akira landed in a forward roll, bouncing once, twice, then impossibly springing back upright, water and flecks of earth coming off him in spinning arcs, his long sword still in his hand. He had lost his helmet and his white-streaked air whirled loose around his head.

The masked shape – could it really be Lord Noboru? – screeched again, a wordless ululation that Kitaro somehow heard *inside* his head, like a Priestess' bone-saw cutting through his mind. It lifted its hands again and the blue-green flicker turned once more to spears of ravening flame, roaring out to strike Akira...

...and flowing around him, like water curling off a rock. For a pair of heartbeats Kitaro saw a sphere of cool milky-white light surrounding his High Lord, pale and translucent as a morning mist, and in that instant the agony in his mind was swept away.

The grass scorched and charred in an arc at Akira's feet, and a fresh wave of steam pulsed outward from him, rolling across Kitaro like an eruption from an overheated bath-house.

The unnatural flame guttered out, and the masked figure spoke, in a human voice that squealed like a plaintive child. "That's not fair! The Moon's slave, here, right after Castle Mouko... not fair!"

Akira slid forward, his sword rising and falling in a precise arc, and the blade went through helmet and mask and the flesh beneath, down into the neck and chest, slicing through the layers of steel and leather as though they were silk. A terrible gurgling howl came from behind the split mask, and then a massive gout of blood. The bloated figure dropped to its knees, its arms jiggling and twitching; Akira kicked it square in the chest, the armor plate denting in like balsa, and a fresh goat of blood sprayed out of the thing's neck and face as he wrenched the sword free and it fell back the ground, sprattled violently once, and went still.

Kitaro felt a sudden relaxation, as though a tight-wound rope in his heart had uncoiled. He was conscious again of the sound of the rain, of the roaring clamor of the battle around him, of the pain in his body and the stabbing agony-ache in his right arm. He forced himself up with his left hand, breathing in thin gasps through clenched teeth, holding the wounded arm against his torso and not letting himself look at it.

Akira stood over the body of the High Lord of the Jade Dragon Clan, his chest moving steadily as he sucked in deep breaths, his face expressionless, his eyes unfocused.

A rattle of hoofbeats, other men in Wolf gray riding up. "My Lord! Honorable Kitaro!" And there was Lieutenant Juzo, pale and blood-splattered but alive, still holding the banner. "Honorable Kitaro! Are you well?"

Akira's eyes abruptly focused. He caught his loose hair with his left hand and pulled it back, using the rain-wet to plaster it against his scalp. He looked briefly at Kitaro, then called, "I need a horse."

Kitaro opened his mouth to give an order, but there was no need; one of the other riders had instantly dismounted and led his animal over to the High Lord. Without another word Akira swung into the saddle and rode away, calling orders in a voice that echoed across the field like a sacred drum.

Lieutenant Juzo walked his horse closer. "Honorable Kitaro? What... what happened here?"

"I'm... I'm not..." Kitaro broke off, sucked in a long breath, let it out slowly. The pain from his arm was worse by the minute, but the focusing exercise let him master it for just this moment. "I do not know, honorable

Juzo, but I need a horse as well. And someone to bind my arm to my breast-plate. The battle isn't over yet."

CHAPTER 16

LORD KIYOGAMA HEISUKE REINED in his horse and lifted his gauntleted right hand to shield his eyes. The weather had shifted from cloudy dampness at dawn to a steady drizzle and now to outright rain, making everything more than a half-mile away into colorless shadow.

After a moment he turned to his son, riding behind him. "What do you think?"

Asking his son's counsel in public was a show of trust, not just to him but to the soldiers marching with them, a column only three men wide but over fifteen hundred long, stretching back along the farmer's road for more than a mile. Banners fluttered weakly in the wet air, and the rain-haze muted the colors – pale yellow, the Jade Dragon green-and-gold entirely absent. Similarly, the banners were in yellow and showed only his own sunflower-blossom crest. It had been expensive to replace all the banners and have all the armor re-lacquered over the last month, but marching to war with an army in the same colors as High Lord Noboru's forces was an invitation to lethal chaos.

Kiyogama Daihachi kneed his own horse up alongside his father and peered ahead. They were both in full armor, the elaborate panoply of extra plates covering the shoulders and waist and thighs, gaudy helmets shrouding their faces. Kiyogama's helmet was the ancestral one his family's Lords had worn into conflict for over a century – a long slanting dome that rose a foot above and behind his head, embossed with the family crest on both sides. He'd had it re-lacquered as well.

They stood on the southern edge of a series of grain fields that stretched two miles to a series of wooded hills on the northern horizon. Clusters of farmer's houses perched on the edge of the woods, still and silent – the farmers here would seldom have encountered large groups of samurai, and were doubtless cowering inside and praying that the passing army would not afflict them.

Kiyogama's attention was directed eastward, where the landscape sloped gradually upward to a broad saddle between two densely wooded hills. Tiny shapes moved there, barely identifiable through the obscuring rain as samurai. They were coming over the saddle and then slowing, losing cohesion, as they spotted Kiyogama's force.

"The banners show a double spiral. I would say those are Lord Onaga's men," Daihachi said finally.

"Indeed, I believe you are correct. In fact," Kiyogama narrowed his eyes, squinting irritably as water dripped off the brim of his helmet, "I am fairly sure that is Lord Onaga's personal banner at the front." There was a small group of horsemen riding at the lead of the formation, and the oversized banner with them showed the bamboo-leaf crest of Onaga's line.

Daihachi frowned. "That is not as large a force as I would expect, to be accompanying the Lord himself."

Lord Kiyogama nodded thoughtfully. "I would guess that these are the men Lord Onaga has left."

"The battle is already over? Our… that is, Lord Noboru is defeated?"

"That would seem the most likely explanation. Ah, it seems they intend to fight… interesting." The Onaga samurai were shifting into a fighting formation, moving a little raggedly but quickly enough.

Kiyogama considered, stroking his half-regrown moustaches, and then raised one arm and made a sharp gesture to his own men. They too began to fall out of their marching column into a series of rectangular blocks, facing toward the mile-distant threat. The rain-wet grass quickly began squishing into mud as they trampled across it.

Daihachi frowned more deeply. "Does honorable Lord Onaga intend to fight? Surely he can see how hopeless that would be."

"Let us see what he does." Lord Kiyogama crossed his hands over the horn of his saddle and waited. The soldiers on both sides continued to deploy, the disparity in numbers becoming increasingly obvious. Onaga's force was at best only half the size of Kiyogama's.

An armored man with a spear held point-down in his right hand rode out into the open space between the two forces. Water fountained up from the horse's hooves as he went through a dip in the land, then reined in atop a soft berm-shape that was probably the remnant of a long-abandoned erosion terrace. He let his horse turn in a circle before reining it to a halt and raising the spear, brandishing it toward the Kiyogama forces.

"Ah, that is my cue," Kiyogama murmured.

His son opened his mouth to object, closed it at Kiyogama's look. Instead he asked: "What if he kills you?"

"Unlikely, I think." Heisuke held out his hand to one of his escorts, and the man tossed him a spear. The haft smacked into Kiyogama's palm and he spun it back and forth once, twice, getting the balance. Then he slung it under his arm, point-down. "But if somehow this does end badly, I am sure you will be able to lead the Clan well enough." *No man escapes Amatsu's judgment.* It was an old, old saying, and one Kiyogama had sneered at in his youth. These days, religion seemed more important than it once had. Aloud he continued: "We have gambled our survival here, Daihachi; a half-measure now is as bad as never trying at all."

Daihachi nodded tight-lipped, then bowed.

Lord Kiyogama kicked his horse into motion and rode down the long shallow slope, then back up the far side toward the waiting horseman. He drew up on the same berm five paces away, blinking his eyes free of rainwater while letting his own horse circle and blow as the other had done, and then bowed in the saddle. "Honorable Lord Onaga."

"Honorable Lord Kiyogama." The other man bowed as well. Lord Onaga was an older man but short and with an oddly youthful face, soft and round, almost child-like. His armor was as elaborate as Kiyogama's, complete with a helmet that mounted a high peak encircled with a serpentine rendering of a dragon in polished gold, but it seemed oversized, almost grotesque, on his modest frame. He looked past Kiyogama, at the lines of soldiers now fully deployed up the shallow slope. "It seems we meet in unfortunate circumstances."

"Do we? We have the opportunity to converse here, without anyone else overhearing us, even our own men. That strikes me as most fortunate, in truth."

"*Ah so*?" Onaga let out a dry chuckle. "And what should we discuss in this fortunate moment of privacy?"

Kiyogama lifted his left hand and stroked his moustaches again. Water oozed out of the modest bristle of hairs under his fingertips. "Perhaps a way to avoid needless conflict."

The older nobleman laughed aloud. "You expect me to join you in betraying the High Lord? No, don't try to deny it – even in this rain we can both see how you've changed the colors on your men. As you say, we're in private, and this isn't the time for court games, not when we stand in the hard place where all choices end."

Kiyogama raised his eyebrows but did not otherwise change his expression. "You are not here to make a triumphal march. Do you think High Lord Noboru is likely to win, at this point?"

"Doesn't matter what I think. He ordered me to clear a route for retreat, no matter what the cost. I'm a samurai and he's my sworn liege. Why, they'll probably write songs and poems about me, like they did about Kujaku Tominoe!" That was a samurai in the first century after the Dread Eclipse who had famously stood his ground and fought to the death to cover the retreat of his Lord, despite the opposing Wolf Clan commander inviting him to switch sides and save both his own life and the men under his command. He was still remembered as a paragon of the Samurai Code.

Not least, Kiyogama thought with a thin smile, *because so few others, including* my *family, have lived up to his example.*

"Lord Noboru is not deserving of such loyalty," he said aloud. "You were at Castle Hokori last winter, Kitsuya, and at the massacre of the Monks in your own lands. A thousand-year-old monastery burned, the Teachers slaughtered... You know what he is."

"I was there, at the Monastery and at Castle Hokori," Lord Onaga nodded. "And my son is still there."

Ah, Kiyogama thought sadly. *As I expected, really.* Onaga's first wife had proven to have an ill-favored womb, and he had divorced her after their only child to survive infancy had died at age six. His second wife had proven fecund, but she had borne him four daughters and only two sons, of which just one had lived to adulthood.

"I was there," Onaga repeated, his voice bitter and bleak. "I saw you hang your daughter Chiyu with your own hands. And then you left the court in secret... cleverly done, I admit, and your son Goichi stayed behind to endure Lord Noboru's wrath on your behalf. How did that discussion go, before you departed?"

"It was unpleasant," Kiyogama replied. "Afterward, in private, I wept. Is that what you want to hear?"

The older nobleman grimaced and ducked his head, ashamed. "My apologies," he muttered. Then he straightened and spoke more clearly. "Regardless... My son remains in Castle Hokori. I have no choice."

"Do you truly? If Lord Noboru perishes here, your son may survive. There will be no one to order his execution."

Onaga shook his head. "Gamble that he left no orders in the event of his death? He already dispatched a command to kill the Bear heir. I cannot take that chance for my son."

The trap we all inhabit, Kiyogama knew. *Always playing the safest bet, protecting the bloodline.* He looked past the other man, at the waiting lines of soldiers, and sighed to himself. *Lord Onaga knows this is hopeless, but he cannot shame himself before his men by giving up. And that is why he rode out here, with a spear in hand...*

"The Goddess calls on us to show Compassion," he said aloud. "But Heaven also demands that Honor and Duty be satisfied. So, let us decide this matter between ourselves. If I win, your men can swear fealty to me, save for those who wish to follow you into honorable death."

Onaga smiled tightly. "And if I win?"

Kiyogama smiled back. They both knew the spear was his favored weapon.

The two men touched the hafts of their spears together, then Onaga Kitsuya wheeled his horse and rode back to his men, speaking to the subordinates clustered around his banner. Kiyogama Heisuke did not bother to do the same – his son needed no orders. After a half-minute the other Lord rode back out, taking a position fifty paces away atop the berm. He raised his spear one-handed, pointing the blade toward the rain-shrouded sky, and shouted a wordless bellow of challenge.

Kiyogama raised his own spear in response and kicked his horse into a gallop. An instant later Onaga's horse surged forward as well, throwing off a shroud of water-spray.

Rain slashed at Kiyogama's face, stung his eyes despite the sheltering brim of his helmet. He ignored it, ignored the sorrow he felt for Lord Onaga and his own uncertainty for the future, ignored everything but the focused moment and the deep-trained muscle-memory of three decades' experience. It had been a long time since he had been forced to meet a challenge personally, but he had never let his training lapse.

He rose in the saddle, guiding the horse by his knees alone, and took the spear shaft in both hands, lifting it up vertically and then, at an instant guided by mingled instinct and experience, whirling it around his head and forward, stabbing with all the weight of that extra speed.

The foot-long blade punched through Lord Onaga's throat and the smaller man tumbled off his horse, Kiyogama releasing the spear-shaft with perfect timing so it would not drag him off his own mount. Onaga's spear tumbled end-over-end across the grass, throwing up arcs of water as it did.

Kiyogama reined in, awareness returning and with it the sound of his men – and his son – cheering ferociously. The Onaga samurai were silent; after a moment they began kneeling, some of them simply waiting, a few drawing blades and preparing to slit their own bellies.

Well. Lord Kiyogama took in a deep breath, smelling the rain, the crushed grass, his own armor and horse, the faint iron-sharp note of blood from where Lord Onaga lay unmoving.

The final journey
Everyone must take it
Yet we are never prepared

It seems the Lady's judgment of me remains in the future. Now we shall see if Kitsuya kept his word.

The dead Lord's personal retinue had dismounted and were walking toward Kiyogama. Ten paces away, they sank to the wet grass and prostrated themselves.

⛩ ⛩ ⛩

OOKAMI AKIRA FELT THE WORLD go dim around him. Someone called out, "Honored Lord!" and a hand caught his shoulder-plate, steadying him. Briefly his vision went colorless, dark grey at the edges, and then he shut his eyes and straightened up in his saddle. Pain and exhaustion pulsated through his chest and limbs and head, his whole body tingled faintly.

Pain is just sensation, he heard his old teachers saying inside his head. *Weariness is just sensation. The mind rules the body. The soul purifies the mind with meditation.*

Akira opened his eyes and shrugged off the hand on his shoulder. "I am fine," he said, which was a lie. But the escorts needed to hear it.

He was atop one of the Midorisaka hills, the highest central one. He still had his long sword in his right hand; it was coated with blood, and more blood covered his hand and arm on that side. The horse under him was blood-soaked as well, trembling and foaming, probably dying. He could not even remember how many horses he had ridden today. Three? Five?

Cool drizzle drifted across his face, making him blink. The rain was finally slackening, switching between mist and heavier bursts. The sky in the west was brighter, though still shrouded in clouds.

Around him the battle was finally winding down, almost done. To the east, from the crests of the hills all the way downslope and a quarter-mile into the fields below was nothing but churned mud and corpses and abandoned gear, with an occasional wounded man trailing back to the Wolf army camp.

The Jade Dragon army had crumbled after his cavalry pitched into their rear, but not all of them had broken and run; some had tried to withdraw in good order, or formed wedges and tried to drive their way out of the trap. Lord Mugai Hokuto had gathered his last thousand men into a hedgehog formation, waving their banners defiantly, determined to sell their lives as dearly as they could. It had taken an hour of hard fighting to break them.

Now, at last, all the men he could see in Jade Dragon colors were running away or dead. Squadrons of cavalry roamed in the open space between the

Midorisaka hills and the treeline in the west, chasing down every man they could catch. The Wolf Clan infantry were slowly reforming on the crests of the hills, while the Bear army was slowly withdrawing to the smaller line of hills to the north.

I need to speak with High Lord Gotaro, he thought. There were many things he needed to do, but he was tired, so tired, and everything hurt.

Memory returned of the fight with Lord Noboru, of the strange fire, the shock when it struck him and then spilled away. The tingling ache in his whole body had started then, though it had slowly been fading since. It was like the sensation he had felt last year at Castle Oka when Lady Yumiko had cursed him – though it had been far weaker then.

Noise and motion drew his attention, his hand briefly tightening on his sword-hilt. A group of horseman came from the west, riding hard. They swept up the slope, shedding water and mud, and now he could see the banner: Kitaro's crest. His hand relaxed.

Kado Kitaro reined in a few paces away. His right arm was tied against his chest, his face pale and set, chalk-white around his mouth. The arm had to be throbbing with every step the horse took, but he had refused to leave the battle. "My Lord," he called, nodding his head in a substitute for a proper bow. His voice was tight and thready, but clear. "There is an infantry force approaching from the west, beyond that line of forest. Six thousand men or a little more."

Akira felt an odd momentary sensation, a hitching in his chest that caused him to let out a cough-like sound. After a moment he realized it was an urge to laugh. "Who are they?"

"They are flying banners with the crest of Lord Kiyogama, my Lord. But," Kitaro paused, breathed carefully, swallowed. "They are not flying the Ryu crest, and their colors are yellow."

Akira had read the spy reports, and Kaede had sent him copies of the letters she exchanged with Lord Kiyogama. *I believe Lord Kiyogama is sincerely interested in avoiding the destruction of his line,* she had written in the margin.

But then why come here now, with all his strength? Did I miscalculate? Did he trick us?

"Send word to Nomi and to the honorable Bear Lord, Kuma Gotaro," he said. "I want twelve thousand men assembled a mile west of this position, half of them his." He kneed his horse; the beast made a plaintive sound, but it trotted forward as ordered. Like his own body, it would obey until it could no longer do so.

Kitaro turned to follow, snapping orders to his subordinates. Horsemen raced off. After a few minutes, blocks of infantry began to peel off from both armies and move west; their formations were a bit ragged, men stumbling with exhaustion, but they were samurai. They, too, would obey until they could no longer.

Halfway to the distant treeline, Akira reined in and waited. Kitaro pulled up next to him, muttering clipped orders to couriers who came and went; cavalry troops began to gather together, scores and then hundreds, adding heft to the infantry line slowly approaching from behind them.

A final wave of drizzle blew across them, soft on Akira's face, and faded away to the east. Ahead the sky brightened, hinting at the presence of the Sun behind it. It was mid-afternoon now, the battle seven hours old.

Infantry emerged from the mile-distant treeline, ranks of armored men. Most of them in yellow armor and banners, as Kitaro had said, but Akira could see some of them in Jade Dragon green-and-gold, with highlights of darker yellow. The Onaga colors, he realized.

They stopped a half-mile away. After a long pause, a small group of mounted men came forward.

"My Lord?" Kitaro's voice was ragged.

"We will wait for them," Akira replied. He was the High Lord. Lesser nobles should approach him, as supplicants.

An elaborately armored nobleman drew rein five paces away, offering a politely noncommittal bow. Akira gave only a brief nod in return. The man smiled, stroking a sparse moustache with his left hand. "I am honorable Kiyogama Heisuke, lord of Castle Kigi. And you, though I have not met you, must surely be the most honorable High Lord Ookami Akira."

"Yes," Akira said. There was no point denying it. He waited.

Lord Kiyogama looked back and forth, noting the ranks of soldiers extending off to left and right. "This is… quite the welcome. I hope there has been no misunderstanding of my intentions."

"What are those intentions?"

He raised his eyebrows. "Did your most honorable wife not inform you?"

Even in the midst of everything else, the reference to Kaede made Akira feel uncomfortable. With an effort he suppressed the emotions and focused his attention more tightly on Lord Kiyogama. His voice went utterly flat. "I know what you wrote to her. What are your intentions?"

Kiyogama smiled, but it looked strained. "I assure you they are the same as I told her. Which I have proven by blocking the retreat of the Jade Dragon army and taking the life of one of High Lord Noboru's chief retainers." He gestured to one of the men in his entourage. That samurai had a cloth bag resting before him on his horse's shoulders; he rode forward a few paces, dug in the bag, and lifted out a severed head by its topknot.

"This was Lord Onaga, ruler of WestTown and Castle Kajou. He fought bravely to protect the life of his son, held hostage in Castle Hokori. After I took his life, his remaining samurai most honorably swore allegiance to me rather than continue to serve a man like Ryu Noboru."

He isn't directly lying, Akira thought. *But he knows how to shield his true intentions.* Many of the older and more cunning nobles could do that, hiding themselves within endless layers of deception so that Akira could never sense their real nature. It had made it maddeningly difficult to tell who would join the rebellion last year.

He let go of his tight focus on the older man and instead looked at the soldiers lined up behind him. It was a larger army than even strong noblemen typically brought to war. *That is probably his entire strength, nothing held back to secure his home territories, and then supplemented with Lord Onaga's men as well. He is gambling everything on this.* "Do you wish to swear fealty to me?"

Lord Kiyogama's expression went formal, but Akira could sense some of his tension easing. "That is indeed my fervent wish, most honorable High Lord Akira. As this field around us demonstrates," he gestured at the bodies scattered here and there across the wet horse-trampled grass, "to oppose you is folly."

Akira shut his eyes, thinking, then *not* thinking and letting the void take him, sinking into the humming nothingness where he could be free of the body's distractions.

When he emerged it was a little lighter, a few hints of blue showing through the western clouds. Kiyogama and his escorts looked distinctly uncomfortable, a few of the lower-ranking ones almost fidgeting. Akira wondered how long it had been.

Aloud he said, "I do not need your soldiers here. The battle is over. Take them back to your castle."

If Kiyogama was surprised he hid it well, though it showed on his underlings' faces. He bowed in the saddle. "I shall do as you command, most honorable High Lord." He paused, then added delicately: "Do you wish my oath now..?"

Akira stared directly into his eyes. "If you truly wish to swear fealty and save your bloodline, you will secure the Onaga and Oyama lands, crushing and exterminating all there who still oppose me." That was how Lord Musume had proven himself, by ruthlessly wiping out his former allies among the rebels. "And then you will visit me this winter. Without an army."

The older man nodded, meeting the intolerably rude stare without flinching. "Of course. I will be honored to serve you in the field, and to be your guest. I have always wished to see Castle Ookami."

"Not there. The Imperial City."

Kiyogama gaped. He was still staring open-mouthed when Akira wheeled his horse and rode away.

⛩ ⛩ ⛩

THUNDER GRUMBLED FROM THE LOOMING, upward-billowing mass of dark gray clouds that covered the western horizon. Blue-white flickers of lightning ran through the clouds, chasing each other up and down through the layers of the storm. Even from the distance of many miles, the lightning was bright.

That storm will be ferocious when it reaches here. Kobayashi Mitsui stared at it blankly, not really feeling the garden bench under his thighs or the cool, damp breeze blowing in his face. *I wonder, if I sit out here, will a thunderbolt strike me?*

He was dressed in the barely-dried clothes he had left to be cleaned yesterday. He and Satoshi had been forced to abandon Mitsui's blood-soaked shirt and leggings in Goro's apartment, along with the corpses; they had set fire to the place to cover their tracks. Once the fire got properly underway it had drawn plenty of attention – it turned out that Tetsukakka Village had a very well-ordered firefighting gang, which made sense given the presence of so many forges. The excitement over the fire had left Mitsui free to walk home in a loincloth, his somewhat less-bloodstained jacket folded under his arm. Fortunately, in a town full of late-night drinking and whoring there was nothing too unusual about a man walking around in that condition.

He had scrubbed the jacket himself after they came back. He probably should have abandoned it as well, but he couldn't bring himself to leave behind the last remnant of his old life. The bloodstains were stubborn, but he'd managed to reduce them to a vague brown that might have been dirt.

Not the first such stain in that jacket, Mitsui thought. *But perhaps... perhaps the last.*

After a while he stopped watching the approaching storm and switched to watching the silent gardener at his work. The man wore the same tattered straw basket-hat as the day before, though his garment today was a lighter brown. He worked steadily, unceasingly, chopping with a wooden one-handed mattock at the ground around the large azalea shrubs on the garden's southern side. The man's silence was unsettling, but at the same time the slow, steady work carried a sense of harmony, of order forced out of chaos.

"Ah, here you are." Satoshi stepped out of the inn's front door, pausing to eye the distant storm. "I had expected you to be asleep in your room, or perhaps wandering the streets as a naked madman. We got a decent start on that last night."

I suppose he is trying to cheer me up, Mitsui thought after a moment.

Satoshi sat on the bench next to him. They watched the gardener as he continued to labor in silence. The storm slowly grew closer, the morning light turning gray and then fading into a sort of unnatural twilight as the dark clouds mounted higher, taking up more and more of the sky, flickering with lightning

"I managed to recover some documents from our… friend's residence," Satoshi said finally. "They might contain something useful."

He's being careful what he says, even here. As if this old gardener might be a Mask cultist… and who knows anymore? Mitsui shut his eyes and swayed slightly on the bench, feeling as though a vast gulf loomed behind him. If he let go he would fall back into it and never emerge.

Can I start over again, yet again, trying to decipher the codes, to trace the connections? The idea felt immensely heavy, utterly exhausting just to consider.

A memory returned, of an instructor at his training hall when he was a youth, reciting the teachings of the Fourth Emperor: *Despair is a sin, a form of Fear and Laziness. A true samurai never despairs, even in a hopeless situation. Especially in a hopeless situation. The Lady's judgment on your soul matters more than any mortal defeat.*

I am too much of a sinner, honored teacher. I always have been. Too weak, too much a prisoner of lowly emotions to be a proper samurai.

"Four years," he said aloud, suddenly heedless of who might listen. "Four years of following these clues. Four years fighting for my life against these… these Demon-powered madmen. What have I accomplished, except to kill Bozu and Mako and my… my wife, and lose my son?"

I do not forgive you, Akemi's voice whispered in his memory. He trembled, pressing the palms of his hands against his forehead. *I've done all I can do, all any man could do,* he told her memory – or perhaps it was her spirit, still watching him. *The trail has run out.*

An especially loud thunderclap followed close on a flickering strobe of blue-white light. The air had acquired a thick, damp smell. He straightened, staring up into the boiling storm, wishing for the rain to come and let him weep within it, tears unseen.

"We did kill a few of them," Satoshi said diffidently. "Even one of their Voices, if I recall."

That was true. Memory came again: a dim low-roofed cavern, wet gravel crunching under his sandals, wails from the rescued children behind him… and a robed figure with an eyeless white mask, the queasy sensation of his sword cutting through a neck that resisted unnaturally.

"Yes, we killed a few of them. Did it make any difference, in the end?" Mitsui's voice turned cracked, uneven. "They've had my son all this time. With another of their damned Voices, no less! And I know… I know what the Masks do to children."

The sky flashed and rumbled. The light dimmed further as the dark gray, almost black clouds swept overhead. Satoshi rose to his feet, looking up at the storm rather than at Mitsui.

"You'll recall, I asked you not that long ago if the Empire is worth saving."

A gray haze of rain was sweeping across the hills and into the town, accompanied by a gathering roar of noise. Mitsui watched it come, not moving. He breathed deep, tasting the rain, and let it out in a long sigh. "The Empire is worth saving. But… can a fool like me do anything to save it?"

He thought Satoshi was going to reply, but just then a voice called from the inn: "Honored customers! The storm is about to break, perhaps you wish to step inside..?"

The innkeeper stood on the edge of the inn's front porch, hands clasped, leaning forward slightly in a posture of anxious concern. The wooden panels behind him were slid open, showing the inside of the inn's common room, and one of the older maidservants was visible cleaning off the tables.

No doubt he's worried about having to wash our clothes twice in one day, Mitsui thought, and despite himself he felt a smile tug at his lips. *The Empire* is *worth saving, even poor silly fellows like this. Even if I'm no good at saving it.* "Apologies, honorable innkeeper," he called. "We'll come inside at once."

Raindrops began to fall, at first just a few large scattered ones, splattering off their heads and shoulders. Mitsui and Satoshi stepped up onto the porch, beneath the inn's sheltering eaves, and seemingly just a heartbeat later the isolated drops became a roaring torrent of silver-gray. A haze of moisture drifted onto the porch to mist their faces. The gardener vanished behind the wall of water, still silent.

The merchant bobbed a half-bow to them, shuffling inside, but the maidservant replaced him, stepping to the edge of the porch and looking out anxiously into the blinding downpour. "Silent!" she shouted, wiping the spray out of her eyes. "Come in out of the rain, imbecile! Do you want to get sick again? You'll break honorable mistress Ami's heart!"

The gardener resolved out of the rain, stepping slowly up onto the porch and then stopping directly in front of Mitsui. His robe was already soaked through, clinging to the lean frame beneath, and water sluiced off the hem and off the brim of his hat. He lifted one bony, muddy hand and tilted the hat back, revealing sunken eyes in a lean hollow-cheeked face, creased with deep lines that Mitsui recognized as the marks of stress and pain – recognized them because he had seen the same sort of lines on his own face when he looked in that mirror.

Though not nearly so deep and graven as these.

The man's mouth worked, trembled. Finally he spoke, showing broken splinters of teeth. His voice was a ragged, hollow croak: "You… hunt… for Treason?"

Mitsui's heart jolted. He sensed Satoshi going abruptly into a combat stance, hand on sword-hilt.

The maidservant's eyes went wide. "Silent? You can speak?"

The innkeeper hurried back out of the common room, managing to simultaneously bob his head with simpering apology to Mitsui while glaring and shaking a finger at the gardener. "For Amatsu's sake, stop bothering the customers, fool," he snapped. "They don't need any of your nonsense."

"But… honorable master Oku, he spoke!" The maidservant's voice was loud with wonder. "I thought he couldn't talk at all!"

The gardener's gaze had not left Mitsui's face. He was shaking, trembling like a frightened child.

Mitsui found his voice. "Who is this man?"

Innkeeper Oku bobbed his head again, greasily apologetic. "No one, honored samurai. Truly no one. We do not even know his name, hence why we call him Silent."

"If you do not know his name, why does he work for you?"

The innkeeper darted a pained look at the kitchen. "An indulgence for my wife. Ami-*chan* is a pious and compassionate woman. I assure you—"

"He showed up in the pond late last spring," the maidservant interrupted. She patted the gardener's face with her towel, blotting off the worst of the rainwater. He did not react except to blink when the towel brushed across his eyes. "I came out one morning to sweep the back porch and there he was, washed ashore. Gave me a fright, by Amatsu's mercy! Fevered and barely breathing, with a vicious cut in his back. Well, a holy man, honorable mistress Ami said we couldn't let him die, *neh*? The Lord would never forgive us for disrespecting one of His sworn servants."

Mitsui kept his gaze on the gardener's face. Satoshi had not relaxed his posture, watching the gardener as though he was a snake coiled to strike. "A holy man..?"

"Well, of course. A shaved head and he wore a Monk's robes, we've all seen those." Ignoring the hovering innkeeper's distress, the maidservant lifted off the gardener's straw hat, shedding more water. Underneath, the man's head was a shaved dome, the bare scalp marred with old scars. "And he still keeps it shaved, you see? A Monk, as sure as I breath. We nursed him back to health, but he couldn't talk. He understands what we say, but he's never said a word until now. And when we asked him where he wanted to go… well, he just went out to the garden and started working. Poor fellow, whatever happened to him must have been terrible, and from what I hear all Monks are half-mad anyway, apologies, what with serving the Lord Moon."

"Yes, from our own experience I believe that is correct," Satoshi murmured. The man – Silent? – did not react to any of the maid's talk, except to flinch very slightly when she took off the hat.

Mitsui felt an inward flinch of his own. His mind's eye showed him Bozu, laughing, smiling, and then shouting for him to flee in the instant before the Mask swordswoman cut him apart...

He set one hand on the gardener's shoulder, feeling the tremors running through the lean bony frame beneath the wet robe. The innkeeper made a soft almost-exclamation at the breach of public manners. "They call you Silent. But you had another name, *neh*? Before."

The man's mouth twitched, trembling harder. Finally he mumbled, "—es." A heavy swallow. "Yes. Ippen. I was... Ippen."

Satoshi let out a huff of breath. His sword made a sharp *click* as he pushed it up from the sheath for quick drawing. "I know that name."

Yes, so do I. Mitsui still remembered Satoshi's account of the Mask swordswoman's attack, the one that had killed a dozen Wolf samurai and kidnapped a noblewoman. Only the sudden, inexplicable eruption of Kenji's Divine power had spared Satoshi from the same fate.

And the swordswoman had been accompanied by a Monk...

Mitsui held the thin shoulder, breathed deep, readying himself. "Ippen. You are a Mask."

Innkeeper Oku squeaked and fled inside. The maidservant put her hands to her mouth. "What in the world..?"

Ippen's face tightened. His eyes closed and his mouth twisted as though from pain. "No," he gulped. "I... I *was*... they... they had me. I was... there was... there was no *me*." His voice cracked. "I was... chained. In the dark."

Mitsui realized Satoshi was muttering a prayer, a childhood mantra for the Lady's protection. He felt a similar impulse. Instead he cleared his throat, made himself continue, fighting the sudden desperate urge to hope. "And are you still... chained?"

"...no." Ippen opened his eyes. Mitsui realized the wetness on the Monk's face was not all from the rain; there were tears leaking from the corners of his eyes, running down the grooves in his face. "The *Light*... it touched me. And then I... I woke up." He swallowed convulsively. "But I still... I remember. What I saw."

Mitsui's throat had gone dry. "You saw Treason." He realized he had said it as a statement, not a question. *Because I want it to be true, I* need *it to be true.*

"Yes." The Monk's mouth worked again. "And he had... a little boy. With a mask."

For a moment Mitsui's hearing failed and his vision went gray at the edges. His hand dropped nerveless from Ippen's shoulder. The world spun, the Monk fading away from him like a receding shadow in a stage play.

Then Satoshi and the maidservant together were holding him, lowering him to sit in an awkward sprawl on the inn's porch. The maid blotted his forehead with her cloth, and the water in it felt pleasantly cool. He shook himself, opening and closing his eyes, taking deep breaths.

Ippen stood unmoving, still just under the porch's roof, framed by the roaring light-gray wall of rain.

"Where is he?" Mitsui demanded, not knowing if he meant Treason or Taro.

Ippen's voice was low, barely audible over the rain. "Tatarayama Village," he said. "He calls himself Merchant Sankichi."

"Of course he does," Satoshi muttered. "At this point it would be a surprise if he *wasn't* a merchant."

The maidservant stood up, setting her hands on her hips. "I don't know what this is all about, honorable guests, but for the Lady's sake let's get inside and dry you all off before you catch a fever. Yes, you too," she added toward the Monk. "Silent, or Ippen, or whoever you are, I don't know what to think!" She caught the man's sopping-wet sleeve and tugged him forward, and he followed, shambling like a child.

Mitsui picked himself up slowly, waiting on his knees until he was sure the dizziness would not return. He looked at Satoshi and the older man raised his eyebrows in response.

"It seems your Fate is not to slink home in defeat after all," he observed. "Well, I've always suspected we were on a path that ended with sordid death in some remote place."

Mitsui felt a perverse impulse to laugh, though whether it was at Satoshi, at himself, or at Fate itself he could not say.

CHAPTER 17

MUSIC AND SONG AND shouted boasts drifted through the night air. The armies of the Wolf and the Bear were encamped together two miles east of the day's battlefield, and their soldiers were celebrating victory – and survival – with the raucous exuberance of samurai momentarily released from the rules of etiquette.

In the morning they'll all be serious and stoic again, Kado Kitaro thought, smiling in the darkness. *And probably hung over, most of them.*

For that matter, I might be as well. He had spent two hours at the command pavilion, joining in the obligatory toasts and poetry recitations and head-viewing and general boasting. Long enough to not insult the higher-ranking guests when he pleaded weariness and left.

Lord Akira looked like he needed to leave too, Kitaro thought, frowning now. In truth, the High Lord had looked pale and sickly and wretched, dark bags under his eyes and his hollow cheeks darker yet, thrown into shadow by the light from the flaming braziers and dozens of colored lanterns hanging from poles along the length of the pavilion. The High Lord had throttled back considerably on the old tradition of an army's commanders meeting each night to drink and toast each other. But not even he could forbid the custom on the night of a victory as great as this one.

The celebration had not been entirely a burden. The head-viewing had been more than worth the time, and not just because of the chance to cheer the fate of the traitor Konatsu Sabato. The sheer number of heads displayed, and their rank, had conveyed the scale of the Wolf Clan's victory more effectively than any speech. High Lord Noboru's head had been too damaged to be put on display – which was for the best, Kitaro thought, after what had happened at his death – but those brought to the celebration included Lord Onaga Kitsuya's head from the Kiyogama, Lord Mugai Hokuto and his brother Mugai Soto's heads mounted side-by-side with those of a half-dozen senior vassals, Lord Oyama Hiroyuki's head locked in an expression of almost child-like surprise... The only Jade Dragon nobleman who seemed to have escaped the slaughter was Lord Tsuchiya.

The Jade Dragon are beaten. It seemed impossible even as Kitaro thought it. He had grown up in the Gray Wolf, one half of a Clan divided for a century, aware from childhood of the looming strength of the Jade Dragon Clan. Studying the sword in his family's training hall, listening to his father and older brother discuss politics and war, he had believed the best hope was for his Clan to keep holding off the pressure from the Ryu family's might.

In five years, everything has changed. And this is only the beginning.

A throb of pain from his arm, strong enough to be felt through the numbing effect of the many cups of wine he had already drunk, reminded him that this triumph had not been without cost. If he listened carefully he could hear the occasional wail or scream from the hospital tents near the army's baggage train, where Priestesses and peasant physicians labored to save wounded men. And the horizon to the west flickered with scores of lanterns – army servants working with peasants and morticians from nearby villages to gather the thousands of corpses and pile them onto funeral pyres. The day's rain meant there was no wood dry enough to burn tonight, so the pyres would not be lit until tomorrow at the earliest.

Just as well. Seeing all those fires tonight would take some of the heart out of the men. They can mourn their comrades tomorrow, after the celebration tonight. Then he stopped and smiled again, this time at himself. *Look at me turning into a proper commander, worrying about morale rather than my own glory!*

He turned and stepped through the flap of the tent behind him, blinking as he passed from cool darkness to the warm yellow light of a pair of paper-paneled lanterns sitting on small wooden stands. Okada Kazomiru, his chief subordinate in the army's cavalry, rose and bowed, then offered Kitaro his seat. On another occasion he would have declined, but the ache from his arm was getting worse, so he nodded gratefully and sank into the folding camp-chair.

Removing his armor after the battle – especially the plates and greaves on his right arm – had been deeply unpleasant. A Priestess had felt the limb over, clucking to herself, and then pulled and stretched until she was satisfied the bone was set, and Kitaro had gritted his teeth through the whole ordeal, eyes closed and chill beads of sweat oozing from his forehead. He had leaked a few tears as well, though he'd managed – just barely – not to shame himself with any noise.

The other men in the tent had fallen silent as he entered. They sat in a rough circle, some on camp-chairs and others cross-legged on the woven mats that covered the ground; wooden buckets full of wine bottles nestling in hot water sat on the floor around them, along with bowls of rice. They bowed or nodded to him, then waited expectantly for him to speak.

All these men were part of Lord Akira's inner circle, the officers and nobles he trusted to carry out his most secret and dangerous orders. Most of them – Kitaro himself and his two chief commanders Kazomiru and Shungo, Chujitsuna Nomi and his senior officers Tokaze Seikichi and Fuwa Hiroshige, young Hajime Soto who was now the Lord of a province and his chief officers Tokaze Fumiya and Hajime Chikao – had served in Akira's original army in the Nightingale lands. The main exception was Lord Kaneda, the ruler of Castle Zanin, but he was utterly loyal to the Ookami and a distant cousin to Lord Toshiwara, the other man Lord Akira trusted completely.

A pity Lord Toshiwara could not be here, Kitaro thought. The man was handling the siege of Castle Kosaten, doing so alone with a force of barely five thousand men precisely because Lord Akira could trust him to do so. *And it would have been good to have honorable Tokaze Kondo here as well...*

I'm wandering, trying to escape the pain. He cleared his throat. "I apologize for calling you all away from the celebrations."

A round of smiles and chuckles answered him. Old Nomi called: "Let me guess, you wanted to compare wounds now that we're both broken-winged," then threw back his head to empty his wine-cup. His left arm had been crippled during the Nightingale campaign, one of several wounds that probably should have been lethal.

Kitaro joined in the general laughter even though it shook his arm agonizingly. It took him a moment to catch his breath and smooth out his voice afterward. "No, honorable Nomi," he said carefully. He picked up a wine-cup and held it out; Kazomiru filled it. "This is actually something... important." Another careful breath. The pain eased... a little. "We all know what honorable Lord Akira intends to do next."

A silence, and then young Lord Kaneda glanced around and said hesitantly, "He intends to... to claim the Imperial City. To become Emperor."

"Yes," Kitaro nodded. Even amid his weariness and pain, those words brought a thrill, and he had to drink some wine and collect himself before he continued. "Today, fighting at his side, I witnessed... something... of great importance."

He told them all of it, everything he remembered. There were parts that were difficult to describe even though it had happened only a few hours ago, as though the unnatural nature of the event was driving it out of his memory.

When he had finished, a much longer silence followed, broken only by the soft sounds of the men emptying and refilling their wine-cups. Finally young Tokaze Chikao spoke: "You are saying that High Lord Noboru was… a Demon worshipper?"

"Is it so surprising? Lord Akira did say that the Jade Dragons had allied with the barbarians," Lord Kaneda observed. "And the tales that have been coming out of their lands for the last year and more, of Priestesses exiled, monasteries burned down…"

"General Akiyama told me a great deal about those matters," Lord Soto agreed. "It was part of why he fled."

Chujitsuna Nomi coughed, emptied his wine-cup, snorted. "Apologies, but you are all dancing around the true heart of things. The most important part of honorable Kitaro's story isn't the bit about the late Lord Noboru, may the Lady judge him harshly. It's the part about *our* most honorable High Lord."

Thank you, honorable Nomi, Kitaro thought fervently, hiding his relief behind another drink.

Nomi's subordinate Hiroshige frowned as he refilled his commander's cup. "I… apologies, I am not sure I understand. What are you saying, honorable Kitaro? Is Lord Akira… Apologies, are you saying he has some manner of Divine power? What does that mean? Apologies, but…" He set down the bottle and lifted his hands helplessly. "I'm just… just a soldier."

"We are all Lord Akira's soldiers, his vassals, his strong right hands," Kitaro said, suddenly fierce. "And he is… Don't you remember your history? When the Demons arose in the days of the First Emperor, there were two Swords of Heaven, serving the Sun and the Moon."

Hiroshige's eyes went wide. "But that is… I mean, that is just a story," he trailed off.

Kitaro took a breath, then let it out and looked down at his empty wine-cup. "I was at Nagai Kyukai Plain," he said quietly.

"We all were," Lord Soto agreed. "I've… I've tried not to think about it since then." He looked around. "We all have, *neh*? It's not… comfortable, to think about it. But that was the power of the Heavens. It could not have been anything else."

Sober nods around the tent. Nomi ventured: "But that… whatever that was… all right, fine, it must have been Divine, it surely wasn't anything to do with the Demons. It made me remember…" He trailed off, coughed, took another drink. "No matter. But it didn't come from Lord Akira. I was with him, he was as surprised as the rest of us. The... light... it was someone else. That fellow that the Priestesses hauled around in a cage, wasn't it?"

"They fought," Kitaro said, still looking down. "That man, and Lord Akira. Twice, the second time last summer. And it was... it was an even match, both times."

Silence again. Finally Hajime Soto cleared his throat. "So what does this mean for us?"

Kitaro flung down his wine-cup and stood, gritting his teeth against the renewed agony from his arm. "It means," he said, his voice rising hoarsely, "it means we are living in the time when the Throne will be reclaimed! It means the Lady will show Her face to the Empire again, and we will fight the Demons as the First Emperor's men did. It means... it means..."

Lord Kaneda suddenly lurched to his feet as well, and his voice rose in a wobbling shout. "It means the Lady is with us... *truly* with us!"

They all screamed it then, screamed the ancient cheer as though it was new-born into the world and they the first to ever speak it.

⛩ ⛩ ⛩

"MY LORD?"

Akira let out a strangled noise, halfway between a sob and a gasp, as he snapped awake. The interrupted dream flickered in his consciousness. Satsuki, she was drowning, he could hear her choking but couldn't reach her... the dream faded and his eyes started working.

He was seated cross-legged on the woven-mat floor in the front half of his headquarters tent, his left elbow resting on his writing-table, his right hand on the hilt of the long sword he had instinctively reached for before he was even awake.

It was his manservant Kaito who had spoken. The old commoner knelt by the tent's front entrance three paces away, next to a tray with a pair of bowls. Sunlight was leaking in through the tent-flaps behind him and from under the edges of the silk walls.

For a span of heartbeats Akira's thoughts were still unfocused. A confused string of memories paraded through his mind, like isolated beads on a necklace. Kaito helping him take off his armor and scrub down after the battle; the interminable celebration feast that had dragged on until Moonset; writing letters and orders by lamplight, his eyes burning with the effort of focusing through his weariness; putting on a new suit of clean armor, meeting with the Bear Lord under a gray pre-dawn sky, handing the letters to couriers, returning to his tent to summon his commanders.

He had sat down for a few minutes to wait for them to arrive...

"How," he started, and his voice cracked and rasped. Kaito rose and came forward, offering the tray; one bowl was fermented-soy soup, the other rice with a fresh-cracked egg atop it. Akira lifted the soup bowl and drained it with three long swallows, then cleared his throat. "How long?"

"Only until your men arrived, my Lord," Kaito said quietly. "Perhaps a half hour."

Longer, Akira thought, noting the brightness of the Sunlight leaking into the tent. He looked at Kaito and the old manservant bowed silently, expressionless. After a moment Akira picked up the rice-bowl and the chopsticks next to it. He wondered briefly how Kaito had managed to find a fresh egg the day after the battle. Then he stirred the egg into the rice and started shoveling the food into his mouth.

Five minutes later, he stepped out of the tent and paused to let his eyes adjust to the light. The morning sky was an achingly clear blue without a single cloud, but the Sunlight was oddly filtered by the pillars of smoke from the scores of funeral pyres three miles to the west. The preliminary reports showed the Wolf army had lost almost three thousand dead, the Bear half that number. The Jade Dragon casualties were vastly higher, as always happened when an army broke and ran; most of those pyres were for them.

The men waiting for him in a wide semicircle all bowed as his attention fell on them. Some of them were clearly the worse for wear, baggy eyed and puffy-faced after the late-night celebrations, but they were all fully armored and waiting with attention, the old-guard nobles just as focused as the men of his own loyal circle.

Kaito handed him the bundle of orders, and without any introduction Akira began to hand them out. "Honorable Lord Shinsen, honorable Lord Soto, honorable Lord Kuroi… the most honorable High Lord Kuma Gotaro intends to advance through TeaTown to Castle Hokori and besiege it. Lord Kuroi and Lord Soto, you will secure TeaTown, hold it behind him, and send him whatever support he may require. Lord Shinsen, you will move to Castle Kosaten to assist Lord Toshiwara's siege. The castle must be taken to open the River of Many Faces for our supplies. General Akiyama, you will accompany Lord Shinsen and offer your support in persuading the garrison at Castle Kosaten to accept defeat and swear fealty to the Wolf Clan."

The two noblemen bowed and held out their hands for their orders. Akiyama smiled, his expression slightly bemused, as though he could still not quite believe what was happening. "I can certainly try, Lord Akira. But I am not sure how eager Lord Goda Ishiki will be to switch his allegiance."

"Lord Goda is to be killed," Akira said flatly. "I only care about the men."

Akiyama pursed his lips slightly but made no further comment.

Akira picked up his next paper. "Honorable Lord Kaneda. You will take your men, honorable Lord Ito and his men, and two thousand from the main force – honorable Nomi, choose a suitable commander." He watched Ito Kyogo as he spoke, to see if the man would balk at serving a Lord of equal youth and more recent provenance, but Kyogo just nodded, his face a closed box. "You will advance down the River of Slow Turning to secure WestTown and Castle Kajou. Make contact with Lord Kado's forces on the Nightingale border. From there you should be able to secure Lord Oyama's lands as well. You can expect support from Lord Kiyogama and possibly also from the Wakita vassal family at Castle Kujira."

Kaneda accepted the orders with a slightly nervous smile. "Apologies, but… what if Lord Kiyogama refuses to help, or turns on us?"

"Destroy him," Akira said simply. Kaneda nodded and stepped back, his throat moving visibly as he swallowed.

"Honorable Lord Musume, honorable Nomi. You will move your forces east on the Golden Sun Road to Toryu Village." Which was the town at the base of the Emperor's Road that ascended into the Mountains of the Sun to the Imperial City. "I will accompany you."

No one openly reacted, but a faint rustle went through all the assembled men. Someone – probably one of the junior officers accompanying the commanders – muttered in a barely audible voice: "Amatsu have mercy, he isn't wasting any time."

Akira ignored it. "Honorable Kitaro. Are you fit to serve?"

Kado Kitaro looked the worst of any of them, his face pale and haggard, his right arm in a sling and tightly wrapped in silk cloth and bamboo splints. But at Akira's words he stiffened his posture and barked, "I am ready, my Lord!"

"You will send a thousand cavalry with me, under a suitable officer. Five hundred will support Lord Kaneda in the south. You will take all the rest of the cavalry west and north to support the Bear, Lord Shinsen, and Lord Soto. Sweep the lands north of the River of Many Faces, capture or destroy any weakly-held castles or garrisons, and watch for any troops moving from Castle Ryu or the other strongholds to threaten the Bear. You'll have to live off the land until Castle Kosaten falls, but try to minimize damage to the farmlands. Patrol the border with the Tiger and make contact with them if possible. I want better information on what is happening in their lands."

Seneschal Amano should have been back by now, he knew. *I have to know what happened with the Tiger and the Aelfynn.*

Kitaro bowed. "It will be as you command, honorable High Lord!" His voice shook slightly as the motion jarred his arm, but his eyes glittered with fervor. "The Lady is with us!"

Most of the assembled men took up the cheer instantly. The sound hit Akira almost like a physical force, and by the third repetition Musume and Kuroi were shouting as loud as the rest of them.

⛩ ⛩ ⛩

TOMOE DREAMED THAT SHE DROWNED.

Her throat convulsed against the water trying to flood inside, but her body refused to die. She tumbled in darkness, her limbs flailing weakly, every muscle burning, her chest a solid mass of pain. She could not see, could not hear. The Lords' power forced itself through her, a thin spiral of energy that was all her ravaged flesh could endure, enough to force her heart to beat even as the air in her lungs turned foul.

Awareness of her flesh came to her slowly, in bits and pieces. Her hands closed on slimy rock and she jerked, shuddered, coughed violently over and over again. Her clothes lay on her body like iron plating, weighting down every motion. The agony in her chest pulsed in time to the coughs.

Her heart beat on its own, Dakkurru's power no longer forcing her flesh to obey.

She opened her eyes.

Tomoe lay on a tumble of broken rock and shattered wood. Gray daylight showed she was on the east side of the moat, below the looming tower of the keep. The shoreline which had been all close-fitted stone walls was now a pile of broken pieces, and the wall that rose above her was scored with massive gouges where the power of Dakkurru had lanced across it. Splintered remains of oaken beams lay half in and half out of the water; other such beams were mixed with the stone rubble, or floated in the stagnant water of the moat. *Pieces of t'bridge t'Other smashed,* she knew, and looking upward she could see the broken-toothed remnants of it a hundred paces above her.

How is it daylight? T'fight happened after Sunset. The thought stabbed in her head like fire, and she abandoned it.

The water stank, a reek of mud and decay and excrement. Behind the rotten stench were other odors, a stale miasma of ash and smoke.

The Other… is she still alive?

She must be. If t'Lords'd lost her, *I'd know.*

Slowly Tomoe pulled herself upright. Every motion was pain. Her clothing pulled unpleasantly against her skin.

She began climbing across the heaps of rubble, setting her feet and hands carefully, working her way northward – she could see a gap there in the walls enclosing the moat. Everything hurt, every muscle, every bone, every breath. Some of that pain, she realized, was a hunger so intense it was not really hunger at all.

How long was I…?

Gradually, also, she became aware of the frustrated anger of Dakkurru, of the Lords raging at her weakness, at her failure to defeat the False Light. But their anger did not consume and overwhelm her as it normally would, and she realized that was because the damage to her own body was limiting how much of their essence could touch her.

If I'd been at full strength, I could've beaten Kenji, she thought, and gritted her teeth against a rush of her own emotions, bitterness and savage frustration. *The Lords had t'use me too much durin' t'battle. Otherwise he'd be mine now, I'd have my revenge.* Thinking the word *revenge* brought her a twinge of warmth, dispelling a little of the pain. *I don't need t'Other's help – she already lost t'him before I got there! I just need t'find him when--*

—WHEN THE FLESH-SHELL IS NOT DISRUPTED—

Tomoe stumbled and one squelching-wet boot slipped on a tilted rock-surface. "Excrement!" She flailed for balance and her knee came down painfully on jagged rock, tearing the sodden leather of her leggings. Tomoe stayed still for a few minutes, panting, looking around.

"Who's there?"

Her voice was a ghastly croak, and in her own ears it seemed hollow and distant.

The Other stood knee deep in the moat a dozen paces away, her shirt and leggings hanging torn and sodden on her lean bony frame. He cloak and hood were gone, torn away along with much of the sleeve that had hung from her shortened right arm. Tomoe felt a sudden surge of memory at seeing the mangled stump that projected from the sleeve. *I did that,* she knew. It was sometimes hard to remember things that had happened *before*, as though she saw them through a layer of silk. *I cut through her sword-hand. I crippled t'Wolf Lord's woman, and then I brought her t'Dakkurru. I wonder what t'Wolf Lord thought when he found out?* That brought a little more warmth into her body, made it a tiny bit easier to get her feet under herself and straighten up again.

"Forgot you… can't talk," she called to the Other. She looked the woman up and down, noting that her eyepatch had been torn off as well, revealing the scarred empty socket beneath. "Guess… Kenji took you down even… harder than me, *neh*?"

The Other said nothing, her single eye staring. For a heartbeat Tomoe felt sure something flickered within that eye, some kind of intent, or of recognition… but when she looked again it was as blank and empty as a crow's eye. *Must've been me,* Tomoe thought, irritably aware how much her vision and hearing were still muddled.

Abruptly the Other turned and began climbing up the rubble, making her way toward the northern edge of the moat. Tomoe followed, cursing absently at the way her sodden boots kept trying to slide. They were ripping, too, coming apart at their seams. The Other seemed to have less difficulty, moving with the jerky precision of a puppet on strings but somehow always placing her feet correctly.

The moat's north side had been smashed open during the fighting, a section ten paces wide and five deep blown out, leaving a ramp of shattered stone descending twenty paces to the city beyond. Water trickled through the opening, and the stains on the walls to either side showed the moat had emptied several feet of depth. Tomoe stared at the opening and felt a moment of disorientation – the broken lip of rock was covered with sludge, as though the water had been flowing over it for days.

She climbed awkwardly through and down, holding on with both hands. The Other stopped in the opening and looked out at the city, her one functioning eye staring at nothing.

They're listenin', lookin', through her, Tomoe realized, feeling a sullen envy at the Other's greater usefulness to Dakkurru even now. The city looked blurry to her own eyes, smudged with darkness that she slowly identified as fires. There were no sounds of battle; instead she heard the distant rumble of drums and chants, and an underlying note of screams, a relentless wailing from all directions.

Did we win? Is t'fightin' over? It seemed unlikely with both her and the Other out of action, but then again, the city's defenses had already been crumbling.

The Other looked down at her, watching silently, then stepped off the edge and dropped five paces to a large rock with a mostly-flat upper surface. She sank to her knees, absorbing the impact, then rose and jumped again, descending toward the bottom like a cat.

"Show-off," Tomoe muttered, knowing as she said it that it was meaningless – the Other was no more capable of such an emotion than the theater-puppet she so often resembled. Tomoe resumed her own more cautious descent, her body aching protest at the effort, her damaged left hand throbbing. Finally the slope leveled out, becoming a scattering of rocks across what had been a garden.

A Temple garden, she realized, seeing the four-story pagoda tower of the shrine at the far end of the open space. Some of the wailing noises came from there. She started toward them, then stopped as a wave of agonizing dizziness struck her and she sagged to her knees. *I'm a wreck*, she thought, bitter rage like acid in her heart. *I'm a wreck, because of* him, *and...*

"T'damned... t'damned *Light*," she mumbled past clenched teeth.

She felt the anger of Dakkurru rising to an impossible, seething rage that made her chest ache with the need to scream.

—WEAKNESS. PATHETIC WEAKNESS. HATE THEM, HATE ALL—

Dark shapes moved inside the Temple, and then a black-robed figure emerged and hurried toward her, the pale mask with its red tear-marks becoming visible as it drew closer. A trio of others followed, their own masks plain white.

"Honored One, Chosen of Dakkurru!" the Mask priest cried, and sank to the ground whimpering, the others doing the same. "You return to us! Dakkurru's guidance returns!" He held out supplicating hands, and they were covered with blood. "At last! Show us what to do!"

She made no answer. Instead she lurched to her feet and walked past him and his followers. They cowered and gibbered, covering their heads like children hiding from a storm.

Useless, she thought savagely, and the rage of Dakkurru pulsated within her more strongly than her own could ever be.

Because she knew now what had happened, the knowledge placed in her head like a stone in a garden. The army of Dakkurru, all the thousands of tribesmen and Masks, priests and shamans, had seen *it*, felt *it* – the hideous, unbearable False Light that had blazed out from Kenji. *It* had robbed their strength, torn away Dakkurru's guidance, and without Tomoe and the Other they could not regain it. The relentless attack that had been overrunning the city had dissolved into helpless chaos, men abandoning the fight to kneel, weep, faint.

And t'damned samurai rallied, no doubt. How long did t'fightin' go on? Days? Weeks? Is it still happening?

How long was I in that damned moat?

She shook her head, throbbing now with Dakkurru's soaring rage, her skull feeling as though it might burst.

The Other had vanished. *They've sent her t'rally t'troops,* Tomoe knew bitterly. *She's not as… damaged… as I am right now. They can get more use out of her.*

She climbed the steps into the Temple.

Inside the main chamber, three Priestesses were laid out on the floor, their voices cycling from whimpers up to screams and back, their limbs held in place by iron spikes. A fourth Priestess, older, hung from the ceiling by a rope that bound her elbows and ankles behind her back. She spun slowly, tears dripping, mumbling a prayer from a bloody mouth.

Behind her the open-armed statue of the Goddess loomed, ten feet tall. The cultists had smeared it with blood and other things, but it still stood, mercilessly compassionate.

Tomoe flung out her hands, unthinkingly trying to summon Dakkurru's fire, and then dropped to her knees as agony lanced through her body and down her arms, like molten metal in her veins. For a heartbeat she thought her fingers were going to burst open. A brief flicker of green light danced on her fingertips and winked out.

Too weak, she thought, gritting her teeth against the urge to scream or sob. *Need to… to heal. Need to…* eat.

She caught the hanging Priestess' knee and used it to lever herself upright. The old woman moaned in pain, and Tomoe caught her neck and spun her around until they were face-to-face.

"Your unlucky day," Tomoe grated, feeling her lips peel back in a ravenous grin. She put her other hand on the old woman's face, digging her fingernails into the soft skin by her mouth.

The Priestess screamed for a long time.

⛩ ⛩ ⛩

"MAMA! MAMA, LOOK, LOOK AT me, Mama!"

Ookami Kaede smiled at her son and waved with one hand, the motion slightly exaggerated so he could see it from twenty paces away. He was sitting balanced atop the pony's saddle, his feet sticking out to either side, his hands clutching the saddle-brim in front. A groom in baggy dark-colored commoner's garb held the pony's bridle and ran a soothing hand over its nose, keeping it from spooking at the loud small creature on its back; a samurai in the red-edged embroidered gray vest of the Ookami house troops was holding the boy's waist to ensure he kept his balance, while a pair of serving-maids hovered nearby.

Nonetheless Kaede felt her heart jump just a little as the groom began slowly leading the pony around the yard in a broad circle, the samurai walking alongside and keeping one hand on the back of the saddle where it could instantly reach up to grab the boy's baggy coat. Basho laughed delightedly, wobbling slightly with each step of the animal but… *Not falling, of course he's not falling and even if he slips a little, honorable Yuji will catch him.* Okada Yuji had been assigned to her personal escort by Captain Tokage two years ago, and was as dependable as the Sunrise.

Still, it was an effort to make herself turn back to her tea. She was proud of how smoothly she lifted the mug, sipped from it, and then lowered it to rest in her lap on both hands. No one watching would ever have guessed that her heart was jumping every time Basho swayed or let out a yell. Not that anyone but servants and her own vassals was watching right now, but half the servants here worked for the Shinsen and would doubtless report anything interesting to their patron.

She was kneeling on the side-porch of Lord Shinsen Jiro's country house; the side-panels to her guest room were open to let the warm late-spring breeze in, and she had come outside to better enjoy it – and to have a better view of Basho's first adventure in horse-riding. It was the fifth country-house she had guested at since the start of the month; she had officially dismissed the court at Castle Ookami until High Lord Akira returned, and was now pointedly visiting each prominent samurai who had aligned closely with Akira or with her, showing them face and granting them the honor of hosting the High Lady. Subtle work, making sure no one would have time to scheme while the High Lord was away at war, and in the process slowly tightening the strings of personal alliance and loyalty.

And of course every one of them would see she was visibly with child, and would know a second heir to the Ookami would be born soon.

As if summoned by that thought, she felt an inward fluttering motion, the unborn child moving. Reflexively she set one hand over her belly, the curve now noticeable even when she wore formal multi-layered robes like today. After a little while the motion eased and she sipped the tea again.

Basho and his pony were now well down the yard, close to the fresh-built stone wall that marked its farthest extent. Beyond, the landscape was mostly farms, buckwheat and soybeans, and in the distance a village. To the left, wooded hills boasted other nobles' summer homes, built for when they wished to escape the crowding and stink of WolfTown; unlike this new-built one, most of them had abundant trees for shade. The Shinsen had been of the Black Wolves, and like others of that former Clan they had been forced to construct a new residence after the Wolf Clan reunited.

Two residences, actually, since like all of them Lord Shinsen also maintained one in WolfTown itself. She could see the charcoal smudge of the city's presence to her right, lurking on the horizon beyond the lines of forest, and could just barely make out the glint of Sunlight on Castle Ookami's mighty keep. Only an easy day's travel away, yet it was a different world from here, this place of soft clean breezes and buzzing insects, of farmers in broad-brimmed straw hats slowly traversing their fields, of rich night darkness broken only by scattered lamps and cool Moonlight.

There are good parts of being Akira's... of being the High Lady. Visiting places like this is one of them. In her own youth she had barely left the halls of Castle Kuroi and had known of places like this only from the books she read. It was pleasant to realize that some of the things in those books were real.

Sock-clad feet paced softly on the porch. Kaede schooled her face just before a pair of servants came around the corner of the house. One of them was an older woman wearing a robe in the black-on-gray vertical-striped style that seemed to be the standard garb here. She carried a tray with a teapot and a small plate. Kneeling with self-effacing grace, she laid the plate by Kaede's knee – it had a small array of pickled vegetables, delicately sliced and arranged in a fan-pattern that showed off their differing colors – and refilled her teacup. Finished, she bowed and murmured, "This one has been instructed to tell the most honorable guest that honorable Lady Shinsen invites you to dinner in the hour after Sunset."

"Inform Lady Shinsen that I will be honored to attend," Kaede replied, and the servant bowed once more and retreated.

Lord Shinsen's own wife was back in his own lands, along with his younger children. The lady of this house was Lady Sumie, wife of his oldest son Wateru, who was away serving in the war alongside his father. She had dropped hints to Kaede that she was expecting a child of her own, Lord Shinsen's first grandchild.

None of them lived in Castle Ookami – the Shinsen were trusted vassals, having stayed loyal during the Clan's civil war last year. Kaede had not bothered to visit the Musume summer residence, since there was no one living there right now – other than young Keppai, living alone in Castle Kage, every other Musume family member who was not in the field of war at Akira's side was a 'guest' of the High Lord, hostage to Lord Musume's loyalty.

I should try to amend that arrangement, Kaede thought. *Lord Musume knows how fortunate he is to have been spared after the civil war. Keeping his family hostage now just gives him a reason to be resentful.*

The second servant had waited patiently for the other to depart. She was a woman in her early thirties, not particularly memorable in her own right – neither pretty nor plain, though her hair was tied back in a knotted tail that was not a typical style in the Wolf lands. Kaede wondered if servants in the Nightingale lands all wore their hair that way, or if it was a particular affectation of Koko and the noblewoman she had once served.

Koko stepped forward and knelt, setting a portable table – a slightly-curved piece of smooth-finished wood on foot-high legs – next to Kaede. "Your correspondence has arrived from Castle Ookami, honored High Lady."

Kaede looked at the tabletop and the neatly-tied bundle of papers waiting atop it. She nodded and shifted to place her knees under it. "Bring me my writing kit, please," she said quietly. As always, it was hard not to be spiteful toward the woman, even though she knew there was no reason to dislike a servant. *She is not responsible for who her mistress was.*

Koko bowed and went into the guest-room to fetch the papers and inkstone and brush. Kaede lifted the bundles of papers – noting as she did that one of them was tied with a particular knot, the one used by Seneschal Amano's secretary Zenjiro. *Spy reports.*

A shout of laughter brought her attention back to the yard. She saw with relief that Yuji was lifting Basho down from the pony, and restraining the boy when he tried to rush forward and hug the animal's foreleg. The groom led the beast back toward the stable – that was a separate building on the far side of the hill – and the two servants took possession of Basho, chivvying him back to his own room with promises of a snack.

Kaede read her own personal letters first. Her network of correspondence had been growing almost by the month lately, thanks in part to the rumors she had her closest allies start spreading last winter. Very few people really believed that Akira intended to claim the Throne – Kaede was not sure she really believed it herself – but the mere rumor that he might was upsetting countless assumptions and settled patterns within the Wolf Clan's nobility. And now every woman of rank was anxious to form a personal connection with the High Lady, just in case that High Lady might soon be an Empress.

I'll start to answer these tomorrow, she thought, scanning down row after row of delicate, perfect calligraphy that all said more-or-less the same thing in carefully indirect wording. *And I'll do just a few of them each day.* If she rushed to reply she would appear too eager, too anxious, and her letters would lack depth and personal connection.

Koko knelt beside her and laid the writing gear on the table. "Thank you," Kaede murmured absently, still scanning through the letters and stacking them as she finished. The presence of the woman was an… *Irritation, just an irritation*, she told herself firmly. *She's a servant, not even a real person. A High Lady is above being upset by such things, I won't let it show, that would shame me.*

One of the letters was from a long-time ally, Lady Mamiko, a notorious gossip who Kaede had gotten a new husband after she was left widowed and without support by the previous war with the Jade Dragon Clan. Kaede read that letter's four pages more carefully, despite Mamiko's spidery calligraphy that forced her to sometimes pause and reread lines to make sure she was interpreting the characters properly. Much of it was nonsense, but there were always many nuggets of value mixed in. *That bit about Lord Kuroi trying to find a holding for his younger son, that's useful, we still have lands from the Makoto and Akabe that haven't been reassigned… Ah, and this part about the Haruto family sending out feelers to everyone about the status of GreenTown. We need to resolve that this winter…*

I'll answer this one today, she decided, setting that letter by itself. She paused to take another sip of tea, then lifted the smaller stack of spy reports and carefully untied the silk cord holding them together. Zenjiro had shown her the specific knot he used, after Amano had departed for the Tiger lands, so she could be confident they had not been opened by anyone else.

One of the letters was from Haruto Toji in GreenTown, the spy who had been code-named Golden Peony. *Interesting that he's still sending reports, even now that he and his cousin are basically running the city*, she thought. *I suppose he wants to influence us any way he can... Wait.* She reread the document again, making sure she understood. *He's... implying, no pretty much saying, that he reported Lord Katsura's disloyalty before Lady Yumiko's rebellion and suggested taking action. We could have assassinated the Katsura back then, instead of making Motosuke into the Lord of Silk Town.*

Amano knew all of this. She sat back, her frown reaching her face, and looked out at the afternoon landscape, trying to let the natural beauty wash over her so she could think clearly. A lone horseman with a back-banner was on the road that passed through the distant village and paralleled the hills with their samurai houses, and she watched him advance at a hard trot, the horse's hooves tossing up puffs of dust. The farmers in the fields paused their work and bowed as he passed.

This isn't the first time honorable Amano failed to tell us about things... I didn't even know about Haruto Toji until after he left for the Tiger lands. What else has he been hiding? Lord Okaro relied on him, I know... Did he change his attitude after poor old Okaro died? Or was he always manipulating things?

Kaede grimaced as she felt another inner kick. She sighed and set a hand on her stomach. Almost instantly the servant-woman had moved from the wall to kneeling by her side. "Are you well, my Lady? Should I send for a Priestess? There is one in the village, I made sure."

Kaede shook her head. "It is just the usual... kicking. Basho was the same." Despite herself she stared at the women, then forced herself to stop. *She made sure? Why?*

The horseman came up the track from the road, now riding hard as he approached his destination. She could see that his banner displayed the Ookami crest. As she watched he reined in and spoke briefly with a pair of Shinsen samurai; they gestured toward her. The courier dismounted and came across the grassy yard toward her.

Kaede felt a sudden rise of tension, and another kick inside as if in response. *The war... is this bad news? They would not send a courier out here for something trivial...*

The samurai knelt in the gift-giving posture, holding out a knotted paper in both hands. "Most honorable High Lady, I bring a letter from the High Lord."

From Akira. She took the letter with fingers that shook just slightly. His duty complete, the courier prostrated himself and retreated back to his horse.

Kaede pulled the folded paper out of its knot and opened it, sensing as she did a prickling attentiveness from Koko. *It isn't her place to care about this,* she thought angrily, but then she saw the brief lines of calligraphy written in Akira's inhumanly precise style, each character exactly the same no matter how many times he wrote it, as though he was using wood-blocks to stamp them out.

Honorable wife:
I have defeated the Jade Dragon Clan.
I am marching now on the Imperial City.
Prepare to relocate the household and court from Castle Ookami.
Ookami Akira.

A noise escaped her lips, a mixture of a gasp and a half-strangled laugh. "He won, he's really doing it," she whispered.

Koko let out a long sigh and mumbled something. Kaede was sure it was, "Of course he won."

Despite herself Kaede asked, "Would you prefer to be with my honorable husband in the field, Koko-*chan*? Then you could have learned about this directly."

The moment she spoke she felt her face reddening. *Idiot, acting like a child, letting a servant provoke you right after you told yourself you wouldn't! You might as well be the hopeless girl you were five years ago.* Her inner voice sounded suspiciously like Priestess Ritsuko.

The servant-woman bowed in apology. "Honorable Lord Akira takes only his manservant Kaito to war with him." Her voice remained even, though Kaede thought there was a hint of aspersion beneath the politeness. *Scolding me without scolding. And she speaks of him so... familiarly!*

Kaede knew it would be best to drop the whole thing, to pretend neither of them had spoken so face could be restored. But the letter's three blunt lines had shattered her composure, and she couldn't stop herself. "I know who you served, before you joined my husband's household. I may be a fool like Priestess Ritsuko says, but I'm not an idiot. When a new servant showed up out of nowhere I looked into it." Her face was burning-hot, the words tumbling out unstoppably. "You love him, don't you?"

Koko had been enduring the tirade in silence, but now her eyes widened. "My lady?"

"Oh, not *that* way, I know. You love him like a brother or beloved son, the way his soldiers love him." Kaede's voice went almost shrill. "I don't know why. I don't know why! Akira... my husband, he's a statue that walks, he's cold and cruel as ice, how can anyone *love* him?"

The older woman was silent for a long time. Her face had reddened and her hands were clenched in her lap. Finally she said only, "It is not my place to speak of such things, my Lady."

Kaede laughed, a sharp bitter sound. "No, I suppose not. It also wasn't your place to travel halfway across the Empire to attach yourself to my husband's household, but you did that, *neh*?" She shook her head. *I have to stop talking.* But the words kept coming, like a river breaking through a dam. "You did that, after something… bad, I don't know what… happened to your mistress, to Lady Naichin. Akira… my husband, after he found out, he was hiding in his room, not sleeping, not eating, and then you came, and he… got better. Why?"

Koko raised her head and looked directly at Kaede. Her voice rose, sharpened. "Because he loves her."

Kaede sat frozen, staring at the servant. The only sound was the buzzing of insects.

He loves her, even now, even when she is… gone.

"I should have you beaten and expelled from my household," she said finally.

Koko bowed. "That is your right," she replied, cool and self-controlled once more, the armor of the servant. "I swore to serve Lord Akira, and you are his wife."

And Kaede knew her threat was hollow. She would never do it, because Akira knew this woman, he *cared* about this woman, this *servant.* He would notice if she was gone.

With a monstrous effort Kaede turned away, looked out at the field once more, sipped her tea. "He loves her." The words were ash in her mouth. "But I am his wife."

"Yes, my Lady."

"He intends to be Emperor," she continued slowly. Each word was like lifting a weight. "Which means I will be Empress, and our children will become a new dynasty." She forced herself to turn back to Koko and smile. It made her cheeks hurt. "What is love, compared to that?"

The servant offered no answer.

CHAPTER 18

OKAMI AKIRA LISTENED TO the heavy beams of the Bridge of Approaching Heaven thud and echo under his soldier's sandals, vibrating slightly but otherwise showing no strain. The bridge, whose foundations dated back to the days of the First Emperor, had been restored by the Seventeenth Emperor, and he had built well – after five centuries it showed no strain at the passage of so many ranks of armored men.

The clatter of Akira's own horse's hooves was lost in the thunder of a thousand men marching at a steady trot. They were spearmen, their weapons held upright and the steel blades catching the morning Sunlight in staccato waves of bright flashes. Despite the clear sky, the air was cold here in the mountains, even in late spring. Clouds of steam – huffing breath and evaporating sweat – rose from the men's armored forms and puffed out from under the brims of their wok-shaped helmets.

Ahead of them Akira could see a haze of charcoal smoke nestling between the mountain peaks that rose on all sides. That marked the location of the Imperial City, the ancient seat of the Divinely-appointed Emperors, half-ruined and unclaimed by any Clan since the last Emperor had died four centuries past.

On the far side of the bridge the road – they still called it the Emperor's Road – curved around the side of a jagged, thickly-forested mountain. A horseman waited by the trees on the uphill side, his red-and-gray armor hazed with dust and his horse blowing and snorting. The man wore a back-banner, a small silk banner on a thin right-angled frame of bamboo tied to the back of his armor, marking him as a courier. Akira kneed his own horse off the road and drew up by the courier, who bowed in the saddle.

"Honorable High Lord! Honorable Captain Mosuke wishes you to know that the city is secure. The garrison… well, there wasn't much to it. They made no attempt to resist."

Akira brought his horse back down to the road and kicked it into a gallop, passing the column of soldiers. After the infantry came a group of mounted men; he recognized Lord Musume, combing his beard with one hand as he looked around with wide eyes. The nobleman started to open his mouth as Akira rode past, but if he meant to say something he never got the chance. Akira continued past the next column of infantry, on around the shoulder of the mountainside.

Ahead, the mountains on either side opened out into a great bowl, five miles and more across, the peaks on the far side barely visible as gray-green outlines. The ancient city crouched between them, a walled rectangle fringed on either side by croplands fed by mountain streams. The thick twelve-foot-high walls still stood, though they had lost all their smooth stucco and were just bare fitted rock; beyond them he could at first see only the haze of charcoal smoke three miles distant, but as he looked more carefully he could make out structures. His memory called up the maps he had pored over in the basement of Castle Ookami, the ancient drawings of the Imperial City on paper that had yellowed to nearly brown.

The Emperors' city was an oblong rectangle running north to south, the huge main gate in front of him located at the center of the northern end of that rectangle. The key structures – the Forbidden City where the Emperors had lived, the Great Temple of Amatsu and the other shrines, the embassies of the Clans – all lay in the southernmost and physically highest portion of the city, beyond the River of Glad Tidings that split it into two unequal halves. As originally designed the city had seven bridges crossing that river, one on each of the major north-south roads named after the Seven Warrior Virtues, but Akira had reviewed the letters from the Wolf Clan ambassadors here and knew that only three of those bridges still stood.

If the defenders want to fight us, that would be the best place. The walls are too weak. The wide but relatively low walls of the city dated back to the earliest days of the Empire, when fortifications had been crude and simple by today's standards, and they had never been updated. Since the Dread Eclipse they had not even been maintained, and Akira could see places where they had sagged or half-collapsed. The main gate was wide open and had probably never been shut in living memory.

His lead infantry unit was nearly up to that gate now, and with Wolf cavalry holding the entrance they were not even bothering to slow their march or change their formation. They kept their faces properly forward, their ranks in order as he rode past on their right, but the men let out a cheer, a long booming roar: "Ookami! Ookami! Ookami!"

A group of rather hangdog men stood to one side of the gate, some of his cavalry standing adjacent, not quite openly guarding them. The men were in partial armor and had bamboo spears, but clearly were not samurai – the clothing under their armor was torso wrappings and white leggings, and their scalps were half-shaved on the front in the commoner style. They were staring gape-mouthed at the army marching up to their gates; as they noticed him riding past, they dropped to their knees and pressed their faces into the dirt.

A company of horsemen waited just outside the gate, Captain Mosuke among them. Another of Kado Kitaro's young officers who had probably been no more than a Lieutenant at best in the Nightingale campaign. His face was blazing, exultant, as he fell in beside Akira and the rest of the men formed up around them in a loose oval. Together they rode through the open gate – open for so many years, Akira now saw, that the ancient wooden panels were sunk into the ground.

Ookami Akira entered the Imperial City, and his army followed.

At first it seemed a city much like any other, endless rows of mostly one-story buildings, built in the traditional wood-and-paper style with tiled roofs. The first difference he noticed was the streets – they were the same clean-swept, hard-packed earth as anywhere else, but they extended in spear-straight lines, north-south and east-west, dividing the city neatly into rectangles. The second thing he noticed was how many of the buildings were old, decrepit, abandoned. In some places they had actually fallen down, leaving piles of forsaken wreckage.

People emerged from buildings to stare, while those in the street scurried to the edge to make room for the advancing soldiers. Shopkeepers in dark respectable jackets, serving-maids from restaurants and tea-houses with knee-length robes and their hair under kerchiefs, laborers in vests and sweat-stained headbands and loincloths, married women in simple day-robes with their children walking beside them or carried on their backs, street peddlers with their boxes balanced on shoulder-yokes, a dung-collector with the crowd making a circle around him and his cart, even a few samurai in loose-sleeved shirts and pleated pants… all of them staring with the same wide-eyed bewilderment as the guards outside the gate. Some whispered to each others, others fell to their knees and prayed or wept; a few ever tried to cheer, although without much enthusiasm.

The crowds slowly grew as the army marching south, more and more people converging on the Street of Honor as the news spread. The numbers were modest compared to the great crowds that packed the streets in WolfTown whenever the army marched out, and Akira thought briefly of the old records that had claimed a hundred thousand people lived in this place. *No more than one-fifth of that now, probably less.*

Although the crowds were thickening, the numbers of samurai did not increase. He supposed most of the samurai lived in the higher-grade neighborhoods beyond the bridges – he could see individual structures there now, a great gold-roofed pagoda that must be the main Temple, and to the east the irregular outlines of ancient, broken-down structures that had to be the ruins of the Forbidden City. The number of clergy was growing dramatically, however, far beyond what he had ever seen in a normal city. Scores of individual Priestesses in yellow-orange robes, ringing their staffs and chanting, their shaven heads gleaming with sweat. Groups of younger shaven-headed girls, each led by a single adult Priestess, the acolytes wide-eyed and silent. Monks, singly or in groups, watching in stone-faced silence.

Akira made himself look at the Monks. His hands trembled slightly, and he tightened his grip on the horse's reins. *I am not in the Monastery anymore. I am not a student anymore.*

They reached the river. It flowed at the bottom of a deep channel, the sides all ancient fitted stone, each piece larger than a man; low stone railings lined the edges, and hundreds of people crowded against those railings, staring, a few even pointing despite the intrinsic rudeness of such a gesture. The bridge that vaulted across was ten paces wide, the railings and posts lacquered red and white, support pillars rooted in stone foundations fifty feet below. On the far side more people gathered, samurai robes and topknots dominating the crowds, and Akira looked left and right, noting two other intact bridges and the broken-off remnants of four more. People were rushing out onto the other two bridges to get a better view.

For a brief time as he closed the distance to the bridge, he considered whether he was taking too much risk by crossing first instead of waiting for the infantry marching behind him. Then he mentally shook his head. *I cannot show weakness now.*

They crossed the bridge and the crowd on the far side parted before them, rolling back to either side like an opening gate. Their murmuring was a steady low rumble, the samurai using fans to hide their mouths, the common folk holding up a hand for the same purpose or just leaning close to each other.

The sound of his horse's hooves changed. The streets above the river were not dirt but stone, close-fitted flat pieces worn smooth by hundreds of years of walking feet. Akira had never seen that outside of a castle.

Two and three and four-story buildings loomed on either side, their window shutters and panels slid aside, the openings filled with watching people. Some of the buildings had banners hanging from windows and the up-turned corners of their roofs – he spotted the Tiger, orange and black, with the Clan crest and the snarling cat's head of the Tora family. *Embassies,* he remembered. *Everyone has one here. I should find where ours is... and the Jade Dragons.*

Almost every block had at least one Temple or shrine, their pagoda towers rising above the other structures, their front entrances crowded with Priestesses and Monks. Most of them were chanting mantras, and the ringing of the Priestesses' prayer-staffs was a constant undercurrent to the crowd-noise.

Behind him the bridge rumbled with the passage of his infantry, and the crowd-noise turned higher-pitched, more anxious. *It wasn't real until they saw I brought an army,* he thought, and remembered something from his old lessons: *Men will believe what they wish to believe until they are forced to do otherwise. This is why the cunning general can trick even the most clever opponent.*

He emerged from the street onto a broad open square, as large as Castle Ookami's parade-ground. Temples ringed it, all of them huge, the largest on the eastern side atop a man-made sheer-sided mountain of stone, rising high enough that he had to crane his head back to see the statues of dragons and foxes lining the platform's edge a hundred paces above. The open space had been crowded as he approached, but now it was almost clear, people edging back against the surrounding temples.

A broad staircase, steep as a castle's interior stairs, climbed the side of the Great Temple's massive platform. Clergy were coming down it, in a formation that looked almost military in its precision and structure: a double row of young Priestesses, chanting and ringing their staffs, and then two more widely-spaced rows of Monks, hands set palms-together in front of their faces as they recited mantras in unison. Another row of Priestesses behind them, these ones older and fewer in number, and then, finally, a group of twelve – half Priestesses and half Monks – walking together.

At the bottom of the staircase the leading rows of Priestesses and Monks shifted out to either side, forming two lines that opened a clear path through the crowd. The other clergy all around the great square took up the same mantras, the combined chanting now loud enough to be heard over the crowd-noise. Bells began ringing, first a deep tolling from the Great Temple above and then spreading to the other shrines, radiating out throughout the city, a steady deep tone once every ten heartbeats.

The twelve clergy came forward slowly, moving with the hieratic pace they adopted at the most formal occasions, each step and gesture like a slow-motion dance. Their robes were subtly different, he noticed, with extra layers and more embroidery, but otherwise they were Priestesses and Monks like any others, if a bit pale and unhealthy-looking. All of them were at least middle-aged, and some much older than that. They were reciting the same mantra as all the others, and now he could make out the words:

Sacred Lady of Heaven, Blessed Amatsu
Stern Lord of Heaven, Divine Mikoto
Welcome your chosen Son
Bless him with Courage, Honor, Honesty, Compassion
Endow him with Courtesy, Duty, and Discipline
May the Empire prosper with him

A subtle change in the timbre of noise made Akira glance back the way he had come. The lead infantry column had arrived in the square and grounded its spears, motionless now save for the fluttering of its banners in the breeze. Toshiwara Nomi stood his horse at their stead.

Ten paces away, the twelve clergy spread out in a single row, stopped chanting, and sank to their knees. As if that were a signal all the other clergy ceased chanting as well, the sound-level dropping sharply enough that Akira could hear a distant child crying. The temple bells tolled one last time and then fell silent as well, and he realized they had rung exactly twelve times.

One of the kneeling Priestesses spoke. She was a plump, puffy-faced woman, her jowls sagging and her shaven head blotchy, and her voice was thin and raspy. "Who comes to the city of the Emperors, the city ordained by Heaven?"

She and her companions were not looking at Akira, and she seemed to have directed the question generally at all the horsemen standing before her. Captain Mosuke smothered a noise that might have been a laugh.

Akira was momentarily bewildered. Then he looked down at himself and realized: *I left the Ookami ancestral armor with Lord Toshiwara, so he could fool the Jade Dragon spies. These people probably think I'm just one of honorable Mosuke's horsemen. That's why they all keep looking back along the column.* The realization brought with it shame and anger with himself. *I should have thought of this. Symbols matter, all the old writings agreed on that.*

He tapped his heels to his horse and walked it forward, stopping just in front of his men. The Priestesses and Monks all blinked at him in sheer confusion. He became aware of the deep silence that lay on the square, the sense of straining anticipation from the waiting crowd.

Akira spoke clearly, not shouting but pitching his voice to carry. "I am Ookami Akira, High Lord of the Wolf Clan."

A single barking cheer erupted from the men behind him: "Ookami!"

The cheer, more than his own announcement, hit the audience squarely. People stepped back, a few women screamed.

After a long moment, the puffy-faced Priestess swallowed hard and recited: "Great and honorable Lord… Ookami Akira, I am… I am Priestess Motoko, first servant of Amatsu in the Theological Council."

A Monk with a sunken-cheeked face and a mouth set in deep frown lines grated: "Great and honorable Lord, chosen of Mikoto to restore our Empire, I am Teacher Hojo, first servant of Mikoto in the Theological Council."

Akira flinched inwardly. The Monk's voice awoke memories that burned in the scars on his back. He closed his eyes briefly, reciting the mantras.

The two of them prostrated themselves, pressing their foreheads to the smooth flagstones, and the rest of the Council followed suit. All twelve spoke in unison: "The Theological Council welcomes you to the Imperial City."

This is some old ritual, Akira thought, feeling a sudden rush of panic as though he was back at the Monastery, trying to remember his lessons through a fog of exhaustion and pain. *What should I do? Is there a response I am supposed to make?* He had expected to simply take control of the city as he would any other captured settlement.

As always when he did not know what to do, he remained silent. The Council members seemed non-plussed by that, some of them glancing back and forth at each other. Finally they all slowly rose from their prostrations. Some of them found that difficult – one of the older Priestesses couldn't get up at all and had to be helped by the Monk next to her.

After a pause that grew so long that Akira thought he could hear some questioning murmurs from the crowd, the one called Motoko recited: "Great and Honored Lord… Ookami Akira. We of the Theological Council, divinely ordained by the first Emperor, have cared for this city ever since the Dread Eclipse."

Not knowing what else to do, Akira said, "Thank you."

"The Council has carried out its duty since the days of the Eclipse, protecting the dwelling of the ancient Emperors until the Heavens chose a new dynasty. Our devotion to the True Path is now rewarded, as harmony returns to the Heavens and the earth…"

Akira shut his eyes, trying to focus his mind. She went on, reciting more of the same thing, an endless circular repetition of ritual phrases. He didn't know what any of it meant. *Am I Emperor now? No, they aren't saying that. What are they saying?*

A moment of clarity: *This is politics, just like the speeches in court. The war is still underway, I cannot stay here to deal with this. But Kaede understands politics…*

He opened his eyes. "Be silent."

Priestess Motoko broke off, blinking in confusion. The iron-faced Monk next to her scowled more deeply but said nothing.

Akira turned his horse toward Toshiwara Nomi. The old man had dismounted and was looking up at the Great Temple with a wondering half-smile on his face. When Akira's attention fell on him snapped into focus and bowed. "Your orders, honorable High Lord?"

"Secure the city. I will be returning to the field with Lord Musume and his men." Akira looked around the square, taking in the numbers of samurai in the crowds. "Encamp some of your men here, the rest can be housed in empty buildings. Company-sized or larger, and maintain patrols at all times. Put guards in control of all the gates and the Clan embassies. Especially the Jade Dragon one, and track down all the Jade Dragon samurai you can find."

Nomi nodded, his eyes gleaming. "And what do we do with those Jade Dragons when we find them?"

"The soldiers can swear fealty if they wish. The nobles die, by their own hand or ours."

⛩ ⛩ ⛩

KADO KITARO REINED IN, GRIMACING in pain and then smoothing his face so his men would not see any sign of weakness. Thick grass brushed against his legs, his horse snorting at the clouds of insects stirred up by its passage. The weather had turned hot in the last two days, the season preparing to move from spring into summer, and the Sun beat down on the horse's neck and shoulders, on his own armor and helmet. His face and body were slick with sweat, greasily uncomfortable beneath the confining armor, and his mouth felt pasty.

When he was sure his voice would stay even, he dropped the reins over his saddle and held out his left hand to Lieutenant Juzo. "Honorable Juzo, your canteen?"

The young officer unplugged the bamboo-tube canteen and handed it open, and Kitaro sipped the lukewarm water with relief.

He and his personal escort were on the crest of a low hill, one of several running northward, covered in thick grasses and occasional large boulders or clumps of shrubbery. The rest of the company of horsemen accompanying him was in the swale below, resting their animals after a hard morning of riding through the blooming heat. To his east, half a mile away, the Road of Dancing Foxes wound its way northward toward the Tiger lands, following the only water in this area – a thin stream lined on either side by clumps of trees. He could see a merchant caravan heading south on it, a half-dozen ox-drawn wagons with people walking alongside.

To the west, beyond a series of small woodlands, the land flattened out became farms. A few miles in that direction, invisible from here, was Castle Shingi, the stronghold of the Mugai family and the northernmost of the Jade Dragon strongholds. A company of his men were there, keeping watch on the garrison and making sure it didn't move south to make trouble for the Bear army currently besieging Castle Hokori.

I've got men scattered to every corner, Kitaro thought anxiously, still sipping carefully – hard experience had taught him that drinking too quickly when overheated could make him ill. *A company here, two companies there... Thank Amatsu we slaughtered the Jade Dragon cavalry at the Midorisaka hills, or we'd be in serious danger now of being defeated in detail.* It was unavoidable, given his mission and the necessity of living off the land, but he had never spread his men so widely before, and the fear of failure and the shame which failure would bring – to him, to Lord Akira, to Lady Miyu as his betrothed – was a constant undertone to his thoughts.

And something is *happening in the north.* An hour ago they had spotted a pillar of smoke on the northern horizon, a gray-black coil that seemed no closer despite that they had moved several miles closer. In fact, it had been joined by a second one. *Miles away still, which means the fires are large.*

He handed the canteen back to Juzo, picked up the reins. Riding one-handed was challenging, but he was not about to let himself be shamed in the saddle by old Nomi. "Move out!"

They went north in an alternating walk-trot that kept the horses from wearing down too quickly. At first they stayed on the road, but as the hour moved past Noon the traffic increased more and more, forcing them to move off onto the open land to the side. Kitaro's inner concern deepened. Even in wartime there was always *some* traffic on the roads – merchants and peddlers and entertainers going from one town to the next, traveling samurai, couriers on horseback, itinerant Monks, sellswords looking for their next job – but today it was mostly peasants, often with bundles on their backs or pushing hand-carts loaded with belongings. *Refugees, just like we saw fleeing the Jade Dragon lands last year,* he thought, and felt a chill despite the warm day. Peasants did not readily flee their lands, given the penalties for doing so and the difficulty of finding any sort of proper life elsewhere.

They came to a roadside teahouse on the left, tucked in under the trees above the stream-bed. It was crowded with commoners, lining up by the counters or sitting outside on rough-cut benches or simply on the ground, more of them spreading out into the road and along the sides as they continued to trickle in from the north. They watched warily as Kitaro's company circled around them to an open field beyond. As they passed Kitaro spotted a sellsword, a man in baggy shirt and leggings with a pair of swords slung across his back, leaning against a tree-trunk while he ate a bowl of noodles. He halted the march and sent Lieutenant Juzo back to speak with the man.

The Lieutenant returned after a few minutes. "The fellow says he's heading north for work – he's heard the Tiger are in trouble with the northern barbarians and are desperate for soldiers. Plans to head for Castle Tanigawa, he's heard they're gathering troops there."

Kitaro got his men moving again while his thoughts went back to the maps he had seen in the basement of Castle Ookami. He kept the column off the road now, it simply took too long to wait for the refugees to move aside. *Castle Tanigawa is… a lesser stronghold, and well southwest of their seat of power in Castle Mouko. Why would they be rallying troops there?*

Five miles further on they came to a farming village. The croplands stretched to the right of the road up a shallow valley for more than a mile, the rice-paddies feeding off a tributary stream that wound through them and then passed under the road at a simple flat-topped wooden bridge. The villagers' houses were perched on either side of the lowland, but the inhabitants were down by the road with sticks and knives and a handful of spears, gesturing threateningly at the refugees passing them. The refugees for the most part ducked their heads and kept moving, although a few shouted pleas or insults at the farmers.

At the sight of samurai horsemen the farmers blanched, scurrying back from the roadside and then dropping to their knees and prostrating themselves. *Afraid that we'll punish them for having the spears,* Kitaro knew. And in truth there was a part of him that wanted to stop and demand answers. Peasants could only acquire samurai weapons by stealing them… or by murdering samurai.

These are not our people, he reminded himself. *They're Jade Dragon peasants, and Lord Akira warned us not to cause more damage than we can help.* He looked away from the farmers and kept riding, his men following. The stream was too deep and wide of a gully to cross easily with horses, so they had to take over the road and cross the bridge while the refugees shuffled to the sides, watching with dull-eyed wariness as the samurai rode past.

They moved north for another hour, passing two other villages. The smoke-pillars slowly grew closer, rising higher into the otherwise clear sky until they loomed overhead like inverted mountain peaks. The road finally left the waterway and passed through a thick belt of woods, then up a narrow valley, forested hills on either side, here and there interrupted by the bare rock of cliffs. The flow of refugees trickled to a few scattered people and then stopped altogether.

They reached the head of the valley, the trees crowding in close on either side; the combination of the foliage and the now close-looming smoke making the light unpleasantly dim for a few minutes before the road crested and then descended the soft slope, emerging back into open ground. The tree-crowded hill remained close on the left, while on the right an open space of grass and bare rock sloped away, the treeline and the hill beyond it gradually curving into the distance.

A half-mile ahead, the road led toward a wooden fortification tucked in against the rocks and trees of the western slope: a border waystation where the Tiger would have checked travel passes and assessed tariffs. It was on fire, orange flames billowing up from the small keep within and from the towers at two of the corners, sparks rising into the thick churning towers of smoke that merged into a single bloated mass overhead and slowly drifting off eastward. The gates of the place gaped open and Kitaro could see bodies on the ground, though it was too far away to tell whose.

He took his hand off the reins and waved a signal to his men; the company spread out from a narrow marching column into a broad fighting one, the horsemen ranging down the slope on the right, picking their way between the occasional boulders.

Up close, he could see the flames had already spread to the other buildings within the waystation – barracks and storehouses and private homes. The roar of the spreading flames was disturbingly loud, and Kitaro could feel the heat on his face even at fifty paces. The bodies visible within the open gates were a mix of samurai and commoners, the warriors' armor showing the Tiger orange and black. He could see arrows sticking from the bodies and lodged in the waystation's exterior walls.

Lieutenant Juzo pointed at a dark shape just inside the gate. "What is that?"

Two men dismounted and ran in, hunching their shoulders against the building heat. They probed at the shape, then lifted it up – revealing a human body – and dragged it back by the arms.

Kitaro kicked his horse forward, heedless of the heat, and reined in next to the men as they dropped the corpse, muttering curses. It was a man, a man with a flat high-cheeked face and greasy hair worn loose, dressed strangely in leathers and animal pelts; he had died from a deep slash across the torso that had spilled out the contents of his stomach cavity.

A barbarian warrior, just like honorable Tokaze Kondo described, Kitaro thought with an inner chill that made his skin tighten despite the heat of the fire. *But they should be up in the north, past Castle Mouko, not all the way down here on the Tiger Clan's southern border!*

A courier raced up in a spray of dust. "Honorable Kitaro! Captain Tomio has found a trail, heading north along the road."

Kitaro wheeled his horse and shouted orders. The company flowed around the downhill side of the burning waystation, rising to a fast trot as they left the pillar of smoke behind them. Ahead the road curved along the side of the left-hand hill, the lower forested hills on the right at first receding away and then growing closer. The second smoke-pillar was to the northeast, somewhere beyond those hills, still a mile distant at least. The valley was eerily silent except for the thunder of their mounts' hooves.

They passed an arrow-riddled body, a commoner man shot in the back as he was running away. Fifty paces past that, a peddler's cart lay abandoned by the roadside. Then, as they came around the curve of the hill, Kitaro let out a violent oath and reined up sharply; his men did the same, not in orderly precision but in a tangled wave of horrified realization.

For two hundred paces the road was littered with bodies. Men, women, old and young, intermingled with toppled handcarts and scattered belongings. In the midst of the ruin a single wagon was run half-off the road, the oxen dead in their yokes, the driver sprawled across his seat. The only sound was a faint buzzing of flies. The air smelled of rancid blood.

Kitaro felt his sweat congealing on skin gone suddenly clammy. *This is not war. This is… something else.*

Wait… where are the children? Every group of refugees we passed had their children with them.

He found his voice: "Check for survivors." Then, with a prickle of unease: "Captain Tomio, get two squadrons out on our flanks."

The captain shouted orders and the men fanned out, cantering their horses and then slowing to a walk as they approached the treelines. They moved down the valley in a staggered array, weaving in and out of the forest as they looked for enemies. Other soldiers dismounted and walked slowly down the long line of bodies, occasionally crouching to look more closely.

Kitaro swallowed against an anxious tightness in his chest and walked his horse alongside the field of slaughter, carefully steering it where there was no risk it might step on a corpse. The rest of the company moved with him, uneasily silent except for the occasional snort or whinny as the horses caught their riders' unhappiness. Ahead, the lead squadron was past the farthest bodies and swinging back to straddle the road, following as it again curved to the left past a protruding stone bolide as large a two-story house, a few stunted trees clinging to cracks in the upper surfaces.

As they disappeared behind the huge rock, Kitaro felt his unease rise and his heartbeat with it, making his broken arm throb. The instinct of a hundred battles and skirmishes made him rein in and look left, and in that instant an arrow flashed past his head, so close that the point clipped the edge of his helmet and the fletching brushed the edge of his ear.

Two paces away, Lieutenant Juzo let out a strangled gasp as an arrow slammed into his side; the banner sagged as he slumped in the saddle.

The whole treeline was spraying dark-fletched arrows, Wolf samurai shouting and their horses screaming as they struck home. The whole left-flank squadron went down in the space of three heartbeats.

Kitaro opened his mouth to shout for a charge. Samurai instinct, to counterattack an ambush, combined with the bone-deep knowledge that horsemen could run down and slaughter archers. But at the same time the harsh lessons of the last four years surged to the top of his mind. *We can't charge into a forested hillside!*

"Retreat!" He caught the bridle of Juzo's horse even as he tightened his knees and forced his own horse around, cursing at the awkwardness of trying to get a fast reaction with only his legs, then kicked the beast into a gallop. Arrows were still whipping past, black horizontal flashes, horses screaming and crow-hopping as they were hit. One clanged off the side of his helmet, rocking his head violently; another *thunked* heavily into the backplate of his armor but didn't penetrate.

The whole company was turned now, riding back the way they had come. He looked over his shoulder and saw three horsemen coming back around the big rock at the corner of the hill, riding at a full gallop, crouched over their saddles. *Three left of a squadron*, he thought sickly. *That's almost two full squadrons lost!*

Barbarians were atop the boulder, drawing and shooting almost straight down at the riders going past below them. With them was another figure wearing some kind of robe or cloak, arms raised overhead, head bloated and misshapen… *No, that's some kind of head-gear to make him look imposing, like the helmets Lords wear into battle.*

The last three Wolf samurai fell, one dropping out of the saddle with four arrows in him, the other two tumbling to the ground as their horses collapsed in tangled limb-kicking heaps. Kitaro cursed again and turned back forward, leaning over his horse's neck as he kicked it for more speed. Somehow he had managed to keep hold of Juzo's horse, the beast running alongside while its rider swayed drunkenly in the saddle. *He hasn't dropped the banner, he must still be alive…*

The arrows were coming in from behind and above now, the enemy arcing their shots as the distance widened. A few still struck home; he saw a horse lurch and falter as a shaft sank into its haunch, then trip over a boulder it tried to leap and send beast and rider into a tumbling wreck. A man shouted in pain as an arrow struck his arm, another reeled and then roll out of the saddle silently as black fletching sprouted from the back of his neck, striking between backplate and helmet with malignant luck.

Then they were out of range, sweeping down across the lower slope closer to the waystation, the smoke-pillar throwing them into shadow. Kitaro leaned back, slowing his horse with the shift in his weight and pulling the bridle to slow Juzo's horse as well. A quick look left and right spotted Captain Tomio, still on his horse and apparently unhurt despite a bright scar of exposed metal on the side of his helmet.

Kitaro looked back. He could see tiny figures at the edge of the treeline, some of them gesturing defiantly. *They didn't pursue us into the open… which means they've fought against cavalry before. Well, they've been fighting the Tiger for generations, of course they would know…*

He walked his horse alongside Captain Tomio. "How many?" His voice was a dry croak, his body soaked with sweat beneath the armor, his face slick with it.

"We lost… at least two full squadrons," Tomio said grimly. "And the same number are wounded. Those arrows hit as hard as our own, maybe more." He walked his horse past Kitaro and caught the drooping banner from Juzo's hands. The young man tried to hold onto it, then gasped and let go.

Kitaro looked at the arrow sticking out of Juzo's side and grimaced inwardly. "Honorable Juzo, can you ride?"

The Lieutenant was breathing in shallow gasps, his face gray and dripping sweat, but he managed to get his hands on the reins.

Kitaro looked once more at the distant barbarians. The robed figure had walked out of the treeline to stand among them, and it raised a banner – in a strange horizontal shape with pointed ends, but recognizably a banner. The cloth was black, with a strange twisted symbol in lurid green; even at this distance there was something unsettling about it, as though it was moving, and Kitaro shuddered and wrenched his gaze away.

The barbarians raised their bows over their heads, waving them back and forth in time with the banner. Even from this distance, Kitaro could make out their chant: "Dakkurru! Dakkurru! Dakkurru!"

Kitaro turned back to Captain Tomio. "Get everyone moving south. The High Lord needs to know about this at once."

They reorganized into a loose oval, the wounded men and riderless horses in the center, and moved past the burning waystation, alternating trotting and walking to let the horses rest after the galloping flight from the barbarians. By now the waystation was almost completely engulfed in flames, the orange tongues licking off the tops of the walls so the whole thing was a cyclone whirling up into the thickening, broadening smoke-pillar. Flecks of ash landed on their armor and speckled the horses' manes.

Kitaro found himself holding his breath as their formation narrowed to funnel through the belt of forest, suddenly aware of how deadly an ambush would be with the trees only a few paces to either side. When they re-emerged into Sunlight on the far side he felt the tightness in his chest relax so strongly that he went slightly weak. His mind started ranging ahead to what needed to happen next. *If the barbarians have raiding parties this far south, we need to make sure we're moving in greater strength, two or three companies together at least. And we may not be able to make contact with the Tiger on this route, so I'll need to send troops up the Road of Spring Winds as well. Maybe Kazomiru can handle that...*

"Honorable Kado," someone said. Kitaro snapped out of his thoughts and looked at Captain Tomio. The officer was pointing ahead, down the valley toward the next belt of trees two miles away.

A mile distant, a swarm of barbarians had emerged from the tree-cloaked eastern hillside and was spreading out across the little valley. *At least a hundred,* Kitaro thought numbly. *And they have another of those... people... in the strange outfits. How did they get more men in front of us? We left the others far behind and to our west. They couldn't possibly have gotten word to anyone else fast enough to intercept us.*

At the same time the war-fighting part of his mind was thinking coldly: *They've moved into the open, they think they have enough numbers to cut us down.* His voice was loud but calm as he called orders: "Advance, and prepare to charge. We'll cut right through them." And then, lifting the banner up as high as his one good arm would allow, pouring his anger and frustration into the shout: "The Lady with us!"

"The Lady with us! Ookami!" The men roared as they raised spears or drew swords, kicking their horses to a trot and then to a canter. Even the wounded men shouted, Lieutenant Juzo drawing his sword and yelling despite the cords on his neck standing out from the pain.

"Dakkurru! Dakkurru!" the barbarians answered, and then the *whung* of a hundred and more bows, the sky suddenly dark with arrows.

"Charge," Kitaro shouted at the same moment, slanting the banner forward and kicking his horse's flanks, and the beast bugled and surged beneath him, muscles bunching and pushing. The whole company surged ahead, the arrows sleeting above their heads, a few men in the back letting out grunts or screams as they were hit.

Another volley was already in the air, the barbarians nocking and shooting as fast or faster than samurai despite their smaller weirdly-curved bows and odd shooting-style – they were pulling the arrows only back to their cheeks, instead of behind their heads as samurai would. Someone grunted and rolled out of the saddle on Kitaro's right, and ahead to his left a horse tumbled over, two others frantically leaping past its flailing ruin. But the distance was closing, closing, he could see details of the enemy, the belts and straps holding their strange clothing together, the glint of eyes and flash of teeth, and around him samurai brought their spears down level, the foot-long razor-edged blades reaching for the enemy.

The barbarian with the strange headdress – it was a mask, Kitaro realized, a broad oval twice the size of a man's head, carved in a grotesque imitation of a human face and fringed with a tangle of black hair – stepped out in front of the archers, holding another black-cloth banner with its bizarre twisting symbol up with one hand while the other reached out, fingers wide, and then clutched and grasped and swung sideways as though he was yanking a string.

The three horses in front of Kitaro suddenly were pitching forward, their limbs bizarrely immobile. The riders had no time to react before they were slammed to the ground by the massive bulk of their mounts, the horses' limbs breaking with ghastly snapping noises, the beasts screaming in dumb animal terror and bewildered agony.

Blessed Amatsu, lay your sheltering robes over me, grant me the courage to face my fate unflinching...

The prayer ran through Kitaro's mind as he frantically kicked his own horse into a leap, just clearing the hideous tangle, a helmet spinning through the air and bouncing off the shaft of the banner in his left hand, the sandal on his right foot lightly clipping a horse's kicking leg. His horse stumbled and almost fell, limbs churning. A flash of motion on his left, Lieutenant Juzo surging past him and bearing down on the barbarian sorcerer with his long sword held high, rising in the saddle to strike as he came within ten paces.

The sorcerer flung his hand out. Juzo's horse pitched forward, the Lieutenant going over its neck and head-first into the ground, his sword flying free and tumbling sideways across Kitaro's field of vision.

Kitaro seemed to be moving in slow motion, every nerve and muscle straining, the mantra running through his mind the only thing still happening at normal speed. He tossed his banner aside, the silk cloth fluttering as it sank toward the ground, and drew his short sword one-handed, bringing the hilt up above his head to make sure the blade cleared the sheath. His hand and fingers and thumb moved in precise increments, bringing the blade near-level and spinning it in the palm of his hand.

A stunt from the training hall, the kind of thing he and the other youngsters had practiced so they could show off to serving-maids at teahouses.

The sorcerer swung his clutching hand toward Kitaro and tightened it into a fist.

The short sword's hilt fell into his palm, his hand snapped closed around it, and he whipped his arm forward, hurling the blade overhand.

His horse screamed and then it was in the air, and Kitaro came out of the saddle and curled into a ball, trying to shield his sling-bound right arm, and a thought flickered through his mind: *Ah Blessed Goddess this is going to* hurt...

He hit the ground, bounced and then rebounded off the horse's toppling hindquarters, bounced again, clenching his teeth against the scream that tried to force itself out of his throat. And then he was lurching to his feet, blinking against the dark sparks flickering in his vision, grabbing the hilt of his long sword and yanking it awkwardly free.

Two paces away, the sorcerer lay on his back, his grotesque giant mask staring blindly at the sky, Kitaro's short sword transfixing his chest. His limbs jerked and twitched, his heels drummed the earth.

Horseman raced past Kitaro on either side, shouting battle-cries, their weapons red-soaked. The barbarian archers were down or running, falling one by one as the cavalry chased them down.

Kitaro sucked in a breath, clamping down on the pain surging up his right arm and through his body. *Discipline,* he recited mentally. *A samurai never lets pain control him, because he possesses Discipline.*

He limped over to the dying barbarian. Most of the banner was underneath the body, thankfully sparing him from having to see it again. This close, he could see the man's mask was a flat wooden oval, featureless except for the two eye-holes. What he had thought was a carving was… the skin of a human face, stretched out and pinned to the wood.

I think that might have been a child's face, he thought distantly. *And that mane around the edges… human hair.*

The sorcerer had stopped moving. Kitaro hesitated, then put the point of his long sword under the mask and shoved it up and off.

The face underneath was pale and shriveled, the now-blank eyes sunk deep in the sockets, the cheeks hollowed-in, the lips pulled back to show yellow rotted teeth made unnaturally long by receding gums. Kitaro felt his stomach churn; he turned away, momentarily sure he would be sick, but the nausea passed once he put his back to the thing.

That brought the rest of his pain rushing back into his awareness; he stuck his sword upright in the ground and then forced himself to feel his right arm.

Splints didn't break, he decided after a moment. *Maybe it'll be… all right. But I need a Priestess, and so do a lot of the men.*

A clopping of hooves brought his head up. Captain Tomio was resting his bloody sword edge-up on his shoulder, his face still bright with the lingering exaltation of combat but concern showing through. "Honorable Kado? Are you well?"

"No," Kitaro grated. "But I think I will live. Is Lieutenant Juzo..?"

Tomio shook his head, now fully serious. "His neck was broken." He looked around, took a deep breath, and wiped the blood off his sword with the sleeve of his other arm before sheathing it. "I don't know what… *that…* was, but it cost us six men and eight horses. Lost another dozen or more to the archers, but once we reached the scum we slaughtered them like helpless oxen. I don't think any got away."

"Good," Kitaro breathed. *They can't tell their friends what happened... but their friends told* them *we were here. How...?*

He looked again at the dead sorcerer, then looked away.

"Get me a horse," he ordered. "We need to keep moving."

"Our casualties?"

Kitaro shut his eyes briefly, fighting the urge to weep. *Juzo was a good man, brave and honorable.* "We can't do a proper ritual with the other scum just a few miles away," he said aloud. "Collect tokens from the fallen, swords or helmets or personal things... something to take back to their families."

"It shall be as you say, honorable Kado!" Tomio rode away, calling orders. After a minute someone brought one of the spare horses over to Kitaro, and politely helped him mount without drawing attention to it. Kitaro felt grateful, for the help and the man's circumspection.

His arm throbbed abominably, but he did not allow himself to touch it again. *A commander can never show weakness.*

The men were moving quickly, collecting a few things from each of their fallen comrades. He watched them, then looked back north. The pillars of smoke still loomed there, grave-markers of the barbarians' victims, and somewhere beyond those trees were the others who had ambushed him. *Somehow they were able to trap me. How? I must get word to the High Lord. He must know what they can do.*

⛩ ⛩ ⛩

KENJI DREAMED.

He was in the pit again, in the stinking dark, eating the last bits of rice while his sister pleaded in a weak, thready whisper. Her voice went on and on, a fading desperate plea. "Ken-*chan*... thirsty, Ken-*chan*... thirsty..." He covered his ears while he chewed the final few grains, but he could still hear her, whispering endlessly, her hand tugging at his robe and trying to pull him down, down into the endless dark where the Demons waited...

KENJI, said a voice that was not hers, and a wisp of light reached through the darkness.

He was awake with no sense of having woken, and his face was wet. Straw prickled at him and tickled his ear, and he remembered: *It's a barn. We stopped at a farm last night.*

The wetness on his face was cold in the night air. *Am I... crying?* He sat up, the straw crackling softly, and scrubbed at his face with one tattered sleeve. Dimly he could hear the other men in the barn, the deep breathing of sleep, a couple of them snoring, someone muttering through a dream.

Hungry, he thought suddenly, his belly growling at him. He'd been ravenous every day since the battle at Castle Mouko.

He felt in the straw for his swords and his sandals, found them. Then he climbed out of the straw, moving carefully so as not to step on any of the Wolf samurai. Not that he cared whether he woke them or hurt them, but if he did they might be insulted and try to start a fight. He wasn't sure if he'd be able to fight them, wasn't sure if he *could* fight someone now whose soul wasn't shadowed.

And besides, Rei would never let him hear the end of it if he killed any of them. She'd been bad enough about duels and bar-brawls back in GreenTown last year.

He found the ladder down to the barn's ground floor. The smells changed from straw to the thick odors of oxen and manure, the heavy breathing of the half-dozen sleeping beasts far louder than the men above. The barn was almost thirty paces long and half as wide, but seemed larger in the thick darkness, mitigated only by a tiny bit of starlight filtering through cracks in the walls. He made his way down the passage between the animal stalls mainly by feel, and suppressed a curse when he barked his shin on the wheel of a wagon parked at the far end. He vaguely remembered there was a large double-door at this end of the barn, but he didn't want to try to drag that open in the dark; instead he fumbled his way along the wall until he located one of the smaller wooden panels and opened that instead.

Outside the dark was less oppressive – it was after Moonset, but the sky was clear and the ocean of stars threw enough light to show the general shapes of things. From the barn's side-porch he could see the outlines of grain fields and rice paddies stretching out toward the horizon, interrupted here and there by buildings – other farmer's dwellings, sometimes with their own barns and outbuildings. Here, fifty paces separated this barn from a two-story house with a thatched roof and a porch all the way around the ground floor. He knew Rei was in there, along with the higher-ranking samurai in their group – the insufferable noblewoman from the Tiger with her brat and servants, that one-armed fellow Tokage, the snooty old man who always wore robes and whose name Kenji had never bothered to learn, a few other officers. The farmer had cleared out most of his family's rooms to make space for the guests.

From what Kenji'd seen the house was almost as nice as a samurai's residence inside, and larger than many of those. *A rich farmer, who'd have thought it?* Apparently the other families here paid him rent, and with no samurai in the area – there seemed to be some doubt which Clan even claimed these lands – he kept it all for himself. *He's probably sleepless and chewing his knuckles, wondering if we'll report him to the nearest Lord for not paying his taxes,* Kenji thought with an inner chuckle.

His belly growled again and he started toward the house, then stopped. *I walk in there in the middle of the night, one of those fancy nobles' bodyguards is likely to draw on me,* he thought sourly. After an indecisive minute or two, a faint sound caught his ear – the chuckling noises of sleeping chickens. It took less than a minute to trace it to the coop, a small building tucked in behind the barn.

The farmers had collected the eggs before dinner, but he found two they had missed. It wasn't hard to sneak them out of the straw nests without waking the sleeping birds – he'd done that a score of time back in his own childhood village, before...

Before the Masks, he thought deliberately. There was no point hiding from the memories, not anymore, not since the Lady had spoken to him.

He sat cross-legged atop the stone retaining wall that divided the barn from the painstakingly flattened croplands, and cracked the eggs into his mouth one at a time. It wasn't a meal, but it took the edge off his hunger.

When he tossed the empty shells down into the field below, a fox was watching him.

Kenji stared at the animal and it stared back, its eyes gleaming with reflected starlight. Then he grinned at it. "You hungry? I took the eggs already. You can try for the chickens, I guess. I won't stop you. This damned farmer's richer'n a merchant, he won't miss a few chickens."

The fox slunk forward – it moved low to the ground, its bushy tail trailing equally low behind – and then hopped lightly to the top of the wall beside him, circling around him and sniffing at his right hand. He watched it, bemused. *Damnation, when was the last time I saw a fox? Back in the village, when I was... eight? Nine? And no one believed me.*

Excrement. What am I doing thinking about that stuff like some white-haired scum in a teahouse rambling about the old days?

The fox shook its head, letting out a barking snort, and trotted away. He watched it go, then shook his head and snorted. *I'm in a damned strange mood.* He lay back on the grass above the wall, staring up at the sky, all aflame with uncountable stars. People imagined pictures in the stars, the twelve animals of the months and hours and Clans, but he'd never learned them well as a child and had forgotten them since.

If I sleep, the dream might come back, he knew, but that prospect no longer held quite so much terror as it had before. *What's a dream, after facing Her?*

Kenji blinked. The sky was pale gray, pink in the east where distant mountains formed a jagged silhouette. He sat up and regretted it, grimacing and biting down on a grunt as stiff night-chilled joints protested.

The farm was silent around him, the buildings dark gray outlines in the pre-dawn dimness, but he could see the glow of one or two lanterns through the paper walls of the farmhouse. Motion and faint noise drew his attention to the bare-earth yard between the house's back porch and the well; someone there was doing sword-forms, the huff and grunt of effort faintly audible. Kenji smirked at that, but then he caught another sound, a faint metallic chiming. Priestess Rei was in the back yard too, standing well aside from the swordsman.

She's there to do the dawn prayer, Kenji knew. Without thinking about it he hopped down the retaining wall, letting out a louder grunt as his not-yet-awake legs and hips flexed to absorb the six-foot drop, then strolled along the embankment at the edge of the grain-field toward the farmhouse, hands on hips, elaborately casual.

Rei saw him coming. For a moment a smile lit up her face and then it was gone, so quickly that if he hadn't spent so much time with her in the last three years he would doubt it had ever been there. She bowed politely as he came closer. "Honorable Kenji. Will you join me to welcome the Sunrise?"

"I ain't no 'honorable,' girl," he snorted. *What's she doing being all formal..? Oh, she's worried about that fellow.*

The practicing samurai was their commander, the man called Tokage. He was dressed only in a simple sleeping robe – probably borrowed from the farmer – and he had hitched it up and tied back the empty sleeve to keep it from getting in the way of his forms. Those were actually rather awkward, only to be expected from a middle-aged man with one arm and a bit of a paunch even after their months of travel, but the fellow worked away at it relentlessly. It make Kenji tired just to watch.

"Did you sleep badly? You usually aren't awake this early," Rei said, then suddenly reddened and looked away.

What's she worked up about now? "No worse than most nights," he grunted, and then grinned as Tokage briefly lost his balance and had to stop his forms, breathing heavily. "You all right, old man? Can't have you keeling over before we ever reach your Wolf Lord."

The older man looked at him owlishly. Despite the cool of the pre-dawn air he was sweating heavily, drops falling from his tightly-trimmed beard. "I will fulfill my duty to the Ookami so long as I am able to do so," he said finally, re-setting his stance. "A duty which includes forgiving your crude manners, since I must deliver you alive to my High Lord."

Kenji laughed aloud, a casual laugh that felt oddly pleasant. "Damnation, did you just call me out without calling me out? You've got real balls, old man."

Tokage went into a new sequence of forms, raising the sword over his head point-forward, then turning it and cutting downward, stopping the blow two feet above the ground. "I will take that as a compliment," he said, timing the words between his breaths. "Do you wish to join me in practice?"

Rei made a soft surprised noise. *Well, I guess I'm surprised too,* Kenji thought, but aloud he snorted. "I don't do stuff like that." He strolled past the old man and sat cross-legged on the porch. "Any idea when these farmers'll be serving breakfast? I could eat an ox."

"They're just starting to prepare now," Rei told him.

Tokage finished his form and turned to face Kenji, his normal stoic expression momentarily open with curiosity. "You do not practice? Not at all? How do you maintain your skills?"

Kenji shrugged, suddenly uncomfortable with how the conversation had turned. "I've always known how to fight."

"Apologies, but… that is impossible," Tokage said. "Fighting is a difficult skill, it requires many years of practice to master it. I've watched you, swordsman Kenji. I saw your duel with Lord Akira. Your skills are… formidable, I freely admit."

"Excrement, you think I'm lyin'? I don't train, old man, never have."

Rei spoke before Kenji could reply, bowing in apology for the interruption. "Priestess Jun told me, honorable Tokage, that Kenji's fighting skills are a gift from the Lady."

"Some gift," Kenji muttered.

"I see," Tokage said, in a tone which conveyed polite disbelief.

Kenji felt irritated, more than he should have been. *What do I care what this stupid samurai thinks? I could kill him without even getting tired. Well, I could if he was a Mask.* "You damned arrogant samurai are always like this," he snarled. "You think all your fancy armor and trainin' and talkin' makes you special. I've killed a thousand of you. Most of 'em didn't even make me break out a sweat."

Tokage did not react to the goading – apparently he really meant it about fulfilling his duty to the Wolf Lord. Instead he raised his eyebrows. "You are also a samurai, swordsman Kenji, even if you lack a Lord to serve."

Kenji laughed again, not lightly but harshly. "I ain't no samurai."

Tokage was silent for a beat, then turned and went back to his forms. It took Kenji a moment to realize the man was deliberately ignoring his words, since acknowledging them would mean he was a peasant carrying a samurai's blades – technically a crime. *Probably thinks he's doing me a favor, protecting me,* he thought sourly.

Perhaps it was the lack of sleep, or perhaps it was the way Rei was still watching him with anxious curiosity. Or perhaps it was the memory of the fox's breath on his hand. But he found himself talking, his tone almost conversational.

"I used to steal food. No family, no village, what else could I do? It was steal or beg or whore myself."

Tokage continued practicing, studiously ignoring him. Rei flinched. "Kenji, you don't have to—"

"I was… thirteen, maybe. I found a dead samurai," he went on relentlessly. "After a battle, *neh*? He had crawled into a ditch and bled to death. And I picked up his swords. And his money string, to buy food and wine." *And a woman, my first one,* his memory added, but even in this moment of unexpected honesty he shied away from saying that in front of Rei. "And a week later, some other samurai challenged me. Said they weren't my blades. Which, excrement, they weren't, *neh*? So… I killed him." He stopped and ran his fingertips down the long scar that creased the right side of his face, just to the side of his eye. "He cut my face, and then I killed him. A gang boss saw me do it and hired me to work for him, to kill his enemies. They were easier than the samurai had been, way easier. He taught me to talk like a samurai, said it would make me more intimidating… but he really just wanted to get into my leggings. And after all his rivals were dead he tried to rape me, so I killed him and all of his gang too. And the Magistrates who tried to arrest me for it."

"Enough, Kenji," Rei whispered. She was crying, and that brought him up short. He felt an odd emotion then, one he did not recognize at first. He had known it very seldom since his childhood.

Shame.

Like when She looked at me.

"Well, anyway," he muttered. "I don't practice." He stood up, put his hands on his hips, being the swaggering swordsman once more. "I'm gonna go back to the barn and sleep until breakfast."

CHAPTER 19

OKAMI AKIRA DREW REIN and shaded his eyes, stilling his horse with a squeeze from his knees. The hilltop he had chosen was covered in thick grass that sprouted clouds of leaping and buzzing insects, making the horse shy and snort.

From here he could see the entirety of Castle Hokori and the city that surrounded it, two miles and more distant, gilded by the hot late-afternoon Sun. He noted absently that his eyes and head no longer hurt when he focused hard, though his limbs and chest still vaguely ached. He was constantly hungry as well, even though it was a month and more since the battle at the Midorisaka hills.

The flesh does not matter, so long as it obeys and mind and spirit, he reminded himself.

Castle Hokori rested in the center of a raised mesa as large as a small city, perched on the south bank of the River of Many Faces. The outer walls loomed above that river and then zig-zagged their way around the mesa, sometimes above and sometimes below the slope. Within their massive extent – easily a mile across, probably more – could be seen forests, settlements, towers, and the lines of additional interior walls dividing the place into layers of defense. Near the center, the great keep itself loomed – ten stories high, almost as wide at the top as the bottom, as large as entire castle complexes elsewhere. It had been the pride of the Gold Dragon Clan in the last days of the Emperors, and its fall to the Jade Dragons had marked the doom of that Clan.

Right now, the outer layers of the fortifications oozed smoke and bristled with movement – the constant flutter of back-banners from thousands of men in motion. The sprawling city that surrounded the walls showed similar and even worse effects – whole neighborhoods appeared to have burned or simply been torn down, new roads cleared through them, a churn of patterned chaos as men and wagons moved back and forth.

East of the city, just below the hillside where Akira had paused, thousands of tents marked the site of the Bear army's camp. That might have been cropland before they arrived, but now it was a bleak expanse of bare earth and mud, stretching from the riverbank inland for a half mile. A hastily-built stockade wall had been thrown up around it, with a few simple observation platforms – little more than three long beams tied together with space atop for a man to perch and beat on a metal plate if he spotted danger. Some of them were ringing now, meaning they had spotted the army coming up the Road of Auspicious Sunset alongside the river.

Akira kicked his horse into motion, circling back down behind the hill and then galloping across to meet the road ahead of his army's lead column; his escorts followed with the huge Ookami banner, now retrieved from the siege-lines at Castle Kosaten.

The marching column's lead units were from the Wolf Clan's northern army, flying the Toshiwara triple-crosshatch crest on their banners. Lord Toshiwara himself rode at the head, flanked by one of his senior vassals, Toshiwara Takaya; they bowed in the saddle as Akira walked his mount onto the road alongside them. A year ago the nobleman might have tried to make polite small-talk when Akira joined him, to discuss the weather or his health or the prospects for the year's harvest; now he remained silent.

Lord Musume and General Akiyama were farther back in the column with their own men. Which was a relief, since Musume had chattered anxiously all the way back from the Imperial City.

Ahead of them a squadron of infantry in Bear colors hustled up the road, followed by a single armored man, thick-bearded and burly, on horseback. Akira focused on them, automatically wary with allies so recent.

"Honorable Lord Akira," Kuma Hirosada called, bowing. "On behalf of High Lord Gotaro, I welcome you and your soldiers to Castle Hokori." He gestured behind him at the distant spire of the keep. "Regrettably, I cannot yet offer you the castle's hospitality. The Jade Dragons seem intent on insulting your visit." The men with him laughed aloud, a few throwing in comments of their own.

They are hiding something, Akira thought. He waited, but when they said nothing further, he announced: "I wish to consult with High Lord Gotaro about the siege."

He was sure Hirosada flinched, perhaps frowned behind the wall of his beard. "Of course, yes. Please accompany me, honorable High Lord. As for your men… I fear our camp is rather crowded, but there should be room to the east of the castle, or north of the river. We've got full control of the city, which includes the bridges."

Lord Toshiwara cleared his throat. "With your permission, honorable High Lord?"

Akira nodded silently and started his horse forward, his escort following.

They rode through the Bear stockade, first the hospital area with wounded men lying on mats in open-sided pavilions while Priestesses hurried around them purposefully, then into the main camp with its rows of tents between muddy lanes. Groups of men squatted around smoldering fires, boiling rice in small iron pots.

Kuma Hirosada leaned slightly toward Akira. "The first supply ships arrived yesterday," he said quietly. "It was a great relief to us. Between foraging and requisitions we had emptied out the local food supply pretty thoroughly." He glanced back at the gate, where the Wolf army was marching to the left to circle around the stockade. "How many men have you brought?"

He is talking about anything but his High Lord, Akira realized. "Sixteen thousand. The soldiers of Lord Musume, half of Toshiwara's northern army, and two thousand former Jade Dragons under General Akiyama." He had left Hajime Soto with the other half of Toshiwara's force, along with his own men and another thousand of Akiyama's defectors, to hold Castle Kosaten and crush any remnants of resistance in the late Lord Goda's province.

"General Akiyama," Hirosada repeated and then fell silent, looking around at nothing in particular while they passed through the far side of the stockade. Beyond, what had once been a normal road had been widened and trampled into a muddy thoroughfare that cut directly through the city to the castle walls; piles of scrap wood and heaped roof-tiles marked the graveyards of buildings that had perished to make room for war. Squadrons of samurai trotted up and down the throughway, alongside groups of commoners wrestling hand-carts and ox-drawn wagons.

Kuma Hirosada led them along one side of the street where the mud was less severe. "I'm afraid we've had to be rough with the town, but we've managed not to kill too many of them," he said. "And they've been very happy to see our Priestesses. Apparently the late Lord Noboru expelled all the clergy from here."

"Yes," Akira replied. *The Bear don't leave their lands much. I should not be surprised that they didn't know about that.*

Hirosada fell silent again. The outer walls of Castle Hokori loomed closer; Akira could see a thirty-pace-wide section had been knocked down, the rubble turned into a makeshift ramp for men and supplies.

"We stormed the outer walls right after we arrived," Hirosada said matter-of-factly. "Took them, but the scum held us at the inner walls. We knocked this section down with sledges afterward, it was taking too long to get in and out through all their twisty defense passages."

He cleared his throat, looking straight ahead. "Half your northern army... and General Akiyama is sworn to you. I saw what you had at the Midorisaka hills. You could have crushed us, couldn't you?"

Akira saw no reason to reply. The man already knew the truth.

They reached the base of the ramp, and the bear nobleman dismounted. "Apologies, honorable High Lord. We learned the hard way that the horses are too likely to fall on this surface."

They climbed the ramp, dust and gravel and clots of mud under their sandals, passing a long line of commoners carrying bundles into the castle on their backs. Beyond the outer walls, the gardens and orchards had been transformed into another set of camps, mats looted from houses covering grass that had been trampled into mud, panels from torn-down buildings serving as walls and ceilings. More men clustered around cookfires, these ones in full armor and with the grubby look of people who had gone without bathing.

"We need to keep troops up close to the lines in case they sortie," Hirosada remarked. "So we rotate men in and out of the main camp to here."

Akira noted the burned-out remains of towers, the faint odor of ash and death that lurked behind the more obvious smells of mud and sweat and excrement. "How many men have you lost?"

The Bear looked away briefly, and when he turned back his face was expressionless. "About a thousand in the initial assault, and the same or a little less since then."

A fifth of their strength, Akira thought grimly. Sieges were ugly, and assaults on strong castles were worse. Sometimes it was necessary, and he had done it himself at Castle Oka last year... but only because he was able to use the soldiers of nobles he did not trust, preserving the strength of his loyal men.

They reached another set of interior walls. Akira noted with professional interest that Castle Hokori's outer defenses were not integrated into a single whole in the manner of most castles in the modern Empire – instead, each layer of walls and towers was separate and distinct from the next. That made the defense harder to coordinate, since troops could not be easily moved from one section of the fortifications to another, but the sheer size of the complex offered its own advantage – any assault would become scattered and weakened as it struggled to break through the successive sub-fortresses. And at the end, of course, they would face the keep itself.

No wonder the Bear haven't taken it even with a heavy advantage in numbers.

He and Hirosada passed through a gatehouse – this one hollowed-out by fire into a shell of stone walls and scorched beams, with the passage cleared afterward – into an area that mixed gardens with ordinary buildings. To the left was a residential neighborhood, dwellings and bath-houses and a street with long rows of shops. Much of it had survived undamaged, and Akira was surprised to see that the businesses – noodle-shops and weavers and sandal-makers and a dozen other such places – were mostly open for business, their customers a mixture of commoners and Bear samurai. Well down the street, a large crowd had gathered around a pair of Priestesses who were leading a prayer.

Hirosada noticed where he was looking and snorted a chuckle. "Common people will carry on with life in the midst of madness… I noticed it last year when we invaded the Tiger lands. And as I said, they're happy to have the servants of Blessed Amatsu back among them." He glanced up at the looming edifice of Castle Hokori's main keep, now blotting out half the western sky. "We're nearly there."

Another layer of walls loomed ahead of them, and Akira saw that the Bear had constructed a set of crude wooden battlements, allowing them to man and defend the walls from this side. *So they took this wall but couldn't reach the next one,* he thought. *The original battlements on the walls would be designed to defend against attack from this direction, but would be open and defenseless on the far side.* The improvised new battlements were a clever solution, although one that surely required a great deal of work and material. In fact the work was still underway, crowds of commoners and samurai stripped down to loincloths and headbands working to raise wooden beams and hammer cross-pieces into hastily-carved notches.

Fifty paces from the wall, a cluster of oversized tents – one of them open-sided, with a table and several unlit braziers visible within – had taken over what had formerly been a meditation-garden. The fine white gravel was now filthy with mud, and the large carp-pond served to water a half-dozen horses. Several banners rose above the tents, displaying the Bear Clan's ferocious crest and the calligraphy of the Kuma name. A group of samurai stood around the table, heads lowered over papers. There was also a square wooden box on the table, but they studiedly ignored it.

As Akira and Hirosada approached, they finished speaking and exchanged bows; most of them departed, leaving one armored figure standing alone, his fists pressed down on the tabletop.

Hirosada cleared his throat as he stepped under the pale brown silk roof. "Most honorable High Lord Gotaro, I bring you the High Lord of the Wolf." He went down on the dirty mats, prostrating himself.

Akira waited until Lord Gotaro looked up, then bowed politely but not as low as he would have before their last meeting.

The High Lord of the Bear's face was bleak, grooved with weariness and loss. His voice was calm, almost conversational. "As I predicted, Lord Akira, my son is dead. When I arrived outside their walls and demanded they hand him over to me, they gave me his head." He pointed to the wooden box. "And now my Clan is doomed. What worth are your words to me now?"

Hirosada remained prostrated, saying nothing.

Akira shut his eyes, thinking. "You attacked after that."

"Yes," Gotaro said, his voice still calm but thickening slightly. "What else could I do? Revenge is a samurai's duty, and the fight keeps my men and my nobles busy. It buys me time, though for what real purpose I cannot say. I suppose I am just too stubborn to give in to Fate easily."

Yes, buying time, Akira thought, his eyes still closed. *That's what I have to do also. Buy enough time to win the war, the real war.* "What do the Ryu have here? Who commands the defense?"

From Gotaro's tone, the practical question seemed to catch him by surprise. Akira heard him shuffling the papers on the table. "I don't think they have more than four thousand left within the castle now. We killed at least a thousand…" He broke off, and when he resumed his voice had become clearer, more methodical. "At the parley, I was told that Mugai Kosei, Lord Mugai's son, commanded the defense. Apparently High Lord Noboru left him here as a trusted man, which means… which means he is the one who ordered my son's death." Gotaro fell silent, mastering himself, then continued. "We've got no spies in the castle, but we interrogated some prisoners and a few stray servants. It seems there's now a Regency Council inside, a quartet of nobles claiming to speak on behalf of… High Lord Ryu Raizo, Noboru's son."

Who is only five or six years old, Akira knew. "Who are they?"

"Mugai Kosei, of course. Also Lord Tsuchiya Bunta, he managed to scurry back here from the Midorisaka hills ahead of us. Lord Onaga's son Eita, who I suppose is officially the Lord of Castle Kajou now, and Noboru's younger sister Ryu Manami."

Who is the only other survivor of the Ryu bloodline. Akira opened his eyes and focused his attention on the older man. Lord Gotaro blinked and his head rocked back as though he had been shoved.

"Send word across the lines. I want a parley with this Regency Council."

ᕼ ᕼ ᕼ

OOKAMI KAEDE TAPPED THE BARRED window of her palanquin with her folded fan. The guard outside leaned closer, visible as a shadow thrown across the bright rectangles between the wooden slats. "My Lady?"

"I wish to step outside for a moment. Take us to the shrine atop that hill, please."

The motion of the palanquin shifted as the bearers stepped off the road, jolting as they crossed a ditch and then tilting and shifting unpleasantly as they climbed the hillside beyond. The thin slots of vision to either side turned yellow-green with the long grass covering the slope, and the buzzing of insects mingled with the sound of the bearers' huffing breaths. Finally the palanquin leveled off once more and lowered to the ground; Kaede waited for the door to slide open – it would be undignified for the High Lady to open it herself – and then rotated herself out and stood, moving slowly so as not to snag her garments or bump her swelling belly.

Once upright she paused to fan herself, and one of her serving-maids stepped forward and opened a parasol, holding it to shade her. The weather was hot, spring now well turned into summer, and she had been sweating unpleasantly within the confines of the palanquin. *At least I'm not getting nauseous anymore.* It was a pleasant contrast to her last pregnancy.

The hill she had chosen was covered in thick grasses, already starting to turn from green to yellow in the summer warmth, with only a few scattered trees on its flanks. A very old prayer-arch perched atop the hill, its lacquer mostly flaked off to show age-gray wood beneath, and a few paces beyond it was a small shrine, little more than an arched roof on a wooden frame. The roof had lost most of its tiles – she could see piles of broken tile amid the tangles of grass on either side – and the statue within, presumably of the Lady, was so overgrown with moss that it had no recognizable features. She wondered briefly why it had been built here, and how long ago, and why it had been abandoned.

Laughter caroled from nearby, and a smile touched Kaede's lips as Basho ran past her, his arms out at his sides, the servant Koko following him with a smile. Even Basho, though, knew to stay inside the loose circle formed by Kaede's personal guards, all men hand-picked by Captain Tokage before his departure for the Tiger lands last winter. Within that ring her other maids fanned themselves and spoke in soft voices, while the palanquin bearers – muscular commoners dressed in loincloths, loose vests, and headbands to catch the sweat off their shaved foreheads – stretched their limbs and joked with each other and drank water from bamboo canteens.

The Road of Auspicious Dawn, a line of dry hard-packed earth three paces wide, passed below the hill and arced away to the northeast, roughly paralleling the glitter of the River of Blue Silk a mile and more to the north past a thick grid-pattern of rice paddies. In the distance she could just catch a hint of WolfTown's sprawl and the gleam of Sunlight on the keep of Castle Ookami within it. In the opposite direction the road angled southwest away from the river, heading for GrayTown.

The road was packed as far as she could see in both directions, an endless column of people. Samurai in light armor and wok-shaped helmets marched on foot, interspersed with more well-equipped officers on horseback; one man in each squadron carried a silk banner with the crest of a noble bloodline in the Wolf Clan. Palanquins rode on the sweating shoulders of bearers dressed like her own; the lacquered wooden boxes shone in the Sunlight, marked with the crests of the nobles riding within – probably a majority of them women, but plenty of men as well. Younger and more athletic noblemen rode horses instead, though dressed in traveling garb – wide pleated leggings, silk shirts, oversized vests and coats, tall black hats – rather than the armor of their guards.

Every quarter-mile or so, the lines of samurai gave way to thick columns of servants and ox-drawn wagons. The personal households of the nobles, accompanying their patrons' journey.

What a nightmare, Kaede thought.

The weeks since the arrival of that astonishing letter from Akira had passed in a flash, every day packed with meetings from breakfast to late in the evening, trying to make all the arrangements to relocate the Wolf Clan's court and seat of government. She suspected Akira had no idea of the complexities involved in the matter – he probably thought of it like moving an army, just load up the supplies and march everyone out. But a court was a community, or rather a vast muddle of tiny communities that lived together, and each of them with its own stubborn notions of what it should do and how it should be treated.

Just convincing every petty courtier and the wife of every absent noble that they would have to move had required multiple personal meetings. Then there had been the rounds of visits to the estates outside the city, explaining to men like Aoba Kisaburo, who had invested years and immense resources into making his house and lands into a coveted destination for the residents of the court, that their investment was about to lose most of its value.

Then there were the merchants, whose markets and plans and expectations – already disrupted by repeated wars – were now being further shaken by the sudden flurry of rumors about the court relocating. Such men were far enough beneath Kaede's station that she did not have to meet with them herself; indeed, they would never have dared to suggest she shame herself with such a thing. But the successful ones generally had patrons among the nobility – the ones they loaned money to, mainly – and those patrons had petitioned her almost daily.

There had been more practical challenges as well. If the entire court was to be relocated, did that mean moving all the heirlooms of the Wolf Clan – the countless pieces of artwork, the ancestral banners and armors displayed in the castle, the rooms full of records and maps in the basement levels? It wasn't as though there was a lot of precedent to follow – the last time a Clan had changed its seat of power had been when the Jade Dragon Clan had taken possession of Castle Hokori, and that had been close to three hundred years ago. Without any guidance from Akira, Kaede had eventually decided that yes, the records must be moved, because they needed to be wherever the High Lord was. That in turn had meant finding enough wagons to carry all those crates of paper, on top of the other wagons carrying artwork and furnishings and the supplies to feed and shelter everyone during the multi-week journey to the Imperial City...

Akira's second letter had arrived a week ago. It had been just as unpleasantly terse as the first:

Imperial City secure. Chujitsuna Nomi in command.
Move everything there immediately.

'Immediately,' he said! Kaede shook her head and fought down the urge to let out a rather undignified snort. Even with all the preparations she had made, it had taken another six days to get everything ready. She was proud that she had managed it in that time, especially considering how every single samurai of any rank had seemed determined to find reasons to delay things. Even the Priestesses from the city Temple had created complications, insisting on a great ritual of prayer to bestow the Goddess' blessing on the journey, and many of them were coming along as well... including old Priestess Ritsuko, who had bluntly declared she would defy any order to remain behind. "I serve the Goddess, and the Goddess – and my poor dead fool of a friend Jun – commanded me to look after your husband. I can't very well do that if he's in the Imperial City and I'm not, *neh*? Besides," and she had cut loose with her hideous cackle, "I'm looking forward to a reunion with the Theological Council."

Even the servants, who were supposed to simply bow and obey, had created delays – loading things in the wrong wagons, misunderstanding directions. A dozen wagonloads had actually gone out the wrong city gate and ended up across the River of Blue Silk, forcing Kaede to send mounted couriers to track them down and escort them back.

I wonder how long it will *take us to get there.* Armies moved slowly, Kaede knew. She had accompanied Akira's army to the battle at Yotsukado early last year, when Lady Yumiko's rebellion erupted, and had seen in person how much time it took to get thousands of samurai marching each day. But the army had been a miracle of speed and efficiency compared to this sprawling mess.

And what happens when we reach the Imperial City? She had read more than a few books set in that fabled place, but they were legacies from the time before the Dread Eclipse. Everyone agreed the Imperial Palace had burned down in that cataclysm, so where would they be living? Where would the new court be hosted? Was Akira going to just start calling himself Emperor?

I'll have weeks to wonder about all of this, if we keep moving at this sluggard's pace, she told herself. *But if I just let everyone else wonder as well, that will be a disaster. They'll scheme and plot and gossip, because that's what samurai do, especially courtiers. So I'll have to work on them all through this journey, harder than I ever have before.* The thought was daunting, but at the same time exhilarating in a way she could not have imagined five years ago when she skulked in the gardens of Castle Ookami and bit her lip while Lady Yumiko mocked her. *Letters, meetings…* She felt a kick in her belly and set one hand over it instinctively. *Well, I have to be careful not to push myself* too *hard.*

She lifted her gaze, peering back at the distant sheen of red tiles on Castle Ookami's keep, and tapped her chin thoughtfully. *All right, we will have plenty of time on this journey, so how do I use that? Everyone will feel uncertain, lost, without the normal patterns of court life. They will want something familiar, some pattern to hold on to. Hmmm… perhaps I can host a dinner party every night, inviting different guests to each. It won't start until late, though, since it'll take time to pitch camp every evening… well, that's all right, courtiers always prefer their socializing to happen after Sunset.*

If I'm entertaining in the evening, I won't have as much time for correspondence. I can read letters and the spy reports while I'm riding in the palanquin, but writing… well, I'll fit it in somewhere. Thinking about the spy reports was an uncomfortable topic, though, because it reminded her that another letter had finally come in from Seneschal Amano last week. She had forwarded it to Akira, of course, but the contents had still been disturbing. Rather than returning home after his mission to the Aelfynn had failed – she still wasn't sure exactly what had happened there, his previous two letters had been extremely vague – he had decided to travel to Castle Mouko to negotiate further with the Tiger Clan. Who were apparently under even stronger attack from the northern barbarians than usual.

Amano is… a problem. But the longer he takes to come back, the better prepared I'll be when he does. So I shouldn't be unhappy about this, but… She shook her head slightly. *Enough woolgathering.* "Basho-*kun*, it's time to go."

⛩ ⛩ ⛩

OOKAMI AKIRA LOOKED AT THE five people seated opposite him, and thought: *How do I break them?*

It had taken three days to set up the parlay with the Jade Dragon Clan's self-proclaimed Council of Regents – one day to agree to a meeting in the abandoned garden between the siege lines, and another two days for laborers and servants to clear a space there and build a flat, open-sided wooden platform for the meeting to use. It was located on what had been a small parade-ground, with fifty paces of clear space on every side, and the laborers had cut trees and torn down several buildings to leave an unimpeded view back to the walls a quarter-mile distant in either direction. The platform smelled pleasantly of fresh-cut pine and maple, with a hint of charcoal from the large braziers placed at all four corners as a precaution against the meeting running into the evening.

Akira had chosen the Noon Ritual to start the meeting, and a quartet of Priestesses – two from his own army, two from the Bear – performed the prayers and recitations in the center of the platform. The Jade Dragon regents, watching from the far side, seemed uncomfortable with the lengthy ritual.

For his part, Akira wished he could be in his armor. His manservant had gently reminded him that for such a meeting, a formal event arranged in advance, it would have been a breach of etiquette to wear battlefield gear. All the men were in formal outdoor clothing, one step away from full court garb – pleated linen leggings, silk shirts, sleeveless coats with peaked shoulders and embroidered crests. Their swords, the mark of their station as samurai, were the only martial notes to their ensembles. The lone woman, Lady Manami, was of course in court garb.

The Priestesses finished with a jangle of prayer-rings, and servants on either side hurried forward to place flat-topped camp-chairs in two opposing rows – five chairs for Akira, Lord Toshiwara, Lord Musume, General Akiyama, and High Lord Gotaro, and four across from them for the Council. The two groups of nobles lined up, bowed to each other with murmured greetings, and seated themselves.

And Akira narrowed his eyes, focusing on the four people opposing him as each of them introduced themselves with the traditional lengthy recitation of titles and history. His own nobles alternated introductions with the Jade Dragons, which gave him more time to gain the measure of those sitting across from him.

Mugai Kosei was the key, he saw at once. The young man seethed with tightly-leashed anger, and unlike many he did not tremble or flinch in the face of Akira's focused attention. Indeed, he seemed to be trying to do the same in a more limited way, to gain the measure of Akira and his companions. *His uncle is...* was *the Jade Dragon spymaster*, Akira remembered. Amano had made a point of identifying his counterpart.

"I am High Lord Kuma Gotaro, ruler of the Bear Clan. My son is dead at your hands."

Onaga Eita and Lord Tsuchiya Bunta gave off far less secure tones than Mugai, and at Lord Gotaro's words they seemed to shrink a little in their chairs. Eita was at best only twenty years old, short and smooth-faced, full of nervous energy held in check with great effort. Despite his attempt to project stoic control his eyes kept moving, from his companions to the Wolves and back.

Lord Tsuchiya had none of the younger man's tight-ratcheted tension, but the grooves in his face – he was only in his forties, but looked a decade older – spoke of poorly-hidden pain.

"I am General Akiyama Gakuto." The peasant-turned-samurai said nothing further, and the three Jade Dragon samurai all stared daggers at him. Even Lady Ryu Manami looked up briefly, apparently not quite willing to believe it was him.

She sat on the left end of the row of four chairs rather than in the center, which said much about her relatively weak position in the Regent's Council. She was a puffy-faced young woman in a formal multi-layered robe, heavily made-up in the traditional style: pale face-powder on her exposed skin, her lips rouged a deep red, her eyebrows shaved and then drawn in higher on her forehead. Akira thought she was about the same age as Eita, though it was hard to tell through all that makeup, which reminded him uncomfortably of how Kaede looked whenever she appeared in public. Manami sat very still, like a rabbit wary of danger, her feet tucked together under the front of her chair, her eyes downcast and her hands folded in her lap.

"—Lord of Castle Shingi, son to Mugai Hokuto, loyal servants of the Ryu since the days of my ancestor Mugai Fumihisa who won the castle from the White Fox Clan with the edge of his sword," Mugai Kosei finished, with a strong emphasis on the word 'loyal' as he looked pointedly at Akiyama. The general merely smiled in return.

Akira realized that was the last of the introductions. Only he remained.

"I am Ookami Akira, High Lord of the Wolf," he said, voice flat as stone. "I took Lord Noburo's life at the Battle of the Midorisaka hills. I have captured the Imperial City."

Mugai let out a bark of noise that was probably a truncated laugh, while the other two men simply stared, young Onaga Eita momentarily open-mouthed before he recovered his face and flushed in shame at his own lack of self-control. Lady Manami raised her face again, her eyes briefly going wide.

Mugai Kosei found his voice first. "Apologies, but that is quite impossible. It has not even been two months since the Battle of the Midorisaka hills. You expect us to believe you have seized the Imperial City in that time?"

Lord Musume answered, as Akira had ordered him to. "I was present when Lord Akira rode into the Imperial City. The Theological Council has acknowledged him as the chosen of Heaven."

"That's—" Kosei broke off, realizing just in time that if he directly named Lord Musume a liar he could be called out for a duel.

Silence for a time as the four nobles tried to grasp a world that had changed beneath their feet. Finally Lord Tsuchiya softly cleared his throat. "Honorable Lord Akira… we agreed to this meeting at your request." Which was a very polite way of saying they had expected him to offer terms. "Are you telling us you intend to be Emperor?"

Akira looked directly at him, and the man blinked and shrank back slightly. "Yes."

Mugai Kosei let out a snort. "Just like that? As if the rest of the Clans will step aside and allow it? Apologies, but if the only purpose of this meeting is to amuse us, we have all wasted a great deal of time. Honorable Lady Ryu, how long must we indulge this?"

Before the young woman could reply, General Akiyama laughed softly. "Apologies," he chortled, "apologies, but I have to ask if Lord Mugai – your father is dead, boy, so you are the Lord for as many days are left to you – remembers what things were like a few years ago when we both served honorable High Lord Ryu Akurai."

Mugai flushed. "I will not be mocked by a traitor, least of all an up-jumped peasant who knows nothing of Loyalty."

Akiyama smiled thinly. "Come, come, honorable Lord Mugai. You may be a high-born nobleman and I, as you say, only an up-jumped peasant… but we both know that if High Lord Akurai had won the Battle of Nagai Kyukai Plain and crushed the Wolf Clan, it would be the Jade Dragon claiming the Imperial City right now. He had already conquered the Nightingale, he controlled the Bear Clan's heir, and the Tiger were always distracted by the northern barbarians. Who would have stopped us?"

Mugai was silent, fuming. Lord Tsuchiya nodded thoughtfully.

"But Fate… or perhaps the Heavens themselves, from what I saw on that day… chose victory for the Wolf Clan." For a moment Akiyama was pensive, his gaze turned inward. "And now the fortunes are reversed. The Jade Dragon are crushed, the Bear and Nightingale have already chosen the Wolf, the Tiger… well, if Lord Akira's reports are true, the Tiger are fighting to hold Castle Mouko itself."

That drew a stir from all four people on the Jade Dragon side of the platform. Even Mugai seemed momentarily at a loss.

Akiyama set his hands on his hips. "So let us hear no more posturing, Lord Mugai. I know your family has lived for nothing but the Jade Dragon Clan, you and your father and your uncle. But the Jade Dragon are defeated, your father and uncle are dead, the war is over, the Throne is claimed. All we are discussing here is whether the Ryu bloodline will be allowed a place in what comes next."

They had no answer for that, though Mugai clearly wanted to say something. Akira waited through the silence, focusing his attention on Lady Manami. Under the pressure of his gaze she shrank back like a mouse facing a predator, keeping her eyes averted.

"I will be Emperor. Those who wish to live will submit and swear fealty, truthfully. I will execute anyone making a false oath."

Lady Manami finally looked up at that, hesitantly at first, then slowly meeting Akira's gaze. "My nephew... he is only a boy."

"He can swear fealty when he comes of age, if you do so for him now," Akira replied. "And bring him to the Imperial City this winter, as a hostage."

"Such decisions are for the entirety of the Regent's Council," Mugai Kosei interjected sharply. "We can consider these... terms, and give a reply in due time." He looked across at the other three, but none of them answered him immediately.

Akira remained focused solely on Manami, so intently that the world around her faded into colorless gray.

She swallowed and spoke in a soft, breathless voice. "Honorable Lord Mugai Kosei, you will slit your belly immediately."

Mugai shot to his feet, his mouth open, reaching for his sword. High Lord Gotaro rose an instant later, his hand hovering above the hilt of his own blade. "Give me a reason," he growled. Lord Musume started to rise as well, then sat down as he realized no one else was moving.

Somewhere in the distance, shouts rose from the soldiers watching on both walls.

"Sit down, honorable Lord Mugai, you shame us all," Lord Tsuchiya snapped. Onaga Eita, sitting between Mugai and Tsuchiya, was frozen in place, his expression locked into immobility.

Mugai hesitated, his hand a foot from his sword. Kuma Gotaro watched him, quiveringly eager.

After a long moment Mugai slowly lowered his hand. His voice was hoarse. "Is this... the will of the Regents?"

Manami finally dropped her eyes, looking down into her lap. "For the good of the Ryu, please slit your belly immediately."

Mugai looked from her to the other two nobles. Lord Tsuchiya returned the stare calmly. Eita averted his eyes, glancing from Lady Manami to Akira to Lord Gotaro.

Mugai let out a huff of breath and his face smoothed. He bowed sharply to Lady Manami and to Lord Tsuchiya, ignored Eita and Gotaro and the Wolf samurai, and pivoted on his heel, marching to the edge of the platform. There he turned to face them once more, bowed again, and removed his coat. He sat cross-legged and laid the coat to one side, pulled his swords out from under his belt and placed them atop it. Then he loosened his belt and pulled open his shirt, exposing his chest and stomach.

Lord Tsuchiya cleared his throat once more. "Do you require an assistant, Lord Mugai?"

Mugai smiled thinly and looked at High Lord Gotaro. "I took your son's head, at the command of my High Lord. I presume you would be pleased to take my head?"

"I would," Gotaro growled. He rose and stalked to Mugai Kosei's flank, drawing his long sword. He held it out to the side one-handed, miming the moment of letting a Priestess pour purifying water across the blade, then lifted it above his head and held it with both hands, ready to strike.

Mugai drew his short sword and used it to slice off a part of one sleeve, then wrapped the silk cloth carefully around the blade, shortening it into a dagger. Finished, he set it before him with precise care and looked at Lord Tsuchiya. "I would ask that you convey my final poem to my wife and son at Castle Shingi."

Tsuchiya bowed his head. "I shall."

Mugai shut his eyes for a dozen heartbeats, then opened them and recited:

Duty is gentle as rain
Spring is passing
The skies are cloudless

Lady Manami turned her head away. The others watched, visibly impressed by Mugai's stoicism. Even General Akiyama had gone completely serious, his earlier smirk departed.

Mugai lifted the sword, one hand gripping the silk-wrapped blade, the other clasping the end of the hilt. He set at against his bare stomach and thrust inward, letting out a faint gasp.

Kuma Gotaro uttered a war-cry and slashed down and across, taking off the Jade Dragon Lord's head cleanly. It bounced across the wooden platform and the corpse toppled forward into a rapidly-expanding pool of blood. Gotaro flicked his sword, shaking off the faint coating of blood, and sheathed it.

Akira had never taken his gaze off Lady Manami. "I will accept your oaths now."

CHAPTER 20

"LORD AKIRA!" KADO KITARO'S face was pale and thickly beaded with sweat, and he held his horse's reins with only his left hand. Nonetheless he bowed in the saddle. "Honorable Kuma Hirosada! Welcome to Castle Shingi!"

Ookami Akira and Kuma Hirosada returned the bow, then kneed their horses forward alongside Kitaro's. Akira took the opportunity to look at Kitaro's right arm. It still rested in a sling, and the forearm was wrapped tightly in silk bandages and wooden splints. The visible flesh was swollen and dark with bruising. "Your earlier report did not mention an injury."

Kitaro smiled – a very forced smile, but he managed it – and made a shrugging motion with his left shoulder. "My injury does not prevent me from serving, so it was not relevant to the report."

Good men will serve in the face of any amount of suffering, the Second Emperor had written. *Weak men will crumble in the face of the mildest setback.*

Akira looked west at the crouching bulk of Castle Shingi a half-mile away. The afternoon Sun was punishingly warm, and even with the headband he had tied on in place of a helmet sweat was trying to ooze into his eyes, making him squint. Kuma Hirosada was taking the heat even worse; the Bear samurai was in full armor, unlike Akira's minimal back-and-breast and greaves, and looked miserably hot, his face flushed and beaded with sweat under the brow of his helmet, his beard tangled and visibly damp.

The seat of the Mugai family was built on a ridgeline overlooking a small town. It was a bluntly practical fortification, all thick walls and low squat towers, with a central keep that was only five stories high. Decorations were sparse, limited to the bright green color of the roof-tiles and the banners flying on the keep's upper levels, defiantly showing the coiled serpent crest of the Clan and below it, a black maple-leaf within a gold circle, the symbol of the Mugai.

"Report," Akira ordered.

"There are probably no more than five hundred men inside, at the very best," Kitaro replied. "Plus families and servants, of course… From what the locals have told us," he gestured at the village with his left hand, "there was a big ritual in the castle a week ago, the samurai all renewing their allegiance to the Mugai."

Kuma Hirosada grunted contemptuously and spat to one side.

That would be when they learned of Mugai Kosei slitting his belly. Akira glanced behind them, at the long line of infantry marching up the Road of Dancing Foxes from Castle Hokori. Four thousand of his own men and three thousand of the Bear; he had sent the bulk of the force west toward Castle Ryu, along with General Akiyama and his newly-converted soldiers. "You delivered Lady Manami's letter?"

"Yesterday evening, under a parlay," Kitaro confirmed. "The castle is officially ruled Mugai Kosei's widow, Lady Otoha, on behalf of their two young children. She attended the meeting but had a subordinate, Sho Hideki, accept the letter. They both seemed… defiant." Kitaro paused, breathing slowly and carefully, his face tight with the effort of suppressing pain, then continued. "We've been intercepting anyone they send out for supplies or patrols. Also, there was a force trying to assemble north of here a few days ago, about two hundred men near a large village called Enkaku. We scattered them, killed about fifty."

It is good to have men I can rely on, Akira thought. Two years ago he'd have had to give detailed orders for such things, and even a year ago, when he still had to deal with dubious men like Lord Katsura, he would have been wary of scattering his men so widely.

"Any more encounters with those barbarian scouts?" That report had been concerning. Not just because the barbarians had gotten so far south, but also because of the suggestion they could somehow coordinate their actions across distances.

Kitaro swallowed, his left hand briefly moving as though he wanted to clutch his right arm but stopped himself. "Not… not yet. After I got back here I sent honorable Okada Kazomiru back up the Road of Dancing Foxes with five hundred men. I hope to hear back from him soon."

Akira regarded the castle, looking over the defenses, measuring distances. The outer ring of fortifications was not nearly so deep or complex as in a major fortress like Castle Ookami or Castle Hokori, but it was formidable for its size. A direct assault would have to storm through three levels of ramps and gates, under continual barrage from archers on the walls and towers. The large towers would hold sally-forces that could flank and ambush attackers. Akira shut his eyes, letting the void of meditation clear his mind while he analyzed the situation dispassionately.

After a minute he opened them and spoke. "Honorable Hirosada. Lord Gotaro ordered you to complete his vengeance on the Mugai."

The big man nodded. "Quite so, most honorable Lord Akira."

"An assault on this castle can take it, but at the cost of several hundred men. Possibly as many as a thousand, though that is unlikely. I will not waste my men on that, but if you choose to assault, I will support your forces."

"As always, Lord Akira, you speak plainly." Hirosada grimaced thoughtfully. "What of a siege?"

"That would be my choice. But it will likely take several months, possibly the whole winter. The garrison is small enough to make their stores last."

Hirosada nodded, chuckling sourly. "Neither choice is very satisfactory, *neh*? Wasting so much after the war is already over." He looked at the castle. "Perhaps there is another option."

He kicked his horse into motion, riding along the embankments between grain-fields toward the castle. His personal escort followed him, banners fluttering even in the thick heat.

Kitaro watched the man wide-eyed despite his own discomfort. "Is he going to…?"

The bearded warrior reined in a long bowshot from the wall, stood in the saddle, and shouted, a deep bellow that rang across the fields. "I am Kuma Hirosada, sworn personal vassal of High Lord Kuma Gotaro! I am the victor in two duels and have slain twenty-three men on the field of battle! I call on the cowardly Mugai to send a champion to face me, or to follow the rest of their worthless bloodline into honorable death as commanded by Lady Ryu Manami! Refuse, and be branded a weakling and traitor!"

Silence met him from the walls. He rode his horse back and forth, his posture arrogant, mocking. "Come out, Mugai! Find some man who will face death for you!"

Kitaro leaned forward, his pain momentarily forgotten amid the spectacle. "Magnificent," he whispered.

Minutes passed. A mounted courier rode up and delivered a folded paper to Kitaro, who read it eagerly. Akira watched his soldiers march past while the Bear samurai broke out of the column and began setting up camp. Kuma Hirosada shouted more insults at the walls.

Finally Hirosada deliberately turned his back on the castle walls and rode back briskly. He reined in next to Akira and grinned, teeth flashing through his beard. "I'll do it again tonight, and tomorrow, and each day after. And put my personal tent and banner just out of bow-shot from the walls. We'll see how long young Lady Otoha can keep the loyalty of her men."

"Be alert for a quick attack or night raid from the castle," Akira said.

"They should try!" Hirosada snorted, scowling, then suddenly laughed. "You are a most unusual man, Lord Akira. From anyone else I would take that warning as an insult to my own competence. But of course no one else would say it at all."

Akira stared at him blankly. *I will never, ever understand these things,* his mind wailed, somewhere deep inside.

"Well, enough talk. Apologies, Lord Akira, I must see to my men. " The Bear bowed in the saddle and rode away.

Kitaro had been fighting to remain silent until the Bear samurai departed. He was unconsciously trying to flex his right arm and flinching as that pained him. He lifted the folded paper. "Word from honorable Kazomiru at last, my Lord. He has made contact with a Lord Tora Arinobu of the Tiger. The news is… not good."

Akira took the letter, scanned down the lines of calligraphy. *Castle Mouko fallen*, he thought, with a sense of pieces fitting together inside his mind.

Kitaro was visibly struggling to keep his self-control. "It's… Apologies, my Lord, it's just hard to believe that barbarians could take a great castle at all. And so… so quickly." He swallowed. "What will we do?"

Akira had finally lived among samurai long enough to know it was a loss of face for Kitaro to ask that question, but he answered anyway. "We will defeat them."

The other man blinked, then smiled and nodded and visibly drew himself together, breathing carefully as he had before to control his pain. "It shall be as you say, Lord Akira," he said, and made the ritual phrase sound like a prayer.

⛩ ⛩ ⛩

A HAND TUGGED AT HIS sleeve. *Ken*-chan, *thirsty…*

"Kenji? Are you asleep?"

Kenji's eyes snapped open, his hand reflexively grasping for the hilt of his long sword before he realized who had spoken and stopped himself.

Priestess Rei looked down at him with a concerned frown pushing her eyebrows together. They were in the shade of a copse of trees, but even so her bare scalp and forehead were beaded with sweat, and her robes clung uncomfortably. Kenji felt his mouth go oddly dry at the sight, momentarily driving away the unpleasant feel of his own sweat-soaked body and the itchy, swampy discomfort of his shirt and leggings.

The weather had turned hot in the last few days and was worse than ever today, the air thick and heavy, the sky a deep clear blue from which the Sun blazed mercilessly. Even the intermittent wind was unpleasantly warm. *Guess I shouldn't be surprised that She won't show me any slack, when She does this to us all every damned summer,* Kenji thought mordantly. He sat up, grimacing and blinking. "The bitch still hiding under her parasol?"

They had stopped at a roadside teahouse, ostensibly because it was just before the Noon Ritual and the nobles wanted to offer thanks for making it this far safely. Kenji was pretty sure it was just an excuse for the whining Tiger noblewoman to sit in the shade through the hottest part of the day. He glanced downslope toward the teahouse – a tiny wooden building with a linen awning that shaded a few tables set on bare earth – and sure enough there she was, all pale and delicate in her huge robes, huddled beneath the awning while a pair of servants fanned her and another servant hugged and cosseted her little brat of a nephew. The old Wolf courtier – Kenji still didn't know his name – was of course seated at the table next to her, chatting away like they were in some damned castle garden instead of in the back of beyond.

Rei sighed at his crudeness. "Captain Tokage is worried about something."

Kenji rubbed his face, trying to force alertness back into his heat-dulled body. He hadn't meant to fall asleep, but he'd been more tired than usual ever since the fight at the big Tiger Clan castle, and the oppressive heat had pressed down on him like a physical weight. The samurai had to pretend the heat didn't bother them, standing in rows out in the open, but Kenji had no such constraints; he'd climbed the slope above the road to the sheltering cluster of oak trees and sat against the trunk. And his eyes had slid shut…

And Yuki was waiting for him, as she so often was.

He shook himself and stood up, stretching and grimacing at the way his loincloth chafed and his leggings stuck to his skin. "What's the old man worked up about? We're finally just about back in his territory, right?"

They had crossed a river yesterday afternoon, ferried over a few at a time by peasant fisherman. Kenji had only the vaguest notion of the Empire's geography, but he had gathered that this was not the same river as the one by Kaze Village where he and Rei had spent a winter with that sad-faced Magistrate, right before…

Right before Jun died. Right before I fought the Demon. The memories were still vivid, but no longer made his mind flinch and shrink away even when he wanted it to. As if he wasn't allowed to hide from them anymore.

Kenji shot a resentful glance at the Sun blazing overhead, about an hour past midday. *That your doing too?*

This morning they had met up with a squadron of mounted samurai who, after a few tense moments, turned out to be from the Wolf Clan. That had caused great excitement for Tokage and his nobleman boss. Of course they didn't bother to explain why to a mere sellsword, but Kenji had gathered that the Wolf Clan had won a big war and their travel should be safer going forward.

Well, good enough, maybe that'll let us make better time back to the Wolf Lord's big castle. Kenji knew how long that trip had taken going the other direction – weeks and weeks, and that was with just he and Rei walking from morning to night. With these damned noblemen slowing them down it was likely to take all summer.

We could leave, go on our own way again, he thought, glancing at Priestess Rei sidelong. *We'd make better time, and…* The thought trailed off in an odd sense of… reluctance?

Shyness? Fear?

"Damnation," Kenji muttered to himself. He ostentatiously shaded his eyes, peering around for Captain Tokage, and finally spotted the old samurai thirty paces down the road talking to some of his men. *Yeah, that's not a happy conversation.*

He hitched at his belt, checked the positions of his swords, then gritted his teeth as he stepped out of the shade and the Sunlight hit his head like a sledge. A slight shiver went through his body, almost as though he had stepped into a cold wind; it was an effort to keep walking normally.

He and Rei went down the slope and along the road – just a dirt track here, barely wide enough for a palanquin – to the group of samurai. Tokage looked up as they approached, bobbing his head in a minimal pseudo-bow. He had taken off his helmet, and his face was red and sweat-slick. "Swordsman Kenji. Honored Priestess."

Kenji looked from Tokage to the trio of anxious samurai and back. "Trouble?"

Tokage puffed out a breath, glanced at the teahouse and the nobles chatting under the awning. "It seems there are some Jade Dragon samurai on the side-road to the south," he said. "A squadron at least, and less than a mile away. They're not moving right now… well, they weren't moving when Sergeant Seijin here spotted them. But if they come this way they could be here within a half-hour or less."

"What, didn't your fancy Wolf Lord kill 'em all?" Kenji looked south, following Tokage's gesture. The road forked, one branch heading east to a farm village about a mile away, the other snaking its way southward through a jumble of low wooded hills and narrow flatlands. No human settlements were immediately visible there, but he could see the smoke of a charcoal-burner rising from one patch of forest.

Then he felt a shiver run through his frame that was very different from what the heat had done a minute before. A flicker of darkness lurked beyond those wooded hills, coiling in his sight like a snake. Not the terrible massed shadows he had seen in the Tiger lands, but the difference was of size, not of kind.

Rei was talking, polite as always even in the misery of the heat. "Apologies for my ignorance, honorable Tokage, but aren't we close to the Wolf lands now? Why are there Jade Dragon samurai nearby?"

"No need for apology, honored Priestess, you're correct," Tokage said grimly. "We came through this route on the way to the Tiger last winter, and it was perfectly safe. But it seems the new war's shaken everything up... Swordsman Kenji?"

Kenji realized he had started walking south, leaving the samurai behind. *Probably thinks I'm bein' unforgivably rude... to damnation with it.* "Rei," he called without looking back. "Stay there."

"Kenji—" She broke off and then said more firmly: "My duty to the Lady is to follow you."

He grimaced. *She's been bitchy about this ever since that time with the damned barbarians at the shrine.* "Fine," he growled. "But stay out of the way."

The dirt of the road crunched under his sandals, letting out little puffs of dust that drifted in the windless air. Cicadas shrilled from the trees, the noise rising and falling in waves, at the peak even drowning out the chiming of Rei's staff. They passed a narrow footpath branched off into the woods, heading toward the distant smoke-marker of the charcoal burner, and then another path to the right that led to a small hut tucked in to a hillside, a vegetable garden on the open ground below. The door-panel and shutters were closed, no outward sign of life, but the garden was well kept and the thatch of the roof intact. *Probably some woodsman's hut,* Kenji thought. Such folk lived in the fringe territories, the lightly-populated zones at the edges of Lords' provinces and Clan territories.

There was a time when he might have idly stopped and robbed the place, or demanded food, or forced himself on the woodsman's wife or daughter. And generally forgotten about it afterward... but the memories had returned when he had faced the Lady, and now they *burned* whenever he thought about them.

Kenji grimaced and made himself look away from the hut, back at the road winding ahead. It passed into a belt of trees, hills crowding in on either side; beneath the shade of the trees the road dipped and crossed a trickling stream that fed into a small pond almost hidden by the tree-trunks. The oppressive heat momentarily abated and they both stopped. Rei blotted her reddened scalp with her sleeve. Kenji took in a long breath, smelling of mud and plants and a hint of rot.

That was when he heard, faintly, the murmur of voices and the clank of armor.

"—apologies, honorable Captain, but I must ask again. If Castle Ryu still stands, is it not our duty to go—"

A grin tugged at the corners of Kenji's mouth and he trotted forward, not waiting for Rei, out of the trees and back into the blazing afternoon light. Beyond the treeline was a narrow valley, covered in thick grass already turning yellow in the summer. It widened toward the south, and he could see the outlines of houses there, a farming village a mile distant.

The samurai were much closer, only a hundred paces away. *Definitely more than a squadron*, Kenji thought, and felt his grin widen.

There were nearly thirty of them, spread out across the road and into the grass on either side, trudging north with their shoulders hunched against the Sun. Mostly armored, back-and-breast and greaves and knee-guards, but not all had the full array and a few were in simple shirts and leggings; one man had only a loincloth and a vest. A few wore helmets – including the loincloth fellow, which looked so odd that Kenji almost laughed aloud – but most were bare-headed or had headbands wrapped around their foreheads. Two at the front were clearly leaders, one in normal armor but with a back-banner and a wide green headband both showing a maple-leaf crest, the other in a more elaborate suit of armor and helmet with the same crest embossed on the peaked front. They were the ones talking, tension visible in their postures, though they broke off and went silent as Kenji came into their view.

Yep, Jade Dragons sure enough, he thought, noting the prevailing green-and-gold colors of armor and gear and banner. There was a strong note of black as well, which combined with the crest probably marked them as vassals of a provincial Lord.

And shadows hovered over them, layers of sinful darkness, strongest and darkest on the fully-armored officer. On him it was not merely sin but a tight spiral of blackness – of emptiness, *absence* – sliding in and out of his body, of his soul. Kenji actually felt his stomach turn over slightly looking at it, though perhaps that was just the heat. *You've been keepin' bad company, samurai*, he thought, and his grin widened and turned fierce.

They drew up, the junior officer – the one with the banner and headband – barking at them to spread out. The soldiers had a motley assortment of weapons, some of them with spears or bows, others with just their swords, but they all moved like men who knew how to fight. Their momentary alarm turned to puzzlement as they realized they faced only a single man.

Kenji strolled toward them, limbs swinging loosely. "This's as far as you go, scum."

The corrupted officer's face, already red with the heat, purpled in outrage. He opened his mouth to bellow a response... and then the darkness within him recoiled, spinning violently away from reality. His eyes widened and his face went slack; he took a wobbling step back, putting him behind the other officer.

Kenji drew his swords, long and then short, swinging them out to the side. His head was suddenly clear, all the misery of the heat and the lingering dreams and memories swept away. He laughed, the sound echoing off the hills, and the world, the Heavens laughed with him.

⛩ ⛩ ⛩

"MOST HONORABLE HIGH LADY KAEDE." Chujitsuna Nomi bowed low, the gesture made only slightly awkward by the crippled arm tied to his chest. "Welcome to the Imperial City."

The sheer improbability of hearing those words made Ookami Kaede feel slightly dizzy, though escaping the stifling heat of her palanquin might have contributed as well. The Mountains of the Sun were cooler than the lowlands, but the summer Sun beat down just as hard, and the narrow slats of the palanquins resisted the mountain breezes as thoroughly as they did any others.

She paused to gather herself, then smiled a courtier's smile and nodded in acknowledgment. "Thank you, honorable Nomi." She transferred the smile to the older man in court robes standing next to Nomi. "Ah, this must be honorable Daisaku?"

"A great joy to meet you at last, most honored High Lady," the courtier replied. Kaede had corresponded more than once with the senior Wolf Clan ambassador to the Imperial City, and had read the occasional and generally uninteresting spy reports he sent – though of course he thought those were going to Seneschal Amano. Hase Daisaku was an older man, his graying hair tied into a formal courtier's topknot that lay forward on his shaved front scalp – an antique hairstyle Kaede had previously encountered only in her books. He was smiling politely, projecting an aspect of refined elegance, but she thought he looked tired and harried underneath the surface. A few other men and women in court robes stood in a loose row behind him, fanning themselves against the summer heat. *The rest of the embassy delegation*, Kaede knew. *And those groups waiting nearby must be from the other Clan embassies.*

Rather than deal with all of that at once Kaede let herself look around, carefully not showing any overt emotion. It would not do for the future Empress to be gaping like a hayseed at her first clear view of the Empire's oldest city.

In truth, it was difficult not to gape. She had grown up reading about the Imperial City, spending endless evenings turning pages by candlelight. Now she stood in the very square where Prince Katsumono had met his lover at midnight, the night before his older brother was crowned Emperor. Right *there* was the Great Temple, rising like a cliff against the sky, gilded red-gold by the afternoon Sun just as the ancient writers had described.

The great square was crowded. Immediately around her were hundreds of soldiers in Wolf Clan colors and a cluster of silk tents flying the banners of the Clan and the Ookami. Kaede's own huge entourage of servants and handmaidens and guards lay behind her, with the first wave of nobles from Castle Ookami slowly trickling in on horseback and palanquin. Beyond that, hundreds of other people crowded at the outer perimeter of the square: laborers and Priestesses, street vendors and children and Monks, samurai and housewives and even a dung-collector with his wagon, all watching the new arrivals. The higher-class folk like the clergy and samurai tried to seem disinterested, while the commoners openly gaped, but they all watched with equal avidness.

Like when the Emperor's procession would return, in the books, Kaede thought. *Everyone wanting to see the Chosen of Heaven... and if it's a new Emperor, wondering what his reign will bring.*

A noise impinged on her senses, a great tolling beat that rang through the city, and she realized it was temple bells. Peering upward, she spotted the massive bell of the Great Temple, suspended from beams outside the building's open gate. Doll-tiny shapes of Priestesses and Monks swung the chain-hung iron-capped log against it with ponderous rhythm. The noise was too great for just the one bell, though, no matter how massive it might be. *They must be ringing every bell in the city.*

Basho, newly freed from his own palanquin, put his hands over his ears. "Loud!" he yelled.

Old Nomi smiled at the boy. "They also did this when Lord Akira arrived the first time. And the Theological Council came out and recited some big ritual prayer... quite the spectacle."

Kaede continued looking at the Great Temple, careful not to appear like she was squinting or gawping. There were scores of Priestesses and Monks lining the railing a hundred paces up, and she wondered if those were the Council or just the curious. "Will they do the same today?"

Nomi shrugged.

Ambassador Daisaku cleared his throat. "Most honored Lady. The Council had made a number of requests to meet with Lord Akira since he arrived."

Kaede was momentarily puzzled. "Is my honorable husband here? I thought he was still in the field."

"He is," Nomi confirmed. "His latest letter announced Castle Hokori's surrender."

That brought a wave of soft murmurs from the waiting courtiers. Kaede noticed the way old Daisaku's fingers tightened on his fan, and thought: *He is insulted that Nomi knows about this and he does not. A man who thinks too much of himself.*

Whatever Hase Daisaku might have been thinking, his face and voice remained properly smooth and calm as he continued: "I have explained that to the Council, with suitable apologies, each time they send the request. They are always very polite and pious, very respectful, I do not think we need be concerned."

"*Ah so*," Kaede murmured. *So they're trying to exert pressure and demand attention, like any other courtier requesting to submit petitions when the High Lord is absent.* It was somehow both a relief and a disappointment to realize that the most important people in the Empire's religious orders engaged in politics just like anyone else.

And Ambassador Daisaku is showing them face, making excuses for them. Well, he's been here two decades, he probably cares more about their opinion of him than he does about mine. That was something her old books had talked about, the way a man long away from his own Clan could sometimes absorb the attitudes of others. *Hmmm, perhaps I should meet with the Council myself after I've been here a little while, to establish my position? But only if they will come to me as supplicants. If I'm to be Empress I can't go to them, that would establish the wrong balance of power.*

She fanned herself, continuing to smile pleasantly at the courtiers while she thought. "The court has accompanied me here, as Lord Akira commanded. Where shall it be hosted? I seem to recall that the Imperial Palace was largely wrecked by earthquake and fire."

"It is sadly true that the Palace of the Emperors is unsuited to such demands at this time," Daisaku confirmed. "The Clan embassy is a large structure, but not sufficient for such a great need. After the most honorable Lord Akira sent notice you would be bringing the court here, I arranged to expand the embassy into several adjacent structures so it could be large enough to properly house so many honored personages. I also arranged for the usage of one of the shrines as a court chamber."

Kaede nodded. "I am pleased to hear it."

The ambassador smiled and went on: "This entailed a considerable exchange of favors with other Clan delegations and the Council. I will not burden you with the details now, since this is not the proper time for such mundane things."

Which is a strong hint that he wants a private meeting, Kaede thought irritably. She noted that Nomi was giving Daisaku an arch look. *Well, he is the ambassador here, and this is probably his first chance to exert real influence from that position. I should try not to earn his anger without need.* "Of course, honorable Daisaku," she said aloud.

Something, some mother's instinct, made her glance aside at Basho. He still had his hands over his ears and had begun to silently cry at the continued tolling of bells; Koko knelt at his side, trying to comfort him, and allowed a frown to touch her lips. Half intentionally she set one hand over the swelling of her belly. "Is this continued clamor truly necessary?"

Daisaku actually blanched slightly. "Apologies, I am sure it is only intended to honor you, my Lady," he said, and stepped aside to murmur at his companions behind his fan. Within a minute one of the courtiers was moving toward the Great Temple, as fast as his robes and dignity would allow. Kaede watched him go and felt a cool satisfaction beneath her anger at her son's discomfort. *Well, that put him off-balance, which is good.*

She found herself remembering her very first arrival at Castle Ookami, how lost and frightened she had felt, how everyone had either ignored her or joined Lady Yumiko in mocking her. *Was that really only four years ago?*

Aloud she said, "All of us have traveled long and are in need of rest. Once this clamor is over, I will be pleased to take possession of our new residence."

"Of course, my Lady," Daisaku agreed, bowing low, the other courtiers instantly copying him. Nomi, watching the whole spectacle, barely suppressed a smirk.

⛩ ⛩ ⛩

THE SCREAMS OVERLAPPED EACH OTHER, a discordant jumble of agony. Tomoe felt a smile tug at her mouth whenever the noise got particularly loud, though whether it was her own impulse or the Lords who listened through her ears she could no longer say.

She sat cross-legged on what had been the porch of a house. The building had been set afire sometime last night, but fierce overnight winds had blown it down in a heap, smothering most of the fire. A few tendrils of pale smoke still rose from the pile of broken beams and matted straw, spiraling away to the east on a breeze which was a lingering echo of the previous night's ferocity.

The village was built mostly on a steep hillside, the houses sometimes directly above each other, with stone walls to hold up the slopes against erosion and channel rainwater down to the rice paddies in the flatland below. Many of the houses had burned, in whole or in part, and dead bodies choked the stone-lined drainage ditches. Tomoe's perch was on the upper half of the slope, but not at the top; the endless screams came from behind and above her, where the village's shrine had rested under the sprawling, meandering limbs of an ancient maple tree. She did not have to look to see what was happening up there – Dakkurru, looking through her body and the Other's body and more distantly through the shamans and Mask priests, showed it to her.

People hung from the maple tree's spreading branches, twitching and writhing against the hooks that transfixed their chests and shoulders. Some of the screams came from them, when they could draw in enough breath to utter them. Among them were three samurai – the local landholder's mother, father, and wife. The smoking ruins of their estate lay a mile to the east on a lower hilltop.

The shrine itself had been torn down, its pieces scattered, the statues of the Lord and Lady smashed into gravel with iron-headed sledges. Where it had stood the shamans had raised one of their banners, the fluttering leather gleaming with the twisted spiral-symbol of Dakkurru. The Other stood before the banner, flanked by several of the shamans. Her pale doll-face was unmoving, framed by a new leather hood that replaced the one she had lost at Castle Mouko.

A long line of tribesmen wound its way up the hill, each of them dragging a prisoner – men and women, young and old. Mostly commoners, although there were a few of the samurai class mixed in. As each of the prisoners came before the Other, the tribesmen forced them to their knees, and she set her lone hand on their faces.

Many of them simply convulsed and screamed and died, their patterns torn asunder by the massive eruption of Dakkurru's power into their flesh. The tribesmen dragged the corpses away, tossing them down the far side of the hill to join hundreds of others. Flies were already swarming there in buzzing black clouds, and rodents scurried in the heaps of decay.

A smaller number of the people submitted, their souls warping and fraying and breaking under the weight of Dakkurru's pressure. Their screams were even louder… until they stopped, as sharply and suddenly as sliced bamboo. The shamans led those away to join the army that camped in the lowlands to the south.

A few, a very few, somehow resisted completely, defiant even in the face of crushing power. The shamans plunged the hooks through their flesh and added them to those festooning the tree.

Crude, and wasteful, Tomoe thought irritably. *Not like with me—*

The thought cut off as sharply as the recruits' screams. She did not even remember it.

Tomoe looked south, past the village's rice paddies, past the dark smoke-shrouded sprawl of the army that camped in trampled grainfields. Beyond was a landscape of forested hills and green valleys, towers of smoke rising up wherever the tribesmen's scouting parties found resistance.

Miles away, barely visible against the blue-gray haze of the summer horizon, the angular shape of a samurai castle rose above the trees. Not a large castle, just a four-story keep atop a hill, but the Tiger samurai holed up inside it could hold it for months, and there were a score of other such strongholds scattered around the lands south of Castle Mouko, each of them garrisoned and defiant.

On the hilltop a peasant women with her hair in a kerchief thrashed against the tribesmen holding her down. She wrenched her face away from the Other's hand. "Amatsu protect me!" she screamed.

The shamans descended on her with their hooks.

It'll be my turn soon, Tomoe thought. The Other had greater endurance – probably because there was so little of *her* left within her flesh – but even she had limits. And both of their limits were shorter these days, their flesh weakened by the battle at Castle Mouko, the battle with *him* – Kenji, and the False Light that blazed through him. They needed some of Dakkurru's power now to simply function, to keep their hearts beating and their breath moving. Not so much as when they had crawled out of that slimy moat, but they not yet back to what they had been before.

Perhaps they never would be.

Tomoe's hands clenched into fists in her lap.

It had been going on all night and all the day since, Tomoe and the Other alternating in the task whenever their bodies weakened too much from the stress of channeling such power. At first Tomoe had enjoyed it as much as the Lords within her, had gloried in the screams and the tears, had reveled in seeing the light of awareness flicker and fade in their eyes. But by now her enjoyment had faded into indifference and exhaustion.

Dakkurru needs more soldiers, she knew. The tribesmen's numbers were vast, but they were a finite resource, dwindling as they offered more and more of their children to the rituals and more of their own lives to battle. *So we do this, even if it only gets us one out of five... and besides, we'd have t'kill them all anyway, or sacrifice them for t'rituals.* Many of the children in particular were being held for that purpose.

If there were more time the captured children could be put through the initiations which the Cult of the Mask used in other lands. But that took many months, and then years for them to grow old enough to be useful. The war needed soldiers now.

Damned samurai, Tomoe snarled, and in that moment her own thoughts and the rage of Dakkurru were in perfect synchronicity. The tribesmen had swept through the northern territories of the Tiger with relentless speed, but after the near-catastrophe at Castle Mouko had put her and the Other out of action the momentum had dribbled away. It had taken weeks to crush the remaining pockets of resistance within Mouko and its surrounding city. The Tiger had rallied in the south, calling every remaining samurai from twelve to sixty to the fight, a few Lords even putting samurai women and peasant spearmen into their ranks.

And the castles… the tribesman had no mastery of siegecraft, that was why they had never been able to threaten the Empire through the long centuries when Dakkurru was asleep. That was why Tomoe and the Other had been needed. They could break a castle, smash its walls and gates with Dakkurru's hatefire… but there were scores of these smaller castles, including many bypassed in the north when the tribesmen had flooded down to Castle Mouko. Every one of them with a garrison that was now coming out to raid and harass, or to march south and join the rest of the rallying Tiger army.

It would take weeks, months, to crush them all. Tomoe felt the vast frustration of Dakkurru, the Lords' fury at being balked after so much quick success.

Her mind shifted and flickered as information suddenly arrived, placed in her like a statue set on a shelf. Images sent from Mask priests, from the Voices –

The ones still alive. Another Voice had been lost, Selfishness killed in battle with the Wolf Lord, and the boy who was supposed to replace Cowardice was not yet ready.

Tomoe probed at the new knowledge tentatively and after a minute or so it coalesced into something resembling memories. And with that came a sense of greedy observation from the Lords, drinking in the new information.

The news was infuriating. *The Wolf Lord's taken Castle Hokori without a fight,* Tomoe thought, clenching her fists tight enough that the nails bit at her palms. *And he's already got t'Imperial City… by the time we get t'Tiger lands rolled up, it'll be winter and we'll have t'find supplies and hunker down.* Even the loyal fanatics of the tribes, raised from infancy to serve Dakkurru, couldn't fight when starving and freezing.

And that'll give t'Wolf Lord all winter t'get everyone to t'Imperial City, to line 'em all up behind him.

The fury of Dakkurru spilled through her mind, six voices speaking in chaotic overlapping unison: **THE SLAVE OF THE PALE LIGHT MUST BE DESTROYED.**

"Can't do that if we're stuck up here taking castles," Tomoe muttered. She stood and looked uphill at the smashed shrine. The Other was staggering away, weaving back and forth like a drunkard. A dozen paces away she collapsed to the ground, huddling into a ball beneath her cloak.

My turn again. Tomoe stepped off the foundation of the house and walking uphill past the waiting prisoners. She grinned at them and they shrank back from her, whimpering or screaming. The shamans groveled, their huge fur-fringed masks bobbing grotesquely. The Mask priests bowed low but sedately, in the manner of the Empire's people.

Tomoe paused, looking at the red-streaked white ovals of the Masks. *We were supposed t'meet up with them in t'Jade Dragon lands, form a single army that would sweep everyone away like a river in flood. If Selfishness had won…*

Rage boiled again, and she felt the grin on her face turn into something else. The man kneeling before her cowered and whimpered, tears running down his face, and she brought her hand down on his face and felt the rage of Dakkurru sweep through her and into his twitching flesh.

EPILOGUE

KOBAYASHI MITSUI WATCHED THE eastern sky slowly brighten, framing the jagged silhouettes of the Bear Mountains, and contemplated the past. His hand rose half-consciously and brushed across the frayed threads on the front of his jacket, the place where he had removed the embroidered crests to avoid attention from Jade Dragon samurai.

Fifteen years ago he had first been appointed a deputy Magistrate in HillTown. His mother had spent weeks painstakingly embroidering the vest with the crosshatch Kobayashi family crest, the Gray Wolf Clan's snarling wolf-head, and the golden fan that showed his office. She had gifted it to him at the Midwinter Festival, and in the way of mothers all across the Empire she had managed to turn the after-dinner presentation into a chance to complain that Mitsui had not yet found a wife.

Of course, once I did marry Akemi, all mother did was complain that she didn't measure up. I think she even criticized her once for not making me another jacket when Lord Watsuki promoted me to Chief Magistrate. Mitsui's wife, like women all across the Empire, had endured her mother-in-law's venomous comments with honorable silence, even when she was pregnant with Taro.

Mitsui's mother had died, carried away by a late-winter fever, only a few months before his son was born. He had mourned his mother and celebrated the birth of his son, accepting the gifts and funeral offerings of his other relatives and his deputies in the Magistrates' office. Struck by the pairing of death and birth, the ephemeral sadness and joy of existence paired together, he had even been moved to compose a poem, a samurai affectation he normally avoided.

The greatest sadness
Is when everything is good
Yet a void remains

So comfortably secure, so soft. I knew nothing of real pain back then. Before he had held his wife while her life's blood drained out onto his shirt. Before the Masks took his son.

He had thought he could no longer weep over the memories. But last night as he was preparing for bed a jolt had run through him and for no reason the grief had returned with shattering force, as though he was not merely remembering it but living it again. For an hour he had sat insensate in his room, his face wet with tears. When it finally passed and he could think again, he had found himself unable to sleep, his mind chasing itself in endless circles. At some point after midnight he had given up and gone outside, walking back and forth across the packed earth of the inn's front yard, trying to wear himself out.

His legs had grown tired but sleep had continued to elude him. Eventually he had just sat down on the grassy verge of the uppermost of the terraced rice paddies descending from the inn's grounds, and waited for the night to be over.

The three-story inn where they had stopped yesterday evening shared the steeply sloping thatch roof of most rural structures in the Bear lands, which gave it an odd triangular look when viewed from the end. Mitsui was used to multi-story buildings having upper floors that were the same width or even a little more than the ground floor; in the Bear lands such designs were confined to cities.

The inn crouched on a narrow stretch of flatland on the shallow-sloped lower shoulder of a mountain; it was steep and craggy higher up, and at Sunset last night Mitsui had been able to glimpse snow on the topmost peaks. A pair of streams ran downslope past the inn, with irrigation channels siphoning off water for small terraced fields above the inn and larger ones below, descending into a steep narrow valley. There was a village down there, though right now Mitsui could see nothing of it in the deep darkness. The fields were mostly rice paddies, thought he thought the smaller ones above the inn were growing tea-plants instead. He vaguely recalled hearing years ago that tea and metal were the main two things the Bear exported to the other Clans.

A creak of wooden planks drew his attention to the covered porch that ran across the inn's triangular northern end. A human shape, featureless gray-black in the pre-Sunrise dimness, descended the steps from the porch and walked toward him, hard dirt scrunching under sandals. Four years of ingrained instinct put Mitsui's hand on the sword at his waist.

"I suppose that would be fitting, to die by mistaken identity after surviving so much else."

Mitsui pulled his hand away and ducked his head in a half-bow. "Apologies, Satoshi. I slept poorly and wasn't thinking clearly."

The lanky samurai sat down cross-legged, facing east across the valley as Mitsui was. "Did you sleep at all? I heard you leave your room, and that was before Moonrise."

"I was dealing with some… old memories." Mitsui shrugged, trying to make it sound inconsequential.

"Ah yes, memories. Troubling things, those." Satoshi, Mitsui saw, was already fully dressed in his usual baggy shirt and pleated leggings, the latter snugged below the knee in the manner of a patrolman to keep his feet clear to move freely. "I confess I did not sleep well either. Just our fate, I suppose, to approach our next task without proper rest."

Mitsui felt a momentary urge to chuckle. Instead he said, "If the directions we got last night are correct, it will be another four or five days to Tatarayama Village."

"Ah," Satoshi nodded gloomily. "So we can have four or five more nights without proper rest before we face this Voice."

The eastern horizon was brightening, going from gray to a pale yellow. Now Mitsui could make out the village in the valley below, though it was still all shades of gray and black. A few dozen buildings, widely scattered, ranging in size from small huts that could barely house one person to two-story buildings almost as large as the inn. Most of them were close to a narrow lake that snaked down the valley from north to south. Yet another of the myriad lakes and rivers that wound through the hills of the Bear lands, fed by a thousand snow-melt streams from the higher peaks.

He considered the man beside him. Satoshi had plucked a stem of grass from the verge and was idly chewing on it while he stared into the distance. *Waiting for me to be ready to eat and travel on,* Mitsui knew. *I've often wondered if he really means all the things he says. Is it an act, a way to protect himself? Or does he really go through life expecting the worst to happen every day, every hour? Why would a man think that way?* He knew Satoshi had been raised by servants and, in his youngest childhood, a sickly grandmother. *Did that give him a dark outlook on the world? But Yukako-*chan *and her father Tokko were not gloomy people – and they often seemed to treat him with the same bemusement as I do.*

And then he smiled to himself. *Does it really matter why he is who he is? He is my friend. He has stayed at my side through all of this. That is all that matters.*

"Four or five days, assuming the innkeeper was telling us the truth. Our history with such matters has not been good." Satoshi removed the grass from his mouth, regarded the mangled end thoughtfully, and tossed it aside. "Is there any plan for what we will do when we find this Merchant Goro? Or will we simply storm his house and hope for the best? That does seem to have become our standard method."

Mitsui felt an odd half-laugh burst from his lips. He rose to his feet, shaking out his leggings and brushing grass and dust from them. "I suppose it has… I was a Magistrate, a man who took pride in upholding the law. Now I break into strangers' houses and murder them."

"Well," Satoshi rose as well, "I don't believe we've managed to kill any innocent people yet." He brushed off the seat of his leggings. "We've probably just been lucky, though."

I do think that might have been a rebuke, though it's always hard to tell with Satoshi.

The older man continued. "Honestly I'm surprised we haven't wound up hanged by now. And these Bear samurai don't seem like the sort to put up with any nonsense from out-of-Clan visitors… Ah." He broke off and lifted his hands, pressing them together in front of his chest, and lowered his head, murmuring a mantra.

The edge of the Sun came over the mountains, painfully bright. Mitsui slitted his eyes, and after a moment's consideration he emulated his companion, reciting the prayer his mother had taught him as a child.

Humbly we approach Blessed Amatsu
With reverent heart, we present offerings and prayer
We entreat in humility and with deep respect
Teach us to live with pure and Honest heart
Grant us Compassion that is genuine, childlike, and true
Grant that we stay on the path of Honor
Grant that we be strong and Courageous in our deeds
We beseech the Goddess to accept our plea.

Finished, Mitsui looked back at the inn, its massive thatch roof now yellow-gold with Sunrise. He could see the innkeeper sliding open the wall panels on the ground floor. The smell of cooking – charcoal fire, hot sesame oil, rice, the sharpness of fresh-cut onions – drifted from inside.

Satoshi stopped murmuring, lowered his head in a bow, then turned to join him in walking toward the inn. Mitsui eyed him sidelong. "I confess, Satoshi, you never struck me as a particularly pious man."

The lean horse-face did not change. "One cannot stare Demons in the face without concluding that it is a wise precaution to seek a certain amount of purification before death." A pause. "And someone has to be pious, now that we are without Bozu to remind us of our Divine duties."

The memory of the eccentric Monk, coming on top of all his earlier musings, brought Mitsui a fresh stab of emotion that made his eyes water. He forced himself to stop and look at the village below, to watch the glow of the Sunrise creep across the slanted thatch roofs, until he got himself under control – though when he spoke, his voice was still hoarse. "I miss Bozu."

"He was a fine comrade," Satoshi agreed quietly. "What do you suppose he would tell us now?"

Mitsui let out another awkward half-laugh. "He would probably remind us that we are chosen by the Divine Mikoto to fight the followers of the False Path… so we should stop complaining like spoiled children and get to it."

"That sounds correct," Satoshi agreed, and Mitsui thought the man's long mournful face had briefly tried to smile. "Well, whatever the Divine Mikoto may say, we are the most experienced Mask-hunters in the Empire. Complete with all the gear our duties require." He patted the traveling pack that hung at his side. "Shall we get underway, then?"

Mitsui let out a long breath, wiped his face with the hem of his sleeve, and firmed his shoulders. "Yes," he said. "That sordid obscure death won't wait forever."

EMPIRE OF THE SUN AND MOON

WILL CONCLUDE IN

THE WAR OF HEAVEN AND EARTH

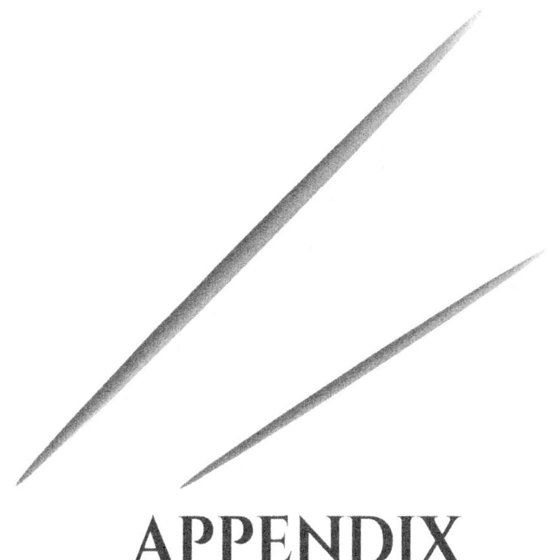

APPENDIX

The Seven Virtues of the Samurai Code

- Courtesy (Moon)
- Courage (Sun)
- Duty (Moon)
- Discipline (Moon)
- Honor (Sun)
- Honesty (Sun)
- Compassion (Sun)

The Seven Sins and the Seven Demons

- Contempt – Keibitsu
- Cowardice – Okubiyo
- Treachery – Uragiri
- Laziness – Taida
- Selfishness – Fudotokuna
- Deceit – Sagi
- Cruelty – Zankoku

The Twelve Original Clans

- Bear

- Gold Dragon (conquered and absorbed by Jade Dragon, Blue Salamander, and Tiger)
- Grasshopper (collapsed bankrupt, conquered by Jade Dragon Clan)
- Hawk (conquered/absorbed by Black Wolf Clan)
- Jade Dragon
- Nightingale
- Ox (conquered/absorbed by Hawk and Bear Clans)
- Peacock (conquered by Wolf and Nightingale Clans)
- Salamander (later divided into Red Salamander and Blue Salamander; Blue Salamander conquered by various Clans, Red Salamander conquered by Jade Dragon Clan)
- Tiger
- White Fox (conquered/absorbed by Tiger Clan)
- Wolf (later divided into Black Wolf and Gray Wolf; reunited by marriage of Ookami Akira and Kuroi Kaede)

The Twelve Arts

- Architecture
- Calligraphy
- Dance
- Embroidery
- Flower-Arranging
- Gardening
- Letter-Writing
- Painting
- Paper-Folding
- Poetry
- Pottery
- Sculpture

ACKNOWLEDGMENTS

Thanks to...

- My readers, for their patience
- My wife and daughter, for their support
- My cover artist nino vecia, for putting together another awesome cover at very short notice

ABOUT THE AUTHOR

Rob Hobart is a lifelong fan of science-fiction, fantasy, role-playing games, Japanese pop culture, and military history. He lives in rural Missouri with his wife and daughter.

Made in the USA
Monee, IL
04 October 2021